G000299416

THE PRAGUE PROTOCOL

The Puppet Meisters Trilogy

Moscow Bound

Dancing With Shadows

The Prague Protocol

THE PRAGUE PROTOCOL

ADRIAN CHURCHWARD

Published in 2020 by SilverWood Books

SilverWood Books Ltd
14 Small Street, Bristol, BS1 1DE, United Kingdom
www.silverwoodbooks.co.uk

ISBN 978-1-78132-968-9 (hardback)
ISBN 978-1-78132-963-4 (paperback)
ISBN 978-1-78132-964-1 (ebook)

British Library Cataloguing in Publication Data
A CIP catalogue record for this book is available from the British Library

Page design and typesetting by SilverWood Books

For Alexander, Casper, Thurston,
Lana, Chloe and David

There are crooks everywhere you look now. The situation is desperate – the final words of Daphne Caruana Galizia, the fearless Maltese investigative journalist who was assassinated by a car bomb outside her house at 3pm on 16 October 2017, within an hour of posting this on her blog.

Joseph A. DeBono & Caroline Muscat, *Invicta: The Life and Work of Daphne Caruana Galizia*

Chapter 1

2018
Day One: 1.35pm, London

David Carey MP loosened his grip on his four-year-old granddaughter's hand as they emerged from the lobby of the apartment block at the end of Selsdon Way in Canary Wharf, en route to a kiddie's birthday party.

The child slipped away from her grandfather and skipped ahead.

'Be careful, Jaffa cake! Mind the road!'

She stopped and turned. 'Here I come, granddad. Catch me!'

She ran towards him.

The MP crouched, placed the wrapped birthday present on the ground and spread his arms. 'I'm ready!'

She crashed into him. 'I love you granddad, millions and millions and millions.'

He scooped her up. 'And I love you too, Jaffa cake, more than the whole wide worl—'

A single bullet, fired from a Blaser R93 Tactical sniper rifle fitted with a compensated suppressor, and located on the roof of the former Tradex Insurance building on the opposite side of the road, tore into Carey's temple and penetrated the pre-frontal lobe.

Blood spatter and brain tissue decorated Jaffa cake's face and her *Frozen* Princess Anna party dress.

The politician tumbled to the ground with his granddaughter still in his arms.

A female jogger stopped and disentangled the screaming child from the MP.

Two men rushed out of the apartment block and knelt by the corpse.

The sniper pulled back from the parapet and dismantled the weapon. She stashed the parts into a sports bag and kept her head down as she hurried to the other side of the roof. It was a short drop to the five-a-side football pitch one level below, where she slid through a hole in the netting which prevented stray balls from disappearing over neighbouring rooftops. She ran down the slope into the underground National Car Park, stopped behind a pillar and scanned the bays for activity: a few vehicles but nobody in sight. She removed her gloves, coveralls and boots, stuffed them into the sports bag and took out a rucksack as she headed for the enclosed pedestrian exit to the Selsdon Way spur road. A waiting biker, dressed in full leather gear with the face obscured by a black helmet visor, grabbed the sports bag from her and roared away on a KTM 660.

The sniper smoothed down her jeans, slung on the rucksack and strolled up the hill into Pepper Street, singing to Fifth Harmony's "Worth It" on her iPhone – in competition with the screaming sirens of the emergency services.

Chapter 2

Day Two: 11am, London

Scott Mitchell sat at the table in the far corner of Caffè Nero opposite Waterstones in London's Piccadilly, sipping an extra hot grande latte and scrolling through his social media feeds.

The bigots were out in force:

> #Manchester #LondonBridge now #CanaryWharf fucking #Islamiccancer

> #Canarywharfslaying when we gonna deport these #ragheads

> Take your frigging #niqab off #TheresaMay and start protecting your own

It was in Scott's genes as a human rights lawyer to advocate freedom of speech, but occasionally his philosophy took a wobble. Were these trolls on autopilot? Didn't they possess the ability to think first and post later or, better, not at all? There hadn't been the slightest hint in the papers or on news websites of any Islamic terrorist involvement in the assassination of the junior government minister.

'Ignorant bastards.'

He checked Heathrow's departure information for any indication that his next morning's flight to Prague might be delayed.

No news was good news.

He downloaded his e-ticket receipt and took a bite

out of his Belgian chocolate muffin.

Colin Fraser walked in, with a folded *Metro* newspaper tucked under his arm.

Scott studied the MI6 officer as he headed his way without stopping at the counter for a drink and something to eat. Smaller than average height, Fraser's willowy frame appeared to have lost another two centimetres since the pair had last crossed paths two years previously in Moscow, and his thinning, mousy hair was greying at the temple on both sides.

The lowered head and slight swagger, however, remained.

No contact for 18 months, then a sudden request for a meeting.

They exchanged perfunctory smiles as Fraser pulled up the chair opposite Scott.

'Pull that next to yours,' Fraser said, gesturing at the adjacent table.

No small talk. Their feelings for each other hadn't changed: barely disguised mutual intolerance.

Scott obliged without comment. The man clearly didn't want anybody to be within earshot. Their nearest neighbour, a 20-something female, was sitting to Scott's right, three tables away on the bench seat that extended the length of the wall. She was on the phone, speaking aloud in Spanish and typing on her laptop.

Fraser placed the *Metro* on the neighbouring table.

'Okay,' Scott said. 'You got me here. Now what? I've got stuff to do.' He had yet to prepare the paperwork for the Prague meeting.

'I need your help, my good friend…'

Scott tilted his head sideways, his eyes widened. What did the man say? 'I need your help'? What had happened to 'you *will* do this' or 'you *must* do that or else'?

Had the spook been on a belligerence management course?

'...You're going to Prague tomorrow,' Fraser continued. 'The press conference with your boss.'

'What about it?' Scott wasn't surprised that MI6 were still keeping him under surveillance.

'I'd like you to confirm something for me.' Quick smile. 'That's all.'

There he goes again: 'I'd *like you to...*'

No way was this the Fraser of old, the spy he'd grown to dislike. The legal warning *caveat emptor*, buyer beware, came to mind; except that it should be Scott Mitchell beware.

'Why should I cooperate with MI6?' He didn't owe them or any other UK government agency anything; just the opposite.

Fraser leant forward and lowered his voice. 'Simple, my friend – I got you off the money-laundering charge in 2016.'

Scott winced. He'd been trying to put that debilitating career-wrecking experience behind him. He, too, leant forward and lowered his voice. 'One: I wasn't *charged.* I was *arrested.* If you guys operated in a due process environment, like us civilised people, you'd understand the difference. Two: you only got me out of what your mates in the police and CPS got me into in the first place. So please don't give me any of that *you owe me* shit.'

Fraser bit his bottom lip and edged back. 'Okay. How about: because I saved your life in Moscow?'

Yeah, that bit was true.

So this was to be the *quid pro quo*?

'Okay.' He glanced at the clock on his phone. 'You've got ten minutes.'

Fraser opened the *Metro* and removed a cream pocket-envelope, from which he took three A-4 landscape photos and gave them to Scott. 'Look at these.'

Scott pushed his food and drink to one side and spread out the photos on the table. They were timed and dated images, taken on different days during the previous month, comprising hazy, but unmistakeable, shots of his Russian oligarch boss, Konstantin Gravchenko. The man was getting into a limousine with opaque windows at the Pest end of Budapest's famous Erzsébet Hid, the Elizabeth Bridge named after the UK's Queen Elizabeth II. Scott knew the location well, from his frequent visits to Gravchenko's office in the city. The second image showed him getting out of the vehicle in front of the Hungarian Parliament building. On both occasions, a woman – late twenties – accompanied him. The third image showed her alone, getting into the same limousine on the opposite embankment on the Buda side of the Danube. He couldn't tell if Gravchenko was inside the vehicle.

He didn't recognise the woman, her face wasn't clear in the images.

'What about them?' The fact that MI6 was also keeping a 24/7 surveillance on the wealthiest person in Russia was of no undue concern to Scott. Gravchenko was without doubt the most spied-on businessman on the planet, such was the West's current paranoia about the activities of any oligarch from the so-called mafia state: the Russian Federation.

'Keep the woman's face firmly imprinted on your mind,' Fraser said.

Scott glanced at it again. 'It's indistinct. She's too far away.'

Fraser pulled a fourth photo from the envelope. 'This is a clear headshot of her.'

Scott lingered on the image. 'Hmm.' He looked closer. Beautiful dark brown eyes; shading towards black.

'Do you know her?' Fraser asked.

'No.' Scott shook his head as he continued staring at her. 'Unfortunately.'

'Are you sure?'

'Positive.' He looked at the other three photos again. 'She's not somebody I'd easily forget.' He eased back. 'So don't keep me in suspense. What do you want from me?'

'I want you to find out who she is.'

Was MI6 running a dating agency?

'Try Google images,' Scott said. 'Their database is bigger than the image gallery in my head.'

'She's doesn't show up anywhere in cyber space.'

'Not a Facebook or Instagram selfie?' He couldn't keep his eyes from her image. 'What's your interest in her?'

Fraser frowned. 'We've been through this before. You know the rules. If you keep refusing to sign the Official Secrets Acts, you're tying my hands. There's not much I can tell you.'

Here we go again.

'And if you refuse to put your question into some sort of context, other than just these images,' Scott said, 'how am I supposed to know what it is you're really asking me to do?'

The two men smiled at each other, as if to say, 'We've boxed ourselves into a corner, where do we go from here?'

Fraser's out-of-character friendliness was unsettling. The man's previous tactics had been to threaten to frame him for criminal activities he hadn't committed. Now he was playing the good cop to his earlier bad cop.

'All I'm asking you to do, Scott, is to find out who she is.'

Yeah, and the rest.

Fraser twice rapped the table with his knuckles. 'That's all.'

He stood up and headed for the washroom. 'Nature calls.'

Scott stared at the photos again. If he refused to cooperate would he end up battling with the devious and dishonourable UK authorities once again? He had no appetite for a repeat of 2016, though he'd faced them down and won the war. He was now comfortably settled in the well-paid position of Chief General Counsel with Gravchenko's World Preservation Foundation, a charity that was aiming to turn the world "green": environmental sustainability for future generations.

A cause much after his own heart, despite his frequent business flights.

Moreover, it was his duty as Gravchenko's lawyer to refer Fraser's approach to him.

The man returned.

'Okay,' Scott said. 'I'll see what Gravchenko has to say, and report back to you...*if* he authorises me to do so, but not otherwise.'

'Good man. We're going to get on fine.'

Yeah, until the novelty of the love-fest wears off, Mr Fraser, and you return to your old ways.

'Do you want me take these photos?' Scott asked. 'Or will you send me the images?'

'Both,' Fraser said as he began scrolling on his phone. 'Here.'

Chapter 3

Day Two: 2pm, London

When Scott entered the lobby of his apartment block Dave, the concierge, waved what looked like a business card at him. 'A woman, a barrister called Diane Costello, came here looking for you while you were out,' Dave said. 'She wants you to give her a bell. It's urgent. *Very* urgent.'

He handed it to Scott.

Diane Costello (Barrister at law)
Areas of speciality: Private Client, Trusts and Wills,
Inheritance Tax Planning

Her chambers' and mobile phone numbers were on the back, along with her email address.

He checked his own phone for a missed call from the number on Costello's card; his details were on his website.

Nothing.

'Never heard of her. Did she say what it was about?'

'Nope.'

'Okay, thanks.' He creased a smile. 'I'll check her out.'

A distraction not welcomed, Ms Costello. There's last-minute research to be done for the Prague meeting.

Rosie was meowing immediately he put the key in the lock of his apartment door, and when he opened it, she ran past him and stretched her legs on the carpet in the common hallway.

'Hey, what about me, eh?' Scott bent down, stroked her and massaged her behind the ears.

She purred.

Therapy for both of them.

'Rosie, baby, what are we going to do with this Fraser guy? He's come back into my life, a chameleon posing as Mr Nice Guy. I can't get a fix on him.' Rosie rubbed herself around his ankles a couple of times before returning to her stretching exercises on the carpet. 'And that's your final word on the subject?' He wedged the door open and went inside; the flooring in the apartment comprised bare oak strips, so there was nowhere for Rosie to have a scratch, except at the oversized pole Scott had bought her specifically for the purpose – and which she'd steadfastly refused to use.

He poured himself a glass of wine, booted up his laptop and checked out Diane Costello's website. Rosie strolled in. Scott waved Costello's business card at her. 'What do you think this lady wants? I've been left a fortune in a distant relative's will? Perhaps she wants me to become a barrister and head up her chambers.'

Rosie ignored him and tucked into her food bowl.

Ms Costello's chambers were in New Square, Lincoln's Inn, the heart of the legal area of London, and Charles Dickens' hunting ground for several of his novels. Costello's reviewers gave her five stars for her expertise in inheritance tax planning.

He called the barrister and was connected to her immediately he mentioned his name.

'Ms Costello, you asked me to call you.'

'Yes, Mr Mitchell, I did.' Her tone was formal. 'Thank you for contacting me.'

'How can I help you?' Scott said.

'Would you be able to meet me, today if possible. Say at four, five?'

'Could you tell me what it's about, please?' And tell me how much I've inherited from a great aunt I didn't know I had.

'I shall do so when we meet.'

Her tone was measured, but determined.

Intriguing, but probably not an inheritance.

'Yes, okay... Let's say 4.30. Where shall we meet? Your chambers?'

Silence.

'Ms Costello?'

'Do you know the Old Thameside Inn by the *Golden Hinde* ship in Southwark?'

It was five minutes' walk from the gym where Scott worked out. 'Yes, indeed.'

'I shall be round the corner, as you approach, outside on the terrace overlooking the river, not the main terrace.'

'I know where you mean, Ms Costello. Shall I bring some ID? It's the fashion nowadays.'

'That won't be necessary. There are sufficient images of you on social media.'

Yes, and not all accompanied by flattering texts. 'Fine. And yours on your website...so we won't end up talking to two different people.' He chuckled at his own joke.

'Four thirty,' she said. 'Goodbye.'

Humourless?' Goodbye.'

4.30pm

The Old Thameside Inn was a converted former spice warehouse, with exposed brickwork and flagstone floors; a veritable tourist attraction in its own right, not to mention its proximity to the famous Borough Market, Southwark Cathedral and the Old Operating Theatre Museum. The inn's large terrace, abutting the replica *Golden Hinde II*, boasted panoramic views over the Thames, east and west, embracing St Paul's Cathedral and the hotchpotch of ancient and modern office buildings peppered around the City of London on the north side of the river.

The main terrace area was packed with groups of pre-teen schoolkids busily scribbling in their notebooks as their teachers explained the history of the reconstruction of Sir Francis Drake's original ship: *Golden Hind*. Scott wondered if any of them would ask their teacher why according to historical documents Drake's original ship was spelt *Hind* but the replica was spelt *Hinde*. He'd never been able to find a definitive answer on Google.

He turned left onto the narrower terrace where there was a single row of half a dozen or so tables banking the riverside balustrade, each with four chairs, two either side.

Diane Costello was sitting alone at the far end and facing Scott.

A woman, with her back to Scott, was alone, two tables before Costello's.

As he walked past her table, he noticed she was wearing earphones and staring at her tablet screen.

He approached the barrister.

'Ms Costello?' She looked like the photo on her website, but without the airbrushing and revealing a jowl on the left cheek. He touched his own, on the right cheek. Instant empathy.

'Scott Mitchell.' She stood up and held out her hand. 'Thank you for coming. Please, sit down.'

They shook hands.

She was big-boned for her apparent height, 1.6 metres give or take; not overweight, though he couldn't see under the table if she was wearing heels. Her shoulder-length ginger hair was crimped, her eyes green.

She glanced behind Scott as he sat down.

'I'll get right to the point if I may,' she said.

'Please do.'

'Mr Mitchell, I'm not a conspiracy theorist. I believe the Earth is round. I believe the Americans landed on the moon in 1969. I believe that Islamic terrorists were solely responsible for 9/11 and they didn't have any help from a *Deep State* unit operating in a bunker in the middle of the Nevada Desert.' She looked over Scott's shoulder. 'So please bear this in mind when you hear what I'm about to tell you.'

Intrigued, was an understatement. 'You have my undivided attention, Ms Costello. May I call you Diane?'

'Yes, Scott.'

'Thank you.'

'Some background first,' she said. 'I am, was, David Carey's personal lawyer in respect of inheritance-tax planning matters. I have been his counsel ever since his wife died of cancer ten years ago. We've become friends and I also now represent his adult children, Stephanie and Jonathan...'

She stopped and gazed across the river; wistfully, he thought.

'Diane, are you okay?'

'Yes, I'm sorry. It was Stephanie's daughter, Chrissy, who was in her grandfather's arms when he was gunned down.' She shook her head. 'Stephanie is devastated.'

'I can imagine,' Scott said. 'The media was full of it last night. It's horrific.' He knew from taking surviving witness statements in the Russian-Chechen conflicts that such traumas had long lasting effects on the families.

She leant forward and whispered. 'Four days ago, David came to see me in what I can only describe as a state of high anxiety.' She looked down at the table, and up again. 'No, it was more than that. It was *fear*.'

'Did he tell you the cause?'

'His life was being threatened but he didn't know who was responsible.'

'Hmm,' Scott muttered. Three days later a sniper assassinates him in London's financial centre. People, unless insane, don't murder without a reason, good or bad. 'What had he been doing?'

'He was investigating suspect trade deals between EU companies and the Russians; sanctions-busting, to be precise.'

Two dangerous pastimes: sanctions-busting and investigating it.

'If there's a profit to be made, people will bust sanctions, and they may become your enemies if you investigate them,' Scott said. 'But they don't usually go around killing government ministers in the process.'

'I agree,' she said.

From Trotsky to Litvinenko, and allegedly the Skripals, the former Soviet Union and the new Russia had never been shy of targeting any of their own living overseas who they deemed to be traitors and a threat to the Kremlin's power base, but, as far as Scott could recall, they'd never targeted a foreign power's government minister. The political consequences and damage to international relations would be incalculable.

So if not the Russians, who had assassinated David Carey?

'Why was he investigating this sanctions-busting in the first place?'

'Prior to being elected as an MP he was involved in trade deals in Eastern Europe, principally Russia and Ukraine. You never encountered him on your own Russian travels?'

'No.' Scott paused. 'No, I don't think so. His name doesn't ring any bells, anyway.'

She looked over Scott's shoulder again, before producing a sealed envelope from her handbag.

'He made me promise to give this to you *personally* in the event of his death or cognitive incapacity by other means.'

Scott jerked his head back. '*Me*? Why? We'd never met. We didn't know each other.'

'You might not have met but, like some of our legal brethren, he was an avid follower of your adventures and, shall we say, *engagements* with the powers that be. He admired your pertinacity and the way you stuck to your principles. Privately, he described you as a veritable David against Goliath; one of a kind.'

'Well, I'm sure there are many more deserving lawyers than me for that plaudit. But I don't understand. What's *in* the envelope?'

'He refused to tell me and said that the fewer people who knew about it, the better it would be...for them. But he also said *you* would know what to do with it.'

Scott sensed the irresistible force of a magnet attracting him into the darkness of the unknown.

He held his hand out. 'Okay, but I don't—'

She pulled back. 'There's something else I have to tell you before I give it to you.'

Scott withdrew his hand, confused. 'Go on.'

'He specifically instructed me to tell you *not* to discuss the contents of this envelope with the police...or members of the Establishment, under any circumstances whatsoever. He didn't trust them. He said that you should never forget the phrase: *quis custodiet, ipsos custodes?* It's Latin. It means—'

'Who watches the watchers?' Scott interjected. 'It's from Juvenal's "Satires".'

'Aha, you have a classical education.'

'Sure. It's the title of episode four in season three of *Star Trek: The Next Generation.* I've got the box set. It's a real *classic.*'

She chuckled, as if to say, 'I asked for that.'

'Why was he so mistrusting?' Scott had every reason not to trust these institutions, but what was the government minister's excuse?

'His illusions were shattered when he understood what went on in the corridors of power, beyond the public's gaze; the brazen betraying of principles, sometimes, allegedly, leading to law-breaking. It didn't matter which party was in charge.'

'*Plus ça change...*' Scott replied.

She was still clutching the envelope.

'He always was a bit of a rebel in Parliament,' she continued. 'Sitting on the back benches and not toeing the party line when it mattered most. He was very persuasive and had built quite a following amongst his fellow MPs. The only way the government could contain him was to invite him into their tent, so to speak.'

'Keep your friends close and your enemies closer.'

'Exactly. He was given a junior minister's post, working with the Foreign Office on Anglo-Russian relations.'

'Sounds like it was right up his street.'

'Indeed.'

Scott stared at the envelope.

'Here.' She handed it to him.

His name was handwritten on the front, along with the words:

Strictly private. To be opened by the addressee only.

He began to open it.

'Scott, please, don't.' She shook her head, quickly. 'Not here. Not in my presence.'

He stopped immediately. 'Why not?'

She lowered her voice, a whisper. 'Think about it. David Carey gave me the envelope fearing his life was in danger. Three days later his fear turned into reality. It's an assassination of a government minister. I'm the family lawyer. I have no doubt I'll be receiving a visit shortly from the police and, probably, the intelligence services...'

Scott thought of Fraser, though the man hadn't mentioned Carey in their meeting. Or would it be MI5?

'...They'll want as much background information as they can get. I don't want to sit here while you open that envelope and discover what's inside. As David said, the less I know about this matter, the better it will be for me.'

Over-concern?

Perhaps, but fair enough.

Scott tucked the envelope into his jacket pocket.

'Okay, I'll—'

Diane put her index finger to her lips and looked over Scott's shoulder again.

He half turned round. 'What? What is it?'

'I've got cramp coming on,' she said. 'I need to stretch my legs.'

'Pardon?' Scott turned back to her. 'What did you—?'

'Walk with me.' She got up and nodded, barely perceptibly, in the direction of the tables behind Scott. 'Come on. Time to depart.'

She hurried past him, back along the terrace.

Scott followed.

The lone woman sitting two tables away had been replaced by three young men, early 20s, nursing beers; their phones lying on the table between them.

Scott stopped to tie a shoelace.

They were chatting about Arsenal's chances in the current football season.

The other tables in their part of the terrace remained free.

Scott caught up with Diane. 'You don't think—'

'I would rather not have to think.'

They headed towards Borough Market and found an empty bench in the grounds of Southwark Cathedral.

'One final thing,' she said. 'David rarely used emails or any other form of digital transmission, apart from his mobile for innocuous calls. He said they all left footprints.'

That was true.

'To take that further, does it follow that his research evidence in his investigation is more likely to be archived in hard-copy format somewhere than on a computer or in the cloud?'

'I believe that's a strong possibility.'

'Any idea where?'

'No.'

Diane's phone rang.

She looked at the screen. 'Excuse me,' she said and moved away.

Scott closed his eyes. Visions of David Carey collapsing in the street with a bullet ripping through his brain while he held his baby granddaughter in his arms flickered in front of him.

Such events happened in Syria, not Canary Wharf.

Russian sanctions-busting and a political assassination.

How would he pitch it to Hollywood?

He opened his eyes, took out the envelope and fiddled with it; his feelings a mixture of anticipation, uncertainty and impatience – *you would know what to do with it.*

She returned.

'Sorry, Scott, but there's an emergency in chambers. I have to leave.'

Scott stood up.

They shook hands, said their goodbyes and she hurried out of the gardens.

He tore the envelope open and pulled out a single sheet of folded conqueror paper on which was handwritten:

Santorini International Securities LLP
Arkady Vladimirovich Orlov
Simone Bisset
Sir Stanton Morgan Bell
Professor Consuela Isabella Marcia Zapatero

None of the names mean anything to him, not even that of the UK knight.

Chapter 4

Day Three: 3pm, Prague

Though operating primarily out of Budapest when working for the World Preservation Foundation, Scott occasionally had to go to Prague. Both cities had suffered the brutal predations of two World Wars, a Nazi occupation and subsequent Soviet invasions, but the intruders had failed to destroy completely two of the most beautiful Central-European capitals. Much of their Austro-Hungarian architecture was still standing, including, in Prague's case, the houses and offices where its most famous author, Franz Kafka, had lived and worked.

He sat outside the *Kavarna obecni dum* café in the city centre, ordered a coffee and a Pilsner beer. The night before, he'd fallen asleep with Carey's list of names repeatedly scrolling across his mind, intermittently interrupted with images of the MP's shooting to death with baby Chrissy clutched in his arms.

Diane didn't want to know what was in the envelope, so he was left with three options: tear the list up and get on with his more than comfortable life; give it to the authorities with Diane's backstory; or investigate the list himself.

He was far too curious to destroy the list and forget he'd ever seen the names. Besides, it was effectively a dying man's last wish that he did something about it.

Giving it to the authorities was a non-starter. Carey hadn't trusted them, and Scott certainly had every reason not to.

That left the third option: what relevance were the names on the list to the MP's sanctions-busting investigation?

His phone rang.

He didn't recognise the number.

'Yes?' he said in English.

'Scott, it's me,' came the reply in Russian. 'Sergey.'

Sergey was one of Gravchenko's trusted lieutenants; Scott worked with him regularly. Like the boss, the man didn't speak English.

'Where are you?' Scott said. 'Are you here? Because if so, I'd like to speak to—'

'No, we're in Paris.'

'What?! The press conference is at 5.30. I—'

'Yeah. Sorry. Something urgent's cropped up. You know how it is.'

Only too well; meetings arranged on short notice and cancelled at the last minute. It was frustrating, but not so annoying as to ever give Scott cause to pack it in. For a fee of US$75,000 a month his patience level was high.

'Okay. But it's too late to warn all the registered attendees individually now. Some will be on their way. I'll cancel it at the venue. Mind you, the media's not going to like it.' The venue for the conference was the Hilton Hotel. Scott's role was to fill in on the legal progress in respect of the Foundation's well-publicised negotiations with Ghana. Gravchenko had offered to help expand the country's infrastructure in exchange for the sole right to manufacture and distribute the Foundation's green products there. It was a win-win proposition for both parties: Ghana would be able to develop its economy with the capital injected – or such of it that was left after the country's corrupt negotiators had taken their commissions – and the Foundation's operating costs would be lower than in other more technologically advanced states.

'The boss isn't cancelling it; he wants you to take the chair,' Sergey said. 'Tell them he's got food poisoning or something. You know what to say. You're the lawman. You know how to lie,' he sniggered.

'Whatever.'

'I don't suppose many will turn up,' Sergey said. 'You remember the last time? In Rome?'

How could Scott forget? They'd reserved a conference room and a buffet for 50, and only ten invitees had shown. But Gravchenko had welcomed the media apathy; it was better than opprobrium.

'Fair enough.' Scott sighed. 'I'll report back to the man later tonight.'

'Have fun.'

Sergey rang off.

Apart from the two isolated occasions when Gravchenko's enemies had accused the Foundation of being a front for an international money-laundering operation, without any evidence being produced, the Foundation had been receiving relatively favourable publicity since Scott had joined in late 2016. There hadn't been any of the anticipated heavyweight attacks from state and corporate anti-green lobbies threatening injunctions, restraining orders and monster damages claims for all kinds of imagined business interruptions allegedly caused by the Foundation's supporters; a few minor litigation skirmishes, that was all.

For his part, Gravchenko had continued to pump millions into the Foundation and instructed his international accountants to put six-monthly *audited* management accounts on the internet. Management accounts were rarely audited and if they were, they would seldom be open to public inspection, if ever.

Scott was again confident that Gravchenko's enemies wouldn't find anything to justify their suspicions.

*

5.30pm

Scott stood at the lectern in the packed 60-seater Tyrolka room while his two assistants, Mariella and Klaus, completed the distribution of a single-page information sheet that he'd hurriedly prepared after Sergey's call, using the internet and the skimpy notes he'd cobbled together the evening before. Gravchenko's promised paperwork, a three-page briefing summary, had gone AWOL with the man himself.

He checked the time and took a couple of mouthfuls of water.

'Good afternoon ladies and gentlemen.' He smiled; no response from the audience. 'For those of you who might not know me, my name is Scott Mitchell and I am Chief Counsel to the World Preservation Foundation. Thank you for coming. I'm sorry that some of you have to remain standing, but we weren't expecting so many of you to attend.' He smiled again; no response. 'I only hope we have enough food to sate your appetites…' He waved in the direction of the nibbles.

'So do I, Mr Mitchell.' The voice came from the front row; a chubby, red-cheeked, middle-aged man with a thick mop of silver hair. He was wearing an ultra-wide tie with an even wider Windsor knot. His accent was English. 'So do I.'

The audience murmured.

The man turned and nodded at them.

'Yes, quite,' Scott replied. 'First, ladies and gentlemen. I must apologise for Mr Gravchenko's absence, I know you expect—'

The murmuring increased.

Scott held his hand up. 'He has been called away at the last minute to an urgent unplanned meeting. Please accept his sincere apologies for his absence.'

Chairs scraped the floor.

'Where is he?' Chubby asked.

'Pardon?'

'Where is Mr Gravchenko, your boss?'

'As I said, Mr...?'

'My name is Henry Wyatt. I write the "Wyatt Non-Fake News Blog". You might have heard of me,' he said smugly.

Oh yes. Scott knew his name, but had never seen the man's face. His profile image comprised the omnipresent Guy Fawkes mask. When it came to the Kremlin's activities, Wyatt was more condemning than the hawks in Washington. His blogs contained wild accusations of corruption, unsupported by a scintilla of evidence. The "Non-Fake News" name for his website was the ultimate irony.

Scott forced a smile and remained polite. 'As I said, Mr Wyatt, Mr Gravchenko was called away to a meeting at the last minute. Client confidentiality, of course, prevents me from saying where he is and what he's doing.'

'So your boss is transparent only when it suits him,' Wyatt said.

Scott gritted his teeth, and held his tongue. 'No, Mr Wyatt. That isn't correct. A well-informed man such as yourself...' the expression "well-informed" stuck in Scott's throat '...will surely appreciate that the confidential relationship between a client and his lawyer is an essential institution of a free society.' He took a sip of water. 'As indeed, is the freedom of expression you enjoy on your blog,' he added with a disdainful smile.

'I'm glad you think that way,' Wyatt said. He stood up with a sheet of paper in his hand; it wasn't the same colour as the information sheet. 'Tell me, Mr Mitchell, have you during your *very long* association with the Foundation...'

Under 24 months equalled a very long association?

'...and Mr Gravchenko ever had any dealings with a company called Santorini International Securities?' He waved the sheet of paper at Scott.

Scott opened his mouth, intending to speak, but nothing came out as he simultaneously conjured up the image of the name on Carey's list.

'Well, Mr Chief Counsel, what's the answer?"

'No...I can't recall ever having done so.' Only answer the question asked – and as truthfully as possible. He hadn't had any *dealings* with the company.

Disconcerting throat-clearing rippled throughout the audience.

Was Wyatt acting alone?

'I see,' Wyatt said, slowly nodding, as if doubting the sincerity of Scott's reply. 'Well, I think you, and the people gathered here today...' he turned and gestured at the audience, and back to Scott '...would be interested to hear that this Scottish company's registered owners are—'

Two companies with the same name? Possible. The name, unknown to Scott until the previous day, coming to his attention from two separate sources within 24 hours of each other? Again, possible. But Scott's gut feeling, bearing in mind Wyatt's anti-Russian muck-raking, leant towards something more disturbing than a simple coincidence.

And a public forum was no place for a prudent lawyer to discuss the matter with a reckless blogger.

Scott held up his hand. 'Mr Wyatt, please. As I've just said, I haven't had any dealings with this company...' he lowered his hand '...and it certainly doesn't feature in today's update on the Foundation's activities in Ghana. So, with respect to your right of freedom of expression, I would like to proceed with the issues that are relevant to the subject matter of this conference. If that's okay with you?'

Wyatt turned back to his audience and threw his hands out wide in a "well I tried" gesture, then back to Scott.

'As you wish, Mr Mitchell. But don't say I never gave you the opportunity to be transparent.'

He stuffed the paper into his pocket and strutted from the room in silence, leaving Scott flummoxed, if not agitated.

6.45pm

Scott emerged from the lift in the lobby relieved that the conference had continued without any distraction after Wyatt had left. But his relief was tempered by the man's reference to Santorini, so much so that the moment he left the conference room he searched the public register at the UK's Companies House; something he'd not had time to do the day before. In strict legal terms it wasn't a *company*, but a Scottish *limited partnership*. Its Edinburgh office address looked like a typical corporate agents' service address, maybe a law or accountancy firm. The two named owner-partners were Dmitry Yazov and Ernst Bauer with a common contact address: a building number in Jerichostraat, Maastricht, Netherlands.

Like the names on Carey's list, the two individuals were unknown to him.

He spotted Wyatt at a table in the corner of the lobby bar, nursing a beer and fiddling with his phone.

Scott approached him.

'May I join you, Mr Wyatt?'

The man looked up and smiled. 'Be my guest.'

'Thank you.'

'Can I get you something?' Wyatt said. 'A beer?'

'No, I'm fine thanks.'

Wyatt laid his phone on the table and relaxed back in his chair. 'You want to know about Santorini,' he said in a confident tone. It was a statement, not a question.

Scott nodded at the phone. 'Are you recording this?' He wasn't sure how the conversation was going to pan out; better to be safe than sorry.

'No, but if it makes you happy, I'll put it in my pocket.' He did so.

'What has Santorini got to do with the Foundation?' Scott asked.

Wyatt's eyes widened. 'Why, *have* you heard of it?'

'I didn't say that.'

'That's right, you didn't,' Wyatt said as he took a sip of his beer.

'So what's the answer?' Scott persisted. 'What has it got to do with my client's affairs?'

Wyatt cradled his beer glass. 'Okay, let's play it your way.' He licked his lips. 'Santorini is a Scottish limited partnership.'

'I know. I've checked Companies House.'

'Then you'll know that the registered owners are Dmitry Yazov and Ernst Bauer...'

'As I said, I checked Companies House.'

'Yazov is an ex-employee of your client's Foundation; he worked in the Paris office until he left three months ago,' Wyatt continued. 'Ernst Bauer works in the Foundation's compliance department in St. Petersburg...'

That was the second time Wyatt had paused at the end of a sentence, as if expecting Scott to say something revelatory.

'And?'

'As you also presumably know, Scottish limited partnerships can be the vehicle of choice for Russian money-launderers.'

Wyatt was right. The UK Parliament was so concerned about the lax registration requirements for such Scottish entities that it had recently enacted legislation to bring them into line with their English counterparts, requiring more transparency as to who was the controlling influence behind a company.

That was the objective, at any event.

'Santorini is no exception,' Wyatt said with a broad

grin and raised eyebrows. 'It regularly launders six-, seven-figure sums, US dollars...through West Africa, *Ghana* in particular.'

Despite the blogger's bullshit pedigree, his reference to the Foundation's employees couldn't be dismissed out of hand by Scott; it merited investigation on his part.

The world knew that the WPF was Gravchenko's baby.

And that would have included David Carey.

'I don't wish to be obtuse,' Scott said, 'but what's all this got to do with the Foundation?'

Wyatt tapped his fingers on the table. 'You're far from obtuse Mr Mitchell. I'm sure you get my drift.'

Scott said nothing.

A phone rang.

'It's mine,' Wyatt said, retrieving it from his pocket.

He looked at the screen and answered.

'Yes? ...Okay, will do.' He disconnected and got up. 'Sorry, got to go, emergency.' He winked at Scott. 'You know how these *unexpected* things crop up.' He pushed his three-quarters full beer glass across the table.

'Here, it's paid for. No point in wasting it.'

7.30pm

Scott called Sergey, after failing to get through to Gravchenko.

'I've finished up here and am leaving for the airport. I'll be back home around midnight. I must see the boss as soon as possible, ideally tomorrow, anywhere will do.'

'Give me ten minutes.'

Sergey ended the call.

Scott googled the street view of Santorini's Jerichostraat address. It was a two-storey terraced house in a street that lined one side of a grass square called Jerichoplein. With its buff brick frontage, it could have been anywhere in the suburbs of an English town, such was the similarity to 1950s-built British homes.

There was nothing suspicious about the two owner-partners having non-Scottish addresses. People living all over the world were registered as owners of UK companies.

Sergey called.

'He'll be in London tomorrow afternoon. The Serpentine in Hyde Park at 3.15. Can you make that?

'Yes. Thanks. I'll be there.'

'Good. Be at the Lido Café.'

'Will do.'

Sergey disconnected again.

Chapter 5

Day Four: 10.30am, Sicily

General Leonid Igorovich Pravda of the GRU, Russian Military Intelligence, sat outside his favourite eatery in Catania – the Bar Francesco located behind the fish market in the centre of town – anxiously tucking into a Sicilian cipollina with cheese, onion and olive, hastily washed down by a double espresso.

His expected carefree enjoyment of a three-week period of R & R had been shattered with the overnight announcement of the imminent arrival of his loathsome boss, Max.

This particular Kremlin lickspittle was never a messenger of good tidings for Pravda.

A diminutive overweight Alfred Hitchcock, cursing in his creased, perspiration-stained white linen suit that was two sizes too big, and wearing a white fedora that was two sizes too small for his bald head, tumbled out of a taxi.

'Get me a beer,' Max grunted as he plonked himself down on a chair opposite Pravda.

'No luggage?' Pravda said.

'I'm going back to civilisation later this afternoon,' Max sneered.

Pravda ordered a beer from Luca, his befriended waiter, and began to relax at the thought of not having to entertain his boss for more than a few hours.

'What have you found out about Santorini?' Max said.

Pravda widened his eyes. 'What are you talking about? What's Santorini?'

'Christ,' Max said, wiping his forehead with a table napkin. 'This *heat*.'

Pravda checked his phone app. 'It's only 35.' He could barely contain his glee.

'Should be against the law. Don't they have air-conditioning on this desert island?'

'Not in the street. Surprising as that may seem.'

The mocking appeared to have escaped Max, who was more concerned with soaking up beads of sweat from his three chins.

Luca brought Max's beer, which he pounced on.

Pravda thanked Luca, knowing that his uninvited guest wouldn't.

'So what's this Santorini matter?'

Max glared at him in between noisy swigs of beer. 'Do you ever read your incoming reports? That's what we fucking pay you for.'

Pravda always tried to read the reports as soon as they came in, no matter where he was in the world and despite any R & R, but he'd been pre-occupied with Max's forthcoming visit and had left his villa that morning without checking what his assistant, Major Yelena Grigoryeva, had uploaded to their secured cloud file, and which he would rarely risk accessing in public.

'IT glitch,' Pravda lied. 'It hadn't arrived by the time I left the villa.'

Max snorted. 'Gravchenko's press conference in Prague yesterday. Your mole, Mitchell, was hit with a question about a company called Santorini International Securities.'

The Kremlin, via Max, had taken Pravda off general military intelligence duties and set him up with the funds to head a small team to obtain as much information as possible about Gravchenko's business affairs. It was obsessed with the notion that the oligarch and the Foundation appeared to be untainted by criminal, or even unethical, activities. Konstantin Gravchenko was up to something. He'd always been up to something. A leopard never changed his spots.

But, Mitchell was far from being a mole. The lawyer had told Gravchenko about Pravda's attempts to recruit him in 2016 and the oligarch had given him authority to tell Pravda everything he wanted to know other than legally privileged information.

'What was the question?'

'Something about whether he'd heard of Santorini in connection with the Foundation.' Max took another large swig. 'Something like that.'

The man wasn't known for his attention to detail.

'Who asked it?'

'An English blogger arsehole. Name of Henry Wyatt.'

Pravda knew the name, and the man's lack of credibility. He was low on Pravda's list of "persons of interest".

'What was Mitchell's response?'

'He said he'd never heard of Santorini and closed the arsehole down.'

Max's voice was getting louder and louder.

Pravda looked at the neighbouring tables; one occupied with three teenage backpackers talking in French, and another table with an elderly couple, the man doing a sudoku puzzle and the woman reading the *Giornale di Sicilia* newspaper.

'Leave it with me,' Pravda said. 'I'll look into it... Santorini and Wyatt. But you could have told me this through the normal channels. No need for the face-to-face.' Why had the genetically programmed xenophobe slithered off his fat backside for a day trip to a "desert island"?

Max leant forward. 'General Pravda, I'm here to help you. I have to tell you in person.' He glanced at the other tables and whispered. 'You understand?'

'Go on,' Pravda said. He didn't need to be a lifetime

intelligence officer to be able to spot not *one*, but *two* rats: the slob sitting opposite and his immediate superior in the Kremlin, whoever that was.

'Patience is wearing thin,' Max continued. 'You've been investigating Gravchenko for four, five years and his charity bollocks for 18 months. What have you got to show for it?'

'Max, I—'

'Nothing.' He glared at Pravda. 'That's what. Nothing.' He wiped the sweat from his face again. 'The clock's ticking, General Pravda. You've got 28 days to get something on the bastard. Twenty-eight days.' He finished his drink. 'Start with Santorini...and get me another beer.'

Pravda's stomach turned. Failure to meet the deadline would mean a dishonourable discharge, being stripped of his bravery-in-conflict medals and loss of pension rights. Perhaps he should have funded his retirement by taking bribes, like so many in service of the fatherland.

'Has anybody ever considered the reason I've not found anything is because there isn't anything there? The man is clean.'

Max slammed a clenched fist on the table.

His empty beer glass jumped, as did Pravda.

The chattering neighbours went silent.

'He's a fucking oligarch! Of course there's something there!'

Pravda squirmed as his left ankle began to shoot pains up his left leg; a wound from his early military career that had refused to heal properly and was now his harbinger of doom.

Chapter 6

Day Four: 3.15pm, London

An illegal drone hovering over the airfield at Gatwick Airport had caused Scott's flight to wait on the taxiway at Prague for two hours, without the passengers being allowed back into the terminal. A second drone at Gatwick had appeared while his flight was over the English Channel and the plane had to divert to Birmingham Airport, 125 miles north of London.

A scramble for taxis and a rip-off payment of £375 got Scott into his Canary Wharf bed at 6am.

Having slept until 1pm, he'd arrived at the Espresso Van Lido Café 30 minutes before the appointed time and taken one of the outside tables by the lake, occupying himself with a brief internet sweep for the principal sites that were concentrating on David Carey's life and death, including the MP's Wikipedia entry. He saved the URLs for a later detailed review.

He glanced around the café area, studying the people sitting at the other tables and squinting at the customers going in and out of the building: singles, couples and groups of three generations.

Were any of the issues in *their* lives as challenging and convoluted as his?

He scrolled through the gallery on his phone where he'd stored the images of the woman from Budapest, having left the hard copies at home.

'Nice day for feeding the ducks,' a Russian voice said from behind.

Scott turned round.

His boss was smiling.

Scott stood up and shook hands with the oligarch. The man's grip was like a vice hungry for its next victim. 'Kostya.'

'Follow me,' Gravchenko said.

They ambled along the lakeside path in a clockwise direction towards the Serenity sculpture, remaining silent until out of earshot of any audience.

'That Wyatt guy can be a real shit stirrer,' Gravchenko said.

His boss must have had somebody in the audience as Scott hadn't told Sergey about the man's appearance.

'Did you expect him to be there?' Scott asked. 'Because if so, you could have warn—'

'He turns up from time to time, if he thinks he's got me on some business deal,' Gravchenko cut in. 'But I've not seen him for a couple of years.'

He walked over to the waterside, pulled a plastic bag from his jacket pocket, took out a handful of birdseed and scattered it over a flotilla of approaching ducks. 'Don't ever feed them bread,' Gravchenko growled. 'It leads to obesity, malnutrition and angel wing.'

'If you say so'. Angel wing? What was that? It was the first time since he'd been working for the man that he'd seen him so relaxed; carefree. 'Does he have anything on you, this Wyatt?'

Gravchenko's eyes stayed on the ducks. 'No.' It was a casual response.

'Have you heard of that company he mentioned, Santorini?'

'No.' He shrugged. 'It's not one of mine.'

There was nothing in Gravchenko's voice or demeanour that led Scott to doubt him.

'I caught up with Wyatt after the conference and asked him for an explanation.'

'What did he say?' Gravchenko was still on the ducks.

Scott told him the story, including the details he'd obtained at Companies House and his google-mapping of the address in Maastricht.

Gravchenko lit a cigarette and inhaled deeply. 'Over there,' he said, and pointed to an empty bench by the Serenity sculpture.

They both sat down.

'Anything else?'

'No, that's about it.'

'I'll check what we've got on these guys, Yazov and Bauer.'

He didn't show any signs of recognising their names; not surprising as the Foundation had more than a thousand employees worldwide.

'Get back to Wyatt,' Gravchenko said. 'I want to know where this money-laundering stuff's coming from.'

'But it's not your company.'

Gravchenko laughed. '*You*, of all people, should know it will be my company by the time the trolls on social media get hold of it. Those parasites don't give a shit about the truth of anything.'

Indeed. He should know.

'Wyatt thinks he's got dirt on me.' Gravchenko squished his cigarette out with his foot. 'I want to know who my enemies are.'

Keep your friends close and your enemies closer.

Unless you want a bullet ripping into your pre-frontal lobe.

Gravchenko got up and walked on.

Scott followed.

His boss took a call.

Scott received a text from Fraser:

Any news?

He looked around, and across the lake.

Was the spook hiding behind a tree?

He responded:

Will get back to you.

And waited for a sarcastic comment, if not abuse.

A “thumbs up” emoji appeared.

Was the man on happy pills?

Gravchenko’s call ended and they carried on walking around the lake.

‘Kostya, did you ever have any dealings with David Carey, the UK government minister who was assassinated four days ago?’

‘No, why?’

Scott told him Costello’s story and about the names on the list. His reasons for not trusting the UK authorities were justified, but that mistrust didn’t extend to Gravchenko, the boss who’d employed him in a high-profile and well-paid job despite his public arrest on suspicion of international money-laundering on a major scale.

‘And what are you going to do about it?’ Kostya asked.

‘I’ve got to check out why Carey was investigating the names. Santorini’s on the list and Wyatt thinks he can link it to our Foundation. I’ve got to show him that he’s straying into defamation territory.’

The oligarch stopped.

‘Yeah,’ he said, pensively. ‘You *do* that.’

He turned away and carried on walking.

Scott was quick to his side. ‘What about the other names on the list? Orlov, Bisset, Bell and Zapatero?’

‘I don’t know any of them,’ Gravchenko said. ‘But I’ll check out this Orlov character. It could be a Russian name.’

‘Thanks.’

'That it?'

'Almost.'

Scott brought up the images of the Budapest woman on his phone.

'Who is this woman, Kostya?'

Gravchenko examined them and stopped walking again. 'Who gave you these?' His tone was calm.

'You remember Colin Fraser, the MI6 spook who hounded me in Moscow?'

'What does he want to know about her?'

Scott told him what Fraser had said.

'No specifics?'

'No. It's a matter of state security and I'm not a member of their club. You know, in 2016 I refused to sign the Official Secrets Act.'

'Refresh my memory.'

'Our existing laws in the UK are sufficient to enable me to be prosecuted for revealing state secrets, provided the state can prove damage. But if I sign the Act, I've effectively signed a *contract* which stipulates that if I reveal state secrets I can be prosecuted, even though the state *can't* prove damage.'

'You Westerners and your rules of law.'

They headed back.

'She's one of my independent researchers,' he said. 'Ecological sustainability. She's looking into the short- and long-term impact on environmental management decisions. I'm going to introduce you to her.'

'Great, I'd like to meet her.' And her gorgeous eyes. 'What's her name?'

'Teresa Stepanovna Volkova.'

'Russian?'

'And Czech. A bit of a handful, but she knows her stuff. You might want to add her to your team at the Foundation.' Gravchenko shrugged. 'It's your call. No pressure. I'm not fazed either way.'

What more could Scott ask for? 'Is it okay if I tell Fraser what you've just told me about her?'

'Sure. I've nothing to hide.'

Chapter 7

Day Five: 11am, London

Sergey called as Scott walked into the serviced office complex by London's Fenchurch Street rail terminus for a pre-arranged appointment.

'Yes, Sergey.'

'Yazov used to work for us. He left three months ago and was killed last month in a road traffic accident in Berlin. A truck driver had a stroke approaching an intersection and careered into oncoming traffic. He took out four vehicles. It was carnage.'

'Poor Yazov.' Damn, a source of evidence gone. 'And Bauer?'

'He's still with us, in St Petes. A good worker. He's also fuming. He knows nothing about Santorini. Never heard of it. But he's had his identity stolen three times in the last two years. This looks like the fourth.'

'Maybe,' Scott said. 'But it could be another Ernst Bauer altogether and Wyatt's information is just plain wrong.'

'Yeah, of course.'

'Is our Bauer on the level?'

'He's got all his records of reporting the ID thefts to the police and the banks and stuff. We're checking them now. They look genuine.'

'He's got to be one unlucky guy.'

'Shit happens.'

'Okay. Thanks.'

Scott disconnected.

*

10 minutes later

There was a framed picture of the late US tennis player, Arthur Ashe, on the wall behind Henry Wyatt's desk. The proud-faced 1975 Wimbledon Champion was holding the trophy aloft for the benefit of the spectators; millions worldwide.

The large-font quote standing in front of a dual screen computer on the desk read:

> 'One important key to success, is self-confidence. An important key to self-confidence is preparation'
>
> – Arthur Ashe

'As Arthur says, Scott, it's all about self-confidence and preparation.'

Wyatt eased forward in his high-backed leather and walnut chair, repeatedly tapping a gold-coloured pen on the desk.

Smugness personified.

'Tell me,' Scott said, 'how confident are you that your information on Yazov and Bauer is accurate?'

A slight frown. 'Their names are on the register.'

'I'm talking specifically about their alleged employment with Mr Gravchenko's Foundation. That's not on the register. So where did you get the information?'

Wyatt swivelled the chair from side to side. 'Come, come, counsellor, you know better than that. We never reveal our sources.'

'Did your source forget to tell you that Yazov was killed in a road traffic accident in Berlin last month and that Bauer's ID has been stolen on numerous occasions? And before you query this information, it's been confirmed with the appropriate authorities. What's more, Mr Gravchenko's never heard of Santorini.' He straightened. 'So what do you have to say about your *preparation* now?'

'Nobody's perfect.'

Especially oligarch bashers who rush to judgement and refuse to let the truth stand in their way of trying to get a viral scoop.

'Which brings me to the next point,' Scott said. 'What's your money-laundering evidence?'

Wyatt scrolled on his phone and handed it to Scott.

'Look at these images.'

Scott took the phone.

They were financial statements issued by one of the world's largest banks, showing that over recent weeks Santorini had been making daily payments of hundreds of thousands, and occasionally millions, of US dollars from its Ghanian account to a string of different companies, none of which Scott recognised at such a fleeting glance.

Did Carey want him to follow the money?

'How's that for a taster?' Wyatt said.

Scott handed the phone back to Wyatt, having memorised the address and sort code of Santorini's bank.

'It doesn't take rocket science to forge bank statements nowadays,' Scott said.

He wanted to end the conversation at that point, but Gravchenko needed to find out who his enemies were, and Wyatt's source would be the place to start. 'Send me three or four images and I'll get them validated.'

He wasn't sure how – with all the data-protection hurdles people had to go through to talk about their *own* bank accounts. He'd give the information to Sergey and let him get on with it; no questions asked.

'Whoa,' Wyatt said. 'Hold your horses. I'm not a charity. I've got *administration* expenses.'

Surprise, surprise.

'How much?'

'Two hundred and fifty-thousand US dollars.'

A unicorn farm in cloud cuckoo land.

'For a few images of dubious bank statements?'

'Only a few, yes, but what you really want is the name and contact details of my source.'

That's at least one thing you've got right, my non-fake-news journo friend.

'Is your source the same source who supplied you with the ill-prepared information about Yazov and Bauer?'

'No, no. Absolutely not.' He shook his head vigorously, as if that would be sufficient to convince Scott that $250,000 was a blue chip investment.

'You're prepared to betray your code of "we-never-reveal-our-source" for a financial benefit?'

Wyatt frowned. 'Needs must. I've got mouths to feed; school fees to pay.'

With friends like you, Mr Wyatt, who needs enemies?

Scott pushed back his chair and got up.

Time to test Wyatt's mettle.

'Of course it's for you to decide what you do with the images, Mr Wyatt, but please, for your own sake, don't be *too* self-confident. Defamation cases can be very expensive...for the loser. Goodbye.'

He left without offering his hand.

Your move Mr Wyatt.

20 minutes later

Scott sat on a bench at the side of the Tower of London, overlooking the Thames and Tower Bridge. He uploaded Santorini's details to the cloud account he shared with Sergey and called Alex, their agent who was based in Nigeria and working on their Ghana project, something he'd been meaning to do since his Prague meeting with Wyatt.

'You must be psychic, Scott, I was just about to call you. Good news.'

Listen first, talk later.

'What is it?'

'Project Conrad is on.'

Gravchenko's favourite book was Joseph Conrad's *Heart of Darkness*.

'That's good.'

'You could be a bit more enthusiastic, counsellor. I've worked my balls off for this.'

And for your hefty commission.

'Yes, you're right, I'm sorry. Well done. A great job.'

'Are you stressed out,' Alex said. 'Have you been overworking...again?'

'Alex, I'm texting you the name of a *fund distributor*, operating in your part of the world. Check it out for me, please.' Alex would know what he meant.

He texted:

Santorini International Securities LLP. It's Scottish

Scott didn't want to risk mentioning the company's name on the phone.

Got it. Will do

'Now,' Alex said. 'Back to the business of the day. The Ghanian government rep and his lawyer want to meet you as soon as possible. They'll be in London in a few days. Can I tell them you're ready to meet?'

'Sure, on 24...preferably 48, hours' notice.'

'Great. Bye for now.'

'Cheers.'

15 minutes later

Fraser was sitting at a table outside the Tower Bridge Café when Scott arrived. They'd arranged the meeting the previous evening.

The spook nodded.

Scott bought a coffee and joined him.

'So, what's the news?' Fraser said.

'Her name is Teresa Stepanovna Volkova and she works for Gravchenko as an independent researcher.'

'What nationality is she?'

'Russian and Czech.'

'What does she research?'

'Ecological sustainability.'

'How did he react when you showed him the images?'

'Nothing special. He wanted to know where they came from. I told him. That's it.'

Fraser placed his phone on the table so Scott could see the screen, albeit upside down, and began clicking and scrolling.

The constant shakes of the head and tutting showed that Fraser wasn't happy with his searches.

'What's up?' Scott asked.

'She's not on the web. No image, nothing.'

'Give it time, you've only spent five minutes on it.'

'No. She's a researcher for Gravchenko, top of Russia's rich list. She's into all this ecological stuff. Must have written papers on it. They'd be on the net.'

'Yeah,' Scott said. 'She may well have written papers on the subject. And, yeah, they'd probably be on the net. But you're just like me, and a zillion other impatient people. You give up searching after the first three pages of Google.' He sipped his coffee.

'Maybe, maybe not.' Fraser stopped scrolling. 'I'll get IT onto it. Meanwhile, I want you to get me the full facts on this Teresa woman: a detailed CV, the URL links to her publications and any websites she's connected with. It doesn't make sense she's not on the web.' He grunted. 'I'll be straight with you, I think your man's holding back something.'

His tone was harsher than in their most recent exchanges, not as aggressive as it used to be in 2016, but heading in that direction.

While Scott had no problem with asking Gravchenko

for more information on her, he wasn't going to tell Fraser that his boss had suggested a personal meeting with her. If the spook knew that he'd be forever pestering Scott to get as much personal information as possible from her directly.

He didn't need the hassle.

Chapter 8

Day Six: 7pm, Sicily

At least somebody up there likes me, General Pravda said to himself as he stood on the threshold of his villa watching Scott Mitchell's taxi turn into the large semi-circular driveway. The lawyer's unexpected request for an urgent face-to-face meeting had been a welcome turn of events after Max's "ticking clock" ultimatum two days earlier.

Pravda had known Mitchell five years and, despite their ups and downs that frequently tested their loyalty to their own country, they'd become trusted friends within the limits permitted by such loyalties.

He opened the rear passenger door as the taxi pulled to a halt, and waited as Mitchell paid the driver and got out with his overnight baggage.

The taxi sped away.

'This R & R suits you, Leonid,' Scott said in Russian as they shook hands.

Pravda's English was patchy.

'Sure. And *you* should try it. When was the last time you took a holiday, or a short break?'

'So what you're saying is, I look like the proverbial.'

'Your words, not mine. Come, let's go inside. Drop your luggage in the hallway and follow me through to the terrazzo outside.'

'Wow!' Mitchell said as they emerged from the back of the villa. 'This is social media imagery. It's stunning, the Med at dusk. What are those twinkling lights in the distance? Fishing boats?'

'Yes, and if you squint for long enough, you'll see a couple of cruise ships on the horizon.' Pravda gestured to a table and two chairs overlooking the sea. 'I've prepared a small snack before we have dinner. Nothing too filling: olives, bread and wine. It shouldn't spoil your appetite.'

'It won't; I'm starving. It's been junk food since I left Gatwick this morning, with a delayed stopover in Rome. I need to cleanse the palate.'

They sat down and Pravda poured a glass of red wine for each of them. 'It's Barolo, your favourite.'

They clinked their glass.

'Cheers,' Pravda said in English.

'To our health,' Mitchell responded in Russian.

'Okay, my friend,' Pravda said. 'What's so urgent?' He knew from their previous meetings that Mitchell disliked prolonged small talk more than *he* did.

'This.' Mitchell took a small sheet of paper from his pocket and handed it across the table.

Pravda studied it for ten seconds, trying to contain any appearance of good fortune at seeing the reference to Santorini.

'What about it?' He laid it on the table in front of him, face up.

'You know that one of our government ministers, David Carey, was assassinated in London six days ago.'

'Yes.' Pravda would let Mitchell do the talking.

'Well, Carey instructed his lawyer, a barrister called Diane Costello, to give me this list of names in the event of his death. It's not the original, by the way; that's in a safe place.'

'Why?'

Mitchell told him the details of his meeting with Costello, and collapsed in his chair with the glass of Barolo in his hand. A relieved man? A trouble shared?

'How can I help you?'

'I've got to find out what Carey was investigating and how these names fit in. Do you recognise any of them?'

Pravda picked up the paper and looked at the names again, more for effect than because he'd forgotten what they were, as he hadn't.

He wasn't going to lie to Mitchell unless his duty to the Kremlin demanded it.

'Would it surprise you to know that we had somebody at your press conference in Prague?'

Mitchell chuckled. 'You, and undoubtedly MI6. All I need now is for the CIA to confirm its presence and I've got the set.'

'So you'll be aware that our agent would have heard the name "Santorini" being mentioned by the blogger Henry Wyatt.'

'That follows.'

'Do you know why Wyatt asked a question about that company? I understand you shut him up before he could explain.'

Mitchell looked perplexed as he fidgeted in his seat and gazed out to sea. Pravda knew the lawyer's body language only too well. Mitchell's mind was ticking over. He was conflicted for some reason.

'Okay, Scott, I don't want to—'

'No, it's alright. Wyatt told me after the conference he had information which showed that a current and, now, an ex-employee of the Foundation owned the company and it was involved in money-laundering.'

Interesting. Give Mitchell something in return.

'We're doing our own investigation into Santorini,' Pravda said. 'The two registered owners are Dmitry Yazov and Ernst Bauer. Are they the employees?'

'Yes.'

'Have you told Gravchenko about Wyatt?' He tapped on the list. 'And this?'

'Yes...to both questions. Neither Carey nor I trust the

UK Authorities.' He took another mouthful of wine.' So you and Gravchenko are the obvious people for me to turn to. I trust you both. In your own ways, you each have access to a vast amount of information about Russian affairs and its people.'

Well, well. Working together with Mitchell and Gravchenko on Santorini, that should confuse Max. 'So what does Gravchenko say about the names?'

'He's never heard of Santorini. Yazov was killed in a car crash in Berlin a month ago and Bauer's clean. He's one of life's unfortunate targets for identity thieves, apparently. It's happened more than once.'

Oh dear. Pravda's short-lived feeling of good luck had come to an abrupt end. If the oligarch was telling the truth, Santorini would be a lead to nowhere so far as Max's ultimatum was concerned; though that didn't mean the company wasn't laundering for other Russians.

'Did Wyatt say anything else about the money-laundering?'

'No.'

The two stared at each other.

Mitchell blinked first.

What was he keeping back?

'Okay,' Pravda said. 'I'll let you know what we find, subject to the usual caveat.'

'Kremlin authorisation?'

'Of course.'

'Thanks. And the other names?' Mitchell asked. 'Arkady Orlov could be Russian.'

'If he is, we should have him on record somewhere,' Pravda said. 'I'll check.'

'Thanks.'

'As for Bell, Bisset and Zapatero, I don't know their names,' Pravda said. 'But if they're involved in sanctions-busting to Russia's advantage, you're going to hit a brick wall at our end.'

'Yeah, I realise that.'

Mitchell's phone rang.

'Yes?'

Pravda checked the names again, while listening to the conversation.

'Yes... Okay... Sure, I can make it... Alright... Yes, see you tomorrow.'

'Duty calls?' Pravda said.

'Yeah. Sorry, Leonid. But I've got to leave first thing in the morning.'

Pravda knew better than to ask about the caller or the destination.

'Tell me,' Pravda said. 'You say that this Costello lawyer didn't know what was in the envelope?'

'That's what she said. I don't have any reason to disbelieve her.'

'Who else knows about the existence of this list, apart from Gravchenko and you, and now me?'

'Nobody, as far as I know. Why?'

'Think about it. You've inherited a list of names from an assassinated politician's investigation. It could be toxic and anybody with knowledge of its whereabouts and its contents may themselves be in danger.'

'That thought had crossed my mind, too. But maybe I was being paranoid.'

'Possibly.' It was more than that. If Russians were involved with the threats and assassination nothing would stop them from tying up every loose end.

Pravda could take care of himself, as could Gravchenko.

Could Scott Mitchell?

Chapter 9

Day Seven: 9.45pm, Madrid

Scott flopped onto his bed in the city's Catalonia Puerta del Sol hotel and closed his eyes, the lids drooping with lead weights. He'd been in the air and airports for a lifetime, hanging around for delayed flights from Gatwick to Rome and on to Catania, back to Rome, and Madrid. There'd been a direct Ryan Air flight from Catania to Madrid, but no available seats.

Wandering aimlessly through duty-free areas while waiting for flights was draining, both physically and mentally; it dulled the senses and sapped the much-needed nutrients from his brain cells.

Thirty minutes earlier Scott had sent a text to Sergey, confirming his arrival and asking for details of the location and time of the meeting with Gravchenko.

There was a knock on the door.

Scott opened his eyes with a start.

Another knock.

'Yes, yes. Patience is a virtue,' he said in English, as he eased off the bed.

Another knock.

'For Christ's sake!'

He pushed aside the spy hole cover, gulped, and opened the door.

Gravchenko strolled in; a quick grin. He looked around the room and peered into the bathroom, all without a word.

Before a bemused Scott could close the door, a young woman stepped inside and hovered.

He recognised her instantly; Teresa Stepanovna Volkova.

Her eyes were more beautiful in the flesh: magnetic, giant brown/black marbles.

He smiled at her.

She reciprocated.

'Right,' Gravchenko said as he emerged from the bathroom and approached them both still hovering awkwardly by the open door. 'Scott, this is Teresa, Teresa, Scott.'

The pair smiled at each other again.

Gravchenko brushed between them on his way out and spoke directly to Teresa. 'Tell Sergey when you've finished. He'll take you back to your hotel. He's waiting in the lobby. Take as long as you want.' He addressed Scott. 'Be in the breakfast room at eight. There's somebody flying in tonight especially to meet us in the morning. He's leaving tomorrow at noon.'

'Wait a minute, please, Kostya.' Scott dashed into the room, retrieved an envelope from his jacket pocket and gave it to his boss. 'The information we discussed the other day in London.' It was the bank account details he'd obtained from Wyatt's images and a summary of the blogger's demand for the US$250K to hang his resource out to dry.

Gravchenko took it, unopened, and walked out punching numbers into his phone.

Scott closed the door.

'Do you mind if I use the bathroom?' Teresa asked in unaccented English. 'I need to freshen up.'

'Er, no, please, go ahead.' Scott nodded in the bathroom's direction, where Gravchenko had left the door open. 'There.'

Why introduce her so late at night?

And who was the *somebody flying in tonight*?

Teresa emerged from the bathroom, looking fresh-faced. 'May I sit down, please?'

'Yes, of course, take the sofa by the wall.'

Boyish with a Beatles-style dark-brown mop top; the eyes dominated the smooth, unblemished olive skin of her face. She wore a lightweight black leather jacket with no bells and whistles and fashionable rip torn denim jeans. Her T-shirt was French matelot style with dark blue and white hoops. A small red leather handbag on a long strap was slung across her shoulder and chest.

'You don't mind if I call you Scott?'

'No, please do. You don't mind if I call you Teresa?'

'No, please do,' she repeated, with an ingratiating smile.

Scott sat on the edge of the bed.

'Mr Gravchenko tells me you're Czech and Russian.'

'My mother's Czech and my father was Russian.'

'Forgive my curiosity, but where did you learn your perfect English?'

'I was brought up in Kent from the age of six. My parents both taught Eastern European languages at London University. Dad died three years ago. Mum's retired now, but she still lives in Kent.'

'Okay,' Scott said. 'Look, Teresa. Please forgive me, but your sudden appearance has caught me on the hop. Mr Gravchenko told me he wanted us to meet. He's suggested we might work together.' His eyes wandered around the room. 'But I didn't expect us to meet like this. I know it's not late for the Spanish, but I've been flying over the last two days. It's catching up. I'm tired.'

'Much the same for me,' she said. 'He didn't tell me we were meeting tonight. I thought it was going to be tomorrow morning.'

That's interesting. 'Do you happen to know who he wants me to meet tomorrow?'

'No.' She licked her lips. 'I'm thirsty, do you have any water, please?'

'Sorry, I'm forgetting my manners. Would you like

something stronger? There's probably wine or spirits in the minibar.'

'No thanks.' Her tone was self-assured. She removed her handbag and put it on the glass coffee table in front of her.

He took a bottle of water from the minibar, poured out two glasses and gave one to her.

'Here.'

'Thank you.'

'Do you mind if I ask you a question?' he said. 'There's something nagging at me.'

'Ask any question you like.'

'Has Mr Gravchenko told you that MI6 are interested in you?'

She widened her eyes. 'Yes.'

'You don't look concerned.'

'I'm not. I've got nothing to hide from them.' She played with the strap on her bag. 'Besides, I work for Mr Gravchenko. It goes with the job.'

She had a point.

'What he hasn't told you, because I haven't had time to tell him yet, is that MI6 haven't been able to find any reference to you or your research work on the internet.'

'That's probably because I write under a pen name, Tessa Green.'

'Any particular reason?'

'I'm shy.' Her eyes sparkled as they grew bigger and a broad grin appeared.

That's one thing you're not, Teresa Stepanovna.

'You have a website?'

'Greentreesforever.com.'

Scott grabbed his laptop from behind him on the bed and found the site. 'Do you mind if I have a quick look now?'

'No, be my guest.' She picked up the hotel information folder on the coffee table and began flicking through it.

Scott raced through a couple of short blogs and read some of the comments, of which there were over 100 for each of them. 'Impressive. You know your stuff alright.'

She put the folder back on the table. 'Thank you. I'm flattered.'

'It's well-deserved praise, not mere flattery.' He pointed to the screen. 'Your commenters confirm this.'

'Not all,' she laughed. 'I've got *some* trolls.'

He sighed. Tell me about it.

'Has Mr Gravchenko seen this?' Scott asked. 'I assume he must have.'

'If he has, he hasn't said anything to me.'

Par for the course.

'Don't worry about his lack of feedback. If he keeps you employed, it means he's pleased with you.'

'That's what I thought. I've completed a few research projects for him and he's given me more to do on the back of them.'

'One thing: your profile doesn't contain your headshot or a fuller image of you; it's pictures from the natural world, mainly flora and fauna. I know it's not mandatory, but why not? Social media gurus keep telling me people like to put a face to a name.'

'That's because my blogs aren't about *me*. It's about how we're destroying the planet, in most cases purely for financial gain. I'm not interested in a beauty parade of duck lips. I'm showing them the results of their destruction.'

Her comeliness had morphed into a stony-faced lecturer.

The outburst took him by a surprise.

A bit of a handful? No. Spirited? That was better.

'This question isn't as strange as you might think,' Scott said. 'But would you mind if I told MI6 about your pen name and website.' He smiled. 'You can guess how much it annoys governments if they can't keep track of the population and their destabilising activities.'

'Tough,' she sniffed. 'These people have got to understand, it's not *me* they should be tracking, but the carbon emitters, the rainforest flatteners and those who claim climate change is all part of a snowflake conspiracy. *These* are the people threatening the stability of society and the future of the world, not *me*.'

Scott held up his hand. 'Teresa, you're preaching to the converted.'

She sank back and pulled a face. 'Sorry, I didn't mean to go off like this. But it makes me so mad.'

'And millions of others, including me...and Mr Gravchenko.'

She moved forward on her seat. 'Yes, you can tell them if you want.' A quick grin. 'The last thing I want to do is to give our spymasters indigestion.'

Intelligent, passionate, focused, determined, fearless – and with stunning eyes.

A recipe for a successful working relationship, or a disaster?

'Thank you,' Scott said. 'It should keep them off my back for a while.'

'Now, can I ask *you* a question?'

'Sure,' Scott replied.

'If we were to work together, how would it be? On what basis? I've been self-employed, a freelancer, since I graduated. And I'm doing alright by it. I'm not into being told by somebody how to do my job. Mr Gravchenko, and my other clients, ask me to do something for them, but they don't tell me *how* to do it. I'm a free agent. I come and go as I please. All I have to do is to get the job done – the end result. How I get there, is up to me.'

Well, that's put *me* in my place.

'Teresa, I also work for the Foundation on a self-employed basis, as a consultant lawyer. Mr Gravchenko isn't concerned with the nitty-gritty of how I carry out his instructions. It's entirely up to me. The only stipulations are: one, that I don't represent anybody who is in competition with his business affairs, and two, that I'm on call 24 hours a day, seven days a week. Apart from that, he doesn't care if I spend my "non-Gravchenko" time bungee jumping from a MIG-29 in the stratosphere.'

She laughed. 'I'd like to see that.'

'*I* wouldn't.'

'Who else do you represent, other than Mr Gravchenko?' she asked.

'Hmm. Interesting question. I suppose I'm pretty much full time working for the Foundation. Occasionally I do *pro bono* work for public interest groups, but... that's about it.'

'Which groups?'

'Animal rights, Greenpeace, Amnesty International and, you know, the usual suspects.'

'They're big groups, worldwide. How do you get the time?'

'I don't actively litigate for them, like I do for the Foundation. I'm more of a back-room researcher, writing preliminary opinions for their legal teams. It doesn't take up too much of my time. And I like to keep my hand in.'

'I'm impressed. A man of many talents.' A huge wide-eyed grin followed.

'*Now* who's doing the flattering?'

She sat up. 'Okay. Where do we go from here?'

'We both need to think about it,' Scott said. 'But meanwhile, let's dot the "i"s and cross the "t"s. Would you send me a copy of your CV, please?'

'I'll show you mine, if you show me yours,' she said with a straight face.

'I don—'

'I'm joking. Of course I will.'

'I was going to say that I don't have a formal CV any longer,' Scott said. 'The internet knows more about me than I do.'

They exchanged contact details, shook hands, perhaps a second too long, and she left.

Scott took a shower, switched on the TV and lay on top of the duvet while he hunted for an English-language news channel.

Images of a conflagration at Madrid's main airport appeared on the screen, with an accompanying commentary:

> At 10.05pm local time, a private jet carrying Dmitry Zletov, the CEO of one of Ukraine's largest oil and gas supply companies and a prospective member of Ukraine's legislative assembly, exploded as it taxied to a halt in its parking slot. Mr Zletov, his female travelling companion, Galina Gusinskaya, and an unidentified male passenger, perished along with the three crew members. It is not known at this stage what caused the explosion...

What did Gravchenko say? *There's somebody flying in tonight especially to meet us in the morning. He's leaving tomorrow at noon.*

Sergey called.

'Hi, Sergey.'

'I didn't wake you, did I?'

'No. I was just watching this news report about—'

'Tomorrow's meeting's cancelled,' Sergey said. 'You can return to the UK tomorrow whenever. The boss will explain later. Goodnight.'

He disconnected before Scott had a chance to say anything more.

Chapter 10

Day Eight: 8.50am, Moscow

Max's ultimatum and Carey's list of names had caused Pravda to cut short his R & R in Sicily and return to his office on the 30th floor of a building in Moscow's international business centre. He'd flown out on the same day as Mitchell, but not before instructing Yelena to drop everything and concentrate on Yazov and Bauer.

The door to his room burst open.

'General, this is doing my head in.'

Yelena waved several sheets of A4 size paper at him. Though his junior in rank, she'd become the daughter he'd never had; consequently his tolerance threshold of her lack of social graces and respect for her superior officer was off the "Richter" scale.

'*Now* what?' he asked.

'Where do we get this stuff from?' She dropped three sheets of paper onto his desk.' Please, look at it, General.'

Pravda picked at a mangled and scrunched-up descendant of a rainforest. The few typefaces of the printed word he could detect resembled what he imagined Klingon text looked like. 'The printer again?'

She grimaced. 'Why do we keep buying this crap? It's the second one this month.'

'No chance of it being operator error, then?'

'Can't we ask three chins for more funds?' she said, hissing.

That's one solution he didn't want. Max, after transferring Monkfish, Pravda's computer-hacking wizard, to his own department in the inner sanctum of the Kremlin's IT hub, had offered Pravda more funds to move to an upgraded office and to install newer state-of-the-art equipment. Pravda had politely refused. He preferred the cosiness of where he was; he knew where the listening devices were located. He also didn't trust Max's government supplier. The Kremlin would plant their bugs in all new equipment. He told Max he could keep costs down by sourcing the IT equipment abroad through cover companies, so the suppliers wouldn't know that the end user was Russian intelligence.

'Why can't I go back out in the field?' Yelena pleaded. 'This desk job is driving me stir crazy.'

'Don't be so hard on yourself. You're good at it.'

'That's not the point. I'm more use to this outfit in the *real* world. Not this virtual...' she waved her hands in the air '...What do you call it? Augmented hallucination.'

'What are you trying to print out?' he said.

'The Yazov and Bauer update,' Yelena said. 'Nothing suspicious about Yazov's road accident.'

'Bauer?'

'It's true about him being a target of identity thieves.'

'Will he talk to us?'

'Can't find him. He's on extended leave.'

'Paid?'

'Full pay for at least six months.'

How convenient.

'Any evidence that Gravchenko ordered this?'

'None so far. It looks like a regional manager's decision.'

'What about the Maastricht address?'

'A work in progress.'

Follow the money.

'We need to get into Santorini's bank accounts.'

'Piece of cake,' Yelena chortled. 'All *you* have to do is tell me where they are – and I'll unlock them for you.' A quick smile. 'Easy huh?'

If Gravchenko was doing something *off the books* he wouldn't be so stupid as to use names that could be linked to his Foundation with three or four taps on a keyboard. This meant that either Yazov had been on a frolic of his own or somebody was pulling his strings.

'Get all you can on that blogger Henry Wyatt.'

'Gotcha. I need a coffee.' She pressed an index finger against her lips and beckoned him to follow her.

They went in silence to the tenants' communal vending machine at the end of the corridor outside their office.

'The unidentified body on Zletov's plane belongs to a guy called Arkady Vladimirovich Orlov,' she said, handing him a coffee. 'Coincidence or what?'

Another name on the list.

They'd been tracking Zletov's movements for months, since their mole in the SBU, the Ukrainian Secret Service, had told them that Zletov and Gravchenko were 'cooking something up', but the SBU didn't yet know what it was. Zletov's death in the Madrid conflagration at a time when Gravchenko was also in the city was, to Pravda's experienced mind, probably one coincidence too many.

'You're sure,' Pravda said. 'One hundred per cent sure?'

'Without DNA, it's 99.9 per cent.'

'Tamara?'

'Who else?'

Tamara was Yelena's current partner, a bisexual who was also sleeping with a man, their SBU mole.

'For our ears only.' She nodded towards their office. 'It isn't public knowledge,' Yelena said. 'The SBU's blocked publication.'

'Why?'

'The source won't tell her.'

Interesting.

'What have you got so far on Orlov?' Pravda said.

'He was a chemical engineer; oil and gas stuff. Travelled on a Bulgarian passport and has an apartment in Varna, on the coast.' She handed him a copy of the passport.

Pravda flicked through it. 'Genuine?'

'So the source says. But I'll double-check.'

'We've got to get to Varna before anybody else does,' Pravda said.

Yelena beamed. 'Parole! Back on the streets at last! I'll leave today. I know somebody who can help me.'

Pravda smiled. 'I won't ask who this "somebody" is, but do you trust this person?'

'With my life...and yours.'

'I hope your confidence is justified, Yelena. We don't know who we're dealing with yet.'

'Stop being so concerned for me, General. I've handled trickier situations than this.'

Yes, she had. She was a black-belt street fighter and one of most acclaimed snipers in the GRU, but she wouldn't be allowed to take a weapon with her and Pravda wasn't fearing a hand-to-hand brawl.

It was the unknown, he feared: who was pulling whose strings?

'Were any members of the plane crew Russian?' he asked.

'Tamara says there were two Ukrainian crew and the pilot was Serbian, but his mother's Russian.'

'Right,' Pravda said. 'Leak it to the Kremlin today, but not via Max. I don't want it to come from us.'

The more Max pushed him, the more suspicious Pravda became of the man's motives. And he couldn't run the risk of exposing Tamara or her source, however remote the possibility.

'Okay, but why?'

'Because we should be able to persuade the Spanish to let our experts join the crash investigation team. Russia has a legitimate interest in finding out why the son of one of its citizens died. And I want the information sooner, rather than later.'

'You think it wasn't an accident?'

'The Kremlin, well, Max, is squeezing us for information on Santorini and Gravchenko. Mitchell's knee deep in investigating the British MP's assassination. Santorini and Orlov are names on the MP's list. Zletov, who we know was going to meet Gravchenko in Madrid, and Orlov, are killed in a plane explosion. We also know that Mitchell was in Madrid at the same time. Question: how many dots can we join?'

Chapter 11

Day Eight: 1pm, London

Scott had spent the early-bird flight back from Madrid analysing more website articles on David Carey. Stephanie lived in the US with her American husband, Tom Burrows, and daughter Chrissy. They were in London on a month's tour visiting relatives and friends when the assassination happened. Scott had made a note to try to speak with Stephanie after the funeral, which, according to the media, was due to take place within a couple of days. Son Jonathan was believed to be wandering around Asia taking images of the natural world in the tropics.

A text from Fraser arrived:

Can we meet at 3.15 this afternoon at the London Eye?

The sooner the better as far as Scott was concerned. He had the additional information Fraser wanted about Teresa. It should be sufficient to keep him at bay for the foreseeable future.

Sure.

3.30pm

Scott wasn't intentionally late. It was due to a passenger falling ill on the Jubilee Line, but Fraser hadn't yet arrived.

He called Gravchenko.

It went to voicemail immediately: 'Leave a message.'

'I'm back in London. We've got the green light on

Project Conrad.' He'd forgotten to tell his boss at their brief encounter in Madrid. 'Speak later.'

'Let's go,' Fraser said as he appeared at Scott's side and gave him a tap on the back.

'After you,' Scott said.

They headed east along the South Bank.

Fraser was two steps ahead.

They stopped at the skateboard park and leant on the railings, as teenagers and young adults performed their tricks.

'Right. I'm going to tell you a few things,' Fraser said. 'To show that our relationship isn't one-sided. But you didn't hear them from me, okay?'

Never look a gift horse in the mouth.

'Understood.' He didn't say that Scott couldn't tell a third party, like his boss; only that he shouldn't betray the source.

'We know that you were in Madrid with Gravchenko.'

Not a surprise. But did they know he'd met with Teresa?

'He was going to introduce you to Dmitry Zletov, the Ukrainian oligarch who died in the plane explosion.'

The possibility had crossed Scott's mind.

'Why?' Scott said.

A young teenager flipped over her skateboard while ascending a concrete mound, lost her balance and landed awkwardly on an elbow. She screamed in pain; she wasn't wearing arm guards.

Fraser began to haul himself over the railings, but stopped as three older kids went to her aid and she quietened down.

'Paramedic as well as a spook?' Scott said.

'Automatic reaction,' Fraser replied. 'I've got twin daughters the same age.'

A cold-bloodied killer who obviously cares for his daughters and young skateboarders? Did Darwin deal with this in his evolutionary theories?

'Are they skateboarders, as well?'

'Not if it interrupts their snapchatting, whatsapping, and whatever else kids do on their phones.'

Scott felt a self-pitying smile emerging as they carried on walking. He'd often considered having children, but the jury had been out for years.

'So, you were going to tell me why Gravchenko wanted me to meet Zletov.'

'No I wasn't,' Fraser said. 'Classified.'

'I don't understand,' Scott said, not angry but irritated. 'Why did you mention the meeting if you're not going to tell me the reason for it?' Was he up to his old tricks again?

'Check out an Australian political website run by a guy called Kevin Shaw,' Fraser said. 'The leaked FBI report about Zletov. Give me your feedback.'

Okay, so don't answer my question; the crumbs from the table will have to do.

'Another thing...' Fraser said. 'The mystery man on the plane with Zletov was a guy called Arkady Orlov.'

Wow! Not mere crumbs, more like the whole loaf!

The plot thickens.

Carey's list flashed before Scott's eyes, with a large pulsating red cross obliterating Orlov's name.

'What caused the explosion?'

'Still being investigated.'

Scott was uneasy. Fraser was giving him a twinge of conscience for not trusting him and not coming clean about the list.

On the other hand: *quis custodiet...*?

'Teresa Stepanovna Volkova blogs under the name of Tessa Green,' Scott said. 'Her website is greentreesforever.com. You'll get most of the stuff you want from there. I don't know about any CV. That may need some more digging.'

Fraser stopped. 'Right, thanks. Now listen to me. I don't want to teach you to suck eggs, but keep your eyes in the back of your head. Your value to Gravchenko is your respectable front,' Fraser said. 'You're the "go-to" international lawyer for this green stuff you're doing for him. But don't be deluded, matey. You're being used by the man.'

No, no, no, Fraser. I'm not going to fall for it.

And while you're so free with your information, Mr Spook...

'I read the other day' – he hadn't – 'that the intelligence services are helping the police with their investigation into the Carey assassination. Is that your lot or MI5?'

Fraser gently squeezed Scott's elbow. 'My friend, please, concentrate on what I'm telling you. Don't get side-tracked.' He took a call.

Scott was slowly taking pieces of a jigsaw puzzle from a blank box, but there weren't yet enough of them to give any hint as to the picture: Fraser had now linked Zletov, and possibly Orlov, to Gravchenko, and Wyatt had allegedly linked the Foundation to Santorini's money-laundering activities.

Pravda's advice came back into focus: *This list could be toxic and anybody with knowledge of its whereabouts and its contents may themselves be in danger.*

5.30pm

Immediately Scott returned to his apartment after the meeting with Fraser, he googled the FBI report:

> Dmitry Zletov amassed a fortune in the late 1990s in the oil and gas sectors. Using aliases, he ended up with 49% ownership of a Bahamian company called UKRUS Fuel Supplies. The remaining 51% is held by the Russian government through a labyrinth of offshore corporations. UKRUS extracts gas from Siberia and delivers it to the

> West. It deals in billions of US dollars, some of which is rumoured to be paid to **[name redacted]**, a Russian oligarch, who could be fronting for Putin personally. Zletov is seeking support in running for office in the Verkhovna Rada, Ukraine's parliament, in the next elections, which must be held no later than 2019.

Since the early stages of Scott's relationship with Pravda, the military intelligence officer had made no secret of the fact that his brief from the Kremlin was to investigate Gravchenko's activities. If the FBI report was accurate and if the redacted name was Gravchenko, *who could be fronting for Putin personally*, was Pravda caught in the middle of a power struggle between Putin and his detractors in the Kremlin?

And why was Orlov on Zletov's plane?

Diane Costello called.

'Yes, Diane?'

'There's something I need to discuss with you. Could we please meet tonight, at my house?'

She sounded anxious.

It could surely only have been about Carey's investigation.

They had nothing else in common.

Of course we could meet.

'Where do you live?'

'Buckhurst Hill.'

It was 30 minutes away.

'Okay, but I don't want to hit the rush hour traffic from the City and I've still got some stuff to do. Let's say 7.30.'

'Alright. I'll text you my address.'

'Fine, see you at 7.30.'

7.40pm

Scott pulled into the sweeping gravel driveway through open electronic gates, to be confronted by what appeared to be a five- or six-bedroomed house in one of the most affluent parts of Essex. He stopped outside the front porch, locked his car and rang the bell. Standard chimes: ding-dong, ding dong. There was no answer, he tried again. No answer. He peeped through the large flat-fronted window to the right of the door. The light was on but the curtains were too thick to see what lay behind them. He tried the window on the left; no drawn curtains. The daylight was fading and the sky overcast – a late summer storm was brewing. All three walls inside were covered with shelves from floor to ceiling, racked with books. A Victorian wing chair occupied each of the far corners. The centre of the room was dominated by two facing three-seater, cloth-covered sofas separated by a glass-topped coffee table, on which were haphazardly-piled books. The house was late 20th century mock Tudor, yet the library room wouldn't have been out of place on the set of Noel Coward's *Blithe Spirit* of some 50/60 years earlier, or Agatha Christie's *The Mousetrap*.

Scott returned to the front door and rang the bell again.

No response.

He called her mobile.

It rang, unanswered.

It was coming from his left.

He followed the noise around the corner of the house to the source – a double garage.

The ringing stopped.

There was no voicemail.

As he pulled the grip on the front of the up-and-over garage door, sirens and the crunching of vehicles on the gravel announced the arrival of the emergency services.

He turned round.

What the—?

Who'd called *them*?

Teams of armed police jumped out of their response vehicles and pointed their automatics at him.

'On the ground, face down and spread your arms!'

'What?'

'Now! On the ground, Now!'

They raised their weapons.

'Okay. Okay.' Scott dropped to his knees like a lead weight. 'Ouch.' Despite his experiences gathering evidence of war crimes in Russian-occupied Chechnya he went cold with fear, as he stared down the barrels of five automatics.

Any attempt to scratch his nose and he was Fraser's *dead* "go-to" lawyer.

'Flat on the ground! Spread yourself!'

He did as commanded and stretched his arms as wide apart as he could. Two of the armed police approached him; one leant over him with the barrel of the automatic two centimetres from his cheek. The other pulled his arms together and secured his hands with wrist restraints.

'Secured!' the officer said, and stood up.

Scott was conscious of other police walking by him as a clunking noise told him the up-and-over garage door was opening.

'And who might *you* be?' a plainclothes man said as he crouched in front of Scott.

Probably the detective in charge. He was calm, soft spoken and non-aggressive. He bore the worn-out face of a prematurely ageing copper who'd seen and done everything – and was thoroughly pissed off with it.

He was surreally comforting.

'Are you the detective in charge?' Scott said.

'Yes, lad. Detective Inspector Martin at your service.'

'My name is Scott Mitchell. I'm a legal colleague of Diane Costello and I have a meeting with her, here, this evening.'

'Guv!' A female voice came from inside the garage.

The detective looked up, and over Scott's head.

'Here, guv!'

'Don't go anywhere.' The detective smiled. 'I'll be back. As Arnie said.'

A sense of humour was the last thing Scott was looking for.

He closed his eyes and let this head flop onto the gravel. 'Ouch, again.'

Armed police didn't turn up on a person's doorstop for routine enquiries.

Diane was either in trouble or it was the inevitable approach by the police and/or the intelligence services she'd told him about.

But why the weaponry?

Crunching gravel announced approaching footsteps.

'You say you're here to meet your legal colleague Diane Costello?' DI Martin said.

Scott opened his eyes. 'Yes, yes. Where is she? She'll vouch for me.'

'Okay, let's get you up,' the detective said. He looped his arm under Scott's and pulled him up.

Scott rose to his feet, and promptly collapsed. His knee was more painful than he realised.

'Jim! Give us a hand!' the detective called out to one of a crowd of uniformed policemen. 'Quick.'

A young constable rushed over and gave assistance.

'Undo Mr Mitchell's restraints,' the detective said to him.

The constable obliged.

'Right, Mr Mitchell. Lean against this car for a moment.' The detective turned to the young officer. 'Stay with him. Make sure he doesn't collapse again.'

'Yes sir.'

Scott rubbed his knee as the detective entered the garage.

'What's going on?' he said to the constable.

The policeman shook his head.

Of course, it was more than his job was worth to tell Scott without permission from his superiors. The detective reappeared, frowning and nodding while on the phone.

He approached Scott and switched the phone off.

'What's going on, detective?' Scott said. 'What's happened?'

'Did you go into that garage?'

'No. I was going to, when you lot arrived.'

The detective looked Scott up and down, as if trying to gauge whether he was telling the truth.

'Are you going to tell me what's happened?'

The detective sucked in air. 'Have you *ever* been in the garage?'

'Detective Inspector Martin, this is the first time I've ever been to this house. The answer is no.' He was losing his cool. 'I've *never*, *ever*, been in the garage. Now would you please tell—'

'Do you think you'd recognise Ms Costello if you saw her again?'

'Of course I would, but why don't you ask her yourself? She'll confirm our arrangement, I'm sure.'

'That might be difficult.'

'Why?'

'Because there's a dead woman in the garage.'

Scott swallowed hard.

'Oh no. Not Diane? We were talking on the phone only a couple of hours ago.'

'Jim,' the detective said to the young constable. 'Get Mr Mitchell a crime scene outfit, please.'

'Guv.' Jim disappeared.

'Is it her?' Scott asked.

'That's what I'm hoping you can tell *me*.'

'So, does this mean,' Scott said, 'that whoever it is in the garage, I'm not a suspect?' Callous possibly, bearing in mind there was a dead body there, but a few minutes previously he'd been the target of a battalion of Colt M4 Carbines – his survival instinct was kicking in.

'Everybody's a suspect, until I eliminate them.'

It was a typical Hercule Poirot response. Scott didn't take it as a personal threat.

Jim returned with a full kit: head cap, overalls, gloves and shoe covers.

Scott put them on and followed DI Martin into the garage.

An Audi boot was open.

'Is that Diane Costello in there?' the detective said.

Scott looked inside.

'Oh, fuck!'

He covered his mouth with his hand to check rising bile.

It was her alright; he recognised the crimped hair and the top she'd been wearing when they'd met at the Old Thameside Inn.

Her face was peppered with small circular red and white blisters.

Scott turned away.

'Are they cigarette burns?'

'That's for forensics, Mr Mitchell.'

Chapter 12

Day Eight: 9.30pm, Essex

'Do you mind telling me, Mr Mitchell, what you and Ms Costello were talking about at the Old Thameside Inn last week?' ADC Chalmers said. His tone was polite, but coming from a stern face with ever-questioning eyes.

Scott wasn't under arrest, but when told by DI Martin that the man heading the Carey assassination, Assistant Deputy Commissioner Chalmers of the Metropolitan Police, would like to have a few words with him, Scott agreed. Despite Carey's warning he jumped at the chance to get to know the "enemy". He'd followed the police in his own car to the local police station, with an armed response vehicle at the rear "for his own protection".

Chalmers' opening question, however, had caught him off balance. Maybe Diane was right to have been suspicious about the girl and the three boys sitting at the neighbouring tables.

He glanced around the small rest room while considering his response. They sat opposite each other in two threadbare armchairs with a footstall separating them. Three of the walls were covered in posters and notices about any and everything: how to become a blood donor, local football club sponsorship, a forthcoming marathon run, a school fete, and a picture of the Home Secretary with darts in it. There was a microwave oven on a makeshift worktop, a rack full of mugs, a fridge and a small sink with one tap. The window on the fourth wall overlooked a well-lit car park.

'She wanted to know if I'd ever come into contact with David Carey in my Russian travels.'

'Why?' Chalmers wasn't blinking, as if scrutinising Scott's every syllable.

'Apparently, he told her he was investigating matters concerning the EU's trading relationship with Russia and he'd been receiving threats which made him fear for his life.'

'What matters in particular?'

'Sanctions-busting, he called it.'

Chalmers eyes narrowed. 'Who was threatening him?'

'He told Diane he didn't know.'

Scott massaged his painful knee.

'Did she ask you anything else?' Chalmers didn't show any interest in Scott's physical discomfort.

If the police had been spying on them at the pub, Chalmers would know that their meeting had lasted for more than a few minutes.

'Yes, she asked if I could offer any ideas as to who might have been threatening him, due to my own Russian connections.'

Chalmers frowned. '*Had* you met him on your travels?'

Scott sensed where the questions were going.

'No.'

'So why did Ms Costello think that you might have some ideas as to who was threatening the minister?'

Play dumb.

'Beats me. I told Diane I'd never met David Carey, much less discussed his trade investigation...which I'd never heard of until she told me about it.'

A slow pensive nodding from Chalmers.

'And that was *all* you discussed with her?'

Chalmers smirked. It was obvious he didn't believe him.

'In substance, yes.'

'Nothing else?'

Scott shook his head. 'No, that was it.'

'What were you doing at Ms Costello's house?'

'She asked me to come to her house this evening as... and I quote, "there's something I need to discuss with you".'

'How?'

'How what?'

'How did she invite you?'

'By phone.'

The man was cross-examining him.

'What time did she phone you?'

'Five forty-five, six.'

'Did she call you on your mobile or landline?'

'Mobile.' Scott grabbed his phone from the small side table next to him. 'Here, I'll check the exact time for you.' He scrolled through the incoming calls. 'Yes, it was 6.02pm.'

'Do you have a call-recording function on your phone?'

'No.'

'What was the *something* that she needed to discuss with you?'

'I never got the opportunity to find out. The first time I saw her was when Detective Inspector Martin showed me her body in the boot of the Audi.'

He shivered at the image of Diane's ashtray face.

'Do you mind if I smoke?' Chalmers asked.

Was the man psychic?

'Isn't it illegal to smoke in here?'

Chalmers ignored the question, got up, opened the window and took out a cigarette, without waiting for Scott's approval.

'Be my guest,' Scott said. 'But please keep the window open after you've finished.'

But if I die of passive smoking, Mr Policeman, I'll send someone to sue you.

Chalmers lit the cigarette and inhaled. 'My penalty for breaking any law is the damage these things do to my lungs.' He blew the smoke out of the window and turned to Scott. 'You know, the problem I have with this version of Ms Costello's behaviour is: why would she have felt the need to discuss something with you after you'd told her that you had never met the minister and you didn't know anything about his sanctions-busting investigation?'

That was one of the questions Scott would have asked if their roles had been reversed. He should have told the ADC that he was too tired and wanted to go home. It'd been a traumatic evening. But such was his hunger for any information about Carey.

'What she wanted to discuss with me may not have concerned David Carey's affairs. She was a lawyer, I'm a lawyer. It could have been about anything; an urgent problem she had in chambers with her colleagues or a legal issue with another client. I don't know. Lawyers do sometimes seek counsel from each other.'

Chalmers collected a cracked mug from the rack, put it under the tap and extinguished his barely smoked cigarette into the water, then left it in the sink and returned to his seat.

Scott stretched his damaged leg and massaged his knee again.

'Are you happy to continue our discussion?'

Chalmers had made the seemingly caring question sound perfunctory.

Don't be too willing.

'Let's see how it goes.'

'You told DI Martin that you and Ms Costello were legal colleagues. How long had you known her?'

'The first time I'd met her was that day at the pub.'

There was no point in trying to cover it up. The truth was easily discoverable with a few questions of Diane's colleagues in chambers.

Chalmers looked genuinely confused. 'I don't understand. You just *happened* to bump into one another there?'

Scott told him the story from Diane leaving her business card with Dave at his apartment block and the subsequent phone conversation to arrange the meeting.

'And you had no idea she was David Carey's family lawyer until she told you at that meeting.'

'Correct.'

'Hmm. Why did she approach you in the first place? You didn't know each other, yet out of the blue she wants to meet with you urgently.' He narrowed his eyes. 'Do you see my difficulty?'

Had this man been a litigator in a previous life? Scott reasoned that had he terminated the conversation at that precise moment, it would have put more questions in the ADC's mind: Why would he not want to answer? He wasn't under arrest or even cautioned. Nothing he said could be used in court if the CPS were to have a sudden brainstorm and charge him for something connected with the murder.

'She knew *of* me, though we'd never met. And like many of my legal peers, she knew about my much-publicised problems with your lot and the CPS.'

A dismissive look from the ADC. 'Why is that relevant to your meeting with her?'

On the face of it, it wasn't relevant.

Time to get assertive.

'Because she also knew, like you lot, that I'm Chief Counsel to Konstantin Gravchenko's charitable foundation. By this, I mean she was aware that I had Russian connections at a high level, at least in the commercial sphere. She thought I might have some ideas about who David Carey's enemies could be in relation to his sanctions-busting investigation.'

Chalmers nodded, though Scott couldn't tell what was on the man's mind.

'Did she give you the impression she thought, or David Carey thought, that Mr Gravchenko might be involved in this sanctions-busting?'

I'm not going to rise to your bait, officer.

'No,' Scott said emphatically.

Chalmers brushed a stray ash deposit from his trouser leg and stood up. 'Thank you for...' He hesitated. 'Helping me with my enquiries.' A cheeky smile. 'I think it's time for us to go home, don't you?' He held out his hand.

Scott stood up and shook it.

The man's grip was firmer than Konstantin Gravchenko's.

'Let's keep in touch,' Chalmers said.

'You know where I live,' Scott said, reciprocating the cheeky smile.

Chalmers led the way out.

It was clear to Scott that the man suspected he wasn't making full disclosure. But what wasn't so clear, was whether the woman or kids at the pub had seen Diane produce the envelope.

'Just one question, ADC Chalmers, if I may.'

Chalmers stopped and turned round. 'Yes?'

'What prompted the police to go to Diane Costello's house, and with an armed response unit?'

'We received an anonymous call that somebody with a gun was prowling around the side of the property, by the garage.'

'A gun? Was she shot?'

Scott hadn't noticed any signs on the body of a shooting, though she was clothed and lying on her side, face forward.

'No word from forensics yet.'

An anonymous prowler-spotter? Interesting. Scott could have sworn that the front garden and garage were hidden from street view by a thick hedgerow at least three metres high.

Chapter 13

Day Nine: 10am, London

The headlines on the newspaper website screamed out at Scott:

David Carey's Lawyer Tortured to Death

A skim through the article confirmed that at least the editor had the decency not to detail the specifics of the torture and, to Scott's relief, not to print that an unnamed person was "helping the police with their enquiries". Such statements often had the habit of quickly turning into media clichéd accusations of no smoke without fire.

There's something I need to discuss with you.

He called Diane Costello's chambers, explained who he was and asked to speak to Paul Northey, Senior Clerk, whose name Scott had found on the chambers' website.

'Yes, Mr Mitchell, Paul Northey here.'

'Mr Northey, please forgive me for calling you like this. I know it's probably the most inappropriate time I could ever have chosen, but quite frankly I need your help. It's about Di...that is Ms Costello's mur...death. I was at her home yesterday evening when the police discovered her. I would like to meet with you. It's not a matter for discussion over the phone.'

Silence.

'Mr Northey? Are you still here? Did you hear me?'

A sigh.

'Yes, I'm here.'

It was a weary tone, rather than annoyance at Scott's

opportunistic indelicacy.

'Would it be possible for me to meet with you today, this afternoon?' Scott said. 'It really is very urgent.'

What did Chalmers say? *We received an anonymous call that somebody with a gun was prowling around the side of the property, by the garage.*

My arse.

'What time?' Northey said.

'To suit you.'

A senior clerk's role was to administer the chambers on behalf of the barristers and negotiate their fees for cases. However, the clerk could be a veritable treasure trove of gossip, rumours and confessions, with diplomatic eyes and ears in every nook and cranny.

'I shall be at the Chapel in New Square at 1pm today. We may talk there.'

Yes!

'Thank you, Mr Northey. Thank you very much. I shall bring my passport and driving licence for identification.'

'That's not necessary. Your website image will be enough for me.'

'Understood. The Chapel at 1pm, and thank you again.'

'Goodbye.' Northey disconnected.

With Carey, Orlov and Costello dead, Scott's focus had to be on the living: Bisset, Bell and Zapatero.

He googled the name Simone Bisset – and wished he hadn't. He got more than 1.53 million hits. There were women of that name spread across all possible social media platforms.

He'd return to her later.

Thank God Sir Stanton Morgan Bell was one of a kind.

The knight was in a minority of members of the House of Lords who bothered to take part in debates, rather than keep the taxi meter running while they jumped out, popped into the House, signed on for their tax-free daily attendance fee of £300 and popped out again.

He'd shown more than a passing interest in Russian affairs. Hansard's official record of debates in the House of Lords confirmed that he'd concentrated on the deteriorating relations between the West and Russia; in particular the economic sanctions imposed by the USA and the EU over the Ukrainian situation. Bell hadn't been backward in coming forward to recommend more haste, less speed and deeper reflection when considering imposing the sanctions. Speech after speech told Scott that the knight was a committed Russophile, though he didn't appear to have any familial or business connections to Russia, except for having mortgaged much of his real estate in Scotland to a loan company reputed to be owned by Russian entrepreneurs. So what? Many Russians in the West were in the mortgage-lending business, but that didn't turn their borrowers into Russophiles.

He couldn't find the knight's direct contact details, only the House's general enquiry number. Any call would be logged, if not recorded. He would resort to other means to arrange a face-to-face meeting with the man.

Professor Zapatero was apparently a well-respected international economist working as a senior adviser to the EU Commission, having published in many prestigious journals – though Scott was sure he didn't know the name. She vehemently argued that Russia was a large, and largely untapped, market that would be ignored at the West's peril. She'd allegedly expressed the view in private that it could be a win-win situation for both sides if the politicians and bureaucrats would divert their talents from meddling in matters they didn't understand – by trying to frustrate Adam Smith's "invisible hand" of market forces – and concentrate on more pressing issues like worldwide security.

Interesting, an anti-bureaucracy advocate working

for the EU Commission – one of the world's largest bureaucratic machines.

Another Russophile?

He printed off the articles on Bell and Zapatero for a later more detailed consideration. A millennial he may have been, but he had an aversion to reviewing documents on a screen. He preferred to run a yellow highlighter over the hard copy text.

He googled "How do I contact a member of the EU Commission and their staff" and found the Commission switchboard on +32 2 299 11 11. It was open from 0800 to 1900 CET.

He called the number, gave his name and profession, and asked to be put through to Professor Zapatero or her personal assistant.

'Good morning, Monsieur Mitchell, my name is Henri Bernard. Professor Zapatero is not available this week. May I be of assistance?'

His English was fluent, but with a strong French accent.

'Monsieur Bernard. I'm an English lawyer...' He paused to see if the man recognised his name. If he did, he didn't say anything. '...And I would like to discuss a personal matter with the professor, sooner rather than later.'

'I understand, monsieur. Please give me your telephone number, business email address and website link, and I will pass this information to her.'

1pm

As Scott entered the Lincoln's Inn Chapel on the first floor above the archways of the centuries-old building the all-pervading calm of the sanctuary embraced him immediately. He rarely attended church but whenever he did, usually only for marriages and deaths, his heart rate decreased and momentarily his troubles vanished.

Three people were standing at the far end behind the

altar, gazing up at the magnificent stained-glass window.

They were way out of earshot.

A single male figure was sitting halfway down the right-hand aisle on one of the dark wooden double-seater pews, against the wall. The entrance to each such double pew was gained through waist-high wooden doors.

The man was leaning forward, as if praying.

He was alone in the chapel apart from the stained-glass admirers.

Scott checked the time, and coughed.

The man turned round, glanced at Scott for a few seconds and nodded.

Scott reciprocated with a nod and approached him.

'Mr Northey?' he whispered as he opened the small door at the entrance.

'Yes,' Northey said in a barely audible tone.

Scott sidled up to him, they shook hands and he sat down.

Northey, small in stature, sported a neatly trimmed salt-and-pepper goatee beard. The dark rings under his eyes betrayed sleepless nights.

'I would like to thank you for agreeing to see me so soon after...'

'Diane's passing.'

'Yes, Diane's passing. Please accept my sincerest condolences and pass them on to her family.'

They both spoke in hushed tones.

'Thank you, I will. You were at the house when the police discovered Diane's body?'

'Yes. Sadly, I was.'

'Did you see her body? The papers said she was tortured, but there weren't any details.' Northey rubbed his forehead with both hands. 'How much did she suffer?' Tears appeared in the corner of his eyes.

Scott wasn't comfortable with the question, though he'd half expected it. How could he tell the man about her face? 'I can't tell you that. I didn't identify her. It was one of the local policemen who knew her.'

Northey gazed ahead at the stained-glass window, as the trio of admirers headed back down the other aisle.

'Thank you for sparing me the details,' he said, wiping his eyes with a handkerchief.

'You were close to her?' Scott said.

He turned to face Scott. 'I'll be frank with you, Mr Mitchell. I was on the point of leaving the chambers when Diane joined us...' He hesitated and wiped his eyes again. 'It isn't a nice place to work...'

Scott hadn't asked for the meeting because he was interested in that type of gossip; nonetheless he let the man speak.

'Go on, please,' Scott said. 'You know this is confidential. Nothing you say will get back to your colleagues. I promise.'

'I'm gay,' Northey said.

Scott wanted to say, so what? But it was obviously a sensitive subject for Northey.

'Forget our laws on equality and non-discrimination,' Northey continued. 'Forget I'm working for a group of lawyers who should know better. Our chambers are rooted in the 1950s. Diane was the only woman among the 11 senior barristers and she always showed me respect, treated me as a human being, as did the junior barristers. But for that, she was targeted by the other seniors; she couldn't do anything right, except of course bring in more fees than all but the top two earners.'

This was the 21st century for Christ's sake. How could it be allowed to happen?

'When did Diane join your chambers?'

'Eighteen months ago.'

'And how long had you been there?'

'Seven years.'

Scott wasn't sure what to say. If he asked him why

he'd put up with it for so long the conversation would drag on.

'I know what you're thinking, Mr Mitchell. But I'm 57, it's not easy for me to find alternative employment.'

'I fully understand,' Scott said. 'And I can only sympathise with you.' He had to get back to Diane without seeming superficial and unfeeling. 'If you have no objection, I would like to try to help you. I have connections with other chambers and could make discreet enquiries about possible openings. I can't promise anything will come of it, but I can promise to try my hardest.'

'That's kind of you. Very kind. But I have to think about it.'

'Of course. Let me know when you're ready.'

'Yes, thank you. I will.' Northey sat up. 'So, how can I help you?'

'Is it alright if I ask you some more questions about Diane?'

'Yes, of course. What would you like to know?'

'How much did Diane tell you about me?'

'She told me she was going to meet with you at the Old Thameside Inn.

'Nothing else?'

'That was all. It's standard procedure in our chambers. We tell at least one colleague where we're going...and whom we're going to meet, unless it's a court appointment of course. It's part of our security procedures.'

'I understand. Did you also know that she called me yesterday afternoon and we arranged to meet at her house in the evening?'

He'd told Chalmers, so why not Northey?

'Yes, she logged the call with me personally.'

'She told me she needed to discuss something with me,' Scott said. 'Have you any idea what it might have been?'

'No. She only said she'd arranged a meeting with you

for 7.30pm at her home. That's all.'

There was nothing in the way Northey replied, or his demeanour generally, that led Scott to believe he might be holding something back.

Scott braced himself.

'I will understand if you don't want to answer the next question due to confidentiality, but do you happen to know if Diane kept any notes about my meeting with her at the pub or what she wanted to discuss with me yesterday?'

'I can't answer. It's not because I don't want to. I just don't know.' He shrugged. 'If she did, she never told me.'

Now for the big one.

'This is one hell of an ask, Mr Northey, but please believe me it could be very important in helping to find out who assassinated David Carey, and who murdered Diane…'

'What is it? Of course, I'll help if I can. It's the least I could do for her.'

The man was genuine. Scott had no doubt.

'I would like to see her files on David Carey.' He gritted his teeth in anticipation. It was an unprecedented request. No lawyer would ever allow an unauthorised person to look at the client files without the client's consent. In this case the client, David Carey, was dead. The files would be held in chambers to the order of Carey's next of kin: Stephanie and Jonathan. 'There may be something in there that would—'

Northey held up his hand, palm facing Scott.

'Please, don't go on, Mr Mitchell. Whatever my views are on the subject, it doesn't matter. The police took away her computer and all her hard copy papers earlier this morning.'

Shit.

That was quick.

'Did they have a warrant, or did David Carey's

children's consent? Press reports say that Stephanie and Jonathan are the executors and beneficiaries of the estate.'

Northey smiled for the first time during the meeting. 'Yes, they had a warrant, but only because on the day after David Carey's assassination they came to collect the files and Diane refused to release them unless they had a warrant. She wouldn't show a single document to them.'

'What time was this?'

'After her meeting with you at the pub.'

Scott remembered her taking a phone call: *there's an emergency in chambers.*

Had Diane been more knowledgeable about David Carey's investigation than she'd admitted to him?

Perhaps a last-minute change of heart had prompted her to set up the meeting at her home.

'Really?' Scott said. 'It was a high-profile murder of a government minister. Terrorism hadn't been ruled out. Didn't the police threaten her with an obstruction of justice charge?'

Northey smiled again. 'Yes, but she dug her heels in; no warrant, no papers. She could be a stickler for doing things properly.'

'How did your head of chambers take it? Sir Philip Nolan QC, isn't it?

'Yes.' Northey smirked. 'He tried to persuade her to hand them over, but she refused until they produced a warrant or she was instructed to do so by Stephanie or Jonathan. Neither Sir Philip nor the police were happy about it but, as you know, a head of chambers has no power to force a barrister to cooperate with the police in those circumstances. "A warrant's a warrant," she said on their first attempt.'

'Okay, thanks. I'll try to speak to Stephanie tomorrow. It's David Carey's funeral today, isn't it? A private affair? Well, so the press say.'

'Yes.' Northey sighed.

'Do you know if Jonathan will be there? He's a bit of a wanderer I understand. An amateur David Attenborough.'

'I'm sorry, I don't. He's a law unto himself. Goes off for months on end filming wildlife and not answering his phone.'

'Does he know his father is dead?'

'Stephanie has been trying to contact him every day since their father died, but I don't know if she's managed to speak with him.'

Scott scratched the back of his head and pulled an embarrassed face. 'You couldn't let me have a contact number for Stephanie could you, by any chance?'

A long shot.

Northey also looked embarrassed: 'I'm sorry, but I can't. GDPR. And in the circumstances of her distress, I'm not going to make an exception, even if I could. I do hope you understand, Mr Mitchell. Nothing personal. But it wouldn't be the right thing to do. If she contacts me, I shall tell her of your request, but that's as far as I can go. I'm sorry.'

Scott reached out and touched his arm. 'Please don't think you should apologise. You've been very helpful.'

Northey stood up, Scott with him.

'I must go back to chambers.'

They both exited the pews.

'Thanks for the chat, Paul. You've been very helpful.'

Especially about the police having seized Diane's files.

'I hope so,' he smiled. 'Goodbye, Scott...and good luck.'

'You too.'

Scott walked up to the stained-glass window, staring at the famous historical figures in each pane but not absorbing them. He imagined a plausible scenario: Diane, the dutiful family lawyer, complies with her client's "death bed" instruction to hand a sealed envelope to Scott with the comment that the police and Establishment weren't to be trusted. Within an hour or so of Diane giving the envelope to Scott, the police demand that she surrenders her computer and all Carey's files to them. She refuses unless they get a warrant. Annoyed at the police threat to charge her with obstructing justice, she goes through the files and discovers either a copy of the list of names, of which she knows nothing, or something else that may have made her curious, e.g. the Russian-sounding name of Arkady Vladimirovich Orlov. Knowing that Carey was investigating Russian sanctions-busting, she decides to discuss her discovery with Scott, before the police appeared with the warrant.

Fanciful speculation or a more than plausible scenario?

Chapter 14

Day Nine: 9pm, Moscow

As Pravda stood in the arrivals hall at Moscow's Domodedovo airport staring at the indicator board for the landed flights, Yelena emerged at the Customs exit before the Varna flight indicated that baggage was in the hall.

She was in a group of 15 to 20 people, carrying only hand luggage.

'Successful trip?'

'You bet.'

Yelena looked like the cat that got the cream.

Pravda led her out to the car park where they jumped into a rented vehicle; his own was being serviced.

Though he didn't fear that the vehicle had been bugged by the Kremlin, old habits die hard and they limited their exchanges to vacuous small talk as they began their 45-kilometre journey north on the A-105 to Moscow's centre.

After 30 minutes of unusually heavy traffic for the time of the evening, they stopped at the Café Stolovaya in the small city area of Korobovo.

It was empty except for two staff.

Perfect.

They ordered coffees with nothing to eat and took a table in the corner from where they could see who was coming and going.

'Orlov's apartment was a goldmine,' Yelena said. 'Bank statements, credit card statements and emails...' She sipped her coffee. 'All sorts of goodies. Some in

Russian, some English, some Bulgarian and some French. It's going to take some time to sort it out.'

Pravda smiled, patronisingly. 'I don't want to dampen your enthusiasm, Yelena, but as far I know, you only speak Russian and very basic Bulgarian. How do you know there's gold in the English and French documents?'

She grinned. 'There's got to be. Because of this.' She took a copy of a Russian passport from a zipped pocket inside her holdall and handed it to Pravda, her eyes widening expectantly. 'Here.'

'What's this?' he said as he flicked through the pages; all clean, no visa stamps.

He stopped at the details page and photo.

The holder was Gulyana Niyazova, a Russian citizen born in Uzbekistan.

'What about her?' Pravda said.

He couldn't understand Yelena's enthusiasm.

'Her name's on some of the credit cards and bank statements and it's plastered all over the other documents. And I know enough to recognise a person's name in English and French.'

'Even so that doesn't necessarily mean that—'

'She's a person of interest to the Kremlin, General. *Great* interest.'

Now she was being melodramatic.

'How can you say that?'

'Because when I tried our portal to check the validity of the passport I got "access denied". After four attempts I got locked out.'

Now, that *was* a matter for concern.

One of the tools they used in their Gravchenko investigation was a high-level access route into many of the government's databases where they were allowed entry without question. Of course, there would be a record of every click they made from the moment of access to the moment of leaving, but the Kremlin couldn't complain because the Gravchenko investigation was its brainchild.

'It could have been an IT glitch,' Pravda said.

'Now why didn't I think of that?' Yelena said disdainfully.

'Okay, we'll check it out again when we get back,' Pravda said. They had other, unorthodox, methods to gain access. 'What else did you bring back with you?'

'All the stuff I found.' She tapped on her luggage. 'It's in here.'

Pravda closed his eyes. 'Let me get this straight.' He sighed. 'You found a bundle of what you say are "gold mine" documents, credit cards and this copy of a Russian passport in Orlov's apartment and stuffed it all in your hand luggage with your clothes.'

'Yes, yes,' she said eagerly. 'That's about it.'

Pravda closed his eyes, blew out air and opened them again.

'What were you thinking of for God's sake?'

Yelena frowned. 'One, I uploaded copies of all the stuff to the cloud. And two—'

'Yelena, how many times have I told you—'

'And two, it came in a diplomatic bag.'

Pravda was flummoxed. 'What diplomatic bag?' He closed his eyes. What had she done now?

'Don't worry. He's the contact I told you about. A hundred per cent trustworthy. He was great. He helped get access to the apartment, hacked into the building's communal Wi-Fi system and set up the scanning equipment. We were working through the night. I couldn't have done it without him.'

Pravda opened his mouth to speak.

'And no, General. I'm sorry, but I'm not going to reveal his name.'

Surely it couldn't get any worse.

'Where did you make the switch?' There were security cameras everywhere.

'Between Customs and Arrivals; in amongst a group of other passengers. Like passing the baton in a relay race. We bought identical bags and practised in Varna.' She beamed again. 'Don't worry, nobody saw us.'

Pravda didn't have time to labour the issue; he'd deal with it later.

He tucked the copy passport in his jacket pocket and checked the time – it was gone 10.30pm.

The traffic was still nose-to-tail.

'Another coffee?' Yelena said. 'And a cinnamon roll to stop you being so grumpy?'

A favourite food of his childhood. His grandma used to make them for him to stop him irritating his mother.

Now Yelena was irritating *him*, but he couldn't be grumpy with her for long. 'Just the coffee, please.'

She went to the counter.

A woman, mid-30s, emerged from the back of the café. She helped herself to a pastry from the vitrine display on the counter and sat down in the corner opposite, where she began reading a book.

Pravda assumed she was a member of staff, but kept an eye on her all the same.

Yelena returned with two coffees.

'Where did you find the documents and the passport?' He lowered his voice and nodded at the woman in the corner.

Yelena pulled her chair nearer to the table.

'That's the strange thing. They were in two large pocket envelopes in Christmas wrapping paper at the bottom of a cat litter bag.'

'Strange?' Pravda had once hidden a birthday present from an extremely curious ten-year-old son in his cat litter bag.

'There wasn't any other sign of a cat living in the

apartment,' Yelena said. 'No drinking bowl, no food, no scratch post, no catnip toys, zilch. That's what made me suspicious about the bag.'

'Perhaps he'd bought it for somebody and had meant to hand it over before he flew to Madrid.'

'Sure. It's possible.'

'Any sign of anybody living there other than Orlov. A woman perhaps?'

He was thinking of Simone Bisset, the name directly under Orlov's on the list. It might make everybody's life simpler if the two were connected.

'Nope.'

'Okay,' Pravda said. 'Time to go.'

They headed for the car.

It was all too easy. It was being handed to them on a plate.

'Just tell me one thing,' he said. 'Your diplomatic source. Is he Russian?'

Yelena hesitated. 'Do I have to?'

'Yes, you do. I'm only asking for nationality; nothing else, I promise.'

'Bulgarian.'

Pravda sighed with an air of relief. A Russian diplomat would be more pliable in the hands of the Kremlin than any foreign diplomat, especially one from an EU member state, which Bulgaria had been for ten years.

15 minutes later

A police car with flashing lights guided Pravda to a halt in a small country road that led off the A-105 to Volodarskoye Shosse.

Pravda and Yelena watched in silence as a uniformed police officer got out of the front passenger seat of his car and walked towards them, shining a torch.

He tapped on Pravda's window.

Pravda slid it down.

'Good evening,' the policeman said. 'I'm Captain Fyodorov. Your documents please.'

Yelena handed her GRU ID to Pravda who handed it to the policeman with his own.

They weren't in uniform.

The captain examined the documents and shone the light on their faces. 'Thank you, General. Wait here please.' He handed back their IDs and returned to his car, where he poked his head through an open window.

The back door of the police car opened and Max manoeuvred his carcass out.

'Oh no,' Yelena said. 'What the f... does three chins want?'

Pravda's left leg arched. 'I'll do the talking.'

Yelena grunted.

Max squeezed himself into the back of Pravda's car, with a medley of curses, snorts, puffs and groans.

'What are you doing in this rented muck wagon?' Max growled.

Keeping away from your ears.

Pravda turned to face him. 'Mine is being serviced.'

Max pulled out his phone, tapped on the screen and showed it to Pravda.

It was a mug shot of a man in his 30s. He had a black eye and swollen lips, with a blood trickle from the corner of his mouth. 'Recognise him?'

'No.' That was the truth. Pravda had no idea who the man was.

'Major.' Max reached across and showed the image to Yelena, who was also now facing him. 'Will you or I enlighten your superior officer, here?'

She glanced at Pravda, and before he could stop her she said to Max. 'He works for me.'

'Doing what?' Max smirked. 'Bringing narcotics into the country in a diplomatic bag?'

Pravda jolted her leg with a hidden hand. 'Max,' he

said. 'You told me in Sicily that time was running out for us to deliver on Gravchenko.'

Max snorted. 'What's that got to do with this man?'

'So let us get on with the job.' He leant towards Max, as aggressively as he could without touching the beast. 'If you're going to hamper us at every step, it's going into my reports. Do you understand me?'

His left leg began to shake.

He knew that one day he'd go too far and Max would delight in crushing him.

'This is your last chance, General Pravda. Do *you* understand *me*? Your last chance.'

He got out and left the door open.

Yelena popped out and closed it.

Pravda took ten deep breaths and turned to her as she climbed back in, head down.

'Right,' he said. 'Let that be a lesson learnt.'

He patted his jacket pocket containing the copy passport and drove on.

Thank God the odious man hadn't demanded to see Yelena's hand luggage.

Chapter 15

Day Ten: 2pm, London

'Thanks for agreeing to see me, Mr Burrows,' Scott said. 'Especially at such short notice. And please apologise to your wife for my calling you out of the blue this morning, so soon after her father's funeral.' Scott had obtained the late MP's ex-directory landline number from a friend in the press and it was public knowledge that Stephanie and her family were staying at his house.

Her husband had taken the call and agreed to meet him in Grosvenor Square, opposite where the US Embassy used to be, after Scott had introduced himself and said he had some information on David Carey that he needed to discuss with the family.

If Fraser was listening in and asked what the information was, he'd repeat the story he'd told ADC Chalmers.

They had a bench to themselves, and were far away from the last of the summer sunbathers.

'What's so urgent, Mr Mitchell, that you couldn't have told me on the phone?'

Burrows' tone and demeanour were formal and showed minor irritation, though not anger.

Scott looked away, searching for the right words. Though he'd practised his opening remark, he wasn't happy with it because it sounded ludicrous. 'There's no other way of putting this.' He turned to face the man. 'Your late father-in-law has...effectively...asked me to investigate his own death.'

'What?' Burrows recoiled. 'Do you mind explaining

yourself?' His eyes looked as though they were going to pop out of his head.

The only people in the UK Scott was prepared to trust with his story were members of the Carey family. Their priority would be to find out who assassinated their father and why. They wouldn't have a more pressing agenda.

So he told a silent, if not stunned, Tom Burrows every detail of his meeting with Diane Costello at the Old Thameside Inn and his conclusion that David Carey wanted him to carry on his investigation into the alleged sanctions-busting, which, Scott hoped, would lead to his finding out why the MP was killed and who was responsible. He also told him about the names on the list and his meetings with Wyatt the blogger, Assistant Deputy Commissioner Chalmers and Paul Northey, plus the news that Orlov was killed in the Madrid plane explosion.

Burrows had listened attentively throughout, barely moving a muscle.

'Would you please give me a few minutes?' he said when Scott had finished. He got up and walked off without waiting for Scott's reply.

'Of course.'

Scott watched as the man strolled around the Square's outer pathway, occasionally stopping and shaking his head. Had he done the right thing? Didn't the family have enough on their plate, without him barging into their lives like a misguided wrecking ball? Should he have left it a few more days before contacting them? But with three deaths in ten days, time wasn't on his side, or anybody's connected to the *toxic list*, for that matter.

His phone rang.

It was Alex in Ghana.

'Yes, Alex.'

'Project Conrad. Sorry about the short notice,' Alex said. 'But they insist on a meeting tomorrow, 11am, at Claridge's, the Brook Penthouse suite.'

He wasn't prepared. 'Yeah, okay. Tell them I'll be there.'

'Great. Will do.'

'Any news on the fund distributor?'

'I've been warned off,' Alex said.

'What?! Who warned you off? And how? Did they get violent?'

The toxic list. The toxic list.

'He's a well-known fixer for all sorts of shady characters. He didn't need to get violent. A twisted smile was enough. You understand?'

Only too well. Scott recalled the late Bob Hoskins' brilliantly acted final scene in the movie *The Long Good Friday* when he got into a taxi and realised too late that it was being driven by the IRA. The three-minute long shot on Hoskins' facial expressions as he was on his way to a certain death told more than a thousand words could ever have done.

'Sorry, Scott, but I'm not going anywhere near this company. It's not good for my health...or my family's.'

'No, no, don't. I completely understand. Forget I ever asked. Sorry to get you into this in the first place.'

'Okay,' Alex said.

'I'll let you know how I get on with the project meeting,' Scott said.

Santorini was at the top of Carey's list of names; now it was at the top of Scott's watch list.

'Cheers.'

'Bye, Alex.'

Scott disconnected.

Wyatt's teasers were one thing, but Alex's life being threatened was far more serious, and immediate.

Tom Burrows returned and sat down again.

'Right, Scott,' he said. 'Listen to me. I'm also an attorney, but not in your field. I specialise in international maritime arbitration...'

Obviously a man who'd recognise bullshit when he heard it.

'Stephanie had been concerned for David for some months. We live in the States and hadn't seen him for two years before we came here, but she spoke regularly with him on the phone or Skype. He liked to tell little Chrissy stories and pull faces that cracked her up.' He stopped and wiped his eyes with a handkerchief. 'Sorry.'

Scott held up his hand. 'Please, no need to apologise.'

Burrows took in a deep breath. 'Stephanie noticed his recent fluctuations in mood when we Skyped: cheeriness interspersed with nervous facial tics and minor hand tremors, fewer smiles and, sometimes, if not slurring in speech, his mind wandered off topic. He wasn't a teetotaller, but he didn't drink that much. She suspected he was seriously ill and was holding back on us. We couldn't get hold of Jonathan, so we jumped on a plane.'

'When did you get here?'

'Two days before he was shot.'

'That was the day after he delivered the envelope to Diane,' Scott said.

'Yeah. That would be right.'

'Jesus—'

'I know what you're thinking, Scott. Had we arrived a day earlier maybe we would have found out about the letter and he would have come clean with us. We could have helped him somehow.' He shrugged. 'But who knows? Life's full of what ifs.'

You can say that again.

'Look, don't take this the wrong way,' Tom continued, 'but are you holding back? Have you told me everything? I've spent the morning checking you out. You're a principled man as far as I can see, but boy, do you like playing with fire.'

'Nothing. I assure you. Absolutely nothing.'

That wasn't strictly true. He hadn't yet mentioned his meetings with Fraser. That was because apart from the spook's enigmatic comment that Scott shouldn't 'get side-tracked' they hadn't discussed Carey at all.

'You mentioned this blogger Wyatt and his allegation that the Santorini company was somehow connected to your man's Foundation. So I assume you've also discussed this aspect with Gravchenko.'

'Yeah, okay, I didn't want to get too bogged down with detail right now. I wanted to concentrate on the UK-specific aspects. As I told you, your father-in-law was adamant that it was the UK police and Establishment he didn't trust. Anyway, Mr Gravchenko has never heard of Santorini. And he's agreed to try to help with the other names, one of which is the Russian Arkady Orlov.'

'Anything else?'

'I've also put out feelers to a contact in Russian Military Intelligence, you know, the GRU. We've worked together before and he helped me to prove that I'd been framed on the money-laundering allegations jointly by the Russians and the UK.'

'You trust him?'

'In something like this, yes. I know he wouldn't deliberately do me any harm or feed me lies. We have a mutual respect.'

'Maybe, but he must have an agenda.'

'Of course, but I can assure you that he's just as keen to find out about the names on the list and who killed your father-in-law as we are.'

'Is that your educated opinion or a known fact?'

Fair question, and typical of a lawyer.

'I'm going to have to ask you to trust me on this one, Tom.' He didn't see why he should go into Pravda's brief from the Kremlin to dig the dirt on his boss.

Tom stared across the square.

'Okay,' he said. 'But just tell me this. If your GRU

contact found out that the Russians killed David, for whatever reason, would he tell you?'

'I believe so, yes. But I'm equally sure he wouldn't tell me the actual names of those behind it, or their reasons. Unless, of course, he had permission from his superiors... which would be most unlikely.'

'Yeah.' Tom sighed. 'I see.'

'When are you going back to the States?'

'Stephanie's taking Chrissy back to Washington the day after tomorrow. My parents will be looking after them. I'll be based in London for the time being, commuting to Hamburg for an unavoidable series of case conferences.'

'You're staying at your father-in-law's house in St John's Wood?'

Tom nodded.

'Before I forget,' Scott said. 'What was he doing in Canary Wharf when he was assassinated? Did he also have an apartment there?'

'No. It belongs to one of Stephanie's old school friends, Laura. They'd kept in touch over the years. He and Chrissy had gone there at the last minute to give a get-well present to Laura's little boy who was too ill to go to the party.'

Fate, whose side were you on?

'So how did the sniper know he'd be there? I mean, no one has said it was a random shooting.'

'That's a million-dollar question,' Tom said.

'How did David, if I may call him that, make this last-minute arrangement with Laura?'

'Stephanie did it, the day before. By phone.'

'On *her* phone?'

'Yeah. David and I were with her at the time.'

'Where did the call take place? David's house or outside?'

'In Selfridges, on Oxford Street. We were shopping. Why? What are you thinking?'

'Short of thinking that Laura is an Establishment or Russian mole, either Stephanie's or Laura's phone was probably bugged, and maybe still is.'

Tom's face – a perfect "oh shit" depiction. 'Yeah, that makes sense. And it's more likely that it was, is, Stephanie's phone than Laura's. Her partner's a Professor of Social Anthropology, or some such, at one of the London University colleges and Laura makes TV documentaries about bird migrations; hardly of interest to the intelligence agencies or Russian sanctions-busters.

'I think you're right,' Scott said. 'And I wouldn't discount *your* phone also being bugged. You're both in the *Carey crucible* with the rest of us...for want of a better expression.'

Another grimace from Tom.

'By the way,' Scott asked. 'Have the police interviewed you and Stephanie yet?'

'Yes, and your MI5.'

'Not MI6?'

'They said five.'

He thought about Northey's comments on the police demanding Diane Costello's files.

'Have they removed any computers or hard-copy documents from the house?'

'Stephanie gave the police permission to search and remove papers. And also his cell phone, but there weren't any computer or other digital devices there.' He shrugged. 'We assume he kept them in his office at the House of Commons.'

Maybe.

'One final question.'

'Yes?'

'Do you have any idea how I can contact Jonathan?'

'No. He didn't turn up for the funeral yesterday. The last we heard was that he was in Asia doing some field studies; like Laura, another wild life enthusiast. But that was a month ago. We've been unable to make contact since and he hasn't posted on social media recently. There's no answer on his cell phone or the landline at his house. Stephanie's left a couple of voicemails telling him to contact her immediately, but without specifically mentioning the assassination. Of course, he might know about it by now, if he checks the internet.'

'If he did, surely he would have called or emailed Stephanie?'

Tom pulled an uncomfortable face. 'You might have thought so, but his relationship with David hadn't been that good for years.'

'Why not?'

'I'd rather not say, if you don't mind. Not now at any rate. I need to speak with Stephanie before I tell you. Family stuff.'

'Sure, I didn't mean to pry. Sorry.'

Was there a skeleton in the family closet that had some bearing on Carey's investigation?

'The press say Jonathan and Stephanie are the executors and beneficiaries under the will. Is that true?' Paul Northey hadn't confirmed or denied it.

'As good as,' Tom said. 'There are also provisions for Chrissy and any children Jonathan might have, but that's not relevant for now.'

'This may be a stupid question,' Scott said. 'You've both had a terrible shock and no doubt are on emotional rollercoasters, but I have to ask it.'

'Go ahead.'

'Have you been to Jonathan's house since the assassination? If only to see if he's there?'

What if Carey left his papers with his son for safekeeping, despite their cold relationship?

'No.'

'Do you mind telling me his address? I'd like to speak to his neighbours. You know, any sightings etc.'

Tom stared at him, as if trying to make up his mind about Scott's intentions.

'I've...*we've*, got to explore all possibilities,' Scott added. 'We don't know what Jonathan knows about David's investigation. It might be nothing, but it also might be a lot more.'

'It's a long shot,' Tom said, 'bearing in mind their relationship. But worth a try, I suppose. It's 25 Rockingham Gardens in a place called Bexleyheath. I don't know the zip code or whatever you call it.'

'Postcode. No problem. Bexleyheath is a London suburb. I'll find it. Thanks.'

'Now,' Tom said in a determined tone, 'here's what's going to happen.'

'I'm listening.'

'I'm not going to worry Stephanie with anything you've told me today. She'll never forgive herself if she thinks her phone call to Laura was responsible for the death of her father.'

'Good point. So you won't ask her to change the phone?'

'No, she'll be innocent of any knowledge of the matters we've talked about, so she won't be able to let slip anything potentially damaging to what we're going to do.'

Interesting. Maybe Tom was going to take an active role in the investigation.

Four hands were better than two.

'So what will you say was the reason I wanted to speak with you so urgently?'

'I'll tell her you wanted to bring me up to date about your meetings with Diane Costello, and that she wanted to know if you had met David in your Russian travels etc. But I won't mention the list. Now's not the time to go into too much detail. I'll also tell her you're having discussions with ADC Chalmers. In other words, you're trying to help us.'

'Won't she ask why?'

'Sure she will. I'll tell her that after your meeting with Diane, you thought you might be able to help find out why David was murdered and who was responsible, because of your well-publicised Russian commercial connections.'

'And she'll accept that?'

'For the time being, yes. She's been hit badly by the assassination. Chrissy is her number one priority. She refuses to let her out of her sight, 24/7.'

God, what a nightmare for her.

'Understood,' Scott said. 'How do you want us to exchange information, bearing in mind your phone might be bugged? Mine is – by MI6, for one.'

'I'll get another cell phone, just for you and me,' Tom said.

'I use prepaid for stuff like this,' Scott said. 'It's not 100 per cent bug proof, but it's secure enough for me. I'll get another one and text you the number.'

'I think we should set up a cloud account that only you and I can access. Use it for documents,' Tom said. 'Tonight, I'll arrange a failsafe contact for you with a guy called Brett Sadler. He's a private investigator. We use him for our maritime fraud cases. He's based in New York. Knows all sorts of people...who know all sorts of other people. Most important, he and his wife, Barbs, are Chrissy's godparents. I've known them since high school. I'll give you his website link.'

'You've really thought this through.'

And in such a short space of time.

'Scott, this stinks – we're teetering on the tip of a very deep iceberg.'

Chapter 16

Day Eleven: 10.30am, London

Scott hurried into Claridge's, where a receptionist told him he was expected. He headed straight for the lift to the Brook Penthouse suite on the 7th floor.

He stepped out of the lift into a mini lobby inside the suite.

Two stereotype dark-suited aides, both black and wearing sunglasses, confronted him.

He was surprised, but not concerned. He'd seen such set-ups before in the movies where the hotel guest had been a VIP, though never in real life in the UK.

'Hello. I'm Scott Mitchell. I've an appointment with Mr Jakande.'

'Unzip your case please, sir,' the smaller aide said.

Scott did so and held it open.

The aide poked around inside. 'Okay. Zip it up.'

Scott did so.

'Show me your passport, please,' the same aide said.

The taller aide stood ahead of him, effectively blocking any further entrance into the suite, his face telling no tales.

Scott handed over his passport.

The aide scrutinised it, lingering on the photo with frequent glances at Scott, as if he were a border guard who'd been trained not to trust his own shadow.

'Okay,' the aide said at last to his colleague, and returned the passport to Scott.

'In here, please Mr Mitchell.' a female voice from an inner room called out.

The taller aide moved aside and gestured for Scott to go through.

'Thank you,' Scott said and walked into the living area.

'Good morning, Mr Mitchell,' said the most beautiful black woman Scott had ever seen. 'My name is Adwoa Twumasi. I am a member of Mr Jakande's legal team.' She held out her hand; too delicate to shake. Scott applied little or no pressure.

'Pleased to meet you, Ms Twumasi.'

'Please come in. Would you like a drink?'

She was wearing a short bright red jacket over a white shirt, and full-length black trousers that covered her shoes.

'If you're having one, certainly. Thank you.'

'Please sit down, over there at that table behind the sofa, take any chair.'

It was a round table, large enough to seat four, with two piles of papers in the centre.

'What would you like? Whisky? Wine? Something else?'

He usually made a point of not drinking alcohol while doing serious business with people he'd never met before. He liked to get to know them first, but Alex had told him that Mr Jakande would be insulted if he refused at least one alcoholic drink.

'A small dry white wine, if I may. I'm driving.' He wasn't.

'You may, Mr Mitchell.'

She poured him a glass of wine and herself a Scotch and soda with ice; she moved with the elegance of a swan gracing a lake as she handed him his drink and sat in the single-seater armchair, at right angles to his left.

Scott raised his glass. 'What do you say where you come from, for cheers?'

'I am from Ghana, Mr Mitchell, but when we are in England, we say what the English say.'

'Cheers,' they both said and each took a sip.

'Ah, Mr Mitchell, thank you so much for coming.'

A tall, suave black man of athletic build appeared from an open doorway at the far end of the room. Scott could see a small dressing area behind the doorway and assumed it was a bedroom. 'My name is Matthew Jakande.'

He stood up as Jakande approached him. He reminded Scott of the images he'd seen of Muhammed Ali in his prime, with not an ounce of fat on display, and Scott instinctively drew his hand over his own abdomen to suppress the early stages of middle-aged spread. The man was dressed "smart casual", in the best Italian style and, unlike many African businessmen as depicted in the movies, he wasn't wearing jewellery. Scott knew little about his private life or wealth. He'd had no time to carry out any in-depth due diligence on the man. He knew only that he was 52 years old, married with two children, and employed by several African states to facilitate international trade deals.

They shook hands.

Jakande gestured for Scott to sit down again and poured himself a gin and tonic, which he took to his seat opposite Scott. 'Cheers, Mr Mitchell.'

'Cheers, Mr Jakande.'

They both sipped their drinks.

Ms Twumasi came to the table and sat nearer to Jakande than to Scott. She slid one set of the papers across the table to Scott and retained the other in front of herself.

Jakande appeared to be content to sip his drink while keeping an eye on the proceedings.

Scott flicked through the papers. They were documents relating to Gravchenko's proposed construction of his Ghanian hub for the Foundation's product manufacturing and distribution service, comprising feasibility studies, political and economic reports, demographics, transportation surveys and everything to be expected for such a project.

'Would you please concentrate on this document for now, Mr Mitchell.' Ms Twumasi produced three single sheets of paper from the bottom of her set and handed one each to Scott and Jakande.

'Thank you.' Scott examined it.

It contained details of three separate bank accounts in three cities: Zurich, London and New York. The bank in each case was AfriCapital Bank of West Africa; Scott didn't know of the bank. The account holders were different companies: Calabar Project Management Limited, Cordoba Coordinators SA, and *Santorini International Securities LLP.*

He lingered on the Santorini name and held his tongue, desperate not to give any sign of prior knowledge of the company. He didn't recognise the other two.

He could see out of the corner of his eye that both Jakande and Ms Twumasi were staring at him.

Did they have somebody at the Prague press conference who'd witnessed Scott's public exchange with Wyatt about Santorini?

It took every effort to refrain from downing the rest of his wine in one gulp.

'What's their relevance?' he said, looking at Ms Twumasi.

Were these guys engaged in money-laundering with the Russians?

'It is part of the Memorandum of Understanding,' Jakande replied.

'Mr Gravchenko must pay US$25 million into each account before any contracts can be signed,' Ms Twumasi added.

Scott wasn't completely naïve. He knew that several economies in African countries operated on a money-up-front basis and it didn't always find its way to the contractually nominated recipient.

But *US$75 million*?

Spell it out, Mr Jakande. 'And what are these payments supposed to represent?'

'There is nothing *supposed* about them,' Ms Twumasi said, with no sign of having been insulted at Scott's choice of the word. 'The first account is for consultancy fees, the second is for facilitation fees and the third is a deposit on the performance bond, to be forfeited if Mr Gravchenko does not complete the contract.'

Though the third account was Santorini's, it wasn't using the same bank as that shown in Wyatt's documents.

'And you have prepared the paperwork to support this...this fiscal arrangement?' Scott said.

'It is in your bundle of documents.' Ms Twumasi smiled.

'As a matter of interest,' Scott said. 'Who's behind each of these company account holders? Mr Gravchenko will want to know.'

And *I* would like to know the name of the thug who threatened Alex.

'They are necessary cogs in the machinery that will ensure the smooth-running of Ghana's economy,' Jakande said, without any hint of irony. 'As far as Mr Gravchenko is concerned he will be dealing only with me. He has no need to concern himself with who oils the cogs.' A broad grin appeared. 'Your client is a Russian oligarch, Mr Mitchell. I have no doubt he will understand.'

2pm

'What the...?' Scott exclaimed as he flicked through the news sites while waiting for a large glass of Sauvignon Blanc at Tompkins' ground floor lounge bar at South Quay in Canary Wharf. A split image of a news broadcaster on one side and a picture of a smiling Henry Wyatt on the other appeared:

The police have confirmed that the man who fell to his death from the roof of an office block in Canary Wharf at 11 this morning was Henry Wyatt, an anti-Russian blogger who had been attending a private meeting in the building. The police have not released any details of who else attended the meeting or how he came to be on the roof. In other news…'

Oh Christ. Not you too.

They were falling like ninepins.

He hadn't checked the media since leaving Claridge's, having been pre-occupied with the news that Santorini was involved in Project Conrad.

He uploaded the report of Wyatt's death, and a summary of the Claridge's meeting with the emphasis on Santorini, to the cloud account he shared with Sergey, and texted the man:

Check the cloud. Will call later to arrange a meeting

The wine arrived.

He called Henri Bernard, Professor Zapatero's assistant.

'Monsieur Bernard. It's Scott Mitchell again. I'm sorry to trouble you, but have you managed to pass on my message to Professor Zapatero yet?'

'Yes, Monsieur Mitchell. She will call you when it is convenient.'

'Thank you. Would you please tell her that the matter has become very urgent?'

'Yes. Of course.'

'Thank you. Goodbye.'

'You are welcome, monsieur. Goodbye.'

They disconnected.

He received a text from Fraser:

Where are you?

Canary Wharf. Why?

At home?

No, Tompkins Bar at South Quay. Outside

Stay where you are. I'll be there in 10 minutes

Scott was supposed to have sated the man's appetite with the information he'd given him on Teresa's website.

Okay.

He finished off the glass and repeated the order; not a clever way to prepare for a meeting with MI6, but Wyatt's death had upped the stakes considerably. He needed liquid fortification.

Fraser appeared earlier than expected and invited Scott to walk with him around Millwall Dock.

Scott paid the bill, leaving the second glass half full, and went with the man.

'What do you know about a company called Santorini International Securities?' Fraser asked.

'What do you know about Henry Wyatt?' Scott wanted time to consider his reply. He'd expected a question about the newsworthy Wyatt.

'You first,' Fraser said.

'If you say so.' He wasn't going to get any more thinking time. 'I presume you had somebody at the Prague Press conference.'

He waited for Fraser's response.

Nothing.

'Well, anyway. Wyatt asked me a question about the company.'

'What *about* the company?'

'If I'd ever had dealings with it.'

'Had you?'

'No.'

'Is that what you told him?'

'Yes.'

Fraser hadn't yet confirmed whether MI6 was there. Was he testing him?

Deflect the man.

'Was Wyatt's death an accident?'

'No,' Fraser said without hesitation, and unexpectedly.

'Any idea who might have killed him?'

'Take your pick. He made enemies easily.'

Something wasn't right. Fraser was releasing information too willingly; he was taking their "bromance" too far. 'So he was *a person of interest* to you?'

'You're forgetting,' Fraser said. 'It's give and take between us. I repeat. What do you know about Santorini?'

'According to Companies House, it's a Scottish limited partnership with two registered owners, who are—'

Fraser held up his hand, stopped and turned to Scott. 'Yeah, yeah, we know all that public stuff... But what do you know that's *not* on the register?'

Give and take maybe, but Scott wasn't ready to reveal everything. Fraser might conceivably be genuine, but his masters in their ivory tower on the Albert Embankment certainly wouldn't be; Scott didn't trust them any further than he could throw them. 'Nothing.' He turned away and walked on

'Really?'

'Really.'

'Okay,' Fraser said with a sigh. 'Then I'm telling you now, the company is a money-laundering vehicle for the Russian government.'

So Wyatt was right about its activities, if not his snide view of the identity of the launderer.

'Russian *government*? Not the mafia?'

'Is there a difference?' Fraser said.

'Some say not.' At least he wasn't trying to drag Gravchenko into it, as Wyatt did.

'By the way,' Fraser said. 'Did you check out that FBI report on Shaw's blog? You know, the redacted Russian oligarch who's a front for Putin.'

A Gravchenko dig?

'To be accurate,' Scott replied. 'It said that the oligarch *could be* fronting for Putin.'

But never let the facts stand in the way of your scheming, Mr Fraser.

'Is there a difference?' Fraser repeated.

Chapter 17

Day Eleven: 6pm, Moscow

Pravda stopped by the statue of Lenin in front of the central pavilion in the VDNKh, the Exhibition of National Economic Achievements, located in a park north of Moscow centre on Prospect Mira, and scrolled absent-mindedly down the newsfeeds on his phone.

A group of early teenage girls were sitting on the low marble ledge in front of the statue, eating ice creams and chatting about boys.

A text from Yelena:

Wyatt murdered in London earlier today

A searing pain from his dodgy ankle warned him of problems ahead.

'You look as if you're about to give birth to kidney stones, boss man,' Monkfish said.

Pravda looked up and smiled. 'Monkfish? Is that really you hiding behind that beard?' The lad was pushing a mountain bike.

They hugged.

It was a prearranged urgent meeting at Monkfish's request.

'Fancied a change from the clean-cut youth I once was.' He scanned the area and his eyes fell on the young girls who, to Pravda, looked uninterested in what Monkfish had to say. 'Let's go for a walk,' Monkfish said.

'Okay.' Pravda eased his body away from the plinth, with a few tempered groans.

‘The old trouble?’

‘Time’s catching up with me. Chronic arthritis, operation threatened, and…well, you don’t want to hear about my ills.’

They mingled with the crowds.

‘How’s Christina?’ Pravda asked. He hadn’t been in contact with either Monkfish or his girlfriend since Max had taken Monkfish under his wing to work for the Kremlin.

‘I don’t know. We’ve separated. After those bastards kidnapped her, she said she didn’t want to have anything to do with them again. She says she’ll always love me, but not enough to be at their mercy all the time. She’s living with a cousin in Slovakia. I don’t blame her.’

The Kremlin had sacked her from her job in the Ministry of Internal Affairs and taken her into custody, for no lawful reason but to use her as a bargaining tool with Monkfish: ‘Work for us and we’ll let her go.’ He didn’t have any alternative.

‘I’m sorry to hear that,’ Pravda said. ‘She’s a good kid.’

There was a gap in the crowd.

Monkfish stopped by one of the flowerbeds that bordered each side of the Central Alley and laid his bike on the ground. He produced his phone and crouched at the foot of the bed, taking images.

‘Beautiful aren’t they?’ he said. ‘Come closer and look at these.’

Pravda approached Monkfish and tried to crouch, but it was too painful. ‘I know,’ he said. He took out his phone, eased down to a sitting position at Monkfish’s side and also began taking images of the flowers.

‘Boss man, your shadow, Max, and his shadows, they know *everything*,’ Monkfish whispered. ‘*Everything* we did, *everything* you’re doing now. *Everything*. You wouldn’t believe what technology they’ve got. What they can do. They're way ahead of the sci-fi films. It's awesome, shit awesome scary.'

Pravda continued taking the photos, fiddling with his phone, pretending to adjust distance and definition.

He glanced at Monkfish. The lad's hand was shaking as he too carried on filming.

'Surveillance is everywhere,' Monkfish continued, as he covered his lips with a handkerchief and pretended to sneeze several times while he spoke. 'They're using a system nicknamed "El Chapo". You know, it's how El Chapo, the Mexican drug lord, was caught by the FBI.'

Pravda knew that.

'It interrupts data on your phone before you send it encrypted through VPN or whatever,' Monkfish continued. 'It's tied up with the Pegasus system and zero dial technology.'

Pravda knew more about the other two systems. They were being openly developed by the NSO group, an Israeli organisation. Ostensibly only intended for lawful government usage to prevent crime and terrorism. Laudatory in the current dangerous climate of jihadism, but what if the government misused it and spied on its own law-abiding citizens with no objective other than to find out what they were doing as they went about their innocent daily lives? China for one was moving that way with its increasing use of surveillance technology on its entire population, under the guise of making the state safer.

'It's undetectable,' Monkfish said. 'We can't hide anything from them. Everything I did for you, the stuff on the net, was being monitored, every click on a site, every tap on the keyboard. Snowden? Assange? They're amateurs. If you're on the net, open or dark, the Kremlin will find your trail, and you. And much quicker than I thought. I'm telling you, boss man, it's Orwell's *1984*. You've got to believe me.'

They both got up and carried on walking.

Did that mean that Max had known the answers to all the questions he'd put to Pravda before Pravda had responded?

If so, "shit awesome scary" was an understatement.

'And how much do you know about what I've been doing since you joined Max?'

'Nothing, nada. They've not told me anything. I'm not working on the Gravchenko project.' He shrugged. 'I suppose they know we've not been in touch. But that's all.'

'Why have they taken you into their confidence? About the extent of their capabilities I mean.' Was this disinformation by the Kremlin? Or worse, had they turned him?

'They haven't. Found out by myself,' Monkfish replied.

'How can you be sure they don't know you've found out? Maybe they're setting you up.' Pravda had always prided himself on being a rationalist, not a conspiracy theorist, much less a teeterer on the borders of paranoia, but occasionally his intelligence training nudged him into those areas.

'I can't be sure of anything.' Monkfish kneeled down and pretended to fiddle with the gears on his bike. 'And there's something else.'

'What's that?'

'The teckies are at war with the Neanderthals.'

'I don't understand.'

'It's all about resources. Everybody knows the economy's going down the tubes. Yeah, even somebody like me, a guy who doesn't know the difference between a bull and a bear on the stock market. The teckies want more rubles to smarten up our existing super-smart cyber capabilities and the Neanderthals want to spend them on increasing our military hardware.' He got up and adjusted his saddle. ‘Might be water-cooler stuff, but the teckies have my support all the way. Give us the ability to pull the plug on our enemies and bring them to their knees without slaughtering them. Isn’t that what you guys call soft power…?’

‘No, it’s asymmetric warfare,’ Pravda said.

‘Whatever. Anyway the Neanderthals want the hard power, the real stuff, the power to turn the world into a nuclear wasteland for the next zillion years.’

Pravda had his work cut out for him.

‘It’s a no-brainer, boss man. We’re all gonna be screwed…one way or the other.’

Chapter 18

Day Twelve: 9.45am, London

Scott unpacked two newly acquired mobile phones and laid them out on the kitchen worktop: an iPhone and a Samsung, as Rosie gave them her sniff of approval. The iPhone was for Tom Burrows and the Samsung was to be a replacement for an earlier one which was playing up.

With his regular phone he'd be carrying three phones around with him.

How did drug dealers manage?

He texted Sergey.

Ready to meet with the boss as soon as possible

Why was Fraser goading him about Kevin Shaw's Russian oligarch?

Did the man have evidence that it was Gravchenko?

If so, why didn't he say so?

Sergey replied:

Day after tomorrow. Budapest. Evening?

Agreed. Thanks. Sergey.

He checked for a number in his contact list and used the Samsung.

'Hi Duncan, long time no speak.'

'And you are?'

'Oh yeah, sorry. It's Scott. Scott Mitchell. I've got a new phone.'

‘Hello, stranger. How long’s it been? Six, seven, *ten* months? I was beginning to think you were dead. What have you been doing with yourself?’

‘This and that. Look, I’ve got a favour to ask. Do you still lunch in the Chandos off Trafalgar Square?’

‘Regular as clockwork. Why don’t you pop down today, and buy me a few beers? I’ve given myself the afternoon off.’

‘You’re a star. I’ll be there at 2.30.’

‘Great. Usual booth.’

‘Cheers, Duncan. See you soon.’

‘Look forward to it.’

Duncan was a parliamentary reporter who’d spent 25 years commuting between the Houses of Parliament and every pub within spitting distance of Nelson’s Column. What he didn’t know about the nation’s MPs and members of the Upper House wasn’t worth knowing.

They’d become friends during Scott’s troubles with the authorities in 2016. Instead of looking for a scoop, he’d been a comforting counsellor. Duncan had less respect for the lawmakers than Scott did.

Scott had rewarded him with non-attributable information about his experiences with the UK intelligence services, which Duncan was using for a book he was writing about the abuse of power.

2.40pm

When Scott arrived Duncan was sitting in his favourite booth, at the far end of the pub on the right adjacent to the side-street opening, and guarding two pints of lager.

‘Thanks for agreeing to see me, Duncan,’ Scott said as he peered into the adjacent booth to satisfy himself it was empty.

He sat opposite his friend.

‘You’re up to something...again. I wouldn’t have missed it for the world.’ Duncan pushed a glass across the table to Scott. ‘Cheers.’

They clinked glasses.

'Cheers,' Scott replied.

'Your adventures brighten up my day.'

'Do you mind if I get straight to the point?' Scott said.

'Why change the habit of a lifetime?'

'I want a face-to-face with Sir Stanton Morgan Bell,' Scott said.

He studied Duncan's reaction.

No sign of disquiet or surprise.

'I don't suppose you're going to tell me why.'

'If it ever becomes public knowledge, you'll be the first member of the press to hear from me,' Scott said. 'I promise.'

'Fair enough.' Duncan took a swig of his beer. 'I could introduce you, if that's what you want. But I can't guarantee he'd be willing to—'

'No, no. You're better off out of it. There mustn't be any link to you.'

'Aha, the plot thickens. This is what I like,' Duncan said. 'Classic Scott Mitchell.'

'Yeah,' Scott said, without enthusiasm. A classic a hole in the head.

'He's a routine guy,' Duncan continued. 'Leaves the House at the same time every day, at 4pm. He doesn't work nights. He walks across Westminster Bridge and gets a taxi to his town apartment off the Clapham Road.'

'Why doesn't he get a taxi this side of the bridge?'

'He says it's the only exercise he gets.'

'What does he look like nowadays? His Wiki image must have been taken over 40 years ago when he was in the Guards.'

Duncan scrolled through his phone. 'Here you are. A shot from my rogues gallery. Taken a few months ago.'

Scott smiled at the picture. 'What's with the carnation in his buttonhole?'

'Old school.' Duncan smirked. 'Standards are slipping,

don't you know?' he said with an affected upper-class accent.

Scott returned the phone and checked the time. 'Is the House sitting today?'

'Sleeping, more like. But yes.'

3.55pm

As Scott emerged from Westminster tube station he spotted the hunched figure of the knight and his carnation across the road, turning right out of Parliament Square and heading for the bridge. Though tall, he looked far from the proud, strong and sturdy military colonel he must once have been.

Scott watched as the man made his way through the early homeward-bound commuters as if apologising for encroaching upon their space, preferring to step off the kerb into the oncoming traffic rather than assert his own right of way.

A sad-looking spectacle, far from what Scott had expected.

Scott hurried across the road and caught up with him.

'Sir Stanton, may I have a word with you, please?'

Bell glanced at him with a surprised look. 'What? Who are you? What do you want?' he said. His voice was barely audible, and he didn't wait for a reply.

'My name is Scott Mitchell, sir. I'm a lawyer.' He held out his business card. 'Here, please, take this.'

Bell did so and stopped and studied it; fellow pedestrians passed either side of them.

'I don't know you, do I?'

He looked Scott up and down.

'We've never met before, have we?'

'No, Sir Stanton, we haven't.'

'Well then,' he said, tucking Scott's card into his pocket and walking on, with a quickened pace.

Scott could smell whisky on the man's breath.

He hurried after him. 'I'd like to talk to you about the late MP David Carey.'

Bell stopped abruptly and frowned. 'What about him?'

They were halfway across the bridge, obstructing more and more people who were eager to get home.

'Let's talk over here, by the railings,' Scott said and led the way.

Bell grunted and followed him.

'Did you know David Carey?' Scott asked.

'Young man, you are taking too much for granted.'

So sudden; a changed man. His voice was more assertive and he'd lost his hunch. Scott was confused.

'I don't know what you mean. What am I taking for granted?'

'Are you Carey's family solicitor?'

Yes and no, was the truthful answer. He was working with Tom Burrows, but he hadn't been formally retained by the family. Anyway, he didn't want to get bogged down in technicalities.

'I have good reason to believe that your life is in danger, sir.'

'Is this a threat?"

Why should it be a threat?

'Just the opposite. I'm trying to save your life.'

Bell frowned again; possibly assessing Scott's degree of sanity.

'Look, here's my driving licence and the photo ID with my home address. You can check me out on my website and with the Solicitors Regulation Authority. I've never been more serious in my life. You must believe me, Sir Stanton, you are in very serious danger.'

'Are you working for the security services.'

'No.' Strange question.

'For the police?'

Not so strange.

'No.'

'The media?'

'Certainly not. I'm—'

'Alright. Give me an hour or so to check you out when I get home. I'll text you, one way or the other.'

An hour? When I get home? It's 2018. You can do it now, here on Westminster Bridge, on your mobile.

Then again, perhaps not.

Old school, Duncan had said.

6.45pm

Bell showed Scott into the living room. There was a half empty bottle of malt whisky on the table. Newspapers, documents and files were strewn across the table, under the table, on chairs and on the floor. The window blinds were half closed and blocked out what appeared to be a view across neighbouring greenery; maybe a park.

'Find somewhere to sit and pour yourself a Scotch,' Bell said, slurring.

The last thing Scott wanted to do was to drink alcohol while trying to extract information from the man, but Bell looked like a man who'd open up to his drinking partner.

Scott poured himself a small glass, as instructed, and toasted the knight.

'Here's to your continued good health, Sir Stanton.'

How long that would be, Scott daren't hazard a guess.

Bell brushed a bundle of papers from a chair onto the floor, sat down and poured himself a large glass, ignoring the toast.

'Why is my life in danger?' he said.

The knight would need some background.

'Did you know David Carey well?' Scott asked.

'No.' Bell took a large mouthful. 'I never met him.'

What? Maybe this wasn't such a good idea.

'He was upsetting the Russians,' the man blurted out. 'Mad fool.'

Maybe it *was* a good idea.

'Upsetting? In what way?'

'Digging into matters that didn't concern him.'

'What matters?'

Bell blinked at Scott. 'Why do you want to know?' He took another mouthful. 'Who's going to kill me? The same person who killed Carey?'

Scott wished he'd brought a recording device with him. None of his three phones had the app, or if they did, he hadn't found it yet. Memo to self – sort it.

'Do you *know* who killed Carey?' Scott said.

'The Russians!' Bell exclaimed. 'The bloody Russians! Who else?'

'Why did they kill him?'

'To silence him, of course.'

Wow! This man had to be nurtured.

'Do you have any evidence of this?' Scott topped up Bell's glass. 'Sorry to prattle on like a boring solicitor going through the ropes, but I *am* a boring solicitor going through the ropes.'

Carey stumbled to his feet. 'The bathroom beckons.'

'Do you feel alright?'

He left without replying.

Scott picked up a newspaper and flicked through the pages. It was a Scottish daily of August the previous year. An article on page 5 was headed: SIR STANTON MORGAN BELL SEQUESTRATION THREAT. He read on. The knight had incurred gambling and other debts totalling over three million pounds. He was in imminent danger of losing his estates that had been in his family for hundreds of years.

Bell returned and poured himself another large glass.

'Russians,' he said, pointing at the newspaper article.

'What do you mean? What about the Russians?'

'They bailed me out. Paid off my debts, took a mortgage on my estates and...'

He stared into thin air.

'And what?'

'Now they're turning the screws.'

'What do you mean?'

'Are you sure you're not from the police or the intelligence services?'

'I give you my word, Sir Stanton. I swear.'

'And this will stay between us?'

That was more difficult, much more difficult. While he had no intention of telling the authorities, Tom Burrows, Gravchenko and General Pravda were different matters.

'I give you my word that I will never discuss whatever it is you want to tell me with the authorities but, quite frankly...' Now was the time to offer something in exchange. 'I might want to discuss it with certain people, not in any way connected to the UK authorities, but who have *personal* interests in finding out who killed your Parliamentary colleague and why.'

'*Personal* interests?'

'Family members.'

Bell stared at him, tears appeared.

'I'm not going to lie to you,' Scott said. 'So if you want me to go, I shall leave, right now.' He felt sorry for the man; being screwed by the Russians wasn't something Scott would have wanted at the top of his bucket list, irrespective of whose fault it was.

'No, no, stay. I want you to hear me out.'

The man was searching for a sympathetic ear. Scott had seen it in the witness box hundreds of times. 'Of course I'll stay, if that's what you want.' He poured himself another small drink.

'When they offered to buy me out of sequestration, they took a mortgage on my estate.'

'Yes, you said that.'

'That wasn't all. They asked me to lobby for the releasing of the sanctions in my speeches in the House.'

Not entirely unexpected and not illegal, on the face of it.

'Yes, it's in Hansard.' Scott sipped his whisky. 'It surprises me though. I can't find anywhere that you've ever had any interest in Russia, its history, culture, people. Didn't your fellow members ask why you were making these speeches?'

A faint smile. 'Yes. I told them a cock and bull story about a distant maternal ancestor being a member of the court of Czar Nicholas the First. I said I couldn't remember her name, but my grandfather used to sit me on his knee and tell me stories about her, despite the generation gap.'

Scott chuckled. 'Didn't anybody fact-check it, as they say?'

'If they did, they never confronted me with the results of their...fact-checking.'

'Did anybody know it was the Russians who owned the mortgage on your estate?'

'Not at first. But now it's on the internet. I don't know how they found out. It was done through a series of offshore companies and trusts. As far as the authorities and my lawyers were concerned it came from a Swiss entrepreneur who went to school with my father.' He took another swig. 'God knows what they think now.'

Oh what a tangled web we weave.

'I still don't understand why you say the Russians are turning the screws.'

The atmosphere darkened and Scott sensed gloom surrounding Bell.

The man put his glass down and dropped his head into his hands.

'I told them I had connections with the intelligence services. Schoolboy behaviour, I know—'

You can say that again.

Scott guessed the rest. 'And they asked you to get classified information for them. Whatever you could.'

'Yes.' He looked up at Scott. 'That's exactly what they did. They said my speeches weren't good value for their money. They threatened to frame me for espionage if I didn't.'

Not entirely dissimilar from Scott's problems of 2016, but he was a lawyer, with a strong constitution and powerful Russian friends who helped him. Bell didn't strike him as having a strong constitution, or if he did when he was a young guardsman it was no longer apparent. And he wasn't a lawyer. As to the man's friends, Scott suspected they would have avoided him like the plague as soon as the sequestration threat was made public. It wasn't an attractive advertisement for the landed gentry.

Scott sucked in air between his teeth. 'You might not like this question, but your answer could help me to advise you what to do from now on.'

'What's the question?'

'*Did* you give them any confidential information?'

Bell laughed, a little manically.

'No, how could I? I don't know anybody in the secret services. I never have done. Even if I wanted to betray my country, which I assure you I don't, I couldn't.'

Scott closed his eyes.

The wretched man had conned the Russians.

Not the best of career moves.

Chapter 19

Day Thirteen: 8am, Moscow

Yelena arrived out of breath, looking flustered and dishevelled.

'Some bastard's nicked my bike. I tried to call you. Your line's dead. What's going on?'

'Nobody has stolen your bike, Yelena,' Pravda said. 'Calm down. It's being serviced, that's all.'

'What!? Who's servicing it? It doesn't need a service. I can do it better than any of our twat mechanics. You know I can. I do all my own servicing.' She stamped her foot like a spoilt child. 'Nobody touches my Harley. That's the deal, General.'

Pravda smiled sympathetically. She was wedded to her bike. She scolded him whenever he tried to sit on it – sometimes to wind her up.

'No taxis around. Traffic's a nightmare, gridlocks everywhere. I had to take the metro. It's years since I've used it.' She pulled a face; her speech was picking up pace. 'I don't know where anything goes, all those lines all over the city… I want my bike back.' She looked around the disused factory building. 'What are we doing here in this dump? Why all this way out of town? It's Siberia.' She frowned at him. 'And you look like you've seen a ghost, General. Where were you yesterday?'

Pravda was so concerned about Monkfish's news of the Kremlin's all-pervading surveillance capability that he'd spent the previous day planning his next moves and the best way of trying to work in complete secrecy.

Yelena,' Pravda said. 'Do you trust me?'

'What sort of dumb question is that?'

'With your life?'

'Second dumb question,' she said without hesitation. 'What's this ab—?'

'Can I trust *you*?' Pravda continued. Was this totalitarian nightmare causing him to doubt everybody? He hated himself for putting the question to the person he trusted most apart from his estranged wife, Anna, and young son, Stepan.

'General, this isn't only your third dumb question, you're insulting me and you're beginning to scare me. These questions aren't you. What's going on? Are you in trouble?'

He handed her a sheet of paper and put his index finger to his closed lips.

She snatched it, and read it.

He'd anticipated her irritation and had written instructions as follows:

DON'T SPEAK

SWITCH OFF BOTH OF YOUR PHONES AND GIVE THEM TO ME.

She mouthed, 'What the fuck?' but did as she was told.

He removed their sim cards and laid the phones and cards on the concrete floor.

He repeated the exercise with his own two phones.

'What the...?' she blurted.

He glared at her, and drew his left hand across the front of his neck.

She glared at him, wide-eyed, but promptly shut up.

He pulled a hammer from his rucksack and smashed the phones and sim cards to pieces.

'That's us off three chins' New Year's card list,' Yelena whispered.

Pravda scooped up the pieces and put them in a plastic bag in his rucksack for later disposal.

'Right,' he said, standing up. 'You asked if I was in trouble. We're *all* in trouble.'

He told her Monkfish's story, without specifically naming him, saying that it came from a trusted source. The less she knew, the safer it would be for her.

She responded with her "this has got to be a wind-up" face.

'I couldn't be more serious,' he said.

She began walking around the unit, kicking the walls. 'No, no. no. They wouldn't dare.' Kick, kick, kick.

'Here,' Pravda said. 'Take these.' He handed her two replacement phones.

She grabbed them. 'The bastards.'

'The iPhone, you can use for general traffic,' Pravda said. 'Working with our team on the Gravchenko investigation. Carry on as normal. I don't want to arouse any suspicions.'

'Oh yeah,' Yelena said, as she fiddled with the phones. 'What are you going to tell three chins about these? He's probably pulling his one remaining hair out.'

'I've put our old numbers and contacts on them.' Pravda already had access to everything on Yelena's team phone. 'So, it shouldn't be a problem.' He smiled. 'Don't worry, you'll get your New Year's card from him.'

She pretended to vomit, and held up the Android.

'Same procedure as before. It's only for use between you and me, nobody else, in extreme emergencies, and I do mean extreme emergencies. Only for sending and receiving texts. They don't have any apps or internet access. You must never, ever, use it for anything else at all, especially phone calls. In a minute, I'll show you another layer of protection with a secret code system to be used when we send texts to each other. If it's not followed we'll know the phones have been compromised. Do you understand me, Yelena?'

'No, I don't,' she said in a dismissive tone. 'I don't understand any of this shit.'

'Look,' he said, ignoring the response. He knew that despite her protestations she would do as ordered. 'We don't know how much information Max got out of your Bulgarian diplomat...'

Yelena winced.

'Do they know about what you found in Orlov's apartment? Did he tell them you uploaded it all to the cloud?'

As added layers of security, he'd printed out everything in triplicate and shut down their cloud account. He'd put one set in a luggage locker at a railway terminus, buried the second set at his dacha under a rock garden, which he'd used before on other missions with Yelena, and hidden the third set in a watertight container in the bank of a small river that separated his back garden from neighbouring land.

He would open a new cloud account as soon as it was safe to do so.

'He wouldn't say anything,' Yelena said. 'He'd probably tell them we met by chance at the airport.'

Her voice lacked conviction. 'Maybe,' he said. 'But we're going to assume that they do know you uploaded something. So, don't, under any circumstances, try to contact him. And blank him if he tries to contact you. He'll be under as much surveillance as we are.'

'What about when he gets back to Bulgaria?'

'If my Kremlin source is right, soon nobody on the planet will be able to escape their tentacles.'

God, he was sounding like a tagline for a 1950s Hollywood B-movie.

Chapter 20

Day Thirteen: 1pm, London

Scott stopped and admired the chrome motorbike being proudly displayed in the shop window opposite Sotheby's on New Bond Street in London's West End. The small placard propped up against the front wheel described the bike as a 1936 George Cohen Norton Special – one of only three in existence. He wasn't a bike enthusiast, but was trying to divert attention from the blood seeping from his gums.

Twenty minutes earlier, his Welbeck Street dentist had extracted an infected wisdom tooth and sent him away with a meagre supply of cotton wool pads to stem any "unlikely" flow, but instead of allowing the pads to do their trick he allowed his tongue to agitate the yet unsealed hole.

'Excuse me, Mr Mitchell.'

Scott turned round.

An overweight man in his 30s, in chauffeur's livery, complete with hat, smiled at him.

'Who are *you*?' Scott said. 'And how do you know my name?'

'Somebody would like to have a word with you, if you don't mind, please sir.' He stood aside and gestured at a dark blue SUV parked across the road outside Sotheby's.

The rear window slid down and a face appeared.

It was ADC Chalmers.

Scott had wondered how long it would take for the Assistant Deputy Commissioner to get back to him after the debriefing at the Essex police station.

He crossed the street, half looking forward to continuing his intellectual chess game with the man. Perhaps the ADC had news on Carey he would like to share with him.

'Would you please get in, Mr Mitchell,' Chalmers said.

The chauffeur walked round to the kerbside rear door and held it open for Scott.

'Are you *asking* me or *telling* me?'

'Neither, I'm *advising* you,' Chalmers said.

Well, that's a new one.

Scott's curiosity prevailed over concern and he got in.

The vehicle eased away from the kerb and headed down New Bond Street in the direction of Piccadilly.

The ADC was in uniform.

'Where are we going?'

Chalmers leant forward to the chauffeur. 'Park in Berkeley Square, please, Monty.'

'Yes sir.'

'Why there?' Scott said.

'You'll see,' Chalmers replied.

Within a few minutes they were in the square, where Monty got out and went for a walk.

'Right,' Chalmers said. 'I'm going to tell you what we know and you're not going to say a word until I've finished.'

Scott dabbed his gums with a tissue and checked it for blood: minor seepage.

'Are you injured?' Chalmers asked.

'Wisdom tooth extraction.'

Chalmers nodded.

'We know you met Sir Stanton Morgan Bell outside the Houses of Parliament yesterday at 4pm and walked across Westminster Bridge with him. We know that after you split up, you went to Starbucks in County Hall, Belvedere Road and stayed there, alone, until you received a call at 6.25pm. We know that you took a taxi from there to Sir Stanton's apartment near Vauxhall Park, arriving at 6.45pm. We know that you left the apartment at 10.30pm and went home by taxi.'

He stopped.

Police surveillance for a while was to be expected, but Scott hadn't realised it would be so detailed. He was more concerned, though, that they were now able to link him with Bell.

'So what?'

Chalmers puffed his chest out.

'We also know, Mr Mitchell, that at 6.57 this morning Sir Stanton Morgan Bell was found dead in his apartment by his cleaner. He had ligature marks on his neck and may have been finished off with suffocation by a pillow.'

Scott felt the blood drain from his face, and it wasn't because of the tooth; he was literally lost for words.

He tensed his muscles to prevent the body shakes.

Orlov's pulsating red cross on Carey's list flickered in his mind and another one landed on Bell's name.

'Now, listen,' Chalmers said. 'Because I'm only going to give you this one chance.'

'I'm all ears.'

How could he not be?

'Unless you tell me, here and now, what you discussed with Sir Stanton Morgan Bell on Westminster Bridge and later at his apartment yesterday, I shall arrest you on suspicion of his murder—'

'Murder?!' Scott went cold. 'What the hell are you talking about?'

'And if you apply for bail,' Chalmers continued, pointedly ignoring Scott's outburst, 'I shall object and tell the court about your being present at Diane Costello's house when we discovered her body. And just so you understand the seriousness of your position, I shall tell the court that because Carey – linked to you via Diane Costello – and Bell were current members of the Houses of Parliament we cannot discount terrorism.'

Jesus. It was a nightmare. 2016 reprised.

Scott closed his eyes and acknowledged that a magistrates' court would err on the side of caution and refuse bail. UK lower courts rarely, if ever, granted bail in murder cases, much less if tainted with terrorism. He could be taken out of action until the case went to a higher court, which could be for 14, 28 or more days, despite the evidence against him being circumstantial, motiveless and wholly uncharacteristic.

And in order to convince a high court judge that the prosecution was baseless he'd be forced to disclose the existence of Carey's list to the police, the very people he was trying to hide it from.

He opened his eyes and studied the humdrum lives walking by.

The social media trolls populated his thoughts:

#Scott Mitchell's at it again. It's murder this time

#Scott Mitchell commits #treason

#Mitchell done for murder of a #lordoftherealm

He turned to Chalmers.

'We talked about the estates he mortgaged to pay off his gambling debts. It's in the press and on the net.'

'Why *you*?' Chalmers said. 'You're a Russian specialist working for Mr Gravchenko. What do you know about Scottish mortgages.'

'Apparently,' Scott said, 'the people who lent him the money were Russians. He thought I might have a word with them because he was having difficulty in finding the repayments. He confided in me that he'd returned to gambling and that was due to be made public, again, any day now.'

'What did you tell him?'

'I said I didn't know anything about Scottish law and their mortgages, but I would see if I could help on the Russian front.'

'Did he give you their names?'

'He was going to let me have details of the lending companies involved and their individual owners today.'

It was Chalmers' turn to gaze out of the window.

Had Scott done enough to convince the man?

At least he hadn't broken his promise to the poor man – nothing about the spying.

'Was Sir Stanton a client of yours?' Chalmers said.

Tell the truth, as much as possible.

'No.'

'A friend or colleague?

'No.' He could see the ADC's mind trying to work out what his relationship had been with the man, which of course was the key to their meeting.

'Had you ever met before yesterday?'

Scott wanted to say yes, but it wouldn't be too difficult for the police to check, especially as they would now get unrestricted access to Bell's paperwork. 'No.'

'So did you arrange the meeting?'

There was nothing for it but to brave it out. Any digital communication between them could be checked. It might not be easy, but they would eventually find its absence in both Bell's and his own phones, or from the service providers' records, and Scott's explanation would be seen for the lie it was.

'A third party, who knows...knew, him, set it up. Sir Stanton told the party that he wanted to meet me to discuss some legal problems he had involving Russians.' Scott was careful not to mention the party's gender.

'Who was that?'

'The third party wishes to remain anonymous.'

'Mr Mitchell, I don't see how I could have made your

position any clearer. This is a murder enquiry, possibly terror-related. You are the prime suspect, the *only* suspect. I suggest you be more cooperative.'

No, no, no. There was a chink in Chalmers' armour.

Scott reasoned that whether Chalmers was a good cop or bad cop he wanted to find out what Scott was up to more than anything else. Although the man might get that information if and when Scott's bail appeal reached the high court, Chalmers wouldn't want to wait that long. He'd prefer to keep him under intense surveillance 24/7, rather than having a mute Scott Mitchell sitting in a prison cell for an unknown period.

He took a deep breath, and extended his hands out in front him with wrists touching.

'Book me – Danno.'

As well as being a Trekkie, Scott also enjoyed his dad's collection of the original *Hawaii Five-O* series.

Chapter 21

Day Fourteen: 11.45am, London

It was a sign of the times that police armed with automatic weapons were to be seen strolling in pairs throughout the nation's international airports, and Heathrow was no exception. "It's a matter of national security" as Fraser would often say to Scott.

The British public were varied in their opinion as to whether the police should be armed, a practice that was taken for granted in many other countries.

Scott's eyes fixed on these guardians of the nation's security every time he glanced up from his phone in the departure lounge, while waiting for the indicator board to flip into action with details of the departure gate for the Budapest flight.

Assistant Deputy Commissioner Chalmers' failure to carry out his threat to arrest him on suspicion of murder had propelled Scott's reasoning into overdrive, and fantasy land: the armed police had been deployed specifically to protect the population from the harm being done by Scott Mitchell's stubborn refusal to disclose to Chalmers everything he knew about Carey and Bell.

He checked the location of the security cameras as they peeped and poked into every corner and mouse hole of the airport's infrastructure.

He clutched his iPhone to his chest and sent a WhatsApp message to Tom:

New phone. 5 and 7 have left the debate.

Tom would understand that it meant Bell and Wyatt were dead. They'd agreed a communication code at their Grosvenor Square meeting: Carey was 1, Bell 5, Zapatero 3, Orlov 2, Santorini 8, Bisset 4, Costello 6 and Wyatt 7. The numbers had been chosen at random. Although nothing could ever be 100 per cent secure with 21st-century digital transmissions, neither Scott nor Tom could see how the code could be broken without the combined ability to crack WhatsApp's end-to-end encryption technology, a knowledge of Carey's list and the use of the word *debate* as a collective description of the names.

Ten seconds later a call arrived on his regular phone.

He didn't recognise the full number, but the opening digits were +322299, the same as the EU Commission.

He let it ring.

Meanwhile, Tom replied to Scott:

Understood.

Another box ticked.

The EU ringing stopped.

Scott waited five minutes for a voicemail.

Nothing.

Two policemen were within earshot, lingering with their backs to Scott.

This was absurd; he was on the verge of jumping out of his skin very time he came face to face with a uniform.

He pulled the Samsung from his hand luggage and texted the EU number.

Regular phone not working. Call/text this number if you've tried to contact me – SM

The same number called.

'Yes?' Scott said.

The police moved away without so much as a glance at Scott.

'Are you Scott Mitchell?'

The lady had an accent. It could have been Spanish – and a hundred other languages.

'Yes, I am.'

'Mr Mitchell, I am Professor Zapatero.'

Extreme caution had to be the order of the day.

'Forgive me, Professor, but I must be certain it's you. Would you please send me a selfie and an image of your identity card, driving licence or passport, date and time stamped?' She would have had at least one of the ID documents with her. Mainland Europeans, unlike most UK citizens, were brought up to carry a form of ID with them at all times. He'd checked out her headshots on her own and the EU's websites.

'*Si*, I will do it now.'

'Fine.' Scott disconnected.

Zapatero's images arrived via WhatsApp.

It was indeed the professor.

His phone rang. 'Are you satisfied?' she said.

'Yes, Professor. Thank you for responding so quickly to my call. I would like to—'

'Mr Mitchell, I shall be coming to England tomorrow. Will you meet me in London?'

Gravchenko was unpredictable, Scott couldn't be sure he'd be back from Budapest the next day.

'Tomorrow could be difficult for me,' Scott said. 'The day after would be better.'

Yes, I understand. The next day in the afternoon will be convenient for me.'

'Good. I—'

'I will tell you the time and place. Goodbye.'

There was a certainty in her voice.

It was as if she knew.

What on earth was he letting himself in for this time?

6pm Budapest

He was delayed at Budapest's Ferihegy airport, due to a computer malfunction at the immigration kiosks, and he arrived late at the Sofitel Chain Bridge hotel in a fluster. He'd arranged to be there by 5.15pm and he'd been unable to call Sergey to warn him of the delay because of a lifeless phone battery and a mislaid charger. He needn't have worried. When he checked at the reception desk Gravchenko hadn't yet arrived. While the hotel concierge charged his phone, Scott sat in the lobby's spectacular atrium, waiting for his boss.

He glanced at the upper floors of the hotel, eight or nine. The doors to the individual rooms were set back behind the continuous walkway which extended around all four sides of the atrium, fronted by an equally extensive waist-high balcony. Scott squinted as the balcony on each floor began to fill up with men in black suits wearing sunglasses, earpieces and carrying phones; resembling fans at a Blues Brothers convention. He counted five on each face of each balcony; 20 per floor.

What the...?

The hotel staff on the ground floor at the reception desk and those preparing the tables in the open-plan Terrassa restaurant on the mezzanine floor remained untroubled by the spectacle.

A fleet of four limousines pulled up outside and Gravchenko appeared from the front passenger seat of the first vehicle, with two men stepping out of the second car. They split and opened the rear doors of the first vehicle from which emerged a tall Indian-looking male, elegantly dressed in a classic Savile Row pin-stripe suit with a bow tie and a smaller Asian-looking male, dressed in a casual jacket and trousers with a collarless shirt. Several more people, including two women and Sergey, got out of the remaining vehicles.

Flanked by the two men from the second vehicle, Gravchenko, the Indian and the Asian led the group into the hotel.

As usual, Gravchenko was on the phone.

Scott stood up and glanced again at the Blues Brothers. They were leaning over the balconies and scanning the ground floor, while on their phones or fiddling with their earpieces.

Gravchenko finished his call, said something to his two colleagues and beckoned Scott over.

Scott approached the trio, his hand ready to shake whoever offered first.

Gravchenko turned to both his guests. 'Gentlemen, this is the man I've been telling you about, Scott Mitchell, the Foundation's Chief Counsel.' He spoke in Russian. He turned to Scott. 'This this is Mr Shastri from Mumbai and this is Mr Murat from Astana.'

'Astana is the capital city of my beautiful country, Kazakhstan,' Mr Murat said in Russian with a proud smile. 'You must allow me to show you around it one day.'

Scott shook hands with both men. 'Pleased to meet you, gentlemen. And, yes, Mr Murat I would very much like to see your country. I've heard so much about it,' he lied.

Mr Shastri smiled and nodded politely without saying anything.

'We'll talk shortly,' Gravchenko said to Scott.

He turned and guided his guests away.

Scott headed back to his seat.

The Blues Brothers were dispersing.

Sergey came over to sit with Scott.

'Who are those black suits up there?' Scott pointed to the balconies as the last few were disappearing into one of the rooms.

'Security.'

'Whose security?'

'Mr Shastri and Mr Murat.'

'Who are they?'

'Very important people.'

'What are they doing with Mr Gravchenko?'

'The boss will tell you.'

'Fair enough. How long will he be with them?'

Sergey shrugged. 'You know the boss as well as I do.'

Indeed, he did. He could be there all night. 'Fair point. It's just that I've come straight from the airport. I need to find a hotel.'

'No worries,' Sergey said. 'It's taken care of. We've done a deal with this place. Reserved three suites for guests on a semi-permanent basis. You can have one of them. We only need two this week.' He smiled. 'The boss would probably let you live in one of them permanently if you wanted to.'

'What do you mean?'

Sergey leant towards Scott and lowered his voice. 'You know he's got a hell of a lot of respect for you and your capabilities, don't you? And he's not an easy guy to please.'

True, he could be difficult sometimes, but he was always an attentive listener to whatever Scott had to say. Still... 'There are plenty of lawyers out there far more experienced than I am.'

'Yeah, maybe,' Sergey said. 'But the boss doesn't trust any Western lawyers...except you, and the Russian lawyers don't have the international experience that you guys have.'

Sergey was right about trust. Once you'd earned it a Russian would be your friend for life.

'Besides, our lawyers are all *yes* men.' Sergey sniffed. 'Me too. Nobody dares argue with him...but *you* do. He admires that. He likes your spirit.' He grinned. 'Even when he ignores your advice...'

Scott gave a wry smile, recalling the occasions when

Gravchenko's activities had been proven commercially right after ignoring Scott's more cautious legal advice.

'...You've got closer to him than I've seen any other Westerner,' Sergey continued. 'He thinks of you as part of his family, Scott.'

Flattery? Yes. But it could be a two-edged sword. 'If you say so.'

'You'll see,' Sergey said.

'See what?'

'I can't say anything now. He'll tell you when he's ready.'

'Well I only hope I can justify all this respect.'

'No sweat, you keep doing what you're doing and you'll be surprised how grateful he can be.'

Was Sergey speaking his own mind, or was he the messenger?

Sergey's phone rang.

'Yeah, okay. Will do.'

The call ended.

'Right, he'll meet you outside on the terrace in five minutes. Off you go.' He tapped on Scott's luggage. 'I'll have this checked into your room. Unless you want it now?'

Scott patted his jacket pocket. 'They're still charging my phone at the front desk.' He stood up. 'I'll get it now and check in.'

'Okay,' Sergey said. 'See you later.'

'Thanks, Sergey.'

Scott checked in, left his luggage at the desk and headed for the terrace, glancing at Gravchenko's group, but with no reciprocation from the oligarch.

20 minutes later

It was dusk when Gravchenko appeared. Scott was sitting at one of the tables on a half-empty terrace, with a small beer and scrolling down a news timeline.

Nothing to get excited about.

He stood up as Gravchenko approached with an unlit cigarette in one hand and a lighter in the other.

Instead of shaking Scott's hand the man closed in on him, grabbed both his arms and kissed him on both cheeks. 'Okay, tell me what's on your mind.' The oligarch sat down while lighting the cigarette and inhaling half of it in one go.

Scott stepped back, surprised. His boss had never greeted him like that before, never on any occasion, even when he'd successfully fought the anti-green lobbies in court.

He sat down, with Sergey's words ringing in his ears: *you keep doing what you're doing and you'll be surprised how grateful he can be.*

Scott reached into his jacket pocket, fumbling for a piece of paper.

He handed it to Gravchenko.

'What's this?'

'Have you had a chance to look at the Project Conrad documents from the Ghanaians yet? I uploaded them to the cloud after the meeting in London.'

'No,' Gravchenko said, looking at the paper.

'It's Mr Jakande's Memorandum of Understanding.' He studied Gravchenko's eyes as he spoke. Nothing untoward. 'He insists you deposit $25 million into each of the three accounts before they open negotiations.'

The oligarch knew enough English to be able to get the gist of a piece of paper asking him to transfer funds to bank accounts.

Gravchenko curled his lips.

'The first and second accounts, in the names of Calabar and Cordoba, are for consultancy fees and facilitation fees respectively,' Scott said. 'The third account, in the name of Santorini...' He stopped, waiting for a reaction to the name. Gravchenko didn't bat an eyelid but continued to scrutinise the document. 'It's a down payment on a Performance Bond,' Scott said.

'Any of it refundable if I don't go ahead with the deal before I sign the contract?'

'Only the down payment for the Performance Bond,' Scott said. 'No deal, no need for the Bond.'

Gravchenko extinguished his cigarette.

'Kostya, two things I think you should know: Wyatt was murdered a few days ago, thrown off the roof of a building in Canary Wharf. It's in my report to Sergey.'

Again, Scott paused for a reaction from his boss.

Nothing but a faint smirk.

'What else?'

'MI6 have confirmed Wyatt's story that Santorini is a Russian laundromat.'

'What about Calabar and Cordoba?'

'I didn't discuss the Ghanaians with Colin Fraser. He only told me about Santorini because he knew that Wyatt had asked me about it in Prague. I don't know what he knows about them.'

'Have you investigated them, yet?'

'Hardly had time. It's next on my due diligence list.'

'Okay,' Gravchenko said with a dismissive wave of the hand and no sign of concern. 'Now, what would *you* do with this demand from Jakande, if you were in my position?'

He lit a cigarette.

This question had been expected.

'Well, you mustn't pay anything to Santorini, that's for sure. You could split Santorini's $25 million between the other two companies, but only after we've carried out extensive due diligence on them.' He sipped his beer. 'Or you could tell him no deal and that you'll find another way to boost Ghana's economy.'

Whoops. Had he gone too far with his last suggestion?

'But that's a bit risky,' Scott said. 'He could call your bluff and you might lose your flagship investment.'

Gravchenko's serious face slowly morphed into a wide grin.

'What's so amusing?' Scott said.

'You're learning.'

'From the master?'

'If you like.' Gravchenko stubbed out the cigarette. 'Tell this Jakande clown I'll pay the $75 million into a Ghana government account with a top-five bank in New York, London or Zurich. What the Ghanaians do it with after is their problem. No Mickey Mouse companies. Ghana government only. If Jakande doesn't like it, he can take your excellent legal advice, and fuck off.'

Kostya was right. He was indeed on a learning curve.

'But if he *does* take my advice?'

'He won't,' Gravchenko said emphatically.

Scott recalled Jakande's words: *Your client is a Russian oligarch, Mr Mitchell. I have no doubt he will understand.*

Gravchenko took a call.

Scott jumped up and began stamping his foot.

Gravchenko looked at him, while still on the phone.

'Cramp,' Scott said.

Gravchenko returned to his phone conversation.

Scott stomped around.

The terrace area had filled up; no empty tables and many people within ear shot.

Gravchenko ended his call.

'I need to get the blood flowing,' Scott said. 'Can we go for a walk?' He dropped some money by his empty beer glass.

'Sure.' Gravchenko scooped up his lighter and cigarette packet from the table and joined Scott as they crossed the road to the river embankment and headed in the direction of the InterContinental Hotel.

'I didn't know you suffered from leg cramps,' Gravchenko said.

'Only when there are too many people listening to our conversation,' Scott said.

Gravchenko smiled. 'Okay, what else is on your mind?'

Scott told him about his meeting with Bell, the knight's subsequent murder and ADC Chalmers' threat.

True to form, Gravchenko listened without interruption.

When Scott finished they stopped at the railings and silently took in the evening's descent on the Danube with its lit-up pleasure boats and chugging tugs.

Gravchenko's phone rang. He connected and immediately lowered his voice.

Scott moved further on, to give his boss space and himself time to reflect.

Two laughing seven- or eight-year-old boys whizzed by on skateboards, followed by a man in his early twenties, also skateboarding, and shouting at them in what Scott surmised was Hungarian.

Fraser's non-specific references over the years to Gravchenko's allegedly state-harming activities came to mind. Nothing that his boss had done during the time Scott had been working for him had given the slightest indication that the man might be anything other than transparent with him. The Foundation was the most transparent international institution Scott had ever encountered. And Gravchenko's point-blank refusal to submit to Jakande's payment demands certainly wasn't the action of a Russian mobster.

Gravchenko caught up with Scott. 'Follow me.'

Scott did so and they sat at a dining table on the terrace of the Corso restaurant further along the embankment.

They were the only diners.

A waiter appeared immediately from inside.

'Good evening, Mr Gravchenko. It's a pleasure to see you here again.' He spoke in English, with an Italian accent.

Gravchenko shook hands with the man. 'The usual please, Lorenzo,' Gravchenko said in heavily accented English.

'And for you, *signore*?'

'The same,' Gravchenko said before Scott could say a word.

Scott smiled. Gravchenko was known for being a control freak whenever he was at a meal with family, close friends and work colleagues. He didn't mind if you didn't eat and drink all the food he'd chosen for you, but you had to be seen to taste it.

'You ought to write a book,' Gravchenko said without a prompt. 'A thriller.'

'What?'

Where had *that* come from?

'This Carey saga. You don't have to make it up. Just change the names and write it. James Bond is escapism, nobody believes it's real. Your story is unbelievably believable.'

'Kostya, this isn't a game.' He didn't want to argue with his boss, especially when he was in such a good mood, but the whole thing was beginning to do his head in. 'I wake up in cold sweats, having dreamt I'm next on the hit list: Carey, Costello, Orlov, Wyatt and now Bell. Five people dead in 14 days, four of them murdered.'

Lorenzo brought the food, comprising a large plate of antipasti for two with a fish sauce that smelt like heaven.

Two small beers followed.

'Will you be having a main course tonight, Mr Gravchenko?'

'No thank you, Lorenzo,' he replied without looking at Scott.

'*Grazie*.' Lorenzo left.

Gravchenko tucked a napkin into his tieless shirt collar and scooped spoonfuls of pasta onto his plate.

Scott followed suit.

'Who are the suspects...apart from me?'

Scott choked. Gravchenko had asked the question without a hint of personal concern.

'You're Russian, that's enough to make Fraser and

his mates blame you and your lot for everything from climate change right back to the Great Fire of London.'

'When was that?'

'Sixteen sixty-six.'

Gravchenko sniffed. 'Ask him what's it like to live with chronic paranoia.' He scooped up more food. 'What about this police commissioner, Chalmers? What does *he* think about us corrupt Russians?'

'He hasn't said. But he damn well knows I'm not telling him everything.'

'Is this Fraser guy looking for Carey's killer, like Chalmers?'

'I can't be sure.' Scott told him about Fraser advising him not to get distracted. 'But with the public assassination of a government minister, followed closely by the less public killing of a knight of the realm, I'd imagine that all available resources are being pooled by our government, and this includes our intelligence agencies.'

'Alright,' Gravchenko said. 'What do you want from me?'

Tell me it's all not real, only a nightmare.

'Let me throw your earlier question back at you. What would *you* do if you were me?'

Gravchenko lit a cigarette. 'Carry on as you are, but keep your wits about you. If you *were* getting too close to the truth you'd be dead by now.'

Scott shivered. 'You don't think I should drop it?'

'No.'

'Why not?'

'Because this Chalmers guy isn't going to let you.' He took a deep drag on his cigarette and exhaled slowly. 'He thinks you've got something he wants.'

'I have.' Scott looked away. 'Although I'm not sure I want it anymore.'

Gravchenko nodded. 'You know how they work. You've been through it before. You aren't in control. They won't leave you alone until you've outlived your usefulness. If they're the good guys they'll hold a retirement party, and kick you out the door. If they're the bad guys, they'll throw you to the wolves.'

This was much the same as Scott's view.

Either way, it wasn't a future to hope for.

'Besides,' Gravchenko said, '*I* want to know what Carey was digging up. Santorini's been linked to my Foundation.'

He had a point.

'And if I find credible evidence that Chalmers and his mates are the bad guys?'

'Then you've got him,' Gravchenko said, with a broad grin.

'Blackmail, you mean?'

'I'd call it your life insurance policy,' Gravchenko replied. 'He's not going to risk hurting you if he thinks the evidence you've got will be made public on your death.'

Well, that was one way of rationalising it. Pity he wouldn't be alive to see Chalmers' expressions when the man's dirty deeds were being tweeted around the universe.

'Okay, let's take Chalmers out of the picture for the moment,' Scott said. 'What if it's some other actors who are responsible for the murders?'

He was being deliberately non-specific because he didn't want to give his boss the impression that he was persuaded by the Western script of blaming the Russians for everything, although he couldn't easily dismiss the notion that, possibly, the Russians were involved with the killings, despite Carey's warning not to trust the UK authorities.

'Do you have any information that these *other actors*, whoever they are, know what you're doing?'

'No.' He hesitated. 'Well, Alex has been warned off investigating Santorini.'

'Who by?'

Scott shrugged. 'Some local fixer.'

Gravchenko lost the softness in his face. 'Alex is working for *me* on Project Conrad. This *fixer* should know this.' He stared long and hard at Scott. 'If he doesn't he's soon going to find out.'

Scott didn't know what to think, but he reckoned he looked like a deer caught in the headlights.

The softness returned to his face as Gravchenko tucked into his food. 'Don't worry. I don't have to resort to violence to get my message across.'

Thank God for that.

'Anyway,' Gravchenko said. 'You're going to tell Jakande that we're not dealing with his dirty laundry.'

The boss had got it all sewn up. It was so easy for him, but he wasn't in the firing line, like Scott.

Or perhaps he was – every day of his life.

'What about General Pravda?' Gravchenko said, unexpectedly.

'I tried to contact him, and Major Grigoryeva,' Scott said. 'But their lines are dead. I don't know how to reach them. I haven't got their email addresses.'

'They've got yours,' Gravchenko said. 'It's on your website. They'll get in touch when they're ready.'

'You think so?'

'Unless they're both dead.'

You didn't have to say that, boss. I've got enough to worry about.

'Right.' Gravchenko wiped his mouth with the napkin, threw it onto his plate, and stood up. 'Let's go.' He put a wad of Hungarian forint notes on the table, considerably more than the meal could have cost, and started back along the embankment to their hotel.

Scott hurried after him, not sure whether he was comforted or more anxious.

'Everything's shit in this world,' Gravchenko said. 'That's why I'm going to change it.'

What did he say?

'I have a new job for you,' Gravchenko continued. 'The Foundation's running smoothly.' He turned to Scott. 'Don't worry about Jakande. He's testing how far he can go with me.'

'You mean you don't want me to act as the Foundation's Chief Counsel any longer?' Was his boss concerned about his ability to do his job with the Carey investigation on his mind all the time?

'Listen to me,' Gravchenko said. 'Shastri and Murat are two of my new venture partners. We're engaged in multi-billion dollar funding of worldwide education about environmental sustainability for the future. It's going to be on a scale the world's never seen before, and we need somebody to administer the project. Black Rock is the biggest asset fund manager in the world; it manages up to $10 trillion. We're going to get access to more than that figure, double, treble. I want you to administer the project.'

Scott pulled up sharply. '*Me*, an investment fund manager for billions, trillions, of dollars? I'm flattered, Kostya.' Are you out of your mind, Konstantin Gravchenko? 'But you've got the wrong guy this time. I don't know anything about fund management and financial investments. Not a jot, well not at *that* level.'

Gravchenko stopped and fiddled with a cigarette. 'Your role won't be to manage the funds. I've got experts to do that. I want you to oversee the appointment of our professional advisers at every stage of the venture: lawyers, accountants, architects, real estate agents, brokers, anybody that can help further our objectives. You're to make sure that they do what they say they can and they deliver on time. Nobody above a certain level is to be recruited and nothing spent until you've signed off on it. Also, I want you to do as much due diligence as you can on my partners, back to their great-grandparents if you have to. I don't want any skeletons in the closet. I want to know everything about them, and everybody else I'm taking on at a senior level.'

I've got experts to do that...I don't want any skeletons in the closet.

First person singular, not plural.

This was going to be Gravchenko's personal project, nobody else's.

That's how Gravchenko operated.

'Kostya, I'm a lawyer, and yes I could oversee the appointment of law firms, but I'd be totally out of my depth evaluating the capabilities of the other professionals. To be blunt, as much as I enjoy working for you, this new task isn't something I'd like to spend my time on. You wouldn't be making the best use of my abilities, my skill sets, as we say today.' He laughed, nervously. 'In fact, you wouldn't be making *any* use of my skill sets.'

He broke away from Gravchenko and returned to the railings overlooking the Danube.

What on earth was the man thinking?

'I know you can do the job.' Gravchenko was at his side. 'I trust you 100 per cent and I don't have the time to do it myself. You can appoint your own team of helpers – I'll fund everything.' He chuckled. 'You'll have a private jet at your disposal 24/7 in case Chalmers tries to screw you.' He lit the cigarette. 'You'll be out of the country before he can tie his boot laces.'

Scott's head was spinning.

He imagined being chased down the runway at London City airport by SO19, the Met's armed response unit, as he dashed for the jet, with only Rosie as hand luggage.

Fodder for a novel indeed.

Gravchenko's tone and enthusiasm was such that Scott knew it would take all his persuasive powers to convince his boss that he wasn't the right man for the job.

But it would be disrespectful to summarily dismiss the idea without further information.

'How many current partners do you have in this venture?'

'Thirteen.'

'That's some unlucky number.'

'I'm not superstitious,' Gravchenko said.

'Are they Russian, apart from Mr Shastri and Mr Murat, I mean?'

'No. You'll meet them all and learn more about the project.'

'When? Where?'

'A week, ten days. Prague. Sergey'll let you know.'

Ten days to make such a life-changing decision.

He thought of the book *Ten Days That Shook The World*, by the American journalist John Reed who personally experienced the beginnings of the main Russian Revolution in 1917.

Would Gravchenko's new ambition shake the world?

'This is so sudden, Kostya. I need time to reflect on this. For a start what happens to me if I don't take the job, and you don't want me to carry on with my Foundation work?'

'You can still work with the Foundation, but take more of a backseat and go public only when you need to.'

Fraser's comment, *your value to Gravchenko is your respectable front*, came back to him.

'Can I go public on any of this, yet?'

'In what way?'

'Well, for a start. Can I tell MI6? If they know what you're doing, and that it's not going to lead to Armageddon, perhaps they'll back off.'

Gravchenko nodded slowly, as if he was about to agree. 'No. Not yet. There's a lot of opposition out there to anything that'll change the status quo. I need to do a bit more persuading the major detractors.'

Scott sympathised with Gravchenko's philosophy about saving the world, but thought it too simplistic, if not utopian.

'And don't worry about your legal fees for the Foundation's work. You'll still get your $75,000 a month.'

'Yes, but—'

'And if you take this new job, you'll be paid $300,000 a month for consultancy fees and as much as you want for expenses, no cap. As I said, I trust you 100 per cent.'

'What? In addition to the Foundation's $75,000?'

Was he dreaming? $375,000 a month?

'Sure. And as Chief Administrator of the project you'll get a one-off appointment fee of $10 million; a golden handshake, you guys call it – tax paid of course.'

Scott was so overwhelmed that he was sure he was going to be physically sick.

With his legal reputation fully restored after the *annus horribilis* of 2016, he was being offered a job which would boost him into the stratospheric arena of the world's top-earning footballers.

His phone announced an incoming message from Tom.

'Excuse me, please, Kostya.'

Gravchenko wandered off and made a call.

A face with a caption underneath appeared:

This man's son runs 8.

Santorini's code number.

Scott froze at the face.

Oh Jesus! No.

Chapter 22

Day Fifteen: 10am, Moscow

'Right,' Pravda said as he picked up a black marker for his white board. 'Let's see what we've got.'

'How long are we going to be working from this Godforsaken place?' Yelena said.

They had returned to the factory unit on the industrial site where Pravda had smashed their phones to pieces. He'd ripped out electric cabling and sockets that had been abandoned by previous users, including the lighting and heating conduits; anything that could conceivably have been used to transmit digital information or listen in to human conversations.

'We'll be gone by winter, I promise,' Pravda joked.

They'd spent the previous 36 hours in a temporary but safe environment to upload the Orlov documents to several different newly created cloud accounts. They used unregistered devices and a convoluted Wi-Fi routing system at a trusted friend's apartment. He lived alone and was hospitalised for five days after a road accident. Whatever Monkfish's super surveillance fears, Pravda refused to accept that the Kremlin had yet managed to capture internet communications from every single building and device in the country, though he couldn't ignore the possibility he and his team could be prime targets of such intrusions by rogue elements in the Kremlin.

Yelena took two thermos flasks from her rucksack and handed one to Pravda. 'Coffee. Make the most of it,' she said. 'It's all I've got.'

'Thanks.' Pravda filled the plastic cup and put the rest

of the flask on the workbench. The place was as void of furniture as on their previous visit, not even a chair; only a workbench fixed to the wall, and the white board and easel that Pravda had brought.

'Where are the toilets?' Yelena asked.

'Round the back. Only the one, and it's not five star.'

'I'll give it a miss, thanks.'

Pravda wrote two headings across the board, followed by:

Arkady Orlov	*Dmitry Yazov*
Credit card	*Debit card*
(Santorini/Nigerian Bank)	*(Australian Bank)*
Debit card	
(Indian Bank)	

'Okay, here's where we are at the moment,' Pravda said. 'How far have you got into these accounts?' Yelena had found references to a bank sort code for a Santorini account and one thing had led to another.

'Orlov used Santorini's bank account in Lagos for the credit card payments,' Yelena said. 'The Indian bank is based in Mumbai. Lots of transactions but I haven't yet analysed them. Yazov's Australian account is clean. Nothing, in or out. And not because he's dead. It looks as though it's never been used. But this is only the start. There's a hell of a lot of tracking to do with other accounts I've found.'

'And what about Santorini itself?'

'It's been spreading money around the globe like confetti.'

'Where does it come from?'

'Most of it from China, Kazakhstan and the US. Hundreds of millions of dollars. Maybe a billion, who knows? I'm still counting.'

'And it's funnelled through West Africa?'

'Yeah. Mainly Ghana and Nigeria, but there's got to be others. There's too much money.'

Pravda circled the Santorini name on the board and drew a line down to a point at the bottom where he wrote:

From China, Kazakhstan and America →
Ghana and Nigeria → ???

He turned to Yelena.

'Then where?'

She laughed and poured herself a coffee. 'Give me the pen, please.'

Pravda did so as Yelena approached the board, coffee in one hand and pen in the other. She wrote after the arrow:

87 different countries, and counting...

'We're going to run out of countries soon. Are there any on the moon?' she said.

Pravda massaged a spasm in his leg.

'It's no quick deal cleaning up a billion dollars under the radar,' Yelena continued, handing back the pen and climbing onto the workbench.

'Yazov's dead,' Pravda said. 'So we're—'

'At a dead end,' Yelena said, and laughed at her own joke.

'Okay. So what about this Gulyana Niyazova? Have we got anything other than her passport image?'

'Copy application forms she's submitted for travel documents. To Canada, Spain and the UK.'

'When?'

'All within the last year.'

Interesting.

'Do we know if she ever visited those places? Because

there aren't any visa stamps on her passport and it's more than two years old.'

'Still wading through the stuff.'

'There's another possibility,' Pravda said.

'What's that?'

'She could have used another passport. One that doesn't need visa stamps...at least for the EU countries: UK and Spain.'

'Maybe,' Yelena said.

'What's her job?'

'Student.'

'How old is she?'

'Passport says 28.'

'Any other images of her?'

'Not found any.'

Pravda began to limp around the unit.

His leg knew something he didn't.

It was going to be a monster task to pull everything together without being able to employ their full resources – the other team members, their computer systems and field agents – but he wasn't willing to put everybody else's lives in danger where there was a hint of becoming ensnared in the Kremlin's super-surveillance web.

'Any news on Jerichostraat?'

'I was expecting a report any day,' Yelena said. 'But because of all this surveillance I've told my contact to hold back.'

'You didn't say *why*, did you?' Pravda shot back.

'General, please, give me some credit. Lesson learnt at Domodedovo, remember?'

Yes, he was being unnecessarily harsh with her.

'Sorry, Yelena. I'm tired.'

'No sweat.'

Pravda pointed at the board.

'What do we know about Calabar and Cordoba, apart from the emails we found?' Pravda said.

There were numerous emails addressed to Orlov from an unnamed source with a Chinese URL, directing payments of $50,000 to be made to each of "Calabar" and "Cordoba", at regular monthly intervals. It had been going on for more than three years, but there weren't any bank account details.

'I've found two companies with those names, with the same Nigerian operating address,' Yelena said. 'They're registered in the Marshall Islands. I'm trying to get hold of the corporate details. They might lead us to something. But you know the Marshall Islands; nominees, smoke and mirrors and bullshit all over the place.' She sighed. 'I mean, how does this Gulyana Niyazova, a *student*, fit into this dirty money operation?' Yelena said. 'What's she studying? How to launder a gazillion dollars without getting caught?'

'Where did you say she applied to travel to?'

'Canada, Spain and the UK.'

Pravda approached her and tapped her on the knee as she was sitting on the worktop. 'Do you remember those two unsolved murders in Canada and Spain about six months ago?'

'You're joking. People are murdered every day somewhere in the world. Why should I remember any of them?'

Yes, it was coming back to him.

'A Russian-Canadian businessman was blown up in a car park in Vancouver and a Spaniard was found at the bottom of a gorge in the Cañón de Añisclo in the Pyrenees with a crossbow bolt through each eye.'

'And?'

'The Russian-Canadian was involved in real estate fraud and the Spaniard conned a Russian entrepreneur into investing in a Ponzi scheme. The woman lost $3 million.'

'So what?' Yelena said. 'Real estate fraud happens everywhere and these Ponzi wotsits involve loads of suckers, not just one. But they don't go around killing the guys that con them...well, most of them don't.'

'No, but it only takes one person to do it, put out a contract.'

'I still don't understand what this has got to do with Niyazova.' She jumped down and frowned. 'Are you trying to say someone paid her to kill them?'

Pravda was only half listening to her.

'And four more have been murdered in the UK these past two weeks – all connected in some way to Russians: Carey, his lawyer Costello, Bell, who was bank-rolled by Russians with a mortgage, and Wyatt who spent his life condemning President Putin and the Kremlin on his website.'

'So now you're saying Putin's behind these murders,' she said in a mocking tone.

He ignored the sarcasm.

'What I'm saying, Yelena, is that our Uzbek student has just moved up our priority list. Don't forget, we still haven't been able to gain access to the Ministry database and verify her passport details. We've got access for other passports, so we can be reasonably sure that it's not an IT problem.'

Severe cramp gripped his leg.

'But when it comes to investigating Gulyana Niyazova we're *persona non grata* and my question is, why?'

Chapter 23

Day Fifteen: 11.15am, London

'How sure are you of this?' Scott said to Tom, as they both stared at the image of Arjun Shastri on Scott's phone.

'Absolute certainty,' Tom said. 'It came from the FBI, via Brett.'

'What's the son's name?'

'Kabir is his first name. I don't know if he has any others.'

They were sipping Starbucks' coffees in Paternoster Square opposite St. Paul's Cathedral.

Scott had grabbed the first available plane in the morning from Budapest, having lied for the first time in his life to Gravchenko. He hated himself for it. The man had expressed 100 per cent trust in him only a few minutes before Tom's image had arrived and what did he do?

Immediately betrayed that trust.

He'd told Kostya he'd received a request from his aunt to return to London urgently. His uncle had been involved in an accident. Scaffolding fell from a building onto a crowded pavement where he was a walking and he was in intensive care. They were his closest relatives since his own parents had been killed in a road crash two years previously.

Tom was back in London seeing the probate lawyers about David Carey's estate.

Scott had no idea of the veracity of what Tom was saying and wanted to check it out thoroughly before he said anything to Gravchenko. Whilst he believed that Tom was being truthful with him, he didn't know how many information channels it had come through before reaching the FBI.

'Did they ask Brett why he was interested in Santorini?' Scott said.

'Of course. He told them a client in London wanted information on it, but he couldn't say anything else at that moment as it was a highly sensitive matter.'

'And they readily accepted that, without further questions?'

'Brett's fraud investigations take him all over the world. He can be useful to the FBI, on an unofficial basis. They respect that.'

The FBI had much greater resources than Scott did; he had to keep Tom, and consequently Brett, in the loop. They were all on the same side.

He stared at Shastri's image again and took a deep breath.

'I met this guy last night, in Budapest.'

'I'm glad you told me,' Tom shot back.

That's odd; there was no surprise in his voice.

'Oh, why?'

Tom tapped on his own phone. 'Because of this.' He pushed the phone across the table for Scott to study another image. 'Brett sent it earlier this morning,'

Scott didn't know whether to laugh or cry. The surveillance was relentless. It was a shot of him shaking hands with Shastri at the hotel and Gravchenko standing between them, smiling.

An image of a bulging sack bearing the legend "£10 million Golden Handshake" and swinging over a funeral pyre lingered in his mind.

'Santorini is using the US to swamp the world with dirty cash,' Tom said.

What could Scott salvage from this?

'It may be a naïve question, but are the FBI saying that Shastri senior is himself involved with his son's money-laundering, or knows what his son is doing?'

'Not naïve at all. But I don't have the answer.'

'Well, thanks for this, Tom. You've given me a lot of food for thought.'

I want you to do as much due diligence as you can on my partners, back to their great-grandparents if you have to. I don't want any skeletons in the closet.

And what if the skeleton is your partner's son?

'I won't ask you what you were doing with Shastri in Budapest,' Tom said. 'I know you'll tell me when the time is right – but I recommend that you prepare yourself for a visit from the FBI.'

3pm

Professor Zapatero called as Scott had finished typing the two words "Arjun Shastri" into Google. It produced over three million hits.

'Yes, Professor.'

'Mr Mitchell. Tomorrow afternoon I have meetings in a Regus office at 100 Pall Mall in London. I can see you there at 2.30. Do you know where it is?'

'Yes, certainly.'

'Good, please ask for me at reception.'

'Yes, Professor. I look forward to seeing you. Bye for now.'

'Goodbye,' she said abruptly, and disconnected.

Rosie jumped onto the keyboard and nestled down for a sleep, repaying Scott no doubt for being AWOL so often. Her adopted foster parent, 14-year-old Leanne, the daughter of Dave the concierge, had returned her to Scott 'just for a couple of hours while I go shopping with me mates.'

He realised how fortunate he was to have such a cat-loving neighbour, especially as his foreign trips were increasing. Rosie certainly appreciated her new servant and was often reluctant to return to home.

'Come on, come on,' he said as he gently lifted her from the keyboard and let her down in front of her food bowl, only to scamper away into his bedroom with a lasting meow, as if to say, 'I'm going for a kip, don't you dare disturb me.'

It took 15 minutes to find an image and a short biography of the Arjun Shastri Scott had met in Budapest. He was a self-made Indian multi-billionaire, born in Mumbai (formerly Bombay) on 27 November 1960. He was educated in the US in oil and gas and business management. After making a mini-fortune as a foreign exchange dealer in the UK in the late 1980s, he'd returned to India where he established a reputation as a political lobbyist for thermal power. He invested in numerous companies at the cutting edge of sustainable development technology and, with international backers, soon controlled one of India's largest conglomerates dedicated to finding alternatives to fossil fuel energy. Allegations of share price rigging and bribery of officials had appeared from time to time, but nothing had ever been proven.

He was married to a famous Indian architect, with one child, Kabir, born 7 January 1985. There wasn't any further information on Kabir in his father's profiles and neither did he appear to have his own individual profile anywhere on the net.

Scott found more than 50 people on social media with the exact name Kabir Shastri, but he didn't know what he was looking for.

What was the personal profile of a 33-year-old international money-launderer supposed to say?

The quickest way to Kabir would have to be through his father.

While in Google he checked out Murat as well.

Hao Murat, allegedly worth more than US$10 billion, was of Chinese ethnicity on his mother's side. He was born in Mongolia in 1955 and moved to Kazakhstan in his early teens, when his mother unexpectedly died of a brain tumour. He was educated in London and Australia in international politics and international trade. He'd built his empire on commodity trading. He knew anybody who was anybody in Kazakhstan and Chinese political circles and was effectively a Mr Fixit between Kazakhstan and China. He'd been sentenced to ten months imprisonment in 1980 for attempted bribery of a government official in Macao but was released after three weeks. He lobbied forcefully in Kazakhstan against closer ties with the USA, preferring instead to deal with China, a heavy importer of Kazakh oil.

He was married with five adult children, four boys and a girl; none of them named in the summary.

These two oligarchs seemed benign enough – bribery and corruption charges with minor criminal convictions, were becoming increasingly common and often disregarded by investors.

They were mega-successful capitalists in their own right.

But team them up with 11 other equally successful oligarchs?

Who knew what power they could exert over national economies?

Maybe Gravchenko's utopian idea wasn't so utopian after all.

Time to put something to the test.

He texted Fraser:

Can we meet today?

It was the first time since Carey's assassination that Scott had taken the initiative with the man. It would be interesting to see how he responded.

*

5pm

'I'm not going to beat about the bush, Fraser. You've been pumping me for information, I've supplied it and you've responded with some crumbs from the table.'

'You'd get a whole loaf if you signed the Official Secrets Act.'

They were sharing a bottle of wine in the famous St Christopher's Inn pub in Borough High Street, a traveller's coaching inn dating back to the 16th century.

'What do you know about an Indian guy called Kabir Shastri?' Scott said.

'Why do you want to know?'

Scott expected that response.

'I'm not going to tell you.' He couldn't, without revealing information that might lead to a discussion about Arjun Shastri. Gravchenko wasn't ready to go public on the mega deal yet. Sure, the FBI had a photo of his boss with Arjun but they could have been discussing anything. Oligarchs meet with other oligarchs; nothing strange in that.

Fraser pulled a face. It wasn't one that confirmed he knew of the man and wanted desperately to know what Scott's interest in him was. It was more like he was frustrated that their new bromance wasn't producing as much information as he had hoped; irritation rather than full-scale annoyance.

Fraser polished off his wine and poured another glass, for each of them.

'Never heard of him.'

Scott believed him.

'I would like a favour, please.'

'What is it?'

'See what you can find out about him.'

'Anything specific, your honour?'

You never give up, Mr Fraser. Dig, dig, dig.

'Yes, *everything*.'

It was going to cost him, but he had to find out if Shastri the Elder had any knowledge of his son's criminal activities; the answer should help him with his approach to Arjun when they met in Prague.

7 pm

'You sure about this?' Robo said to Scott. 'Not having a millennial moment are we?" One hundred per cent sure,' Scott said. 'They found the list, copied it and put it back...in the wrong place.'

Scott had arrived home from his meeting with Fraser and been hit with a sense of dread as soon as he'd opened the front door.

'And nothing nicked?'

'Seems not.'

They were surveying the living room area of Scott's apartment from outside on the third-floor balcony, having found a Finnish language radio station on the TV to muffle their speech. Robo was Scott's personal trainer, trusted childhood friend and Mr Fixit. He was used to Scott's Russian escapades and one of the few, amongst Gravchenko, Pravda and Duncan the journalist, who'd stood by him when he'd been hounded by the authorities and social media in 2016. Scott had told him snippets of his current predicament. He needed somebody to talk to, somebody he trusted with his life and who was totally disinterested in the events.

Robo scratched his head.

Scott flipped through the pages of Tom Wolfe's *The Bonfire of the Vanities*. 'I put the list in here, between pages 296 and 297. I found it between 438 and 439. It must have dropped out when they were going through the bookshelf and examining each one in turn. There's no way they could have known exactly where I'd lodged it. I check it every time on my return from a trip abroad or popping down to the supermarket.'

'That's a bit OCD.'

'People have died because of the list, Robo.'

'I don't understand you sometimes,' Robo said. 'You're this hotshot worldly wise lawyer. You've uploaded the list to the cloud, but you keep the original. A piece of paper that you say kills people.'

Scott didn't take offence. 'You're right. I should destroy it. Trouble is, I'm a lawyer. It's drummed into us from our first day at law school: never destroy original evidence. In some cases it might be a criminal offence to do so; in others, you never know when you might need it.'

'Okay, if you say so.' Robo scanned the room again. 'And you reckon it was the spooks?'

'Think about it.' Scott said. 'According to Dave the whole block's CCTV system was disabled. The management company's tech guy said it wasn't an accident, glitch, virus or whatever. It was deliberate, a professional job.'

'If they were *that* professional, why didn't they reactive it after they'd done their spooking?'

'No idea,' Scott said. 'Run out of time? Disturbed?' Who knows?'

'Who's got keys to this place?'

'Only Dave and me.'

'Why Dave? Management companies don't usually have keys to all the apartments, do they?'

'You're forgetting, Dave's daughter, Leanne, looks after Rosie when I'm abroad. Sometimes she cat sits, other times she takes her home with her. Depends how long I'm away for.'

'Do you have a cleaner?'

'No. The place never gets dirty.'

'Ha, ha. Don't tell my missus that. She'd be round here like a shot and find a skipful of dust in 30 minutes.'

'What about your laptop? Anything dodgy on there you don't want people to see? The spooks always download stuff in the movies.'

'I'm sure they did. It's been moved, not much, but sufficient to show someone's been sniffing around. But in answer to your second question, all legally privileged stuff for Gravchenko, and anything else they might be interested in, is safely locked away in the cloud, including my ongoing research into the names on the list.'

'An inside job?' Robo said. 'Another apartment owner, tenant?'

'What?' Scott laughed. 'I'm such a threat to MI6 that they're investing their ever-dwindling resources in monitoring little old me 24/7?' He patted his mate on the arm. 'Why bother? My mobile's bugged 24/7 and I don't have a landline. I use my credit and debit cards for everything; all easily traceable transactions. And in 2016 they froze my accounts and seized all my paperwork and computer files. They think they know more about my every move than I do.'

'Only *think*?'

Scott grinned.

'Right,' Robo said. 'You got somewhere to stay tonight? I don't want you to disturb anything, not even the dust. Leave it exactly as it is. I've got some detecting and de-bugging to do.'

'Yeah, Dave's got an empty service apartment, I can use that.'

'Okay,' Robo said. 'We'll get this sorted tomorrow. I'll send over the boys first thing. It shouldn't take all day.'

The fact that a stranger had been rifling through Scott's apartment was trauma enough, but the knowledge that the names on the list were no longer secret caused him far greater concern for the welfare of last two alive: Simone Bisset and Professor Zapatero.

Chapter 24

Day Sixteen: 12.45pm, London

It may have been a bright late-summer's day with a clear blue sky in London's Green Park, but Scott's thoughts were enveloped by dark clouds as he sat on a bench preparing for his meeting with Professor Zapatero while being continually distracted by the name of Kabir Shastri and the break-in.

Shastri the Younger had appeared on the scene from nowhere and risen to the top of Scott's list of major headaches in no more than a day and a bit. The thought of somebody being an existential threat to Gravchenko's mega plan for the future of mankind was, in itself, a major worry for him. However, if Shastri the Younger was free to pursue his illicit activities, and an apparently credible connection could be found between Gravchenko and Santorini, the mega plan could be destroyed. Scott would not only lose out on a $10 million golden handshake and $4.5 million annual income, but also his beloved Foundation might go with it.

The often ill-informed and agenda-driven perceptions of public opinion, aided and abetted by social media polarisation and bigotry, was becoming a powerful tool for making or ruining people's lives. The public were no longer prepared to accept that due process and the rule of law should be the sole arbiters of what was right and wrong.

2.35pm

'What do you want to tell me that is so urgent, Mr Mitchell?'

The hired mini-boardroom wasn't what Scott had expected in a 2018 Regus serviced office set-up. Instead of the state-of-the-art wall monitors, Wi-Fi access, side table with soft drinks and over-wrapped biscuits, flip chart facilities, intercoms and modern art prints, there were two expensive-looking cloth-covered armchairs, a fish tank, one phone and a restful Constable painting of the East Anglian countryside.

Scott studied the professor while trying to assemble his thoughts for the hundredth time since Bell's murder. She was tiny, no more than 1.5 metres at a guess, black hair in a bun, thin-faced with a cold demeanour and immaculately dressed in a dark blue business suit; a severe 21st-century Miss Jean Brodie.

She tilted her head to one side as if to say, 'Get on with it'.

'I have credible evidence that your life could be in imminent danger,' Scott said.

She tapped an unopened cigarette packet on the wing of her armchair.

'You are a lawyer, Mr Mitchell. How *credible* is your evidence?'

'I assume you know of the assassination 16 days ago of our government minister, David Carey?'

'*Si.*'

A slight increase in her blink rate?

'I also assume you know that *three* days ago, a member of the House of Lords, Sir Stanton Morgan Bell, was also murdered.'

'*Si.*'

Definitely no increase that time.

Scott was deliberately dragging his questions out; it helped him keep track of her reactions, physical or otherwise, which for the moment gave little clue as to what she was thinking.

'And, presumably, you are also aware that David

Carey's lawyer, Diane Costello, was brutally tortured and slain in her own home *eight* days ago? The killer, or killers, used her face as an ashtray.'

He was trying to provoke her into breaking the cold silence that was beginning to irritate him, though he was determined not to mention Carey's list unless he could be certain she was an innocent in the matter.

The list didn't distinguish between the good and the bad guys, assuming such a difference existed.

She winced, stopped tapping and gripped the cigarette pack.

She looked as if she was going to crush it.

'Yes,' she said in answer to Scott's question about the murder of Diane Costello.

Time to pile on the pressure.

'Professor Zapatero, both David Carey and Sir Stanton Morgan Bell were heavily involved in Russian matters…'

Her eyes narrowed.

'Albeit for different reasons. But what they had in common was an interest in the trading sanctions imposed by the EU, and the US, in response to Russia's Ukrainian and Crimean activities.'

He waited.

Surely her interest was aroused by now?

She straightened up in her chair and transferred the cigarette pack to her other hand. 'Why is this a matter for me?'

Okay, if you want to play hardball.

A text arrived from Robo:

All clean

Relief, to an extent.

'Do you mind if I respond to this message, Professor?'

'No, please do.'

Thank you.

He replied to the text:

Thanks. Catch you later

Sorry about that.

She nodded. 'So, what is your concern?'

'Well, according to my research, Professor, you have publicly expressed your view that the termination of much of the West's trading activities damages not only the Russian economy, but also ours. You have effectively accused us of commercial myopia.'

She smiled for the first time. 'Commercial myopia. An interesting expression. I shall use it. *Gracias*, Mr Mitchell.'

People are being murdered, for Christ's sake.

'I'm sorry, but I've not come here to improve your excellent English language comprehension. You must take me seriously.' He leant forward. 'You're on a *hit* list, Professor.'

'A *hit* list?' She frowned and jerked back.

He was conflicted; concern for the woman and at the same time wary of the extent of her involvement.

'A metaphorical one, I mean.'

She lost her smile. 'I will be serious. You are correct, I have said those things about the sanctions. But why would the Russians want to kill me? I am on their side.'

'I'm not saying it *is* the Russians. I'm saying that people who had the same interests as you in the subject, and in Bell's case also went public in his House of Lords speeches, these people are being murdered.'

'And this Diane Costello,' she said. 'Did she have the same interests in these matters?'

Her tone was dismissive.

'The connection,' Scott said, 'must surely be that she was David Carey's lawyer and whoever killed her thought she had some knowledge of what her client was doing.'

'And what *was* David Carey's interest in the trading sanctions?'

She stared at him, eyes wide open, as if about to hang onto every word he uttered.

She knew something.

She was testing him, probing him.

'That's what I'm trying to find out,' he said at last.

'Look, Mr Mitchell, there are many, *many* people in the West,' she said, 'who have the same views as me and speak to the public about them. Is everybody to be killed?'

'No, of course not, but in this case, I think you are in danger.'

Because your name is on the dreaded list, but I'm not yet convinced of your role in this, so I'm not ready to tell you about it.

'And I am asking you again,' she said. 'Tell me where is your *credible* evidence? This is only your speculation.'

Fraser rang.

Scott looked at the professor.

She nodded without any facial expression of her thoughts.

'Thank you.'

He turned toward the fish tank and answered the call in a hushed tone.

'Yes?'

'Can you talk?'

'No.'

'I won't be around for a few days. So I'll tell you now.'

'What?'

'Your man, at St Christopher's.'

'I'm with you.'

'He's *not* a person of interest.'

That didn't mean Fraser didn't know his name.

'Okay, thanks. We must meet when you get back.'

'You can be sure of that.'

Fraser disconnected.

'Thank you, again.'

Scott wasn't going to get much further with Zapatero at that moment.

'How long will you be in London for?' he said.

'I am going to Amsterdam tomorrow morning.'

Well, he'd met her and planted a seed, he hoped.

'Would you please promise me you'll at least think about what I've said? In return, I promise I will try to find more credible evidence.'

'Not *more*, Mr Mitchell, *some*.'

Chapter 25

Day Seventeen: 8am, Moscow

One minute General Pravda was limping past the Bolshoi Theatre, aided by a walking stick, the next he was waking up, bound and gagged in the boot of a car. That was what it felt and smelt like; he couldn't be certain as his eyes were taped over, though the bouncing around and faint whiff of exhaust fumes were persuasive. Earphones or muffs prevented him from picking up any sounds.

His ankle was agony, but he couldn't struggle free to reach the painkillers in his jacket pocket.

In an attempt to estimate how far he was travelling, he tensed his leg muscles to lessen the ankle pain and began counting the seconds, although he couldn't gauge the vehicle's speed. Also, despite knowing the approximate time he'd blacked out, he had no idea how long he'd been unconscious.

Apart from the throbbing ankle and smell of exhaust fumes, his sensory deprivation was complete.

The vehicle came to a halt after he'd diligently counted 3,342 seconds; under an hour. It seemed a lifetime before the boot was opened and he was yanked out. He steeled himself, unable to speak with the gag still in place.

Somebody pulled him on his feet and he promptly collapsed as his injured ankle buckled. He could hear only the faintest of voices, not enough to decipher clearly what was being said, except that it was Russian.

He was gripped on both arms and dragged forward.

Where was his stick?

A few steps further across what felt like loose gravel

underfoot, he sensed he was being manhandled through a doorway and into a building. The floor was firm, possibly tiled. The soft-soled shoe on his good leg searched for, and found, what he thought were gaps between tiles.

His captors stopped and untied his hands, which he shook to increase blood circulation.

They removed the gag and earphones, leaving only the blindfold in place.

The smell of bleach was overwhelming.

'Sit here, General Leonid Igorovich Pravda of Russian Military Intelligence.'

It was a harsh male voice; a sneering tone.

'Sit here.'

He was pushed down onto a chair.

'My ankle is killing me,' Pravda said. 'I need my tablets.'

'This isn't a fucking pharmacy.'

Searing pains shot up his leg.

'They're in my pocket.'

'Take off the blindfold,' the voice said.

Pravda closed his eyes as somebody ripped it off.

He winced, rubbed his eyes and blinked several times.

He was in a small hangar-like building, about 10 x 20 metres. The floor tiles were crimson, possibly porcelain ceramic; the walls grey metal with corrugated shuttering interlaced at stages by wooden struts. There were no windows and only one small entrance/exit door. The ceiling was suspended and made of white fibreglass tiles. Portable arc lights occupied the two top corners, with a third set in the middle of the building standing behind a two-seater, stained buff Dralon-covered sofa that had seen better days. The whole set-up, including the walls, confirmed it was a portable structure, except for the porcelain floor tiles.

A TV monitor, the size of a home movie screen, stood on a table in front of the sofa. Cables tracked back from the monitor and across the tiled floor to a machine on wheels: it was a generator. Two people dressed in combat fatigues with full-face balaclavas and wearing sunglasses sat either side of the TV. They were hefty enough to be male, but Pravda couldn't be sure.

Each held a Kalashnikov across his lap and wore white surgical gloves.

Pravda took the tablets from his pocket and turned round.

Five further individuals stood behind him in a cluster. They were disguised similarly to the two men at the monitor, also armed with automatics.

'Does anybody have a water bottle, for my tablets?'

No response, except silent stares.

Stay calm.

He popped two tablets into his mouth and swallowed hard with the few drops of saliva he could find in his arid mouth.

One of the men in the cluster peeled away and stood in front of Pravda, blocking his view of the monitor.

'Where's Orlov's documents?' It was the same man who'd spoken earlier. The only voice Pravda had heard since his capture, discounting the indecipherable exchanges of the men who'd dragged him from the vehicle.

So this was how is it was going to be.

'Who's Orlov? What documents?'

The man pulled a pistol from his belt and swiped Pravda across the temple.

He and the chair crashed to the floor.

The ankle agony transferred to his head.

'We don't have time for your games.'

Pravda pulled the chair towards himself and tried to get up.

The thug kicked him in the groin and stamped on his injured ankle.

'Aaagh!' Pravda couldn't stop himself from calling out. The pain was excruciating.

'Get up!'

Determined not to show any sign of weakness, Pravda used the chair to help himself up and sat down again.

'Okay, one more time,' the thug said, the pistol still in his hand swinging freely by his side. 'Where's Orlov's documents?'

It was no random kidnap. Whoever they worked for wanted the documents more than they wanted to kill him. Of that, Pravda was certain. Okay, so he'd have to endure a beating; it wouldn't be the first time.

'Who *are* you people?'

It had to be Max's doing. He was the only person apart from Yelena and her Bulgarian diplomat who knew they'd been to Varna, unless the arsehole had told others.

The thug appealed to the ceiling. 'What's up with this guy?'

As quick as a flash he thrust the barrel of the pistol into Pravda's left eye and pushed until his head doubled back over the chair. 'Last chance.'

He pulled back.

Pravda plopped forward, massaging the eye socket.

'The documents. Where are they?'

The sound of the men behind sliding back the bolts of their Kalashnikovs was unmistakeable. Not a clever move. Their leader was a standing target in the firing line. It would only take one half-body collapse by Pravda and a stray bullet.

They couldn't have been military trained.

Keep the man talking.

'They're out of the country.'

'Don't insult me, General. You'd have stored back-ups in the cloud.'

'Ask your Kremlin masters.'

A three-second silence.

'What do you mean?'

He couldn't see through the mask and the expression

on the man's face, but the voice betrayed uncertainty.

'They cleared out the back-ups from my cloud account. It's empty.'

Sow the seeds of doubt.

The thug moved away and began walking in small circles in front of Pravda, tapping his own temple with the gun barrel as if knocking thoughts into his head.

Pravda turned round.

The others were hovering and mumbling – more uncertainty?

He turned back.

The thug was leaning against a sidewall, between Pravda and the monitor.

'You've got 24 hours to produce the documents,' he said, in a casual tone, as if he didn't have a care in the world.

Strange. Why the sudden change of mood?

Pravda straightened, trying to mask the signs of ongoing pains in his ankle, temple and eye socket. The tablets had given up on him. 'Can't be done. I'll need a few days at least.'

This would give him enough time to have it out with Max once and for all. Either he stopped interfering in the Gravchenko investigation or Pravda would pack it in – and explain to Putin why. He'd find a way to get a personal meeting with the President.

The thug nodded at the two men by the monitor.

One of them pushed a switch at the back and the screen began flickering.

The other made a quick phone call.

'Twenty-four hours,' the thug said and waved his gun at the screen.

A head shot of a bruised and bloodied face appeared on the screen.

It was in real time.

Pravda couldn't make it out.

The camera slowly eased back, to reveal a youngish man in an ISIS-style orange jumpsuit.

He dominated the screen.

Pravda gulped – no saliva appeared.

It was Yelena's Bulgarian diplomat.

The man's eyes were half closed; a total lack of awareness, probably drugged.

The camera continued to pan back, until it revealed a scaffold in the background, mounted on a makeshift dais with a noose slung over the cross bar.

Pravda jumped up.

'No! No! Are you mad?! He's a diplomat! You wouldn't dare.'

The screen went black.

The image lingered in Pravda's mind.

'You bastards. You total bastards.'

'It's in your hands, General Leonid Igorovich Pravda,' the thug said softly. 'Twenty-four hours.'

Pravda felt a pinprick in the back of his neck and blacked out.

2.30pm

'You've got to rest up that ankle for at least two weeks, General,' the nurse said.

'Thanks for your concern, Lyudmila, but I can't spare a week, let alone two.'

'And your left eye's still bloodshot, we need to look inside, not to mention that bruising on your temple. Those must have been some stairs you fell down.'

Lyudmila knew the rules. No questions asked when the GRU popped into their special clinic for patching up.

'The painkillers will do the job,' Pravda said. 'And can you find me a temporary walking stick, please?'

The kidnappers hadn't returned it to him when they'd unceremoniously dumped him, still half anaesthetised, in a quiet back street off Red Square.

'If you don't get that eye seen to, you'll need a *white* stick as well,' she said and left the room.

Pravda called Max on his new phone.

The Kremlin lackey answered immediately.

'Who's this?' he growled.

'It's General Pravda. Call the hounds off, Max. I'm warning you. I've had enough of your interfering. If you don't I'll—'

'What are you talking about?'

'You know damn well. If anything happens to that diplomat, I'll see you in hell.'

'General Pravda. I've no idea what you're going on about. Where are you? We need to meet. Worms are eating your brain cells.'

You'll be begging for those worms, Max, when I've finished with you.

'I'll see you on the steps of the museum in Gorky Park at 4,' Pravda said.

'Take some tranquillisers before we meet,' Max said. 'I don't want a one-sided conversation with a corpse.'

Pravda disconnected before he went too far.

He texted Yelena on his dedicated phone, after initiating their agreed code sequence:

> Be at Gorky Park at 4. Museum steps. I'm meeting three chins. Don't approach. Shadow us

She replied immediately, acknowledging the code:

> Will do.

4.15pm

Pravda had misjudged the time and arrived 15 minutes late.

A crowd of people were gathered in front of the museum steps.

Emergency vehicle sirens drowned out conversations.

As Pravda limped towards the throng, armed police swarmed the area and pushed the crowd back,

Yelena was applying the kiss of life to a body which was splayed out on the ground motionless, his head in a pool of blood.

The medics arrived and took over.

Yelena got up, spotted Pravda approaching, wiped her mouth with the back of her hand and spat out saliva.

'He's just taken one for the FSB,' she said.

'Max?'

'Yeah, R.I.P. three chins...you old bastard.'

'How?'

'It was like slow motion. One minute he was standing, the next his head snapped back and he dropped. It was a sniper.' She pointed to a cluster of trees in the distance. 'I reckon from over there.'

'Did he say anything?'

'We know too much.'

'What?' Pravda didn't understand the context.

'That's what he said: "We know too much".'

'Nothing else?'

'Nope.'

Who's *we*?

Chapter 26

Day Seventeen: 11.35am, London

'Do you really want to do this?' Robo said as he and Scott sat in their car staring across the street at Jonathan Carey's house.

'I've run out of ideas. It's my last resort. There might be something here. I need credible evidence. It's the only thing she'll accept.'

'So why don't you tell her about the list of names?'

'I'm not ready to. How do I know she's not one of the bad guys?' But anyway, if I were her, I wouldn't accept it at face value. Anybody can quote a list of names. And even if I show her the slip of paper they're written on, she couldn't be sure it came from Carey. She's only got my say-so.'

'Okay, you're the boss,' Robo said. 'Let's go.'

They crossed the road and approached the front gate.

'Are you sure he's out?' Robo said.

'As near as. He didn't turn up to this father's funeral. His sister thinks he's in Indonesia, the jungle, somewhere.'

'Is there a back way to this place?' Robo said.

'Google maps says so. There's an alley running along the back gardens of the whole terrace.'

Robo laughed as they reached the front door.

'What's the joke?'

'I'm going to be the first black man who's already lawyered up when we get nicked for breaking and entering.'

'What's your being black go to do with it?'

'You kidding me?' Robo said. 'Black guys get arrested

first, then the cops ask questions. White guys get asked questions first, sometimes they get arrested.'

He was right, in a way. According to government statistics, black men, as distinct from black women, were three times more likely to get arrested than white men.

'We won't get nicked,' Scott said. 'Not when I tell them who I am and that we're working for an Assistant Deputy Police Commissioner on a matter of national security.'

That was the last thing he'd do if they got caught.

'Whatever,' Robo said. He bent down and peered through the letterbox.

'Jesus Christ!'

'What?'

Robo moved away. 'Take a look.'

Scott did so.

'Moses! How did *that* happen?'

The hallway was covered with unopened mail and flyers; not unusual when the occupant was away for a long period of time, but much of it was at the far end of the hall and halfway up the stairs – a feat impossible to achieve through a narrow letterbox without the aid of a pencil thin missile launcher.

'Hello! Anybody there?!' Scott said.

The door eased open.

'What the?'

He looked up.

Robo's hand was pushing the door open.

'Now, here's a question, your honour,' Robo said. 'Are we breaking and entering if the door is already unlocked?'

He slipped by Scott and went inside.

Scott followed and closed the door behind him.

'Hello! Hello! Anybody in?! Your door was open!'

They both stood still, silent, listening for a response – nothing.

Scott recognised the layout. It was a standard small immediate post-Second World War suburban two-storey terraced house: front room, dining room and kitchen at ground floor level, with two or three bedrooms and a bathroom upstairs.

Robo went upstairs while Scott checked out downstairs.

The front room was devoid of furniture but littered with half-open cardboard boxes and their contents: clothes and trainers, strewn around the room as if hit by a tornado. He couldn't find any labelling or other marking on the boxes.

'Scott! Get up here. Quick! Quick!'

'Coming!' Scott bolted upstairs, scattering the mail deliveries under foot.

'Here in the back room!'

'What?! What's happened?!'

He dashed into the room.

Robo was staring at a body lying on an unmade single bed.

'He's breathing,' Robo said. 'But he didn't wake when I shouted for you.'

He was male, mid-20s, wearing a 'save-the-whales' T-shirt and boxer shorts, no footwear.

As with the downstairs room, the place looked like the same tornado had ripped through it: three bottles of water, a spilt glass of juice, an open laptop with a decapitated keyboard, earphones torn apart, a rucksack with the contents spread out next to it, cigarette butts, local newspapers, a mobile phone and a box of bloody tissues.

Scott leant over the body and immediately jerked back.

'What?' Robo said. 'What is it?'

Scott pointed at the neck. 'There, look at those.'

Robo took a look. 'Bites or stings of some sort?'

'No mate,' Scott said. 'If I'm not mistaken, they're cigarette burns.'

It was Costello all over again.

Scott gently tapped the lad on the shoulder.

The boy grunted and opened his eyes, blinking for focus. 'No. Not again. Leave me alone, please. I've told you, I don't know anything.'

Before Scott could answer the lad closed his eyes and his head flopped to one side, as if going into an instant coma.

'It's him, Jonathan Carey,' Robo said. 'Here.'

Scott turned round.

Robo handed him the passport. 'It was over there, with the backpack.'

Scott flicked through the pages and compared the image to the lad on the bed. 'It looks like him, and the name fits: Jonathan Edward Carey.'

Scott tapped Jonathan on the shoulder again. 'Jonathan, wake up, please. We're here to help you, not to hurt you.'

Jonathan screamed and clutched his stomach. 'Aaagh!'

'What? What's the matter?' Scott said.

'My stomach! My stomach! It's killing me!'

Jonathan eased his T-shirt up.

'What the fuck?' Robo said.

Scott fought to hold down vomit.

Jonathan's stomach was also covered in cigarette burns.

The sadist. The absolute sadist.

It had to be Costello's killer.

He turned to Robo who was punching numbers into his phone.

'What are you doing?'

'Calling an ambulance.'

'No, no. Don't,' Scott said. 'No 999.'

'What do you mean? The guy needs a doctor, now.'

'I know,' Scott said. 'I know, I know. But not 999.' He glanced at Jonathan who was staring at him plaintively.

Scott pulled Robo back from the bedside and lowered his voice. 'We need to be discreet. This kid's life is in danger. If we take him to an NHS hospital they'll inform the police. It's obviously torture.'

'So what do you suggest we do, Doctor Wise Guy?'

'You take him to that no-questions-asked clinic of your mate's while I dig around this place to see what I can find.'

Robo widened his eyes. 'You sure? It's going to cost you...a grand a night – and that's just for the duvet. Medics extra.'

'No problem.' Jonathan was Scott's closest link to his father. He had to be kept healthy and away from prying eyes for as long as it took.

'Okay, it's *your* money,' Robo said.

He called the clinic and made the arrangements. 'They're on their way'.

'Text me when he's settled in,' Scott said. 'And I'll let his brother-in-law know.'

'Okay.'

Scott began his search in the other bedroom. Wardrobe doors were hanging off their hinges and the drawers pulled out; clothes scattered across the floor, picture frames with their backs removed, the mattress on the single bed ripped to shreds, a bedside table smashed to pieces, and a makeshift table and drawers, apparently fixed to the wall, had been torn away from its mountings to reveal a large a metre-square hole in the wall where the brickwork had been gouged out – but nothing to see.

The bathroom looked untouched. He tried to prise the bath's side panel away without causing any damage. He couldn't.

He went down to the kitchen.

There was no sign of a disturbance.

No. Not again. Leave me alone, I've told you, I don't know anything.

There wasn't any use in speculating what the bastard wanted from Jonathan. Scott would have to wait until the boy was in a better state.

He went through the cupboards and, finding nothing, turned to the mail and flyers littering the hallway and stairs.

He gathered them up and dumped them on the kitchen worktop.

One envelope stood out amongst everything else.

It was addressed to Jonathan personally and it bore the following text in large red capitals:

> THIS IS NOT A CIRCULAR OR SPAM MAIL. DO NOT IGNORE.

The sender's address on the back indicated that it was from a debt-collection company.

He opened it, convincing himself that it was his duty as the self-appointed Carey family lawyer to counsel his "client" in times of threatened legal proceedings. It was typical of such letters Scott had seen before.

The threat was indeed there, alleging three months' arrears of payments of instalments for a unit in a local storage facility. A statement of account was attached to a legal letter.

'Rob!' He was still upstairs with Jonathan.

'Yeah?!'

'I've got to take my car and check something out. Will you be okay with Jonathan until the ambulance arrives?!'

'Sure, no problem!'

'Cheers. Call me when you get settled in!'

'Will do!'

*

45 minutes later

The large reception centre of the storage company was empty.

Scott pressed the bell on the desk.

A middle-aged man with a pock-marked face emerged from an adjoining glass- fronted office. He stubbed out a cigarette on an ashtray lying on the desk.

'How can I help you?'

'Hello,' Scott said. 'I need to get into my unit, but I've lost my keys.'

'No problem.' The man switched on a desktop computer. 'What's the unit number and your name?'

Scott took out the invoices and checked the number. '12E. I'm Jonathan Carey.' He reckoned it was better to say that than say he was the family lawyer, or a friend. Everybody was worried about the GDPR and data protection; they wouldn't tell you the time of day unless you produced ID or a sample of your grandmother's DNA.

Overkill gone mad.

'You got ID?' the man said, staring at the screen.

'Sure, look at these three invoices. My details are on them.' He didn't produce the debt collector's letter.

The man skimmed them, and sniffed. 'I mean driver's licence or latest utility bill with your home address on it. Something like that.'

Scott was trained to think on his feet.

'My licence is with the DVLA, speeding endorsement. And I forgot to bring my utility bill.'

'Hmmm,' the man said. 'No keys. No driver's licence. No utility bill. Not your day is it?'

'What can I say? Stuff happens.'

'Oh yes, Mr Carey, stuff happens alright,' he said as he tapped on the keyboard and squinted at the screen.' Oh yes sir. Stuff definitely happens.'

'What are you talking about?' Scott said.

The man lifted the access flap on the desk to get to Scott's side.

'Follow me.'

Scott did so.

Relieved. He was going to open the unit for him.

'Do you have a master key?' Scott hadn't seen the man bring a cutting tool that would have been required to snap a padlock. His own storage unit in Docklands was accessed by a toughened padlock that Scott had put on himself. The owner had told him they weren't allowed to have master keys, for privacy and security purposes. In an emergency they'd smash the lock off.

'No key needed,' the man said as he stopped outside unit 12E and slid back the bolt.

There wasn't any lock on the door.

'After you,' said the man.

Scott went inside.

It was empty, nothing except a few nuts and bolts lying on the stone floor and two reels of black gaffer tape in the corner.

'Come for your bolts and tape have you?'

Scott checked the date on the debt collector's letter.

It was two months old.

Bugger.

'You've seized my stuff to pay off the invoices! I've been abroad for three months. You could have at least waited 'til I got back.'

'Not us, the police.'

'What?' Scott's heart sank.

'Five days ago. Had a warrant. Cleared you out. Took 'em a couple of hours. They weren't happy bunnies. What's in those cabinets? Stonehenge? They were moaning about getting hernias. Right load of whinging wusses.'

Chapter 27

Day Eighteen: 10.55am, London

If it wasn't Fraser skulking around in the back of Scott's mind, it was Chalmers. They were playing tag with him. It had to have been the ADC who'd authorised the search warrant for the seizure of Jonathan Carey's goods at the storage unit.

Something had triggered the Commissioner's curiosity.

Something they'd found in the papers seized from Diane Costello's chambers or the computer files and other stuff they'd taken from David Carey's house; not to mention the list of names, which of course mentioned Santorini and Bell. Fraser was working on Santorini and Chalmers on Bell.

The stage was getting crowded.

Robo was going to let Scott know when Jonathan was fit for visitors.

He texted Tom for a second time. He'd tried the night before, without connection success.

The wanderer has returned. Talk later

The reply was immediate.

Great, thanks

He called Pravda.

No response; line dead.

This was the third time in recent days that Scott had been unable to make a connection with Pravda.

The same with Yelena.

They'd disappeared off the face of the earth.

Fraser sent a text:

Be at The Balcony coffee place upstairs at Waterloo Station @2pm

2.05pm

'Okay, Fraser said. 'When were you going to tell me?'

No smiles.

'You said you wouldn't be around for a few days,' Scott said as he scooped the froth from the top of his cappuccino with a spoon – his first of the year – and took his time in swallowing it, while waiting for a reply.

They had a panoramic view of the terminus, sitting as they were side by side at the bench overlooking the station concourse.

He stared at the giant clock that blocked part of their line of sight of the departure indicator board covering platforms 12 to 18.

'Never mind that,' Fraser said. 'When were you were going to tell me about this?'

Fraser produced the FBI image of Scott in Budapest.

Scott scrutinised it, as if he hadn't seen it before.

'Hmm. That's interesting,' he said innocently. 'Where did you get it?'

Scott returned to studying the clock.

'The guy on the left,' Fraser said. 'The guy you're shaking hands with. His name is Arjun Shastri.' He stopped.

Scott turned to him.

'Your point being?'

'But you must know that, mustn't you?' Fraser continued. 'I mean, you're bosom buddies in this image.'

The man's return to his former sarcastic ways indicated the end of their short-lived ceasefire.

'Okay, Gravchenko introduces me to an Indian billionaire. So what?'

'It's like pulling teeth with you. Doesn't our goodwill mean anything any more?'

'The goodwill left from platform 18 at the beginning of this conversation.'

Fraser frowned. 'What do you mean?'

'You never answered my question when I asked if you people were working with the police on the Carey murder.'

Fraser grimaced. 'You got a short memory for a sharp lawyer. I told you not to get side-tracked.'

'I'm not getting side-tracked. I'm talking about Assistant Deputy Commissioner Chalmers. Don't tell me you don't know him. He's in charge of the Carey investigation. Are you two sharing information?'

To give Fraser his credit, he didn't bat an eyelid.

'Shastri,' Fraser tapped the image. 'Tell me about him.'

The man was a tough nut to crack, and Scott may have queered his pitch for future exchanges.

What was Otto Von Bismarck supposed to have said, but didn't?

Politics is the art of compromise.

'Okay,' Scott said. 'According to Wikipedia, Kabir Shastri is Arjun Shastri's son. But I didn't know that when I met him in Budapest. In fact, I've only met the man on that one occasion. Neither before, nor since.'

Fraser's body language appeared to soften. 'According to our American cousins Kabir is behind Santorini. You know about the company's money-laundering, so why did you ask me about the old man if it wasn't because you knew his son was running the operation?'

Good question.

Scott searched for a good answer.

What did Tom say?

Prepare yourself for a visit from the FBI.

Or their puppet, Colin Fraser.

'As I said, I hadn't heard of Arjun Shastri until Gravchenko introduced me to him in Budapest. When I returned to London, the FBI showed me the photo you've just shown me and told me about Kabir's involvement with Santorini.'

Fraser froze.

'Oh dear. Did our American cousins forget to tell you that one of their agents showed me the photo?' Scott revelled in Fraser's ignorance. 'Tut, tut, that's not very friendly is it?'

Fraser gritted his teeth and squirmed.

'I wanted to know what you knew about Arjun Shastri, so I could decide if he was somebody that perhaps Mr Gravchenko shouldn't be seen with, for fear of the public coming to the wrong conclusion if this man and his son were money-launderers.' Scott shrugged. 'That's all.'

It contained elements of the truth.

However, the answer to the next question – What was Mr Shastri doing with Mr Gravchenko in Budapest? – wouldn't be met with the truth, only a resounding lie, Scott decided.

Fraser kept staring at the photo and biting his lip.

He'd been humiliated.

'It doesn't look good, does it?' Fraser said.

Scott relaxed with relief.

The expected second question hadn't come.

'What do you mean?'

The professionalism of the photo or the context?

'Your boss, and *you*, hobnobbing with the old man. The father of the brains behind one of Putin's major laundromats.'

Hobnobbing? How quaint.

'Two questions,' Scott said: First, how do you know that Arjun Shastri has any idea what his son is allegedly up to? Second, how do you know that Putin has heard of Santorini?'

Scott's phone rang.

It was Robo.

'Yes?'

'Five tonight.'

'Thanks. I'll be there.'

Scott disconnected.

Jonathan Carey was ready to talk.

'Sorry about that,' Scott said to Fraser. 'Now, where were we?'

Fraser snatched his phone and got up. 'You're digging a big hole for yourself. Catch you later.'

5pm

Robo had left the clinic by the time Scott arrived.

Jonathan was in a private ward that wouldn't have been out of place in a five-star bijou hotel in any major European city. He was sitting up in bed reading a travel brochure.

'How are you feeling?' Scott asked.

Jonathan waved the brochure at Scott. 'Like I need a holiday on a deserted beach in Thailand.'

He was chirpy.

'Haven't you just come back from three months in the tropics?'

'The jungle, rainforests, yes, but that was work.' He waved the brochure at Scott again. 'This is R & R.'

Scott sat down by his bedside.

'I didn't bring you anything,' Scott said. 'Grapes are bit too clichéd, sorry.'

'Your friend says you're spending over £1,000 a night on me. I reckon that covers the grapes, thanks. I don't know when I'll be able to pay you back. But when Dad's estate is wound up, you'll get back every penny. I promise.'

Scott was glad Jonathan had got so quickly to the point of their meeting.

'That's okay. How much has Robo told you about us, me?'

'Not much. You're a lawyer helping Tom trying to find out why Dad was killed, that's about it.'

Well done, Robo.

'I'll fill you in with some more later,' Scott said. 'But first, can you tell me what happened at your house? From the beginning.' He would let his own role seep out in dribs and drabs, depending on how the conversation went.

Jonathan eased himself up. 'Aaagh. It's the chest, the burns.'

Scott glanced at the dressing on his neck. 'There as well? Shall I call the doctor?'

'No, no. It's okay. It's much better than it was. They're going to wash me and change the dressings in an hour. Anyway, I've dealt with worse in the jungle.' He gestured at the space-age TV on the wall. 'And with no widescreen in my tent.'

'So what happened?'

'I got home from Heathrow at two or three in the afternoon. As I turned the key in the lock, I got shoved forward and tripped over the mail on the floor. A man in a balaclava stood over me, shouting, "Where's the stuff? Where's the stuff?" Another man stepped over me and disappeared. I said, "What stuff?" and the man kicked me in the groin.

'Was he English?'

'An Afrikaans accent, at a guess. I've been there on safari.'

'Jonathan, I don't know much about South Africa, but isn't the accent in Cape Town different from that in Jo'burg?' He wanted as much information as possible; it would help with building a full profile.

'Yes. Cape Town sounds more English. It's softer than Afrikaans, like you get in Jo'burg.'

'Okay. Sorry to interrupt. Then what happened?'

'He was a big guy, built like one of those rugby players, as tall as a Redwood. He slammed the front door and dragged me upstairs. The other one came out of the front room and followed me with my rucksack and stuff.'

'Did this other man say anything.'

'Not then, no. But he did later.'

'Go on.'

They took me into my bedroom, stripped me down to my T-shirt and shorts, and threw me on the bed. The other one disappeared again and I heard him smashing the rooms up.

'Did you say anything to them?'

'Of course. I asked them who they were and what they wanted.'

They ignored me, at first.

'Then what happened?'

'The kicker asked where my dad's papers were. I asked him what he was talking about. He kept asking me the same question. He lit a cigarette and burnt me. Every time I said I didn't know what he was going on about he burnt me.'

Jesus Christ.

'The pain was unbearable. I didn't know whether I was coming or going. I'm sure I lost consciousness a couple of times.'

'So when did he stop? Did you tell him something, make something up, to stop the pain?'

'I was about to do that when the other guy burst in shouting they had to get out, quickly. He had his phone in his hand. Someone had called him and told him to leave, fast—'

'Sorry to interrupt, again, but what were you about to tell him?'

'I've got a storage facility. I was going to tell him to look there. I just wanted the torture to stop, I'd give them my key and...' He grimaced. 'I don't know what I expected to happen next.'

'Did your father keep some of his papers there?'

'No. He never asked to. He wouldn't ask. We were never that close.' He paused.' It's been over a year since we spoke. We parted on some bad words.' He wiped a tear away. 'I came back for Dad's funeral. I read about it in the press. My phone was broken, the flight was delayed and, well, one thing after another. What do they call it? A perfect storm. Everything went wrong.' He wiped his eyes again.

Scott waited, respectfully, for Jonathan to continue.

But he didn't.

'Do you mind telling me?' Scott said after a short silence. 'What do you keep there?'

'My lifetime travelogues. You know: diaries, articles, magazines, brochures, photo albums – don't use phone images – etc. I'm going to write a book about my trips one day.'

Enjoy your reading ADC Chalmers.

Scott told him about the debt collector's letter, his visit to the storage facility and the police seizure of everything stored there.'

'Oh no! You're kidding! No, it's all I have.'

'No backups anywhere? In the cloud?'

'I don't do tech stuff.'

Like father, like son.

'Well, don't be too upset. You'll get it all back when the police realise your father hadn't stored any of his papers there.'

'But when will that be?'

'Tom will be here soon, in the next couple of days. He's in Germany. We can discuss it with him. He'll get his lawyers on to it.'

Scott could ask the police himself, but it would be like a red rag to a bull. Best to stay out of that aspect.

'I don't know if you realise,' Scott said. 'But your other rooms, apart from the bathroom and kitchen, look like a tornado's been through them. In the front room they tore open all the boxes and searched inside them; threw the contents, clothes, shoes, all over the place. What were they for? The boxes weren't labelled.'

'They belong to a friend. He runs a charity that sends them overseas, mainly to Africa for the kids who have to walk miles to school, half naked and in bare feet. I let him store them there. I never use the room.'

'Okay. I'll get some help to tidy up your place, that's if you don't mind.'

'Haven't you done enough for me? I can do it when I get out of here.'

There was no way Scott was going to allow Jonathan to return home. The thugs hadn't finished their job and they didn't know that he hadn't got this father's papers.

'We can discuss it with Tom.'

'Okay. That's a good idea.'

'Before I forget,' Scott said. 'Was the other thug also South African?'

'No, Scottish, through and through.'

'Regional accent?'

'They all sound the same to me.'

Scott smiled. 'Me too.'

'And they left, straight after the call?'

'Yes. And in an almighty hurry. '

'Did you hear any of the phone conversation?'

'No, I think he took it downstairs. Not that I was in any condition to—'

'Of course not. I understand.'

'They wore balaclavas, you say?

'Yes.'

'Did they wear gloves? The place could be full of fingerprints.'

'The Scotsman did, but the guy that burnt me didn't.'

'Any distinguishing marks on his hands, wrists?'

'No...' He hesitated. 'No, I don't remember seeing anything.'

8.30pm

A text from Sergey arrived.

> Pack your bags – one/two days. Be at Stansted tomorrow morning at 9:00. You're going to Geneva, by private jet. A member of the crew will be waiting for you at Isle F with the paperwork

Scott replied.

> Okay

He sent a text to Tom:

> Wanderer fine. Message me when you're available for a meeting. Will be abroad for one/two days

He tried Pravda and Yelena again – still no response.

Tom's reply arrived.

> Thanks. Will do.

Chapter 28

Day Nineteen: 2pm, Geneva

'What's this place?'

'Ah, so you *are* alive. I was beginning to wonder. You haven't said a word since we left the airport.'

'Sorry, Sergey. I've a lot on my mind.'

'It's the boss's brainchild,' Sergey said as he stopped at the entrance barrier while the guard manually raised it for him.

The large advertising hoarding at the entrance announced the forthcoming construction of the headquarters of a pedagogical institute for the World Preservation Foundation. It was in four languages: French, German, English and Russian, with images. The names of the developers, architects and other essential contributors to the construction process comprised French, German and Chinese companies.

They eased along a temporary road, flanked by building materials and machinery as far as the eye could see. The road took them up to the main building; one of the 18th- and 19th-century villas that populated the shores of Lake Geneva.

Gravchenko appeared from a small outhouse as Sergey pulled to a halt at the side of the villa. He was wearing green coveralls, steeped in dust, and a white face mask. He was holding a dustpan and broom; the pan was loaded with dog poo while an excitable brown and white Cocker spaniel nibbled at his trouser legs.

Sergey took the dustpan and broom from Gravchenko and enticed the dog away.

'Well,' Scott said, 'that's a sight I thought I'd never see.'

Gravchenko loosened his face mask to his neck, and lit a cigarette. 'Follow me.'

They walked round to the front of the villa and down a grass slope to a bench under a large spreading tree.

'This is some tree, Kostya. What is it?'

'Lebanese Cedar. It's over 200 years old.'

'Beautiful.'

'See that building over there, across the lake?' Gravchenko said.

'Yes, what is it?'

'It's the World Trade Organization building.' He turned to Scott. 'And we're going to shake them up with a tsunami. They won't know what's hit them.'

As eager as Scott was to hear Kostya's plans for the future, his immediate concern was the Shastris, but, as before in Budapest, his boss's tone told him to bide his time.

Passionate, if not hyper.

'In what way? What's this all about?' Scott waved vaguely at the villa behind them. 'I've seen the notice board at the entrance, but can you give me some details? What's this pedagogical institute?'

'If we're going to change attitudes from obsessive materialism to sustainability, we're going to have to educate the younger generations, away from the self-absorbed brainwashing they get from the current world political leaders and international corporations and towards more green and socially equable philosophies.' He took a deep drag on the cigarette and blew out smoke rings. 'This institute is to be the first of many, worldwide.'

'I understand, but your aspirations are going to cost more than Black Rock's $10 trillion. You're talking about a project investment that's going to take generations to come to fruition, assuming it ever does.'

'I know that, but I'm determined to lay the foundations.' Gravchenko gazed across the lake. 'This world is shit, absolute shit.'

Scott preferred to think of it as the curate's egg – good in parts.

'One thing, Kostya. The democratic West is going to be hard enough to persuade to give up their foreign holiday flights, but do you honestly think you'll be able to persuade people like Putin and the Chinese?'

'It's all about people power.' He shook his head. 'Don't worry, I know how to buy it, even in Russia and China.'

Buy it? How much would it cost to buy the hearts and minds of 1.5 billion people?

Sergey pulled up in a golf buggy. 'Lunch is served.' He placed a hamper on the bench next to Gravchenko. 'Let me know if you need anything more.'

'Thanks, Sergey,' Scott said.

Gravchenko put the hamper between them and opened the lid. 'Help yourself.'

There weren't any plates or cutlery, only the food and napkins. Scott tucked in to chicken wings, salmon sandwiches and a bottle of beer that had a screw top.

Alright. Who would Scott be dealing with?

'Who are the members of the group?'

'They'll all be there in Prague. Currently two each from Russia, that includes me, and from India...'

Scott said nothing. It wasn't the right moment.

'...and China. And one each from Kazakhstan – you've met Murat – Hong Kong, Malaysia, Australia, Germany, Sweden and Brazil.'

'All male?'

'No, four women, from: China, India, Malaysia and Brazil.

'None from the Middle East, where the oil money is?'

Scott chuckled to himself. Wouldn't that be ironic? Using their oil money to get rid of fossil fuels.

'I've invited two: one from Saudi and the other Iran—'

'The arch enemies.'

'It doesn't matter. They prefer to spend their money on spreading Islam.'

'It's a pity. All that money.'

Scott wondered if Kostya was religious. Many Russians, irrespective of wealth, followed the Russian Orthodox Church's teachings, though he'd never discussed the topic with his boss.

'I don't need God's help to recreate the world,' Kostya said.

Well, if that wasn't the ultimate expression of self-confidence, Scott didn't know what was. He finished his beer.

'I've got some news on Santorini and Shastri.'

'I'm listening.'

'But first you should know that somebody broke into my apartment and copied the list of names.'

Gravchenko chuckled.

'What's so funny?' Scott was in no mood to laugh about it.

'I'm going to enjoy reading your novel.'

Definitely not the time for jokes, boss.

'Look,' Gravchenko said. 'Unless you know who did it, there's nothing you can do about it. Nothing at all. Don't work yourself up into a rage, go on a guilt trip or whatever else you feel like doing. The genie is out of the bottle. You have to live with it.' He gave Scott a friendly tap on the arm. 'Stay calm, or you'll worry yourself to death.'

The man was right of course.

He was slowly losing control over his destiny, but he couldn't do anything about it.

'Now,' Gravchenko said, 'what's the news on Santorini and Shastri?'

Scott told him about the FBI information on Kabir

Shastri and their photo of the Budapest meeting.

'So you see the problem,' Scott said. 'Whether or not Arjun knows what his son's doing, if the public, or any authorities gunning for you, find out about this, it could seriously damage the Foundation's objectives.'

Kostya's face lost its happy sheen and he frowned. 'How sure are you of this?'

'MI6 and the FBI are convinced by it.'

'Fake news?'

'We won't know that for sure until we get to the bottom of it ourselves,' Scott said.

Gravchenko wiped his mouth with a couple of napkins as Sergey returned to collect the hamper and rubbish.

'Right,' Gravchenko said. 'Ask Arjun about it when you meet him in Prague. Tell him your source, no need to mention any names, and say that you're telling him about his son in case he didn't know. You're an experienced lawyer, you'll be able to see from his reaction if he did or didn't know. Either way, he'll deny any knowledge of it. Blood is thicker than water. Go along with him and tell him that he's got to find out how deep his son is involved, because if it's true it's going to upset his partners in our project. Let me know what he says.'

'Do you want me to tell him I've told you?'

'No, say you only just found out and didn't have time to speak to me before you left for Prague. You wanted to tell me face to face; it's not something to be discussed on the phone or in emails.'

They strolled up the hill to the villa.

'So? The job offer?' Kostya said.

'Kostya.' Scott waved his hands around the scenery. 'All this. It's a massive project. I'm not sure I'm equipped to...'

The man laughed. 'Do you want more money? Name your price.'

Now that was scary.

He'd never seen the oligarch show his hand, in any negotiation with anybody, at any time. He'd always bargain from a position of strength, or perceived strength.

Kostya grabbed Scott around the shoulder and pulled him hard.

'Scott, you're part of my family now. It's my job to look after you.'

Blood is thicker than water.

Scott was about to mention Zletov and Kevin Shaw's redacted FBI report when a Russian language text arrived on his regular phone:

Must meet in Malta, Very urgent. Dr Snitkina

Dr Snitkina?

Aha! Yes!

It was Major Yelena Grigoryeva. She'd used that alias in 2016 when he'd visited his friend Sophie Menke in hospital, after somebody had tried to kill her on the Moscow Metro. Yelena had been guarding her.

'Problem?' Kostya asked.

'It's from Major Grigoryeva.' Kostya knew who she was. 'She wants to meet me urgently, in Malta. I've got to go. Something's up. I've been trying to contact her and General Pravda for days.'

'Take my jet. It's only a couple of hours. If you leave by five you can be there at seven,' Kostya said. 'It's at the airport waiting for instructions.'

'Thanks, that'd be great.'

'Do you want Sergey to go along with you?'

Kostya couldn't be more helpful.

Was that because he was now a member of the family, or for some other reason?

'Thanks for the offer Kostya, but I don't want to spook the General. He likes a one-to-one.' He assumed Pravda would be there.

He booked a room at the Preluna Hotel in Sliema and replied to Yelena:

Preluna Hotel in Sliema at 10am tomorrow?

Yelena replied immediately:

Agreed

He turned to his boss.

'Thanks again, Kostya. I really appreciate this.'

'Don't forget, keep your wits about you,' he replied in the tone of a father cautioning his son.

Chapter 29

Day Twenty: 10am, Malta

'Darling, it's so lovely to see you again. I've got so much to tell you,' a woman's voice said in Russian.

Scott looked up from the glossy Preluna Hotel brochure he was studying while sitting in the hotel's reception area.

'What the...do I know you?'

The woman leant into him and gently pulled him up from the chair. 'Play along with it,' she whispered in his ear.

My God, it was Yelena!

He stood up and smiled as she looped her arm in his and led him to the exit, effusively planting kisses on his cheek; touchy-feely.

Long-lost millennial lovers?

She was oozing femininity with her light-coloured skirt and top, high-heeled shoes, sheer tights and a modern clutch bag. The first time he'd met her, in 2013 on a cold winter's night in a Moscow Hotel car park, she'd been in military uniform and keeping a psychopathic killer at bay. Thereafter, he'd only ever seen her in jeans or multi-pocketed cargo pants, with a rock and roll T-shirt, and a gun secreted in her boots, except on the one occasion when she'd been masquerading as the white-coated Dr Snitkina – but still with a gun hidden in her boots.

Scott was mesmerised.

Her eyes were everywhere and her body trembled each time she drew herself into him.

He played along, responding with hugs and smiling like a Cheshire cat.

They crossed the road to the waterfront bar.

'Here,' she said, 'Sit here.'

She chose a table at the far end, overlooking the sea and away from the other customers.

'What would you like to drink, eat?' Scott asked.

'A Coke, that's all,' she said softly, as she looked around.

The ebullience had faded as quickly as it had appeared.

The waiter approached.

'A Coke and a herbal tea, please,' Scott said.

The waiter nodded and disappeared.

'The General's missing. Three days,' Yelena said. 'He's never done it before without warning me up front. It's shit everywhere. We're all in danger.'

If Scott hadn't seen it himself, he wouldn't have believed it possible. Her whole body was weaving and bobbing with her eyes swivelling everywhere, while at the same time tapping the fingers of her left hand on the table, manically, as if on drugs. It reminded him of the mania displayed by Claire Danes in her brilliantly acted scene in *Homeland* when the FBI turned up to search her house.

'Look, Yelena, stay calm. You're a nervous wreck. I don't understand.' Something's happened for the General to disappear like this. Something out of character.

'You remember Orlov. On your list,' she said. 'Died in the Madrid plane explosion.'

'Of course I do. In fact I'm still trying to work out what he was—'

'We found loads of documents: credit cards, bank statements, transfers and stuff in his apartment in Bulgaria.' Her eyes stopped on Scott's and widened.

Orlov?

'Lots about Santorini,' she continued.

Now *that* was interesting.

'We got into the bank accounts. It's a mega money-laundering outfit. Hundreds of millions of dollars whizzing round the universe. We've got paper trails: names, dates, account numbers, amounts...well, some of it. There's lots more stuff to go through.

She punctuated each statement either with a manic grin at Scott or by scanning the customers as they came and went.

The waiter brought the drinks.

Yelena grabbed the bottle of Coke, ignored the accompanying glass full of ice and downed most of it one go.

He had to calm her.

'Okay, okay, Yelena. That's fantastic news. I think the time's come for us to swap information.' He leant forward and gently touched her arm. 'But what's it got to do with the General's disappearance?'

'He was snatched off the street in broad daylight three days ago. Outside the Bolshoi Theatre. The bastards were masked.'

'What!?' A GRU general kidnapped on Moscow's streets? He didn't disbelieve her, but who'd be crazy enough to do it?

'They stuck something into his neck, anaesthetised him. Bundled him into a car. Took him to some industrial unit and interrogated him...with pistol whipping persuasion.'

Scott listened in horror.

Yelena shrugged. 'So far, no sweat. The General's a hard case. Been there, done that.'

'What did they want from him?'

'They showed him a real-time video of my source, a Bulgarian diplomat. He helped me at Orlov's apartment. He'd been beaten up and was dressed in an ISIS type jumpsuit...in front of a hanging scaffold.'

Scott's bile was rising.

'They gave the General 24 hours to give up the Orlov documents, or they'd hang my source.'

Images of Jihadi John's ISIS viral video of him standing behind one of his kneeling prisoners and pulling a knife across the condemned man's throat came back to haunt him.

Who *are* these bastards?

Scott sighed. 'The 24 hours is up. What's happened to your source?'

'I don't know. Can't get hold of him. No news anywhere.' She banged the table. 'I can't get hold of him!'

'Okay, okay.' He tapped her arm. 'Try to stay calm, Yelena. Please. It's not doing you any good.' He tapped her again. 'We have to keep cool. Otherwise we won't be able to think straight.'

She sighed deeply and withdrew her arm. 'Okay. Okay.'

'Tell me about the General?' Scott said. 'What happened to him? He must have come out of it alright, as he lived to tell you the tale.'

'Yeah. They dumped him back in the city centre, same day. He thought Max was behind it. You know about Max?'

'Sure. The General told me. He's a member of the *siloviki* and in charge of your investigation into Gravchenko.'

'*Was* a member.' A tortured smile. 'He was shot dead in front of us in Gorky Park a couple of hours later.'

What had Gravchenko said about the Bond movies, *escapism*? Yelena's whole story was becoming more unbelievable by the second.

'How far does this stuff go up the food chain?' Scott said.

'That's what we were trying to find out when the General disappeared.'

'Would the Kremlin kill one of their own?'

She stared at him as if he were mad.

'Sorry, silly question.'

'And it gets worse,' Yelena said. 'A whole lot worse...'

What could possibly be worse?

'And you've got to believe me. This is from a trusted source who told the General. The Kremlin's got eyes and ears everywhere, From the Ukrainian border to Vladivostok, the Arctic Circle to the Caucasus. I'm telling you. They can trace, crack, hack, turn on, turn off all digital communications devices and platforms. They can break any encryption service: VPN, WhatsApp, ghost phones. And stuff that's not been invented yet. You name it, they can do it. It's total Orwell.'

She took a cigarette from a packet in her clutch bag.

Another shock. Yelena was a health and fitness fanatic, apart from the occasional sugar drink, always in the gym and she never smoked.

She lit it with a novelty lighter shaped like a pistol, inhaled deeply and coughed her lungs up. 'Fuck this,' she said, and extinguished the cigarette, which she scrunched up with the packet and its contents.

'So that's why I couldn't get through to you guys recently.'

'Yeah. We've dumped our old phones and got new ones.'

It didn't matter if the Kremlin couldn't do everything Yelena said it could. All a government needed to do, to totally control the people, was to get them to believe they *could* do what they claimed; scaremongering was an oft-used tool of manipulation, especially political.

'Do you reckon they know you're here, with me? Could they have picked up our texts?'

She looked around the bar for the 99th time.

'I was here when I sent the texts. I bought the phone in Malta.' She toyed with her glass, and shrugged. 'But who knows?'

'Okay.' Comforting to a degree. 'Do you reckon they know you've left the country?'

'Can't be sure. But I've got a way to get out of Russia; the General doesn't know about. I've used it before. Got the trick from guys who operated in the Cold War days. And if the Kremlin's stalking me they're going to be monitoring internet-connected devices, CCTV, phone lines and stuff. Dodged the CCTV and didn't use the phone; also turned off its locator. Even left my ID docs at home.'

'Good.' He knew enough not to ask her how she did it. 'But how did you get into Malta?'

She shook her head.

Another stupid question.

'So tell me more about the General's disappearance. When did you realise he'd gone?'

'Max's shooting. We didn't want to hang around and talk to the police, with them asking awkward questions.'

'I don't blame you.' The last thing they needed was the police taking their names as potential witnesses.

'I went back to the office, but the General didn't feel too good and went home to rest. Said he'd see me next day.'

'But he didn't?'

'No. I tried to get him early in the morning. He didn't respond. I thought he might have relapsed after the kidnapping. I went to his dacha. It was the day his cleaner comes. She said she didn't think he'd been there all night. The bed was made, which he never did if he could help it. No sign of life.'

'Have you checked with his ex-wife? She lives in St. Petersburg, doesn't she?'

'Not easy, with all this surveillance. And I don't want to scare them. It's got to be business as usual. But if he is with them, he would have got a message to me.'

'I understand. If the General hasn't given these guys the documents, or access to them if they're online, where are they now?'

She told him about the locations Pravda had hidden them in.

'Yelena, I need to see these, sooner rather than later. Do you reckon you can get me copies without being discovered? I don't mean the hard copies. Cloud account access would do.'

'Yeah, maybe. But, I'll think about it. I don't want anybody to access the accounts until I'm 100 per cent sure the Kremlin's asleep.'

He laid his hand on her arm. 'I don't want you to put your life in any more danger than it is now. There have been too many killings connected to the list. If you can't do it, I'll have to think of another way.'

He told her about the break-in.

She was tapping her fingers on the table, like a jack-hammering leg. 'I've got to get back to Moscow asap. The team's getting edgy. They're thinking the General and me are keeping them in the dark.' She forced an embarrassed grin. 'We are, for their own sakes. And now he's keeping *me* in the dark."

Scott thought for a minute. Unless he's dead.

'It may be that the kidnappers aren't working for the Kremlin,' he said.

'Yeah, I know. This is some complicated shit.'

He leant forward and lowered his voice. 'I've got an extra-special favour to ask you.'

'Oh yeah, what's that?'

'I want to tell Gravchenko about this. I know we're on opposite sides in one sense, but we're also on the same side in another: we both want to know what's going on. I was the one who told the General about the list of names in the first place.'

'I know. You can tell him everything. And you can also tell him we haven't found any dirt on him, after five years of investigation.'

Scott squeezed her hand. 'Thank you, Yelena.'

She sighed.

'Another thing,' Scott said.

'What?'

'Do you know why Orlov was on the same plane as Zletov? Was he also going to meet my boss? I keep forgetting to ask him.'

'We don't know.' She looked at him, as if wanting to say something more, but deciding against it. 'Not yet found his name in the documents.'

Ah, but what had she found out from other sources?

She averted his gaze.

Scott decided not to push it at that moment.

'I've been thinking while we're talking,' Scott said. 'Whichever way we look at it, secure digital communication between us is going be nigh on impossible.'

'I know, so how do we deal with it?'

'As you said. Go back to Cold War days. No telecommunicating. Face to face only.'

'How?'

'I can't expect you to try to get out of Russia every time something urgent crops up, so I'll come to Moscow. There's nothing suspicious in my going to the Foundation's Moscow office. I haven't been going there that much recently, but I'll get Gravchenko to tell them that I'll be paying more regular visits, to sort out some legal issues. Something like that. Then we can meet in person, in secret.'

Sergey texted him:

Click on this link

It was an English language breaking-news website.

The scrolling text drained Scott's blood from his face.

He thumped the table. 'For Christ's sake! Didn't I warn you?! Didn't I warn you?' he said in English.

Chapter 30

Day Twenty-one: 8.45am, Paris

Scott stared at the news link Sergey had sent to him the previous day, while he waited patiently for a note to be delivered to his room in the Le Tsuba Hotel located in Paris's 17th arrondissement, two-minutes from the Arc de Triomphe and the Champs-Elysées:

> At 7.45 this morning CET Professor Consuela Zapatero's car crashed into a wall in the Place de l'Alma underpass in Paris when a passing motorcyclist shot into her chauffeur-driven vehicle. The driver was killed instantly. Professor Zapatero received non-life-threatening injuries...

How's that for credible evidence, Professor?

The note arrived with a time and address: 11.30am at a private apartment in the École Militaire in the 7th arrondissement.

It was across the Seine from his hotel. He would take a lazy stroll there while working on his opening speech and line of questioning.

Yelena had left Malta the previous afternoon on her clandestine, and dangerous, journey back to Moscow, after Scott had told her about the attack on Professor Zapatero.

Neither of them had said goodbye with a smile.

Scott had flown to Paris that same evening after receiving a text from the professor requesting him to meet her there, urgently.

Of all the names on Carey's list, Santorini had been the most prominent: from the Prague press conference to

Pravda's kidnappers demanding Orlov's papers; papers that, according to Yelena, confirmed Santorini to be a mega money laundromat. Moreover, Wyatt's circumstantial link to the Foundation, through Yazov and Bauer, might be sufficient for the court of public opinion to be convinced that the Foundation was Gravchenko's baby and involved in money-laundering, despite strong denials of any connection.

The situation wasn't helped by Scott's deep concern for General Pravda's well-being.

11.30am

There was no sign of a protection detail in the street outside the apartment block, but as soon as Scott's finger aimed at the buzzer to the professor's apartment, he was pushed into the wall, face first.

'Please do not struggle, monsieur,' a female voice said in polite accented English, as a hand gripped him tightly by the back of the neck so he couldn't move his head.

Another hand patted him down and removed his wallet from his jacket pocket.

He wasn't carrying anything that would cause concern to security personnel.

Apart from the hand holding his neck in place, the body search was gentle. It wasn't a random mugging.

He waited, saying nothing.

'Okay, monsieur, you can turn round,' the female voice said in English.

An armed woman and two armed men, all three in uniform of some sort, stood in front of him.

'Sorry for that, Monsieur Mitchell,' the woman said, again in English, and handed him back his wallet. 'You can go inside now. Second floor.' She stepped away. 'The lift does not work today.'

A safety precaution or lack of servicing?

'*Merci*.' Scott straightened his clothes.

One of the armed men opened the door for him.

The other was on the phone.

Scott's limited French was enough to understand the words 'He's coming up now.'

The professor opened the door to him, her left arm in a sling.

Outwardly she looked confident, not shaken up.

'Thank you for coming to see me.'

He wouldn't have missed it for the world.

'I'm sorry about your driver.' Scott didn't know what else to say. He hadn't known the driver and he barely knew her.

She nodded. 'Follow me, please.'

She led Scott into a sparsely but expensively furnished living room with Rothko prints on the walls, dark oak flooring, a leather-covered two-seater couch and two matching high-backed chairs; an aquarium, three floor-to-ceiling pine book shelves, fully-stocked, and two glass coffee tables.

'Sit here, please.'

She pointed to one of the chairs, separated from the couch by a coffee table.

Scott obliged.

She sat on the couch.

A young woman walked into the room.

'Would you like something to drink, monsieur?' she said in French.

'A glass of still water, please,' he replied in French. 'And a green tea, if I may.'

'*Oui*, monsieur.'

She turned to the professor.

'An orange juice, Jamila, please.' She also replied in French.

The young woman nodded and left the room.

Scott waited for Zapatero to speak first, though he was urging to scream at her.

'You are right,' she said, pointing at her sling. 'This is

the credible evidence.' She spoke in a tone of controlled anxiety.

'The question for me is,' Scott said, 'why *you*? But before you answer, Professor. I owe you an apology. When we last met and I told you about the metaphorical hit list, I wasn't being honest with you. It's a *real* hit list and your name is on it, with others, two of whom are dead.'

Her face dropped.

'But why? What list? I don't understand.'

Scott told her the history of the list and of the deaths of those on it or associated with it, and about the break-in at his apartment.

'But why didn't you tell me when met in London?'

'Yes, I realise now that maybe I should have done but I wasn't sure why your name was on the list. To put it crudely, I didn't know whose side you were on.'

She straightened. 'Are you sure now?'

'The Paris attack has convinced me,' Scott said. 'Sorry for doubting you.'

'And the other names?'

'Well, Santorini is a Russian money-laundering vehicle.'

Her eyes flickered at the mention of the company.

'Arkady Orlov, he was connected to Santorini, and I'm still trying to find out who Simone Bisset is.'

He still didn't know where to begin, with so many similar name hits on the internet.

The professor fidgeted uneasily in her chair and bit on her bottom lip.

Scott pretended not to notice it.

'So there you have it, Professor, but I'm still none the wiser as to what somebody thinks you've done to warrant an assassination attempt. As we discussed in London, it doesn't make sense that the hit was ordered by Russians; you'd argued vociferously for the withdrawal of the sanctions imposed on them.

She leant forward and lowered her voice.

'It is important we talk in confidence, Mr Mitchell. The strictest confidence. You must never repeat anything I say, to *anybody*, unless I authorise it. Do you understand me?'

Her eyes challenged him.

'In principle,' Scott said, 'I can guarantee not to repeat anything that you say, though I'm not prepared to commit perjury if I'm called to give sworn testimony about it.' It was a worst-case scenario, but he doubted he would ever be subpoenaed to give such evidence. Who knew about the meeting, apart from Jamila and the security guards?

She bit her lip again.

'Although,' he said, 'I could always refuse to answer and claim lawyer-client privilege. That is, if you're about to ask for my legal advice on something.'

'I want to ask you for legal advice,' she said without hesitation.

Cute.

There was a knock at the door.

'Come in,' she said.

Jamila brought in a tray with the drinks, a selection of biscuits and some napkins.

She put them on the coffee table and removed the tray.

'*Merci*, Jamila,' Zapatero said.

Jamila nodded and left the room.

'Please, help yourself.'

'Thank you.' Scott picked up his glass of water and a biscuit.

Zapatero didn't touch her drink, but selected a chocolate biscuit and napkin.

'Before you say anything further,' Scott said. 'Now you're my client, I have to advise you that I have told my other client, Konstantin Gravchenko, about my concern for David Carey's investigations and he has agreed to help me investigate the matter. This is because somebody has allegedly linked his Foundation to at least one of the actors involved in the investigations.'

'How is this a matter for me?'

'Well, it may be that what you want to tell me is something that could affect Mr Gravchenko's Foundation. If it did, I'd be duty bound to tell him, and that would conflict me.

A less scrupulous lawyer wouldn't have warned her of that.

But Scott was Scott, and she was to be his client, at least for the length of their conversation.

If she accepted the caveat, he wouldn't be conflicted.

'I understand.' She stared at Scott, as if weighing him up. 'You may tell Mr Gravchenko.'

Relief.

He'd worry about telling Yelena, and Pravda if he ever appeared again, later.

'I have helped David Carey with his investigation into the sanctions-busting,' she said, as she leant forward to pick up her glass of orange juice.

Her hand was shaking.

She took a sip and quickly put the glass back on the table.

What was the American expression? "It came straight out of left field."

If Scott's eyes had opened any wider they would have obliterated the rest of his face.

'Let me explain, please.'

Be my guest, Professor. Take as long as you like. All night if need be. I'm not leaving here until I get to the bottom of this matter.

'Of course,' Scott said.

'I first met David Carey 18 months ago, at one of the EU's social functions. He knew of my opposition to the sanctions. He told me of his experiences in Eastern Europe and Russia, before he was a Member of Parliament...'

Costello's information confirmed.

'It was small talk, nothing else. I never met him again until six months ago. He asked me to help him. He was investigating the sanctions-busters and he wanted to know if I had knowledge of them from my own research into the economic effects of the sanctions on both the West and Russia.'

She paused.

He sensed her doubts creeping in about how much she could confide in him.

Keep going, please keep going.

'This *is* in confidence, Professor Zapatero.'

'I wanted to help him, because although I do not agree with the sanctions, I also do not agree with the sanctions-busting. It creates a black economy that distorts the markets.'

Scott wasn't an economist, but he could see why and how some black economies could literally be lifesavers for some countries.

'I understand. So what did you do?'

'I gave him extracts of confidential information from my research papers. I had sourced them in the EU Commission's libraries of proceedings. I did not apply for permission to make this information public.'

Slowly, slowly. Don't spook her.

'And you would like me to advise you of your legal position in connection with passing this information to David Carey?' he said in a light, matter-of-fact tone.

'Yes...please,' she said with hesitation.

He drew in a deep breath. 'Well, to do that, I need to know how and where you got your information from.'

She raised her eyebrows.

'Why?'

He wanted to say: because, Professor Zapatero, your answer to this question could lead me to finding out if there's any link between the sanctions-busters and

Santorini. If there isn't, it would be another box ticked. But she would immediately recognise that he wasn't advising her on her legal position.

'Because, if you obtained the information in a lawful manner, except for not asking for permission, you probably wouldn't have committed any serious offence and the information could be used in evidence in a prosecution against the sanctions-busters. But, if you obtained it, and have used it, unlawfully, for example in a breach of the terms of your employment contract with the EU Commission, you might get some smart-arse lawyer...' he said dismissively '...who's got it in for you and who might try to prosecute you for an illegal act. But there's the remotest of possibilities of that happening.'

It wasn't bullshit, but he wouldn't get any more than a "weak pass" in an exam for expounding a general principle that was vaguely related to the question asked. 'That's my understanding of *English* law, at any rate. EU law might be different.'

And don't ask me about Spanish law.

She screwed up her face. 'I see. I will think about it.'

Bugger. He'd lost her.

'But this is not everything,' she said.

It gets better.

'Please, do carry on.'

'Two weeks before his death David gave me his dossier, as he called it, about his investigations. He gave it to me for safe-keeping. He was convinced he was under surveillance and he didn't trust anybody. People were threatening him. Telling him to stop the investigation.'

Scott's heart raced, 16 to the dozen.

'Do you mean the *hard* copy dossier?'

'Yes. He didn't trust digital transmissions.'

'That's what Diane Costello told me.'

The professor had Carey's papers, dossier.

He'd found the Holy Grail.

Which of the 1,000 questions should he ask first?

He leant forward.

'Professor, do you have this dossier with you. If so, may I—'

'No, I do not,' she said apologetically. 'The dossier was stolen from my apartment in Brussels the day before David was assassinated.'

No! When one door opens, another slams in your face.

'So you were targeted?'

'The police say it was a random burglary, probably a drug addict.'

'Did this *drug addict* take anything else?'

'Nothing of any monetary value. A few cheap mementos that my ten-year-old daughter, Sarah, bought back from her holiday trips: sea shells, badges, model dolphins, that is all. But the burglar did damage the furniture with a knife.'

'Did you tell the police that sensitive papers had been stolen?'

'No, I did not,' she said emphatically.

'Was that because you obtained the information unlawfully, illegally?'

'Are you still my lawyer?'

'Yes.'

'The answer is, I prefer not to tell you.'

Scott laughed. 'You're learning. But seriously, a drug addict who steals only boring sanctions-busting information and a few cheap holiday trinkets? How much does that sell for in the local bar?'

'Yes. It is a stupid explanation. If I think about it too much, I shall be paranoid. I will not trust anybody.'

Quis custodiet ipsos custodes?

'You didn't have time to make your own copy, by any chance? Bearing in mind how important the dossier was.'

'Yes, I did, I uploaded it to my cloud account.'

Brilliant!

'Would you allow me access to this account? The information in the dossier might lead to David Carey's assassin and the reason why the others were killed and somebody is trying to kill you.'

A long sigh and she sank back into the sofa, a twisted look on her face.

'No, I am sorry.'

'But why not? I'm not asking for the password. You can access it for me and I will read the documents in your presence, under your supervision.'

Why tell him about it if she had no intention of letting him get at the information?

'I don't have access any longer.'

What?!

'I'm sorry,' Scott said. 'I don't understand.'

She took another sip of her orange juice and replaced the glass immediately on the table. Her hand was still quivering.

'I set up the account with my ex-partner, Sarah's father, so he would also have access, if something happened to me.' She pointed at her sling. 'I did not trust anybody else.' She frowned. 'But now he has changed the password and will not tell me what the new one is.'

What the heck is going on here?

'My partner and I have separated. We are now fighting a very angry custody battle for Sarah. It is a new development. Something has happened to him these last few days and he is being very uncooperative. It is so sudden.'

Scott needed to speak with him.

Tread carefully.

'Does he live here in Paris or Brussels?'

'No. He lives in Tel Aviv with Sarah. It is stable for her there. Her father's parents are there. Mine are no longer alive. I commute between Barcelona, my family home, Brussels and Strasburg. But I am prepared to settle in Brussels, where there are many good schools for her,' she said wistfully.

Oh, Jesus.

Emotions versus rationality.

'What is he doing in Tel Aviv?'

He is a visiting Professor of Marine Conservation at Tel Aviv University.'

'What's your partner's name?'

Scott could see a trip to Israel coming on.

'Dr Alan Fleischmann.'

He knew the name Fleischmann from somewhere.

'Does *partner* mean he's your husband?'

'No, we are not married.'

'I'm certainly not a family lawyer, but does that fact mean you will have a greater entitlement to custody, as Sarah's birth mother?'

He needed as much information as possible, in order to work out how to approach Dr Fleischmann.

'What is it you lawyer's say? "It's not straight forward." The lawyers are fighting over which law applies and the correct legal forum. Do you understand what I mean?'

Only too well.

'Of course, and I am truly sorry that you have all this trouble. Really I am.'

'I do not know what to do,' she said. 'I'd give up everything to get Sarah back.'

He wasn't a family counsellor, he didn't want to get involved.

'Do Sarah and Dr Fleischmann know about what happened to you yesterday?'

'Alan does. He hasn't told Sarah. He doesn't want to worry her. At least we agree on *one* thing.'

'Will he be coming to Paris, or Brussels, to visit you?'

'It is not necessary. I am not badly hurt.'

Scott screwed up his face.

‘What is it?’ Zapatero said.

‘Look, Professor, I know you have other, more important, matters on your mind, but you mustn’t dismiss the attempted assassination on you yesterday. There’s no escaping from the fact that you’re on the hit list.

‘What are you saying to me?’

‘I’m saying that it is *very* important that I get access to the dossier. So, I’d like to meet with Dr Fleischmann as soon as possible.

‘Good luck with that,’ she scoffed.

‘If you don’t ask, you don’t get.’

She massaged her sling.

‘Yes,’ she said. ‘I understand. Alan will be doing research in London tomorrow for ten days. I shall call him today and tell him you are advising me on the documents and you would like to discuss the matter with him. Would that help?’

And some!

‘Please, that would be very kind of you. But please don’t mention any names on the phone. Like you, I’m in danger of becoming paranoid, but better safe than sorry.’

‘I cannot guarantee he will see you.’

‘You can only do what you can do, and it’s much appreciated.’ Scott took a sip of his tea. It was cold, though he didn’t show it.

‘By the way, who knew you were helping David Carey?’

‘Nobody, except Alan.’

‘And whoever tried to kill you yesterday,’ Scott added.

She closed her eyes.

Somebody had discovered that Professor Zapatero was feeding David Carey with the sanctions-busting information and that she had his dossier. That was a plausible explanation for the theft of the dossier and the attempt on her life. As far as the public knew, she was effectively the sanctions-busters' lobbyist in the EU, with her advocacy for economic growth over international politics. Nobody knew about her double life, except Carey himself...and Fleischmann, a man with whom she was in a bitter child custody dispute.

People in custody disputes have been known to do the craziest of things.

'There is *one* thing,' she said.

What more could there possibly be?

'Please, tell me.'

'There is a lobbyist for the lifting of the sanctions. He is a pest. He is like...how you say? The dog with the bone. His name is Roberto Silvano Pappalardo.'

Scott hadn't seen his name in any of his searches.

'Do go on, please.'

'He is a Maltese national and likes to be called Bobby. There are rumours in the EU. They say he is connected to that company called Santorini.'

It gets better and better.

'Do you remember any particular names in the dossier? Individuals or companies?'

'I did not read it when David Carey gave it to me. I had other things on my mind. I only skimmed it when it was in the cloud account.'

'But did you see the name of Santorini there? And how about the other names of Sir Stanton Morgan Bell, Arkady Orlov and Simone Bisset?'

'I only remember Santorini.'

'Why that specifically?'

'It's a name I know. Santorini is a Greek island. My parents owned a villa there when I was a teenager.'

'Do you remember what David Carey said about the company?'

'No. I'm sorry.'

She was looking tired, flagging.

'Okay, I shall leave you alone now,' Scott said. 'I'm

sure you could do with a rest. You've been very helpful. Thank you.'

'Thank you for coming to see me, Scott.'

She led him to the front door.

'One last thing, if I may,' Scott said.

'Yes?'

'This Bobby Pappalardo pest character. Could you find out more information about him? I'm not asking you to break any laws or confidences, but to keep an ear out for rumours. You know the kind: water-cooler gossip in the Commission's corridors of power? Do the rumours have any substance?'

'What? Rumours about the sanctions and the Russians, you mean?'

'Anything, rumours about anything involving the man, his public life, his private life, anything. I want to build a profile on him.'

'Yes, I understand. I will try for you.'

'Thanks, but please do be careful, he may be dangerous.'

'The Commission is giving me protection, 24/7.'

Chapter 31

Day Twenty-two: 9.45am, Moscow

Pravda had made Yelena accompany him on a 35-minute walk from Park Krasnya Presnya to his favourite artisan café, the English-language named *HuggaMug Café*, on Arbat Street in the Bohemian district of the capital.

She'd displayed the annoyance and reluctance of a small child by lagging two or three paces behind him at every opportunity and conducting the episode in silence.

'So, *General* Pravda,' she said as they sipped their coffees at one of the only two tables on street, the other being unoccupied. 'Are you going to tell me why you vanished into thin air three days ago?'

Her tone was that of a mother admonishing her teenage son who'd stayed out all night without warning.

He sympathised and accepted that he had only himself to blame. She must have been worried sick about his absence; it coming so soon after his kidnapping outside the Bolshoi Theatre.

'We're not going to be able to undertake a complete review of the Orlov papers if we remain in Moscow,' Pravda said. 'Or anywhere in Russia, for that matter. Too many eyes and ears.'

'Tell me something I hadn't worked out for myself,' she said dismissively.

'I've been setting up an alternative, temporary, base in Budapest.'

'What?' She frowned. 'You just jumped on a plane at Sheremetyevo, or wherever, and flew to Hungary without telling me or the rest of the team? You know that Max...'

she paused '...whoever's replaced him, monitors all our traffic. Passport control tells the FSB. Bang. Suspicious activity. Pravda's left the country without telling the team. What's he up to? Let's investigate.' She shook her head. 'I don't understand you.'

Pravda bit his lip to stop himself from smiling at his protégé.

'Not quite,' he said. 'But I'm not going to tell you how I got there.'

Did she smile at that revelation?

The grumpiness melting?

Pravda had employed one of his emergency escape routes. None of them was foolproof; they all carried risks, risks he felt compelled to take in the current climate. He'd left Moscow three hours after Max's assassination and rented a vehicle for cash and with a false ID. Many vehicle owners were only too pleased to earn their living off the books, and they couldn't give a damn about who the hirer was. It had taken him ten hours to drive to St. Petersburg where, as pre-arranged, he'd left the vehicle with a friend of the owner. From there he'd taken a 150-kilometre drive to the border with the Estonian town of Narva – again with the pre-arranged help of people who lived in the black economy – and from where he crossed the border hidden in the back of a truck stacked to the limits with contraband vodka, including a couple of crates each for the two underpaid Russian border guards and their counterparts in Estonia.

Once in Narva, an old Estonian secret service friend flew him from a local abandoned airfield to the country's capital Tallinn, from where he took a chartered jet to Budapest, using a fake Estonian passport.

It had been exhausting and costly, but time was against him.

'They're everywhere, the bastards,' Yelena said, looking up and down the crowded pedestrian area. 'I bet they're looking at us now.' She waved at the CCTV cameras. 'Hi comrades!' She turned back to Pravda. 'So how do we get to Budapest without being noticed?' She waved her hand at the CCTV system again. 'With all this around. Do we use Steve McQueen's escape tunnels?'

Pravda chuckled. Everybody in Russia must have been allowed to see *The Great Escape* after the collapse of the Soviet Empire. 'He used a motorbike.'

She widened her eyes. 'A Harley?!'

'No.'

'He should have done. He wouldn't have got caught.' At last she was lightening up.

'We *hide* right in front of their faces,' Pravda said. 'We fly out from Moscow on a regular passenger plane, using our real IDs, with genuine short-stay visas.'

'What the f—?'

'We tell the team we've got something on Gravchenko and we're going to do some digging in Budapest, to confirm it. Max's replacement will be listening in, but they won't object because that's where Gravchenko's based and we'll be doing what they want us to do – finding some dirt on the man.'

For the first time that day, Yelena exhibited a broad grin.

'We'll make sure they see our instructions and reports going backwards and forwards between the two cities. Business as normal.'

'Okay, I get it,' she said. 'When does Max's 28 days expire?'

'In ten days, by my reckoning.'

'What happens to us if we've haven't dug up anything?'

'I'm not sure,' Pravda said. He didn't want to frighten her unnecessarily. 'But it wouldn't surprise me if it was all Max's doing in the first place. The *siloviki* threaten him if he doesn't find anything and he threatens us.'

'Covering his arse, as usual,' Yelena sniggered.

'Perhaps, but it didn't work. He gets killed and the threat dies with him.'

'Another coffee?' she said.

'Good idea. And I *will* have a cinnamon roll this time. Thanks.'

She got up and as she passed by him she squeezed his shoulder. 'I forgive you, General Leonid Igorovich Pravda. I forgive you. But please never do it again.'

Over-familiarity for sure. Not the way to address her superior. Nonetheless, he wanted to hug her. Nobody was indispensable, but he was damn sure he couldn't operate without her, and her trust.

His eyes welled up.

Though he'd tried lightly to instil the idea in Yelena that the ultimatum had died with Max, it would remain on his list of issues until events convinced him that it was no longer valid.

Yelena arrived with the coffees.

'How are we going to get a set of Orlov's papers to Budapest?' she said. 'The FSB might let us go there, but it doesn't mean they won't search our luggage on the way out.' She hissed. 'What's to stop them letting us through with our hand luggage but searching our suitcases before they get into the hold, and nicking or copying the papers?'

'They're in Budapest,' Pravda said. 'And uploaded to new cloud accounts. I'll give you the access codes when we arrive there.'

'What, all three sets?'

'No, only one. The other two are still buried at the dacha and in the river bank.'

'But how did you...I mean. You must have taken a hell of a risk to pick them up from the railway locker and smuggle them out of the country. You remember the shoot-up in 2016 when Scott Mitchell tried to do the same sort of thing?'

Yes, he remembered Mitchell's foolhardy acts only too well, but the lad had survived.

'Yelena, I'm not going to tell you how I did it; for your own good. But I *shall* tell you if we ever have to do it again. I promise.'

She shrugged. 'Okay, you're the boss.'

No grumps, no growls, no "you-don't-trust-me" outbursts. She'd forgiven him.

Pravda's retired Estonian secret service friend, who'd flown him to Tallinn, had been operating a channel for getting sensitive documents out of Russia for years. He'd set up a company called the Narva Educational Institution. He worked out of his apartment in that city and distributed information about high schools and universities in Estonia, most of which he'd cut and pasted from the internet. He was respected for only charging the Estonian equivalent of $5 per pack. He obviously wasn't in it for the money. He'd made enough of that in his years of moonlighting in the intelligence services and later as a security guard to wealthy families, until somebody had disintegrated his spleen with an automatic.

Pravda had downloaded from the net 50 pages on crystallography, in French. He'd used a friend's Wi-Fi connection, putting 20 on top of the Orlov bundle and spreading the remaining 30 throughout the rest of it. Then he'd sent them by international courier to the *French Dept. Narva Educational Institute* at the PO Box number provided. He'd described the contents as *educational research papers* and given a false return address in Moscow.

If the package was intercepted or lost, it wouldn't be fatal as he still had the other sets buried in his garden.

'Right,' Yelena said. 'My Malta trip with Mitchell.'

'I'm listening.'

She told him everything, but refused to tell him how she'd left Russia and got back in, undetected.

'Well, did I do right? Or what?'

Pravda whistled, softly. It was a hell of a risk, no matter how secure she thought her exit and re-entry route was. And there was no way of knowing if the Kremlin was shadowing her but had decided not to intervene.

Still, what else should she have done?

For all she knew, her boss could have been dead.

'Well, General. Don't prolong the agony. At least put me out of my misery.'

'Why Scott Mitchell?' he said.

'We know each other. You respect him, he respects you. We're both working on the Carey hit list. Who else do I go to when you're lying dead in a mushroom patch riddled with bullets?'

Lying dead in a mushroom patch riddled with bullets.

Yelena had a way with words.

'You did the right thing,' Pravda said. 'If our positions were reversed, I would have done the same.'

The look of relief on her face was palpable.

'I'm sorry to say that Scott Mitchell is now probably the only person we can trust with our confidences. You were right to open up the channel with him again.'

'Phew,' she sighed. 'What about the people helping you in Budapest? Can we trust them?'

'No guarantee, but I've tried to limit the risks. I've put them into cells, units. No cell knows of the existence of the other. I've got the Hungarian immigration officials, who are helping us, in one cell. The real estate brokers who've found our office for the Gravchenko investigation in a second cell; another broker who's found a smaller office where we can concentrate on Orlov – I call it the Orlov Office – in the third cell, and a city gofer who'll do anything for us at the appropriate price.'

'So that's everything covered.'

'Not so fast.'

'What do you mean?'

'You're probably too young to remember, but in 2002, Donald Rumsfeld, the US Secretary of State for the Defense Department, made what was his most famous sound bite. He said that in strategic planning concepts there are "unknown unknowns".'

She pulled a face. 'What are they?'

'They're future outcomes, events, consequences, things we can't predict when we're planning a course of action. A lot of people laughed at him at the time. But it makes sense. You can't know all possible eventualities.'

'Doesn't apply to computers and chess games. Don't they keep beating the Grand Masters now?'

'Yes, they do. But we're not dealing with logical minds. We're dealing with the irrational actions of humans. And in our case these are humans who've shown they're willing to kill to get what they want. If that's not irrational, I don't know what is.'

'I bet it's rational to psychopaths,' Yelena said.

Chapter 32

Day Twenty-three: 10am, London

Scott had spent the previous day tidying up a loose end. He and Tom Burrows, who'd interrupted his business meetings in Germany, had persuaded Jonathan Carey that he would be safer in the States for a while, visiting his sister and niece. It was far too dangerous for him to remain in London while his attackers were still at a large and hadn't got what they wanted from him.

Jonathan had reluctantly agreed and Tom introduced him to the probate firm who were dealing with his father's estate, after which they instructed another firm of specialist lawyers to press the police for the return of the cabinets and contents they'd seized from the storage company.

Meanwhile, Scott arranged to clean up Jonathan's house from top to bottom, get the boxes in the front room collected by the charity and replace the locks, including on the window catches.

Jonathan agreed to stay with Tom at his father's house for a few days until he was to fly to the States.

Scott called Dr Fleischmann on the number provided by Zapatero.

'Hello?'

'Is that Dr Fleischmann?'

'I am *Professor* Fleischmann, yes.'

Whoops, nothing like getting off on the wrong foot.

'Sorry, Professor Fleischmann, my name is Scott Mitchell. I believe Professor Zapatero has told you to expect a call from me.'

‘What do you want?’ Fleischmann said in a gruff tone.

A smile in your voice, perhaps.

‘I’d like to discuss something with you, face to face. The professor has told me you’re in London this week. Could we meet, today? It’s very important.’

‘What’s so urgent that you want to discuss it with me, *today*?’

‘Didn’t the professor give you any idea?’ Perhaps she’d misjudged him and he hadn’t understood what she’d meant by “documents”.

‘I wouldn’t be asking, if she had.’

This was heavy going.

‘When we meet, I shall tell you, Professor Fleischmann.’

‘You work for Konstantin Gravchenko’s World Preservation Foundation. Is that correct?’

‘Yes. In fact, I—’

‘I will talk about the Foundation, Fleischmann said. ‘You will *not* talk about the custody case. Those are my conditions. Take it or leave it.’

Yes sir! Even Gravchenko didn’t adopt such an attitude. He would always listen to what the other side had to say even if he’d made up his mind long before the meeting had begun.

Interesting, though, bringing the Foundation into it.

‘Yes, that’s okay with me.’

‘Be at the Pavilion Café at the Greenwich Maritime Museum at four this afternoon.’

‘Thank you, Prof—’

The line went dead.

4pm

Fleischmann was typing on a tablet when Scott arrived. He recognised him from his profile image on the university’s website: early fifties, a full head of smartly groomed dark brown hair and wearing a navy blue suit, cream shirt and a black tie with spots. With his rimless glasses he resembled a mature 1990s accountant, rather than a 21st-century science professor who was trying to look cool.

Scott stood at his table.

'Professor Fleischmann, I'm Scott Mitchell.' He held out his hand.

'Sit down,' Fleischmann said, gesturing to the seat opposite him, but not offering to shake Scott's hand.

'Thank you for agreeing to see me at such short notice,' Scott said.

'If you mention one word of the custody case, I shall walk out of here. Is that clear?'

Fleischmann locked on to Scott with challenging eyes.

'You made that abundantly clear on the phone. I haven't come here to talk about your custody case. I'm not a family lawyer. I'm a—'

'You're a human rights lawyer who, with your Russian oligarch boss, wants to turn the planet green.' Fleischmann swivelled his tablet around so that Scott could see the screen, showing the Foundation's home page.

Scott pretended to show an avid interest in it.

He'd seen it a 1,000 times before.

'What about it?'

Fleischmann took the tablet back.

'There's no water there,' he said.

'Pardon?' What was the man talking about?

'The rivers, the seas, the oceans. There's nothing on your website about them. Seventy per cent of the planet is covered with water and the oceans hold 95 per cent of it. They contain organisms that are essential to the world's food chain.' He slammed the tablet closed. 'Yet your Foundation has ignored the topic, completely ignored it.' He leant into Scott. 'We die if we don't have water and these organisms, Mr Mitchell. *We die.*'

Fleischmann sat back, with a "what-are-you-going-to-do about-it" look.

"Unexpected" was the understatement to beat all understatements.

The course of the discussion had thrown Scott completely.

'I'm a Professor of Marine Conservation. The leading authority on the topic,' Fleischmann continued. 'Your Foundation wants to save the planet. Give me a $5 million grant so I can fund my university's research into marine conservation and I will give you the cloud account holding the Carey dossier.'

Now Scott had the measure of the man. Two days earlier somebody had tried to kill the mother of his child; the information in Carey's dossier could lead to who was responsible for the attack, but Fleischmann was more concerned with furthering his career.

Chapter 33

Day Twenty-four: 6.45pm, Prague

Security was tight at the entrance to the Cuckoo restaurant's private dining room on the top floor, with its airport-style body scanners followed by a hand "pat down" from the tallest person Scott had ever seen, a Russian-speaking Croatian called Boško.

He was well over two metres.

'What about the women?' Scott asked Boško. 'Who gets to pat *them* down?'

Boško grinned widely and waved his hands at Scott.

Scott shook his head. 'I don't think so.' He could see the comments on social media after a secret video of Boško's wandering hands appeared with a photo-shopped image of Gravchenko and the Foundation's logo in the background.

'I do it,' a woman's voice said in English.

Behind Boško's torso and elderly woman, fiddling with a phone, was sitting on a chair in the corner.

'That's great,' Scott replied.

'My mother,' Boško said.

Scott nodded to her and went into the room.

He was the first attendee to arrive.

He grabbed a glass of orange juice from a tray held by an eager young waiter, while monitoring the staff as they completed the settings at the 13-seater table in the centre of the room: five places either side, two at the top and one at the other end. He walked round the table and examined the name tags, each also bearing the diner's country. He and Gravchenko were to sit at the top, with Arjun Shastri at the far end. Hao Murat would be sitting halfway down on Scott's right, with his back to the window, in between the two women investors from China and Malaysia.

'Aha, my friend, we meet again,' a Russian voice said.

Scott looked up as Murat approached him with a wide smile and his hand held out.

'Hao,' Scott said, shaking his hand. 'Welcome to Prague. Is this your first time here?'

'Yes, I only arrived this morning. There are lots of places I must visit and take images before I return to Astana.' He took his phone from his pocket and waved it at Scott. 'How did we live without these for so long, eh?'

The room was filling up as more guests arrived and Scott was conscious that his eyes were wandering while his conversation with Murat continued. He didn't like that habit in other people and tried to curb his own inclinations do it.

Arjun Shastri appeared at the entrance door, and was having difficulty getting through the security checks; the alarm wouldn't stop beeping.

'Excuse me, Hao. Mr Shastri needs some help.'

'Oh. Yes, yes. You go.'

'Arjun, what's the matter?' Scott said in English. Although Arjun spoke Russian to Gravchenko in Budapest, every Indian bureaucrat, entrepreneur and lawyer Scott had met in his travels spoke near perfect English grammar and syntax, despite having a heavy accent.

'I sometimes have trouble with these contraptions,' Arjun replied. 'I have a few metal plates in my body.'

'Let him through, please,' Scott said in Russian to Boško. 'I will vouch for him.'

Though for how long, remained to be seen.

Boško moved aside.

'Thank you,' Shastri continued in English. 'I'm sorry I should have told you.'

'I don't see why,' Scott said. 'I didn't realise the security would be this strict.'

'Well, that's Konstantin Gravchenko for you.' Shastri looked around the room. 'Am I the last to arrive?'

'Yes, it would appear so, apart from Mr Gravchenko, that is,' Scott said.

'Indeed, apart from Mr Gravchenko.'

Scott called Sergey.

'Hi Sergey. How far away are you? We're all here.'

'Stuck in a tailback on the outskirts of the city. A truck has shed its load. We can't go forward or back. The boss says you'll have to keep them happy until we arrive.'

Here we go again. 'How long do you reckon?'

'Good question. I'll update you when I get more information.'

Scott sighed. 'Okay.'

'Mr Gravchenko has been delayed,' he said to Shastri. 'Traffic jam. I'm going to start things off. You're sitting at the other end, down there.'

'Okay. We must speak later,' Arjun said.

Scott nodded.

You can bet your life on it, Mr Shastri.

He moved to the top of the table and tapped a knife on his glass. 'Ladies and gentlemen, may I have your attention please?' He addressed them in English. 'I certainly hope you all speak English, because regrettably I don't speak some of the languages I've seen indicated on your name tags this evening. My—'

'I don't speak English,' a male voice called out, in English. 'I only speak Australian.' A large heavily built man with a glass of champagne in his hand beamed at Scott.

Everybody laughed.

'Ah yes,' Scott said. 'Bill Rogers, isn't it?' He'd remembered the name tag.

'That's me, matey. Bill Rogers at your service.'

'Thank you, Bill. I'm looking forward to chatting with you.'

'Okay, I know when to shut up, even though I'm Australian.'

More laughter.

'For those of you who might not know, I'm Scott Mitchell, Chief Counsel to Mr Gravchenko's Foundation. The prime purpose of this dinner is a sort of getting-to-know-you exercise. Some of you may have met before, but I believe this is the first time that you're all together under one roof. Mr Gravchenko is on his way and he'll be speaking to you about this exciting new project that he hopes you'll all be getting involved with. Unfortunately, he's stuck in traffic, so he's asked that we begin our meal without him.'

'Does he speak English or Australian?' Bill said. 'Because I sure as hell don't speak Russian.'

'He's bringing a Russian-English interpreter with him.' Although Scott spoke Russian fluently, he wasn't a professional interpreter; that was a specialised discipline in itself.

Scott turned to Boško. 'Would you please tell the staff they may start serving?'

Boško nodded and trotted off.

Thankfully, there was little rumbling of discontent and the guests were quick to find their places, enticed no doubt by the immediate appearance of two wine waiters.

'Scott, matey, if ever you want a good ski package in Australia, Bill Rogers is your man.' He was Scott's immediate neighbour in the first seat on the left-hand side.

'Thanks Bill, I might take you up on that one day.'

'My pleasure, Scotty.' He nudged Scott and winked. 'Mates rates and all that.'

Scott smiled. 'What line of business are you in?'

'The markets call it the entertainment and leisure industry. We negotiate music distribution rights throughout the Asian Pacific area. We also own a string of five-star hotels, with casinos. The Asians are gambling mad.' He winked at Scott again.

'Interesting,' Scott said. How do you know about Mr Gravchenko and our Foundation?'

Bill nodded in Hao Murat's direction. 'I've been discussing with Hao the possibility of expanding into China. We got talking. One thing led to another. You know how it is.'

'Yes, it's been the story of my life,' Scott said. 'One thing leading to another.'

And how.

'Of course,' Bill continued. 'As the saying goes, "Behind every successful man, there's a woman." But in my case, there are three.'

Scott wasn't sure what he was getting at. 'How so?'

'My three daughters are passionate about climate change and environmental sustainability.' He grinned. 'So, here I am, about to see what this beautiful city of Prague has to offer me...'

A sudden shattering of glass drowned the diners' table chatter.

Shards rained down on the guests from the skylight.

Half a dozen or more armed personnel dressed in black with balaclavas and the word "Policia" emblazoned on their chests followed on ropes.

'What the fuck?' Bill said.

Nonplussed, rather than fearful, Scott said nothing. He was in charge of the event; if he showed signs of panic, the guests would follow.

'On floor,' they shouted in English. 'Everybody on floor.'

They sprayed bullets in all directions around the room, at the walls, the windows and back up to the ceiling.

'Hands on head! Hands on head!'

'Quick,' Scott said. 'Get under the table.' He didn't know what the police intentions were, but he'd been in stray-bullet situations before.

Bill didn't follow him.

Scott peered out.

Bill was standing his ground, as the other guests dropped to the floor and covered their heads as instructed.

'Who the fuck are you!?' he said.

More shooting, at the food and on the table, where cutlery and dishes shattered and flew everywhere.

'I said, who the fuck are you!?'

Two of the police grabbed Bill, dragged him across the floor and out of the room.

'You bastards are going to pay for this!' Bill shouted. 'Big time! Fucking big time!'

Scott was alone under the table.

An eerie silence fell on the scene.

'Everybody up! Everybody up!'

He peered out.

People rose to their feet and shook themselves free of the plaster and glass that had landed on them in the shooting.

'Hands on heads! Hands on heads!'

The police stood in a line, their weapons trained on the diners.

'What are you doing with us?' Murat said in English.

'I want talk to my embassy,' the Malaysian woman said.

A piercing siren filled the room.

Somebody shouted in English 'Fire! Fire! Building on fire! Out! Out! Out!'

It was Boško's husky voice.

Panic set in and it was everybody for themselves, including the police.

They rushed for the entrance, creating a bottleneck and shouting in a multitude of tongues.

Still under cover, Scott waited until the room cleared.

The fire alarm stopped and he hauled himself out from under the table.

Scott couldn't see or smell any smoke.

Something odd was taking place.

Gunshots rang out in the street below.

He peered through one of the bullet-shattered windows.

Armed police were herding the guests and others he didn't recognise into their vans while paramedics were performing CPR on two bodies in the middle of the street.

He couldn't identify the victims.

Firefighters arrived and disappeared from Scott's view as they approached the front of the building.

Crowds gathered in the street, many taking photos on their phones; passing cars slowed down – their occupants rubbernecking.

Voices on the staircase.

Czech language? He didn't know, much less who they belonged to.

Police or firefighters?

Prudence told him to exit at the other end of the room, where a parted curtain revealed a half-opened door. The logo on the wall at the side of the door read: *požární únik*. The first word was similar to the transliterated Russian for fire: *pozharnyy.*

The fire escape?

He darted through the doorway and down the stairs to the ground floor where he crashed through another fire escape door into a quiet street in the cool night air, in time to see a small red Fiat car with two occupants speed away from the kerbside. He didn't recognise the occupants or the model of the vehicle.

He collapsed against the wall, gathered his senses and called Sergey.

It went straight to voicemail:

'Sergey. We've been raided by armed police. They've shot the place up. A fire alarm and no fire. Everybody ran for their lives. Boško's disappeared. They're taking the guests away in vans. Two bodies, maybe dead, in the street. I don't know who they are. Couldn't see. Call me back as soon as possible.'

A police car approached, driving slowly as if they were searching for something, or somebody.

Scott flattened himself against the wall, hoping not to be seen in the darkness.

As the car reached him, the red, white and blue crossbar lights on the vehicle's roof rack flashed and the vehicle sped away with its sirens wailing.

Sergey texted him:

Get a taxi to Dejvická metro station and text me from there

There was little point in protesting, at least not while he was on the run.

Okay

He hugged the wall as he headed for the T-junction at the end of the street, where night lights from rows of shops and passing trams indicated it was a major road.

He turned right at the junction and followed street signs to the nearest metro station, mixing with the evening shoppers and tourists, occasionally glancing back in the direction of the Cuckoo restaurant, where all seemed quiet.

Over as quick as it had begun?

A row of taxis ahead were queuing outside a hotel for fares.

As he approached the first in line, two police cars screeched to a halt across the road.

He didn't wait around to see what was happening,

but swiftly moved on and gathered walking pace as he weaved in and out of the oncoming pedestrians.

Sirens screamed behind him.

A police car overtook him and slowed down, the occupants scanning the crowds.

He ran down the entrance steps to the Flora metro station entrance, vaulted the access barrier and ran to the nearest train, which was signalling its imminent departure. It was on the green line.

He'd travelled the Prague metro before. The city's public transport system operated on a paper ticket basis, which could be bought in stations, hotels, tobacconists and 100 other places. If he got caught without a ticket, he'd make up a sob story and pay the fine by credit card.

He checked the location of the Dejvická station on the map in the train. He was lucky; it was also on the green line.

He hovered inside the train at the open doorway and looked along the platform; he hadn't had time to check if anybody had been chasing him.

No sign of the police or station staff.

CCTV cameras were an everyday appendage to people's lives in most cities and Prague was no exception. There was little point in getting uptight. If he was spotted, he'd pour out the sob story.

General Pravda had taught him in 2016 how to check for people following him on the metro.

Scott put his lesson into practice while on the green line.

He got out at two stations en route to Dejvická: Muzeum and Malostranská, where he scampered up the escalators and immediately went back down again but remaining on one stair and looking behind to see if anybody was doing the same. When the next train arrived he got on and jumped off at the last second before the doors closed.

Nothing suspicious. If he had a tail, he'd shaken it.

A man was working on one of the ticket barriers at Dejvická and all the others were in the open position.

An official waved everybody through without checking the tickets.

Scott texted Sergey.

Arrived

The response was immediate:

Green Volvo under the Brno signpost at street level. Get in back

Scott did so after a confirmatory nod from the driver.

It was too soon for Scott to rationalise his evening's experience, though it fully occupied his mind. The bullets were real enough, but apart from the manhandling of Bill, the police's behaviour and their body language lacked the usual physical and psychological aggression he'd come to expect, either from personal experience or third-party evidence. The whole point of the psychological aggression was to put the fear of God in the targets, to make them more compliant.

Scott hadn't felt fear throughout the entire raid, though he conceded that the guests, except Bill, might have.

And where was Boško – and his mother?

The car stopped in a leafy suburb outside a high wooden gate, nestling in a three- to four-metre high hedgerow, with CCTV mounted on each side.

The gate opened and Sergey appeared.

Scott thanked the driver in Russian – though he had no idea what language the man spoke as the only noise he'd made throughout the short drive was a grunt – and got out.

The driver turned round and drove away.

'Strange fellow,' Scott said.

'He sees nothing, hears nothing, speaks nothing,' Sergey said enigmatically, and patted Scott on the back. 'Come.'

He led Scott along a half-moon paved driveway to the open front door, where Gravchenko was talking to somebody on the phone.

His boss ended the call, looked Scott up and down, and smiled.

'I'm glad *you're* happy, Kostya, because I'm not.'

Sergey peeled off and disappeared inside the house.

'This way,' Gravchenko said and went inside.

Too exhausted to vent his feelings on the doorstep, Scott said nothing more and followed his boss through the lobby and into a room at the end.

It was a small study or sitting room, with a glass-fronted bookcase to one side and an old-fashioned fireplace on the opposite side. Two fabric-covered armchairs faced each other in a recess, with closed floor-to-ceiling curtains, possibly hiding the back garden. A low wooden table, on which were two ashtrays, one full, the other empty, separated the two chairs. Dimmed chandelier-style ceiling lights failed to identify the colours of the furnishings. Paintings of animals and 19th-century soldiers decorated the panelled walls.

The place reeked of smoke.

Though claustrophobic the room was surprisingly relaxing. He'd recognised the furniture from catalogues: it was traditional pre-First World War Austro-Hungarian.

Gravchenko took one chair and Scott, the other. 'Do you want to freshen up before we talk?'

'No thanks. Not yet anyway.' He did, but an immediate explanation was more important to him. 'Would you please tell me what tonight was all about and where we're supposed to go from here.' The words came out more formally than he'd intended, though he didn't intend to sound disrespectful. But he couldn't understand why his boss was so calm when his mega-deal had taken the biggest hit imaginable.

Gravchenko lit a cigarette.

'This is the ugly side we're up against, ' he said, tapping his cigarette on the side of the full ashtray.

Scott pinched his eyes closed.

'No. I need more than that.'

He opened his eyes.

'I've got enemies,' Gravchenko said. 'They won't stop until they've destroyed me and the Foundation. These are *powerful* people,' he snarled.

Indeed, Scott had just experienced some of them first hand: police armed with automatics arresting 12 international oligarchs who were enjoying a quiet evening meal. It would certainly have taken a powerful group to arrange that and come out unscathed. 'Yes. But—'

'Tonight's raid wasn't official,' Gravchenko said. 'Some of the shooters were real police, moonlighting, but the others were local thugs for hire. They were paid to scare the shit out of all of us. They never shot to kill or injure.'

'What? I don't get it, Kostya. Who paid them?'

'I'm working on it.' Gravchenko squished the life out of his barely smoked cigarette in the ash tray.

'Scott remembered them firing up at the skylight and at the windows, but not at anybody directly.

He could barely keep his eyes open.

'The call I took earlier was from a top aide at the Ministry of Justice. The Czech prosecutor's office didn't know anything about it. My partners have been released and the shooters arrested.

Was there *anybody* Gravchenko couldn't influence?

Stupid thought. He obviously couldn't influence his enemies.

'It was their own dumbass fault.'

'How so?'

'The two people lying in the street. One died. The other one, an innocent pregnant woman caught in the crossfire, luckily survived and will make a good recovery.'

'Who died?' And what crossfire?'

Gravchenko hesitated, most unlike him.

'Arjun Shastri.'

There was a knock on the door.

'Yes!' Gravchenko snapped.

Sergey brought in a tray with four small bottles of water and a variety of nibbles.

'Something stronger to drink, Scott?' he asked.

Arjun Shastri? Scott's stomach flipped.

'Scott?' Sergey said.

'Er, no, no. Thanks, Sergey. This is fine.'

'Sorry there's nothing else to eat,' he said. 'We've not long arrived and I forgot to arrange for the food.'

'That's okay,' Scott said. 'Thanks anyway.'

'Boss?'

'No.'

Sergey left the room.

'I don't understand,' Scott said. 'How did it happen?'

'He pulled a gun on one of the shooters who was trigger happy.'

What was Kostya saying? Arjun never had a gun. He'd been through a body scanner... Scott rubbed his eyes, trying to stay the tiredness and replay the scene in the dining room. Oh shit! Astri's metal plates. Scott had waived him through the scanner before Boško could get his hands on him. What *had* he done?

'Where did he hide the gun?' Scott asked.

'In an ankle holster.'

Scott frowned.

'But why did he bring it and why did he pull it on the police, or whoever they were?'

Gravchenko shrugged.

'We don't know.'

Scott shook his head.

The evening had been a gigantic clusterfuck.

But what was done was done.

'I never got a chance to ask him about his son, Kabir,' Scott said.

Gravchenko lit another cigarette. 'Forget it. He's history.'

Scott wondered if his boss would ever dismiss him as *history*.

'Arjun, yes, but we've still got Santorini to investigate, and that's Kabir's company. I've got to make sure there's no hint of a credible link between the company and the Foundation.' He told his boss what Yelena had said at their meeting in Malta, not only about the Santorini accounts but also about the Kremlin's super-surveillance capabilities.

'Concentrate on Santorini.'

As before, he didn't seem concerned with the Kremlin revelations.

'Which brings me to Professor Zapatero and her estranged partner, Dr Alan Fleischmann, or *Professor*, as he likes being called,' Scott said.

'What about them?'

'Well...' Scott told him about his Paris meeting with her and the subsequent demands of Fleischmann. 'So you see, according to Professor Zapatero, the Carey dossier could well have important information on Santorini and God knows what else.'

Gravchenko extinguished his cigarette and took a handful of nibbles, which he swished down with a bottle of water.

'*You* deal with it,' he said. 'Any way you want. I don't have time. I've got to sort out tonight's shit storm. Restore confidence in my partners. Stop the rumours spreading.

I've got more partners in the pipeline. If I don't sort it now, my enemies have won. I was going public on the new deal tomorrow morning, when everybody'd confirmed their commitment, financially and morally.' He sucked in air between his teeth. 'But the bastards have beat me to it.' He drank another full bottle of water. 'It's on social media and breaking news timelines.'

Scott recalled the people in the street taking photos.

'It's damage limitation time,' Gravchenko said.

'Okay,' Scott said. 'I know how to handle Fleischmann. The man's greed will be his undoing. But how far can I go?'

'It's your baby. Any deal, at any cost.' Gravchenko said. 'Pay the $5 million or do a Jakande and tell him to fuck off. *You* know what you're looking for in the dossier. I don't. And it's in English. I haven't got time for translators.'

Gravchenko took a call.

Earn your money Scott Mitchell.

A completely free rein.

He couldn't ask for more than that.

Gravchenko finished the call.

'By the way,' Scott said. 'What's happened to Boško? Did he get taken in? I think he set off the fire alarm.'

Gravchenko laughed; he was lightening up. 'Nobody takes Boško anywhere he doesn't want to go. Yeah, he set off the alarm. He's on an errand at the moment. He'll be here later tonight.'

Scott half closed his eyes; a mixture of physical and mental exhaustion.

'Is that it?' Gravchenko said.

'Just a couple of things I keep forgetting to ask you.'

'What's that?'

'Who did you want me to meet in Madrid, apart from Teresa of course?'

'The Ukrainian oligarch, Dmitry Zletov. He was interested in joining the new venture.'

‘But why did you want *me* there?’

‘I wanted your first impression of him.’

Okay; a reasonable explanation.

‘And how did Orlov fit in to all this?

‘I’d never heard of him until you told me it was a name on your MP’s list. I don’t know why he was on the plane. Zletov never told me he was coming with him.’

Scott sat up, his mind springing into action again. ‘Talking about Ukrainian oligarchs, have you heard of an Australian blogger called Kevin Shaw?’ He told Gravchenko about the leaked FBI article.

Gravchenko sighed. ‘He’s another Wyatt. Writes bollocks. Some say he works for the CIA spreading fake news. I don’t know.’ He toyed with a fresh cigarette. ‘And I don’t care.’

Why wasn’t Scott wholly satisfied with the glib reply?

Was it tiredness dulling his senses?

Was paranoia seeping into his frontal lobe?

He sank back again into his chair.

‘Alright,’ he said, weakly.

‘Now tell me,’ Gravchenko said. ‘What about my job offer? After tonight’s shit storm.’

Scott had given much consideration to the question over recent days.

He’d decided to accept the offer and nothing that had happened that evening had changed his mind, not even Gravchenko’s response to his question about Kevin Shaw. He wouldn’t forget that particular issue, but would wait until he had a clearer head and carried out his own due diligence on Shaw.

‘Yes, I would like to accept your offer, but I’ve got some conditions.’

‘Go on.’ Gravchenko lit the cigarette.

‘One, I’ll carry on as the Chief Counsel to the Foundation with my current work load and ease in the new duties slowly, bit by bit. Two, my first task will be to interview each of the remaining oligarchs, individually, in my own time and in my own way. You've obviously done your due diligence, as far as you can, on the finances of these people and their sources. I won't duplicate your work, but if I turn up any Shastri-type skeletons in their cupboards, either they go or I go. I realise that Arjun may have been completely ignorant of Kabir's money-laundering but he was, at best, *tarnished by association*, as we lawyers say. When Kabir's role in Santorini becomes public knowledge your powerful enemies will set their trolls loose on social media and link Santorini to Arjun, then to the Cuckoo shoot-out, and you. We have to be prepared for that.'

'I've got it in hand.'

'If you say so.' Scott wasn't sure how his boss was going to manage it though.

'Anything else?'

'Yes, third condition: I'll be responsible for hiring our professional consultants, the lawyers, accountants, real estate agents, business acquisition experts and similar. I'll get a team of experts to help me with the non-lawyer engagements. Fourth: I'll take the increase in monthly fees and expenses on day one, thank you, but not the $10 million golden hello until I'm satisfied with my due diligence on the oligarchs and you've accepted them officially into the team.'

Gravchenko smirked. 'A lawyer refusing money?'

Was this Gravchenko's real feeling or was he teasing?

'Kostya, we can't all be bought.'

The smirk, such as it was, became a grin. 'Anything else?'

Scott yawned. 'Excuse me. Yes, for tonight at any rate.'

'Right.' Gravchenko leant across the table and they shook hands. 'I'll send the contract in a couple of days.'

Gravchenko stood up and opened the door. 'Sergey will take you back to your hotel and drive you to the airport tomorrow.'

'Thanks, Kostya.'

I think.

Chapter 34

Day Twenty-five: 2pm, Budapest

'At least the view's better than the last dump we had in 2016,' Yelena said. 'No brothel under this one.' She opened the window and let in the noises of the river boats chugging up and down the Danube.

'Plenty of time for sight-seeing later,' Pravda said. 'Come here and watch this video.'

They sat side by side in two separate chairs.

'And no holes in the chairs this time,' she said. 'Things *are* looking up.'

'You've been in the office for three minutes and you're acting like a realtor,' Pravda said. 'Watch this.' He flicked on the screen.

Oh how he'd missed their banter during his absence for those three days.

A street scene appeared.

The time stamp on the video showed it was 7.30pm the previous day.

The sign of the Cuckoo restaurant came into view.

Police are herding people into vans; firefighters are arriving and dragging their hoses into the building, paramedics are trying to speak to the people being loaded into the police vans but are being pushed aside, bystanders are looking on, some taking pictures; there's shouting and screaming. The camera pans up from the ground floor up to the third floor and back again several times. Windows are broken, but no flames or smoke can be seen. It moves to the street and focuses on a man kneeling over a still body of a woman, lying flat on the ground, face up. He's looking around, his lips are moving, maybe calling for medical assistance.

'Isn't that Arjun Shastri?' Yelena said.

'Yes.'

Shastri's head jerks up and he collapses onto the woman. The video pans to a group of policemen, just in time to see the back of a person in plain clothes barge his/her way through them and into the shadows. The police make no move to restrain the figure.

'I thought I heard a pop,' Pravda said. 'A gun?'

'I didn't,' Yelena said.

He played the moment back several times, but it wasn't any clearer. There was too much competition.

'Do you reckon that person was a man or a woman?' Yelena asked.

Pravda replayed it again, several times.

'I can't tell,' he said.

Yelena stood up and went back to the window. 'We don't know if the person was the shooter, do we?'

'No.'

'Where did the video come from?' Yelena asked.

'Anonymous delivery, courier, here earlier today.'

'Do you reckon the Czech Prosecutor's got a copy?'

'I've no way of knowing.'

'Well,' Yelena said. 'Despite all this shit on the internet, there's nothing on my timelines about Shastri's death, or injury if he wasn't killed. Lots about the raid; no deaths.'

Pravda sighed. 'I know.'

Was this going to be par for the course – yet another cover-up?

'But I bet *one* guy knows,' Yelena said.

'Gravchenko?'

'None other.'

'If he wasn't bald,' she said, 'he'd be pulling his hair out with rage.'

And what was he going to do with this rage?

The names and images of Gravchenko and his 12 partners in the project were viral on the internet, as were leaked details of the new venture. One online German newspaper, owned by an oil tanker billionaire, had headlined their passport images as:

THESE PEOPLE WANT TO DESTROY THE WORLD

'If the information about Gravchenko's new project isn't fake news,' Pravda said, 'I can see why the Kremlin might think he's a threat to their power base.'

He switched off the monitor.

'And the oil and gas guys will mark him as a threat to their profits,' Yelena added.

Pravda nodded. Five years' investigation and no dirt found on the oligarch. His new venture would capture the hearts of millions of people around the world, but the funding requirements would be in the trillions of dollars. Had Gravchenko crossed the line and resorted to money-laundering to boost the fund?

'What's the latest with the Orlov papers?' Pravda said. Yelena had spent the morning ferreting through them.

'Long way to go still. It's driving me crazy, trying to check and double-check everything. These banks are getting clever with their firewalls and stuff.'

'Now you know what IT hackers have to put up with,' Pravda joked. 'You should have some sympathy for them.'

'I do. I'm *one* of them.'

'Go on,' Pravda said. 'What have you got so far?'

'You remember those emails to Orlov with the Chinese URLs, telling him to transfer funds to Calabar and Cordoba.'

'Yes.'

'They come from Kabir Shastri, Arjun's son.'

'No doubt?'

'No doubt.'

'What about the owners of Calabar and Cordoba?'

'Still a work in progress.'

Pravda received a text on his "open" phone from a withheld number:

> Bulgarian diplomat's body found in Moscow River an hour ago

4pm, London

'Follow me,' a familiar voice whispered to Scott as he waited in the queue at the taxi rank outside London City Airport after his delayed flight from Prague.

Fraser nudged him out of line.

Scott had half expected the man to pounce on him at the earliest opportunity. The news websites and social media had been busy all day with reports on the raid, including a tabloid headline:

LOOK WHO'S WHO IN THE CUCKOO'S NEST

Followed by headshots of all the investors.

And on the front of a broadsheet:

SHOULD WE FEAR KONSTANTIN GRAVCHENKO
AND HIS PARTNERS?

He followed the man to a year-old Volkswagen Polo, illegally wedged in between two buses.

'Get in,' Fraser ordered, and walked round to the driver's side.

The rear passenger door wasn't locked.

Scott got in.

Fraser roared away from the bus lane.

'I haven't got any cash on me, driver. It'll have to be a card, I'm afraid,' Scott said, trying to lighten a heavy atmosphere.

Fraser didn't reply until he brought the car to a forceful halt three minutes later by Pontoon Dock DLR station, again parking illegally.

He turned and faced Scott.

'You've no fucking idea what you've got yourself into. I'm not talking about Chalmers and his bollocks about framing you for Bell's murder and I'm not talking about all that stuff you had with us two years ago.

'So what *are* you talking about?'

Was Fraser warning or threatening him?

'Your mate Shastri was murdered last night.'

Well, a possibility, but as far as Scott knew the Prague's Chief Prosecutor hadn't yet completed the investigation.

'Murdered,' Fraser continued. 'By your boss.'

Piffle.

'Whatever gave you that idea, apart from your pathological hatred of all things Russian? You know, Fraser, you need counselling.'

'Shastri's son confessed to him,' Fraser continued. 'Family code of honour pressure and all that. He's running Santorini for the Russians and he gave his daddy names and bank details.'

'What's that got to do with Gravchenko?'

Scott knew the answer. Kabir's alleged confession would be leaked and social media trolls would do the rest; the attacks and accusations against his boss would be relentless.

'Gravchenko is the middle man,' Fraser replied. 'He's Putin's puppet.'

Not *that* old chestnut.

Now that Gravchenko's new venture had entered the public domain, albeit in an unplanned manner, Scott had no reason to be reticent in his response.

'And here was I thinking you wanted to talk about Gravchenko's new plans for cleaning up the planet... getting rid of all the poisonous influences that are destroying civilisations, if you get my meaning.' He grinned at Fraser. 'You disappoint me, you really do. You've been pestering me since 2016 to tell you what the man is up to. Now it's public knowledge, you don't want to know. Instead you want to spread rumours that he killed one of his new partners—'

'Now listen to me,' Fraser growled. 'You—'

'No Fraser. *You* to listen to me. Gravchenko had nothing to do with that raid last night. He'd be mad to kill Shastri in those circumstances, even if he were that way inclined, which he isn't. He'd be cutting off his nose to spite his face. I know for a fact that he's having to concentrate 24/7 with a hell of a lot money on damage limitation, not only to regain the confidence of the existing partners, but to pacify the concerns of future partners he's got lined up.'

He picked up his hand luggage and grabbed the door handle. 'You don't need me any more to tell you what Gravchenko's up to...click on the news sites in future. He's Mr Transparent, unlike some nearer to home I could mention.'

Scott got out. 'I'll take the train from here. Put the bill on my tab.'

He slammed the door shut.

What did Gravchenko tell him in Budapest?

They won't leave you alone until you've outlived your usefulness.

Fraser and Chalmers were going to try to squeeze every single pip of information about Gravchenko's activities out of him.

Chapter 35

Day Twenty-six: noon, London

The message Scott had been anxiously waiting for arrived:

> Bank instructed to make funds available at your discretion. Waiting for your call. The boss has hired Teresa Volkova to help with damage limitation. You can tell her everything you know.

Teresa?

> Thanks Sergey

Then it came to him. Dr Fleischmann was cited in one of Teresa's blogs that Scott had read on her website in Madrid. She'd cited extracts from his published articles in support of her arguments for marine conservation.

He called her.

'Hi, it's me, Scott.'

'Right first time,' she said. 'That's what it says in my contact list. Congrats on your new job.'

'Congratulations on yours. What are you going to do?'

'Try to limit the reputational damage.'

'I realise that, but what will you be doing specifically?'

'Usual stuff. Write blogs praising the work of the Foundation and its future aims. I've got thousands of followers and contacts with all the right save-the-planet organisations. We'll use a specialist company to boost its prominence, you know SEO and stuff. Spread the word.'

'Well, I wish you luck. We've got some powerful enemies out there.'

'No worries, I'm a glass half-full person. This is my field. I do my research. Know my subject. Write with conviction.'

Blimey, had Fleischmann's confidence rubbed off on her?

'Teresa, the reason I called,' Scott said. 'You cited an article by a Dr Alan Fleischmann in one of your blogs I read in Madrid. He's a professor also, I believe. You were arguing the case for marine conservation.'

'Yes, I remember. What about it?'

'Do you know the man? Have you ever met him? What can you tell me about him?'

A second opinion on somebody he'd only met once was always welcome.

'No and no are the answers to the first two questions. What can I tell you? He knows his stuff. One of the world's leading experts in marine conservation. Devotes his life to it, so they say. Focused. Doesn't suffer fools gladly. Comes across as obstinate, irascible and plain rude.'

You will <u>not</u> talk about the custody case…take it or leave it.

'How do you know this if you've never met him?'

'Online comments from his fellow academics.'

'He's a visiting professor at Tel Aviv University, isn't he?'

'Yes, but there's a rumour he's applied for tenure there, and been refused twice.'

'Why, if he's such an expert?'

She laughed. 'Apart from the personality disorder? I guess it might be a funding issue.'

'What do you mean?'

'You know how it works. You only get tenure if you're in the right clique or you can attract funders, benefactors, whatevers. I can't imagine what type of clique would accept Professor Fleischmann into their fold. So he's got to find donors to fund the department he wants to set up.'

Know your enemy.

'Thanks, that's helpful.'

'What are you up to, now, Scott Mitchell?'

He could "see" her cheeky smile.

'I'll tell you later.'

I can't wait.'

Another cheeky smile?

'*Paká*,' she said.

Informal Russian for 'goodbye for now'.

'*Paká*.'

He read Sergey's text again.

Okay, Dr or Professor Fleischmann. Time to go head-to-head.

He called the man.

'Yes?'

'Good morning, Professor Fleischmann. It's Scott Mitchell. I've made the arrangements as agreed. Could we meet later today at the bank?'

'What time?'

'To suit you. I just need to confirm it with them.'

'Three-thirty.'

'Leave it with me and I'll call you back in ten minutes.'

'I shall be expecting your call.'

'Thank you.'

Jesus. How much courtesy should Scott expect for $5 million?

He'd agreed with Fleischmann that the deal would be done at the Canary Wharf branch of one of Gravchenko's international banks.

He called the bank and confirmed the time.

Then Fleischmann.

The phone went straight to voicemail.

Scott left a message:

'Three-thirty is confirmed, Professor. I shall be in the lobby to take you through. Please bring your passport as ID. Any problem, please call me. Thanks.'

4.15pm

Scott had called the professor at 3.45 when he was 15 minutes late, but the phone rang without answer or the voicemail facility operating. He didn't chase him with a text, but preferred to sit and wait, outwardly displaying calm. The man's bad manners served only to strengthen Scott's resolve to play hardball. Fleischmann had appeared at 4pm with no explanation for his tardiness; only a barely audible apology.

They sat at a table, opposite each other with a senior bank official, Adrian Hughes, at the head. All three of them operating their tablets.

'Gentlemen,' Hughes said. 'Sorry about the formality, but I have to go through this protocol. I confirm that you have both requested this meeting is not to be videoed or recorded in any way. The procedure will be: first, Professor Fleischmann will show extracts from the dossier, which is located in his cloud account, to Mr Mitchell, who will be entitled to review them for no longer than 15 minutes – a time imposed by Professor Fleischmann, not this bank. I shall leave the room during this period. Then, if Mr Mitchell wishes to purchase the dossier he will press the green button on the phone here on the table and I shall return to the room to facilitate the simultaneous transfer of funds to Professor Fleischmann's bank account in exchange for the dossier, which will be transferred to a cloud account nominated by Mr Mitchell. If there isn't to be an exchange, one of you will press the red button for my return.'

He looked at each party in turn. 'Is this understood and agreed?'

'Agreed,' Scott said.

'Yes,' Fleischmann said.

'One more thing,' Hughes said. 'I am here solely as a facilitator to each side. I do not represent either Professor Fleischmann or Mr Gravchenko, through Mr Mitchell, and I cannot advise either of you. The dossier will remain Professor Fleischmann's property until I am instructed by Mr Mitchell to transfer the funds to Professor Fleischmann's nominated bank account in the name of the University of Tel Aviv. And until I receive that instruction either side may withdraw consent. Is that understood?'

'Yes,' Scott said.

'Yes,' Fleischmann said.

'Good.' He picked up his tablet. 'I shall now leave the room.'

Scott grabbed the water jug.

'Would you like a glass, Professor?'

'No thank you. Let's get on with it. Come round to my side.'

Scott poured himself a glass of water and pushed it across the table to the seat next to Fleischmann. He ambled round the table, the long way, and sat down next to the man.

'Here,' Fleischmann said. 'The dossier contains 127 pages. Here are a few pages of extracts I've cut and pasted.' He slid the tablet towards Scott.

Scott was determined not to show any enthusiasm or excitement at what he was about to read.

The extracts were printed, not handwritten. They contained references to the incorporation details of Santorini which Carey had obviously copied from the register at Companies House.

Underneath he'd typed:

1. Confirmed Russian laundromat, but where does it operate?
2. Who are Yazov and Bauer?

There followed a page and a half summary of confirmed, or rumoured, connections of a UK establishment figure and two high-profile EU figures, all three with their names redacted, to Santorini and other entities, again names redacted, with alleged dates and amounts of payments for "services rendered".

Additionally, Carey had listed brief details of shipping documents which he must have thought were related to sanctions-busting by the redacted names and others, with the URLs of sites where he believed they were hidden.

Well, well, so David Carey wasn't wholly averse to using the internet.

The extracts made no mention of Orlov, Bisset, Bell, Gravchenko and the Foundation.

'Time's up.' Fleischmann took back the tablet and logged out.

'The redacted names, individual and corporate,' Scott said. 'Was that Carey's doing or yours?'

'Mine. They're all fully disclosed in the dossier.'

'I'd like to check out at least one of the URLs.'

'No. As I said, time's up.'

There was enough promise in the extracts for Scott to want to do the deal, especially the involvement of the three Establishment figures and the payment trails.

He didn't for one minute believe that Fleischmann had the intention to scam him and Gravchenko; he wouldn't get far with Gravchenko's money. More importantly, his only interest was marine conservation and obtaining tenure at the university as the world's leading authority on the subject. The money was being paid directly into his university's bank account, not a Ferrari dealer's in Monaco.

Scott sat back and tutted, with an emphasised smirk.

'What?' Fleischmann said. 'What is it?'

'It's of nominal interest.' He shrugged and pushed the tablet back towards the man. 'But I've seen much of this stuff before. In a different context of course, but much the same information.'

'That's *your* problem, not mine,' Fleischmann said harshly. 'I've not come here to play games. You either want the dossier or you don't. Make up your mind. I haven't got all day.'

Scott wondered how the man would fair in a negotiation with Gravchenko. Who'd blink first?

Scott shrugged. 'No, I can't go to $5 million. It's not worth that much to me. Two point five. No more.'

That should get the man at least a five- to ten-year tenure.

For a split second Fleischman's face dropped like a lead weight.

'You're way off the mark,' the man said.

Good, he's ready to bargain.

'Hmm, okay. Show me some more extracts,' Scott said.

'No,' Fleischman said angrily. 'Don't you listen to what I'm saying? This is not a game, Mr Mitchell.'

'Well.' Scott relaxed back in his chair and played with a coaster on the table. 'I'm afraid it's not going to be $5 million, I'm sorry.' He looked at Fleischmann. 'But I *will* go to $3 million and that, as they say, is my final offer.'

'You're mad,' Fleischmann said. 'Completely mad.'

Scott shrugged. 'If you say so.'

'Four million, five hundred thousand,' Fleischmann said.

Got him.

'No, $3 million's the absolute limit. I wasn't joking.' Scott stretched across the table for the red button.

Fleischmann laid his hand gently on Scott's wrist. 'No, wait.'

Scott left his hand hovering over the button and waited, saying nothing.

'Three million it is, then,' Fleischmann said. He removed his hand from Scott's wrist.

'Good. And thank you, Professor Fleischmann.'

He wasn't concerned that Fleischmann may have kept a copy for himself. He couldn't check it out even if the man assured him he hadn't. The original dossier had been stolen from Professor Zapatero's apartment, so it was in a limited public domain. Scott's principal objective had never been to prevent the information from being circulated, but to find out why Carey had been assassinated and to make sure that Gravchenko's reputation couldn't be impugned.

Fleischmann checked the time on his gold watch. 'Let's get Hughes back in.'

Scott raised his hand.

'Before we do, I'd like you to settle something for me.'

Fleischmann frowned. 'Settle what?'

'Your custody case with Professor Zapatero.'

I do not know what to do...I'd give up everything to get Sarah back.

Fleischmann glared at him. 'I told you I didn't want to discuss—'

'I'll give you an extra $500,000 if you agree that the professor can have full custody of Sarah, with you of course having reasonable access rights.'

'One million,' Fleischmann said, without blinking.

'Seven hundred and fifty thousand,' Scott replied. 'I'll lodge the funds with the professor's lawyers with instructions to release them to you when they're satisfied that a legally binding settlement agreement between you and the professor has been reached.'

'It's a deal,' Fleischmann said immediately. 'Now press the green button.'

8.45pm

Before Scott settled down with a large glass of Barolo and hard copies of the dossier that he'd downloaded and printed out as soon as he got back to his apartment, he'd called Professor Zapatero and told her the good news of the custody settlement.

'Thank you, Scott. Thank you very much. I am in your debt.'

'Well, Professor, if it hadn't been for you and your work with David Carey, I wouldn't have got my hands on the dossier and you wouldn't have seen a satisfactory resolution to your custody case. So perhaps we should share the honours.'

'Alright. Let us, how do you say...pat each other on the back?'

'Agreed.'

'Thank you, again, Scott. Thank you very much, so, so...very much.'

Her voice faltered.

Scott's eyes watered.

'You're more than welcome. By the way, any news on that other matter we discussed, the profile?'

'Tomorrow or the next day.'

'Great! Speak to you again shortly, Professor. Goodnight.'

'Goodnight, Scott.'

He texted Sergey:

> Deal done. Dossier uploaded with my summary of the meeting. Plus info on the Indian's son. Speak later

Scott had written his summary in Russian, but the 127-page dossier would have to be translated from the English.

Sergey came back in 30 minutes:

> Boss says well done. Prof now owes us one

And it's on its way, Sergey my friend. It's on its way.

Chapter 36

Day Twenty-seven: 10.30am, Hungary

'You should have given the bastards the stuff,' Yelena said, banging the side of their rowing boat repeatedly with the palm of her hand. 'You should have given it to them.' She glared at Pravda, tears welling up. 'Why didn't you? Why didn't you give them the damn stuff?'

Pravda stopped rowing and allowed their boat to drift idly in the middle of the beautiful Lake Balaton; the people on the shoreline no larger than ants, pedalos racing back and forth, yachts barely moving under a cloudless sky.

While Yelena had been pre-occupied with examining the Orlov documents Pravda had spent much of the previous evening scouring the news sites and social media in Russia and Bulgaria searching for references to the discovery of the diplomat's body in the Moscow River. Nothing. He'd checked with the team back in Moscow for news, again nothing, not a murmur.

If the Kremlin had been responsible for Pravda's earlier kidnapping and the subsequent death of the diplomat, it would have made sure it hit the news, as a warning to others.

The media silence didn't make sense.

Pravda had suggested the 130-kilometre drive to the lake.

It was time to clear their heads after the dramas of relocating from Moscow to Budapest while trying to piece together Orlov's cache of criminal activity.

'Easier said than done.' He sympathised with her.

She still retained guilt for dragging her source into her mission in Varna. Had she not done so – she kept saying – he wouldn't have been beaten up by Max's friends and killed by Pravda's kidnappers. Nonetheless, she had to understand his own position. 'Remember, I told them their Kremlin masters had cleared out the cloud accounts and I'd need a few days to get my hands on copies.'

'That was ten days ago,' she said. 'They weren't going to wait that long.'

She was right, he shouldn't have waited.

But...

'Maybe we're not thinking clearly.'

'What do you mean?'

'We only have somebody's word for it that the story's true. Somebody who withheld their number. A number we haven't been able to trace.' They'd exhausted all means at their disposal, legal and illegal, to try to get the number.

They'd failed.

'Best guess is that all this is linked, and it's either a disgruntled section of the *siloviki* who are using Santorini to build up their pension fund, or organised crime who are working with rogue elements in the West, sanctions-busting.'

'Not the Kremlin itself?'

'No. I don't think so. If it was, my kidnappers would have checked with the Kremlin that what I said was true or not, before taking matters any further. I'm not sure they did.'

'Why?'

'Because if the Kremlin knew that I'd been kidnapped and beaten up while trying to do my job for them, they would have stepped in and dealt with it.'

'Perhaps they *did* deal with it,' Yelena said. 'By taking out Max.'

'Yes, that's a question I'm wrestling with. What were Max's dying words: "We know too much"?'

'Threat or friendly warning?' Yelena said.

Pravda shrugged.

'There are so many questions to answer,' Pravda said. 'Maybe the kidnappers have an idea of what's in Orlov's papers and want to take them out of circulation, for whatever reason.'

'Or use them for blackmail.'

'That too.'

'So my source might still be alive?'

'Look at it this way,' Pravda said. 'All we have is this anonymous text message and a silent media. Somebody is playing with our minds. I don't know who or why.' She was trawling her hand through the water. 'I don't know what else to say, except that until we receive proof that he's no longer alive, I'm going to remain positive.'

Yelena yawned.

'I'm sorry, General, I'm exhausted. You dragged me out of bed at 6.30 and drove 12 million kilometres across Hungary for this...' She waved her hands around. 'A pesky rowing boat lesson.'

Twelve million kilometres.

He laughed. His son Stepan used to exaggerate like that when he was angry, but he was only eight.

'You slept through the whole journey. Think of the beautiful countryside you missed.'

'I didn't need a guided a tour. It's all in Google Maps.'

'Anyway,' Pravda said, 'back to business. What was it that kept you up for most of the night?'

He'd fallen asleep at 11.30 with Yelena's New Orleans jazz music wafting through the wall between their adjoining rooms.

She unzipped her left boot and produced a piece of paper from a hidden pocket.

'This,' she said, handing it to Pravda.

He widened his eyes.

'Hmm.'

It was a passport image in the name of Gulyana Niyazova, not Russian but Uzbek.

'It could be interesting,' he said. 'But there's no reason why she shouldn't have dual nationality.' The Russian law on allowing dual nationality was flexible to say the least. Pravda knew of numerous cases where it had been flouted. Though he didn't know what Uzbekistan law said on the subject. 'She was born in Uzbekistan. I assume at least one of her parents is an Uzbek national.'

'Both her parents are dead,' Yelena said. 'Both were Uzbeks.'

'So how does this take our investigation further?' Pravda said.

'Some other documents say she's a student of fashion design, not money-laundering.'

He chuckled. 'That would make sense.'

'Yeah, but, for a student of fashion design she's got one hell of a CV,' Yelena said.

'What do you mean?'

'She's been trained by Uzbek special forces.'

Pravda slumped.

Here we go.

'And that's not all,' she continued. 'She was charged in Uzbekistan for killing an ultra-pro-Western politician in a knife fight. But surprise, surprise. She was snatched away two days before the trial and ended up in our own Hatsavita Mountain Training Centre with the FSB, and you can bet it wasn't for skiing lessons. My sources say she can kill at 30 paces with the blink of an eye. She doesn't need two, like the rest of us. Yelena threw her hands up. 'I mean, when does this killing machine get time to design clothes? I don't get five minutes to polish my Harley's mirrors.'

It couldn't possibly get any worse.

‘What did we say about her extraordinary rendition?’

‘What everybody says: we denied it, she sought asylum with us on the basis that her murder trial was politically motivated.’

Pravda laughed again. Did anybody believe such nonsense in the 21st century?

‘How do you know all this?’ Pravda narrowed his eyes at her. ‘You didn’t go through our usual Spetznaz channels, did you?’

‘No way. I promise you. Tamara used her Ukrainian intelligence mole. He didn’t know why she wanted the information on Niyazova or who she wanted it for.’ Yelena grimaced. ‘She’s good at pillow talk.’

The picture was becoming fuzzier, not clearer.

Chapter 37

Day Twenty-seven: 11am, London

Scott's alarm clock that morning was neither Rosie nor his phone. An adrenalin rush, which had begun the moment he'd understood the import of Carey's dossier the previous evening and subsided at 3am, had stirred him into action again at 7am.

His preliminary view was that Carey's research had uncovered more details pointing to probable Western involvement in the sanctions-busting than Russian, or at least the Kremlin. Santorini's name was referred to in many of the documents, either directly or via URL links, and Carey thought it might be the hub of much of the activity, but Scott hadn't, as yet, found anything specific that pointed directly to sanctions-busting or money-laundering. There was little on how the company operated or where disclosed funds had come from.

He wasn't disappointed though. Yelena had confirmed her discoveries in Orlov's papers with their emphasis on Santorini's financial transactions that had the hallmarks of classic money-laundering activities. And Scott was also relieved that the dossier was silent on the WPF and Gravchenko personally. In fact, Carey didn't appear to have known that the two registered shareholders in Santorini: Yazov and Bauer, were employees of the Foundation, ostensibly in Bauer's case.

Carey had mentioned Bell's borrowings from the Russian mortgage lenders and suspected the knight could be in deeper than the MP had yet discovered.

How right he was.

Again, the dossier didn't mention Wyatt. That made sense: he was an opportunist, Russo phobic blackmailer rather than a sanctions-buster or money-launderer.

The only mention of Roberto Silvano Pappalardo was his name with a question mark after it, possibly a matter for Carey's future investigation.

What had excited Scott's interest was Carey's reference to a Paris-based lawyer called Bernard Damiron. His law firm comprised himself as its sole principal, with no other lawyers or paralegals. Carey said that Maître Damiron outsourced all the administration tasks. Though unusual for a law firm, it wasn't rare enough to warrant suspicion. Scott knew of small law firms in the UK with a similar set-up, especially those that operated in serviced offices or used a virtual office when operating from home. The intriguing aspect was that Maître Damiron specialised in setting up offshore companies for the rich and famous – and did nothing else.

Somehow, Carey had obtained a copy of the lawyer's client list. The man was a mini version of the Panamian law firm, Mossack Fonseca, whose leaked records resulted in the worldwide publication of the "Panama Papers" in 2016. Those papers disclosed all kinds of secret offshore activities – some legal, some illegal – carried out by some of the world's "elite", as well as the usual lifetime criminal suspects. They included autocratic rulers of countries, politicians, high-ranking civil servants, international corporations, media owners, entertainment celebrities, oligarchs, drug cartels, money-launderers, arms dealers, and a host of other characters who preferred to keep their assets and income streams away from the prying eyes of the general public – and, allegedly, the tax collectors.

Maître Damiron's client list, though much smaller than Mossack Fonseca's, had its share of UK and other EU participants: individuals and corporations. Two corporate names that stood out on the list were Calabar

Project Management Limited and Cordoba Coordinators SA, though Scott hadn't yet found an explanation in the dossier of the roles they played in Carey's suspicions.

Scott discovered in his morning's internet searches against Damiron that his wife, Michelle, was a "project facilitator" who operated in the EU Commission in Brussels and the EU Parliament in Strasburg; but under her maiden name, Michelle Pelletier.

The Damirons were, in effect, nurturing a cash cow: while Michelle was wining and dining the EU elite, her husband was investing the elite's money in sanctions-busting contracts. These contracts, which, again, Carey had obtained from Damiron's client files, showed transactions between his clients and third parties, both of which used offshore entities in the names of nominees. Their subject matter included imports of goods originating in Crimea, exports of goods and technology for the telecommunications and energy sectors to Crimean companies, the buying and selling of financial instruments issued by certain proscribed state-owned Russian banks and their subsidiaries outside the EU, and real estate investments in Crimea; all in breach of the sanctions.

His appetite whetted, Scott paid $100 into the website account of a Serbian conceptual artist called Spiridon Petrović. It was public knowledge, because Petrović openly admitted it, that he indulged in "hacker ethics" which involved the critique of economic, legal and political models which he expressed in artistic formats. He'd hacked into firms similar to Mossack Fonseca, as well as legitimately obtaining information from public registers, and accumulated, so far, 15,000 names of people and corporate entities who were using nominees in offshore companies to carry out commercial activities. His efforts often revealed, sometimes with supporting images of passports – one of which was the

French passport of Simone Bisset – and bank statements, the existence of email instructions from the real owners of the companies or their lawyers to the likes of Maître Damiron.

He interrupted his reading and wrote the name of Simone Bisset in large capital letters on a notepad, with the words "find her before it's too late!" underneath.

Petrović never commented on the revelations. As he said, he "put the facts out there for everybody to see and make their own judgement" at the nominal cost of $100.

Threats of litigation to silence him came to nothing, presumably because it would mean the claimants having to wash their dirty linen in court.

How the man had managed to stay alive was a source of wonder to Scott. People had killed for much less than the public disclosure of their financial crimes.

In particular, Petrović's endeavours showed the Damirons to be the ultimate owners, through a series of trusts and other companies, of a well-known German finance company that used a variety of offshore companies and trusts to take payments for themselves, described as introducer fees, in major loan deals between banks, hedge funds and other investment vehicles. Some of these payments were, however, funds belonging to many of Damiron's clients who were averse to the notion of fiscal transparency. Petrović's list included a British multi-millionaire in the technology start-up industry, who was benefiting financially from the suspicious activities of the German finance company, and several senior advisers to the EU commission.

The information was overwhelming. It would take one person weeks, if not months, to cross-reference everything in Carey's dossier, Petrović's "artwork" and Scott's own internet searches; not forgetting that he had yet to see the Orlov papers.

The more Scott considered the documentation, the

clearer it became to him that some members of the so-called EU elite were swimming in a primeval swamp of criminality, the fear of exposure of which could plausibly drive them to non-judicial resolutions of the problem and, perhaps, with the help of those Russians for whom the rule of law was to be ignored rather than obeyed.

Zapatero called him.

'Scott, I have the information for you. Shall I send it now by WhatsApp? It's encrypted end-to-end, yes?'

Encrypted end-to-end.

Yelena's concerns about the Kremlin's hacking and surveillance capabilities gnawed at him.

A million-to-one chance, maybe.

But why risk it?

'No, Professor, please don't. Where are you?'

'I am in Brussels. At the Commission building.'

'I'll come and get it, right now. By train from St Pancras.'

Silence.

'Professor, are you still there?'

'But...are you sure that's necessary,' she said. 'It's a very long way to come to collect some notes.'

Yes, Professor Consuela Isabella Marcia Zapatero. It *is* necessary. Absolutely necessary.

Carey's dossier had mentioned Pappalardo's name.

Who knew who else was wallowing in the swamp?

'I don't mind. It only takes a couple of hours. I'll check the train times and call you back.'

'Alright. If you insist. But you do not have to do this. I can send it by FEDEX this morning, if you are unhappy with the WhatsApp.'

'I assure you, I don't mind. I'll call you back in 10 to 15 minutes.'

Yes! He shook a clenched fist.

Okay Mr Bobby Pappalardo, let's see what game you're playing.

He booked the earliest train available and called her:

'I'll be on the 12.58, scheduled to arrive in Brussels at 16.08, your time.'

The city was an hour ahead of London.

'Yes, that will be good for me. We can meet at the Brasserie de la Gare. It's opposite the main exit on the north side of the station. Midi/Zuid terminus.'

'Perfect. There's a train that leaves for London just before six. That should give us sufficient time for a coffee.'

'Thank you, Scott. I look forward to our meeting again.'

'No. thank *you*, Professor. Bye for now.'

'Goodbye.'

Yes! Yes! Yes!

4.55pm, Brussels

Professor Zapatero was sitting at an outside table as Scott approached.

She wasn't wearing the sling, so he held out his hand.

She shook it lightly.

'Still painful?'

'A little,' she smiled. 'But it has been worse. How was your journey?'

'As you can see, the train was delayed in getting here. I'm sorry.'

'I know, I have been following on my phone.'

A waiter appeared at their table.

'*Madame*? *Monsieur*?'

'A camomile tea, please,' Professor Zapatero said in English.

'I'll have the same, please,' Scott said.

The waiter nodded and retreated to the bar inside the café.

'Apart from the delay,' Scott said, 'it was uneventful. I wasn't paying attention to the journey. My mind was on David Carey's dossier. It's mind-blowing.'

‘I am glad it’s helpful to you.’

‘How are things going with the custody case?’

‘Yes. Good. The lawyers are preparing the settlement papers. David is pushing them. He tells them they must work all night.’

And doubtless their fees will reflect it.

‘I’m pleased for you. It will be another problem out of your way.’

She looked embarrassed.

‘What is it?’ Scott said.

‘It was very generous of you, and Mr Gravchenko of course, to do what you did. I do not know how to thank you.’

‘Thank you. It’s kind of you to say that and I shall pass your comments on to Mr Gravchenko. But we also benefited from the transaction, apart from getting the dossier, I mean.’

‘How is that?’

‘Professor Fleischmann isn’t a fool. He knows that donations at this level come with understandings, if not legally binding conditions. We’ll expect him to keep our Foundation informed on the progress of his research, before he goes public with it.’

‘And you think he will do that?’

‘I’d be surprised if he didn’t,’ Scott said. ‘He wants more money and he knows that Mr Gravchenko is in a position to give it to him...for future projects that will help the Foundation and Mr Gravchenko’s other good causes.’

‘Is the Prague incident a problem for Mr Gravchenko?’

‘You will understand, Professor, that it’s not something I am willing to comment on at the moment. Mr Gravchenko will be making a public statement shortly.’

At least, Scott hoped he would.

The PR team should also *work all night* to get a formal statement out as soon as possible.

Teresa's SEO endeavours won't be enough.

The waiter brought the drinks.

'Well, thank you, again.' She took a brown envelope from her handbag and slid it across the table to Scott, under her bag. 'It's the profile of Bobby. I hope you will find this information as helpful as the dossier.'

'I'm sure I will.' Scott slipped the envelope into his rucksack.

'And I would like you to have this,' she said. 'A little token of my appreciation for your personal efforts in helping to resolve the custody case.'

She handed a small gift-wrapped package to him.

'Oh, Professor, thank you, but you shouldn't have.' He took it from her. 'May I unwrap it?'

'Yes, of course, I hope you like it.'

Scott was touched and reduced to feeling like an excited child unwrapping an unexpected birthday present.

It was a Parker Pen box.

He opened it.

'Goodness me,' Scott said. It was one of the Premier brand. Although he wasn't a collector, he knew of the brand.

'Do you like it?'

Of course he did.

It was too good, too classic, to use.

'Yes, yes. It's beautiful. Thank you so much.'

Fraser texted him.

Call me

Not now, Fraser. Not now. The day's being good to me. I don't need you to spoil the party... Although... I could nail you guys once and for all with what I've discovered.

'Business?' the professor said.

'Yes, I'm sorry. But I think I ought to go now. My

train leaves in 30 minutes or so and I need to make an urgent phone call before I get into a crowded carriage.'

He grabbed his rucksack and slipped the pen box into an inside pocket.

'I understand,' she said and offered her hand. 'Thank you and Mr Gravchenko again for all you have done.'

'You're more than welcome.' They shook hands. 'And thank *you* for this beautiful present.'

She smiled. 'Goodbye, Scott – and good luck.'

'The same to you, Professor.'

Scott walked off, smiling at Fraser's message.

Boy, have I got a few surprises for you, Mr Fraser. Oh yes, indeedy.

The station concourse was noisy with a mixture of messages from the public address system, the shouts and jostlings of 50 or more EU flag- and balloon-carrying teenage schoolchildren, who'd probably been on one of the Commission's guided tours, and the homeward-bound evening commuters.

He found a quiet seat at a table in front of Sam's Café when a female voice penetrated the airwaves with an English language rendition of the EU's anthem "Ode to Joy".

The café's customers looked up and smiled at the source, some joining in.

One of the schoolchildren was towering above her colleagues, presumably standing on a box, and bellowing out the song while those around her waved their flags and balloons. Within moments she was joined by another... and another...and another...and some of the commuters, accompanied by an orchestra which appeared from goodness knows where.

As entertaining as the flash mob was, he couldn't hear himself think.

It scuppered his chances of having a coherent conversation with Fraser.

He texted him:

Not convenient now

A hand appeared over his shoulder and snatched the phone from him.

'What the—?'

Scott turned round to be confronted by three heavily armed men in regulation buff army fatigues with stab vests, though without any facial coverings.

'Please come with us, monsieur,' the front soldier said.

Another one picked up Scott's rucksack.

Scott stood up.

'What's going on? Give me back my phone and rucksack.'

The customers concentrating on the flash mob had turned their attention to him.

The lead man smiled politely and gestured towards his colleague with the rucksack who was making his way the exit. 'Follow him, please, monsieur.'

The third soldier straightened, with both hands on his automatic, which was slung across his chest.

One look from him was enough to convince Scott that arguing with the messengers would be a futile exercise.

He followed rucksack man, with the other two behind him and the "Ode to Joy" ringing in his ears.

'Jesus Christ,' Scott said when he emerged from the station.

The restaurant area where he'd been sitting with the professor was swarming with police and more soldiers, many armed. They were ordering and ushering the customers and onlookers back beyond crime scene tape that surrounded the street-side sitting area.

Emergency vehicle sirens drowned out the "Ode to Joy".

'Oh no! No!' Scott said as he crossed the road with his escorts.

Forensics were erecting a tent-like structure around "his" table.

Professor Zapatero was lying on the ground, in a pool of blood.

'No! No! No!' He headed for the table but was restrained and led to another table in the far corner of the café area, where a man in plain clothes man was on the phone.

Rucksack man dumped the bag on the table and the lead soldier handed Scott's phone to the outstretched hand of the civilian who ended his phone call.

'Please sit down, Monsieur Mitchell,' the man said in English.

Scott glanced back at the crime scene.

The tent was erected.

There was nothing to see.

The professor was dead.

So much for her 24/7 protection.

He sat down and buried his head in his hands.

'Here,' the man said. 'Drink this.' He pushed a bottle of water across the table.

Scott stared at the man.

Where was he?

It was surreal.

'Thank you.' He took a mouthful. 'Who are you?' Scott asked softly. Any aggression had been sucked out of him.

'My name is Victor Mertens. I'm a member of the Belgian State Security Service.' He produced his ID card.

Scott glanced at it – and misted over.

'When did it happen? How?' Scott said. 'I was with her only 15 minutes ago.'

'May I see your passport, please, Monsieur Mitchell?' He shrugged. 'Box-ticking. I know who you are.'

Scott obliged, glancing back at the tent again, hoping it was a dream.

More police had arrived and were studying the ground between the now empty tables.

Police on the perimeters were interviewing people.

The news media trucks with their telescopic antennae scraping the heavens were disgorging camera crews.

It was a circus.

'Thank you,' Mertens said and returned the passport to Scott.

Scott sighed. 'So, what happened?'

'The professor was shot by a pillion rider on a motorbike. We have it on CCTV.'

'Any chance of recognising them? The number identification plates?'

'Both blacked out from helmet to foot. No plates.'

A fully blacked-out motorbike couple had carried out the first attempt on her life in Paris and Scott had read somewhere that the police investigating Carey's assassination were searching for a woman seen giving a sports bag to a blacked-out motorbike rider by the National Car Park in Canary Wharf at the time of the shooting.

'Now,' Mertens said, 'would you please tell me what you were doing here with the professor?'

His tone couldn't have been more polite.

Scott glanced at the rucksack with Bobby's profile inside; he cursed himself for making the error and quickly met Mertens' eyes head on.

Sticking to his policy of keeping as close to the truth as discretion would permit he told Mertens about the professor's bitter custody dispute and Fleischmann's interest in receiving funding from Gravchenko's Foundation, and that they'd met for a general update, before she went away on an unplanned business trip. Also, she'd wanted to thank him personally with the Parker gift for his efforts.

'Why did you so leave so quickly?' Mertens said.

'I had to make an urgent call, and we'd finished our business.'

Mertens scrolled through Scott's phone.

'In response to this text?' Mertens showed the screen to Scott.

'Yes.'

Mertens checked the contact name.

'Who is Colin Fraser?'

'He's your counterpart. He works for our Secret Intelligence Service, MI6.'

The momentary look of surprise on Mertens' face told Scott that Mertens would tread carefully when continuing his questions, not that the man had been anything but polite up to then.

'What did he want?' Mertens said.

'I don't know. I was going to call him, but was interrupted by the "Ode to Joy"; it's there in my text response to him. And then your men snatched my phone.'

'Do you work for MI6?'

'No.'

'So what is your business with them?'

Come, come Victor, you surely must know better than to ask *that* question.

'If I tell you, they'll chop my head off in the Tower of London. It's a matter of UK national security.' He smiled at Mertens. 'But you could always call Fraser and ask him to give me permission to divulge our nation's secrets.'

Scott wouldn't object to telling Mertens what Fraser had been wanting from him, now that Gravchenko's project had become public knowledge.

He took another sip of water, to mask a second anxious glance at the rucksack.

'Wait here,' Mertens said, and he left the table with Scott's phone firmly clasped in his hand.

He got into an empty car and made a phone call.

Scott was tempted to pull the rucksack nearer to him.

He resisted the urge, not wanting to betray his concern.

A black cloud descended on him and he was consumed with pangs of guilt and paranoia.

What could he say to Sarah? *I'm responsible for your mother's assassination.*

If only he hadn't insisted on coming to Brussels to collect the profile.

Was it really possible that somebody could have stolen or copied it from WhatsApp?

What kind of people was he dealing with?

Mertens returned.

'You may go, Monsieur Mitchell,' Mertens said, returning Scott's phone. 'Thank you for your cooperation.'

They shook hands.

'I have Professor Fleischmann's phone number, if you need it,' Scott said. 'I think he might still be in London.'

'Thank you, but we are in contact with him.'

Scott scooped up his phone and rucksack.

'Goodbye, Mr Mertens.'

'Goodbye. Have a safe journey back to London.'

9.40pm, London

Scott was intellectually exhausted when he boarded the train for London at 7pm, an hour later than intended. He slept for most of the journey, apart from a visit to the toilet towards the end where he tucked the Bobby profile envelope down the back of his shirt. He didn't anticipate being searched by the police on his arrival in London, but he wanted to minimise the risk of losing the profile if his bag were snatched by an opportune thief. It wasn't convenient for him to upload the documents on the overcrowded train, where the Wi-Fi connection was intermittent at best.

'You've had a busy afternoon, I hear,' a male voice at his side said as Scott emerged from a crowd at St Pancras and headed for the taxi rank.

He glanced to his left and did a double-take.

It was ADC Chalmers in a light blue linen jacket, black chinos and a tieless yellow shirt.

Was this for Scott's supposed benefit?

Less threatened because the man was out of uniform?

'I see Fraser got my text,' Scott said.

'Champagne?'

Scott stopped abruptly.

'You've either won the lottery or are fiddling your expenses.'

Chalmers nodded towards the bar. 'Come. We've got some catching up to do.'

Here we go: good cop, bad cop. The MI6 man had ended their bromance and returned to type, leaving Chalmers as his substitute.

'Okay, lead the way.'

Scott kept two paces behind as they headed for Searcys Champagne Bar on the first floor while he adjusted the envelope tucked into the back of his shirt.

The four-seater tables were arranged in a single row, parallel to the Eurostar train track.

Chalmers chose an empty one between two other empty tables and ordered a bottle of Perrier-Jouët Belle Epoque 2011 Brut Champagne.

'Are you sure you haven't won the lottery?'

'Look,' Chalmers said, 'I want you to understand my difficulty.' It wasn't said in a threatening or smart-arse manner. His tone was pleasant and temperate.

It was an act, of course, and Scott would remain on as much alert as a few glasses of good quality bubbly would permit.

'Go on.'

'My difficulty is,' Chalmers said, 'I don't know how to suspend my disbelief.'

Play dumb.

'In what?'

'I find it very, no, *extremely* difficult to believe you're not connected in some material way with the murders of Diane Costello, Sir Morgan Stanton Bell and Professor Zapatero.'

Pile it on, why don't you, Mr Policeman.

'The pure coincidences of your being found by the body of the tortured Costello, of your being the last person to see Bell alive before he was murdered—'

'No. The last person to see him alive was the *murdere*r,' Scott said.

'...and of your sitting and chatting with Zapatero immediately before she was assassinated.' Chalmers smirked. 'I mean. Would you believe that such a character in a Grisham or le Carré novel wasn't materially connected with the others? Come on, be honest with me.'

The champagne arrived with a bucket of ice.

Neither of them wanted to taste it, so the waiter poured two glasses and left.

'Cheers,' Chalmers said and raised his glass.

'To absent friends,' Scott said, thinking of Professor Zapatero.

Chalmers raised his eyebrows.

'So be it,' Chalmers added.

They clinked their glasses.

All very amicable – and laced with a poisonous subtext.

'What do you mean by *materially connected*?' Scott said. 'How *material* is this connection of yours supposed to be?'

'What were you doing with Professor Zapatero this afternoon?'

He told Chalmers the same story he'd told Victor Mertens in Brussels.

I'm interested in classic pens,' Chalmers said, without apparent conviction. 'Would you show it to me?'

'Certainly.' Scott guessed that Chalmers wanted to see what else he had in his rucksack. Maybe somebody had spotted Professor Zapatero handing the envelope to him or it was caught on CCTV, despite her attempts to hide it.

He put his rucksack on the table and pretended to look for the present by opening all compartments in full view of Chalmers.

He could see out of the corner of his eye that the man was trying to peer inside the rucksack.

'Yes, here you are.' He pulled the pen and box from its wrapping and handed it over. 'Open it. It's beautiful.'

Chalmers fiddled with it for less than a minute and gave it back.

'Yes, it's a definitely a classic. You're a lucky man. You must have done her a great service.'

An obvious dig for more information.

He finished his champagne and topped up Scott's without asking, before filling his own glass.

A third-rate movie ploy to loosen Scott's tongue.

He played along and took a large mouthful, before catching the waiter's eye.

'Yes sir?'

'Please may we have a litre bottle of still water in another bucket of ice and two glasses.'

'Certainly sir.'

Chalmers frowned at him.

'Well, it can't cost as much as the champers,' Scott said innocently.

'As I said, she was pleased that I helped her get an amicable settlement agreement for her custody case.'

Oh shit, that poor kid.

Scott offered to pour a glass of water for Chalmers.

'No thanks.' He topped up his own champagne glass.

Scott poured himself the water and drank it in one go.

Time to go on the attack.

'Right, I'm tired,' Scott said. 'And as you know, it's

been a harrowing afternoon. Now, I'm going to tell you something. And I don't give a toss if you do or don't suspend your disbelief.'

Chalmers showed no emotion as he took a sip of champagne.

Scott tore a slip of paper from the scribble pad he always carried with him, wrote three names on it and gave it to Chalmers.

'Here's three names of some of the so-called EU elite who are up to their necks in sanctions-busting and laundering their ill-gotten gains. You'll recognise the first one: the English technology billionaire, MBE, who's done so much for the UK and, rumour has it, is buying his way to a lordship; the other two hold top positions in the EU Commission.'

He searched Chalmers' demeanour for every muscle movement as the man studied the list, every frown, facial tic, excessive blinking, heavy breathing – nothing, apart from normal eye movement as he read and re-read the names.

Now for the *coup de grâce.*

'I've got irrefutable evidence of all their criminal activities and of those of many of their elite bedfellows.' He hadn't. 'My team's investigations are ongoing.' With Pravda missing, the active members of his team currently comprised only Yelena and himself. 'But don't get any ideas of trying to stop us.' Chalmers could infer from that whatever he wanted. 'Because the full list of names and details of their criminal activities will be released to the world if I go missing for more than 30 days or die...' He stared at Chalmers who was glaring at him. 'From any cause whatsoever.'

'This is not the fucking *Godfather*!' Chalmers unexpectedly and uncharacteristically shouted. He slammed his fist on the table. 'How *dare* you make such an inference!'

The two bar staff turned away.

Scott flinched, and leant into him, tapping on the table with his index finger as he spoke. 'With all these killings, Assistant District Commissioner Chalmers?!' Of course it's the fucking *Godfather*! It's a never-ending string of the fucking horse's head in the fucking bed scene!'

He had difficulty in stopping his hands trembling as he filled his champagne glass, ignoring Chalmers.

How crowded did the swamp have to be before this man admitted what was right under his nose?

Chalmers dropped the list onto the table and narrowed his eyes.

'We should both calm down,' he said, and poured himself a glass of water.

Scott picked up his own glass of water. 'I'll drink to that.' And took a mouthful.

'What are you asking me to do about it?' Chalmers' tone was back to normal: calm and measured.

Was Chalmers one of the good guys?

'I would like you to understand,' Scott said, equally calmly, 'that the EU isn't just an orchard with a few rotten apples. I've got the document trails, emails, records of phone calls and dodgy bank transfers that infest the swamps and sewers flowing behind the European Union's façade of equality for all, including identification details, birth certificates, highly creative CVs, passport images and a whole load of other stuff that could put these hypocrites away for decades.'

It was a massive over-exaggeration, but it would be a hard task, if not impossible, for anybody to prove the lie.

'Assuming you're telling the truth,' Chalmers said. 'The Russians are no better, probably worse. Are you threatening to reveal *their* dirty deeds in your crusade for the truth?' Still calm, still measured.

'You may be right,' Scott said. 'But my client is *Gravchenko*, not the Russian nation. And he's putting his money, his *clean un-laundered* money, where his mouth is, despite his enemies trying to scare off his venture partners with fake raids.'

Chalmers' expression didn't signify any concern about the Prague raid.

'So you're asking us to lay off Mr Gravchenko?'

Scott chuckled. 'I *would* if I thought it would do any good. But it won't; I'm not that naïve. No, I'm not asking you to do anything. I'm telling you what I'm doing, and have been doing, since we first met.' He took a mouthful of champagne. 'Which of course is what you and Fraser have always wanted to know.'

'Do you expect us to investigate these people without seeing your so-called irrefutable evidence?'

'I don't care what you do with them, but you're not having the evidence. It's my insurance policy.'

'So what's happened to your principle of nobody's above the rule of law? If you really believed that, you'd help us to prosecute them.'

Fair comment, but Scott was no longer so idealistic. His experiences during the recent years had convinced him that the much-vaunted rule of law was honoured more in its breach than in respecting it, when it came to those who had the political and economic power to manipulate society to their own ends.

'*Plus ça change...*' Scott said and shrugged. 'Corrupt leaders and officials have been removed from office, imprisoned and assassinated throughout history...to be replaced by another set of corrupted souls.'

He stood up.

'Time for bed, Assistant Deputy Commissioner Chalmers. Goodnight, and sleep well.'

He picked up his rucksack and walked away.

A heavy burden lifted.

But had he signed his own death warrant, despite his threat of exposure?

Chapter 38

Day Twenty-eight: 7.30am, London

The only word on Scott's mind, as he read the four-page Bobby profile, was "toxic". It wasn't anything to do with the contents of the profile, but because of the description Pravda had given to Carey's list.

Scott's fitful sleep had been punctuated with the thought of why Professor Zapatero had been silenced. However he tried to rationalise the attacks on her it all came back to her name being on the list, and for no other reason. True, somebody could have been monitoring her association with Carey and her passing information to him, but she hadn't been attacked until Paris and Brussels, which was long after her helping Carey and the theft of his dossier from her apartment, but only after the list was copied by Scott's intruder.

Whether his conclusion was rational or he was way off the mark, it didn't matter; he bore the pangs of guilt for not having destroyed the original hard copy of the list.

Pappalardo was a sex maniac according to a witness statement by a 39-year-old divorcee working in the Commission's legal department. Both of them had gone back to his apartment after they'd drunk too much at one of the Commission's social soirées. He raped her and kicked her out, screaming that he was married to a beautiful young French student "half your fucking age, you old bat!"

The rumours went quiet after he paid her compensation of 150,000 euros and made her sign a non-disclosure agreement. Three weeks later she attempted suicide after posting details of the agreement on social media.

He was still seen lobbying in the corridors of power, but, so rumours had it, on the understanding he didn't try to recover the compensation from the victim, who was under medical supervision.

Black and white headshots of both husband and wife were included in the profile.

Then, bang!

Pappalardo's beautiful young French student was Simone Bisset, or her twin. Her image was identical to that in her French passport that Scott had found in Carey's dossier.

Tom texted:

> Back from States. Family doing well. So 3 has left the game. Am in London for a couple of days. Can we play catch-up this morning?

It was good news so far as his family was concerned. It meant that Jonathan had reached his sister safely. Number 3 was their code for Professor Zapatero. As with David Carey, the news dominated many websites.

> 1pm at Embankment underground station. Northern exit on Villiers Street and immediate right into the small park/gardens?

He still had some "tidying up" to do.

Tom replied:

> Agreed

He uploaded copies of Carey's dossier, the Bobby profile and his recent internet searches to the cloud account they'd set up.

He texted Sergey, Russian as usual:

Sad news about Professor Z. Have updated the account with a summary. Will explain later

He texted Yelena:

Dr S. Condition deteriorated. Need very urgent consultation. Where are you?

The "Dr S" was the agreed code for communications between them.

Sergey's reply arrived:

Thanks

Yelena replied:

At Budapest clinic for next 2 months. Will fit you in

Relief – Scott didn't have to go to Russia and spend his time dodging the Kremlin's radar.
He responded:

Tomorrow?

Two months in Budapest?

She replied:

Call me when you arrive at the airport. Dr Spiegelhalter is out of his coma

Dr Spiegel…? Who's…?

He smiled; she must be referring to Pravda.

Thank God.

Great news. See you tomorrow

He googled the sites explaining the security risks of sending a message by a standalone fax and by email on a device using the internet. Whilst neither method was regarded as 100 per cent secure, the consensus was that transmissions via the internet were more vulnerable than those sent over the "old fashioned" public phone line system.

He texted Yelena again:

Do you have access to a stand-alone fax machine, connected to the public phone line system but not the internet?

Perhaps with this latest passport information on Simone Bisset, Pravda might stand a better chance of finding her, without Scott having to approach Pappalardo himself. Pravda had access to all kinds of intelligence databases and Yelena's personal hacking skills were not to be sniffed at. He doubted that Gravchenko could match their resources and retrieve such intelligence information as quickly and easily as the GRU.

She replied in a few minutes:

7pm local time. Will contact when ready

He'd send the Bobby profile to her.

1.10pm

'I've uploaded a dossier which David Carey gave to Professor Zapatero, plus a file on Simone Bisset's husband, Bobby Pappalardo, which I got from the professor yesterday and some internet research. You'll find it very interesting reading,' Scott said to Tom.

'Thanks. I'm—'

'Look, Tom. There's a lot of stuff I haven't committed to a computer file or written down, but you should be aware of it as you read the uploaded account.'

'Go on.'

Scott told him about his meeting with Yelena in Malta, Pravda's reappearance, the previous day's events in Brussels and later with Chalmers.

'Wow, you *have* been busy. And it seems that we're in Professor Zapatero's debt.'

'Yes we are.' Scott stared into the distance.

'Are you alright?'

'No, not really.'

Scott slapped his knee. 'What a fucking shit world!'

'Yes, it is,' Tom said. 'But it's up to people like us... and Gravchenko, to try to put it right. In our own way. And hold those in power to account, as the cliché goes. You and I have got to make sure that David, Diane Costello and Professor Zapatero didn't die in vain.'

'And that Simone Bisset doesn't also.'

'What do you known about her?' Tom said.

'Nothing, except she's the unfortunate wife a sex maniac.'

'Okay,' Tom said. 'Any movement on the Orlov documents that General Pravda and Yelena have?'

'No, but I'm hoping to get more information when I see them tomorrow. And if I do, I'll uploaded it to our account. Pravda and I have each got 50 per cent of a jigsaw. I'm hoping to persuade him that it's time we joined the pieces to complete the picture.'

'Do you think you'll get their cooperation?'

'Yes, I do. I've never seen Yelena so anxious, hyper, when she told me about Pravda's kidnapping, her Bulgarian diplomat's beating up and now the Kremlin's super-cyber surveillance capabilities. At the moment we're each trying to investigate this with one hand tied behind our backs.'

'Could you find out more about this latest Kremlin technology...?'

Whoa!

What relevance was this to his father-in-law's assassination?

'So we know what we're up against and try to find a way to operate under the Kremlin's radar,' Tom added quickly, as if having read Scott's mind.

Scott wanted complete frankness between them. If Tom had an agenda other than to find out who killed his father-in-law and why, niggling doubts could creep in.

'Tom, forgive me for saying this, but if you're with the CIA, FBI or some other US Agency please tell me now.'

Tom looked surprised, if not hurt. 'No, I'm not. But as I told you, Brett has his connections with these people. We're not going to get their help without reciprocating. Do you understand what I'm saying?'

Scott lowered his head, like a mildly admonished child. 'Yes, of course I do. Sorry. It's just that I'm becoming so paranoid that I go through self-ID checks every morning when I wake up. No offence meant.'

Tom laughed. 'None taken.'

'But in answer to your question,' Scott said, 'Pravda and Yelena aren't idiots and if they suspected for one second that I had an underlying motive of getting classified information about their new technology, they'd drop me like a hot potato, and our investigation would hit the proverbial dead end. Sure, they aren't happy with their government's closeness to organised crime and the extra judicial killings, but they aren't traitors and would never betray their country's military secrets – if that's what this cyber stuff is.'

'Understood.'

They got up and stretched their legs with a walk around the gardens.

'Why did you tell Chalmers you had this evidence?'

Tom said. 'Don't you think it was premature, especially as you say that much of it was a bluff?'

The question had been bugging Scott from the moment he'd jumped into the taxi home at St Pancras station.

Why hadn't he slept on it for 24 hours, before confronting Chalmers?

'What was your objective?' Tom added.

'Hmm, yes. On reflection, I'm not sure. It was a decision from my heart, not my head. I'd just seen Professor Zapatero assassinated on a crowded street. A place she wouldn't have been in if I hadn't been so suspicious of everybody and insisted on a face-to-face meeting.' I set her up, as a sitting target...literally.'

'You can't possibly know that,' Tom said. 'She'd been the object of an assassination attempt a few days earlier in Paris. She was on somebody's hit list long before you got involved with her.'

'I know what you're saying and I thank you for it, but I just can't stop thinking about her poor daughter, Sarah. What must she be going through? As if her parents' bitter custody battle wasn't enough. I guess I just exploded.'

Chapter 39

Day Twenty-nine: 3.45pm, Budapest

'Well,' Scott said. 'They look identical to me.'

Having agreed to join forces with a full exchange of information in their Carey and Orlov investigations, Scott and Pravda sat in the latter's "Orlov" office in Budapest examining three passport images on the desk in front of them.

'That's what we think,' Pravda said. 'There can't be any doubt about the headshots; there's not been any attempt to disguise them. The dates of birth are identical, in all three. The places of birth and countries of origin are the same in the Russian and Uzbek passports, but different in the French. To be expected I suppose.'

'So, we're agreed.' Scott said. 'Gulyana Niyazova and Simone Bisset are the same person.'

'On the face of it, yes. But Yelena hasn't yet been able to confirm the validity of any one of them,' Pravda said.

'What about the payments?' Scott said. 'How certain are you on those?'

'One hundred thousand dollars either side of Carey's assassination, and a third $100k the day before Zapatero's killing, were paid into the Niyazova account. One from Santorini, one from Calabar and one from Cordoba.' Pravda shrugged. 'We know that for sure, but we don't have any evidence of what they were for.'

Scott immediately realised that the third payment was made before his phone calls with Professor Zapatero fixing their Brussels meeting; so any leak couldn't have come from his insistence on going there.

He still retained pangs of guilt, though.

The payments may have followed the pattern of thriller stories, where the hitman/woman is paid 50 per cent up front and 50 per cent on the kill, but that wasn't going to impress a court.

'Maybe when we've cross-referenced all the paperwork in Carey's dossier, we'll get a clearer picture,' Scott said.

Yelena burst through the open doorway from the adjoining room, waving several sheets of paper.

'And here's number four!' she said, laying one of the sheets on the desk. 'Another $100k credited to Niyazova's account during the night. I've just picked it up!'

She stood in front of them, grinning from ear to ear.

Scott and Pravda studied it together.

It was Niyazova's bank statement confirming the credit, from another Santorini bank.

'Yeah,' Scott said. 'It's progress, but we still need more documentation, much more. It wouldn't be too difficult for her to produce contracts, shipping documents and whatever...' He remembered the freight forwarding documents he'd skim read in Carey's dossier '...showing they were instalment payments in commodity deals. 'Tom Burrows, Carey's son-in-law, is a maritime lawyer; he specialises in shipping fraud. You'd be surprised at some of the tales he has to tell.'

'And, we'd have to get her into court,' Pravda said.

'Well,' Yelena said. 'While you guys are talking all this court and evidence stuff, you'd better look at this.' She dropped a second sheet onto the desk. 'Five hundred thousand big ones!'

It was a bank statement in the name of Simone Bisset showing a credit of $500k from Santorini, made earlier that day.

'Where did you get this?' Pravda asked.

'I've been up half the night and all morning going through the email instructions in Orlov's documents.

The letters "SB" appear in the transfer instruction sent from Kabir Shastri's email account to Santorini, you know, from that Chinese URL. It's addressed to our old friend Ernst Bauer, or his clone.'

She dropped the last sheet on the desk. 'Look.'

Scott and Pravda stared at it without saying a word.

The email was in Russian:

> Now for the big one! Send $500k to SB. Usual terms. Cal and Cor to reimburse.

It was sent six hours after Professor Zapatero's assassination.

Scott shook his head as he re-examined the passport images, bank statements and email while half listening to snippets of a conversation between Pravda and Yelena:

'A million dollars? ... Another hit? ... Putin? ... the head of the FSB? ... Who then?'

The weight of the evidence in Carey's dossier didn't point to any identifiable reason to kill Russian politicians or other high-ranking Russian officials; the documents favoured financial corruption in the EU hierarchy. The killings to date had all been of people who had, or might be thought to have had, knowledge of that corruption.

The silence from Pravda and Yelena was deafening.

Scott looked up.

They were staring at him.

The last words he recalled were, 'Who then?'

They were stone-faced.

'No, no. Not *me*. It's absurd.' He shook his head vigorously. 'Why would someone pay a million dollars to have *me* killed? How would it serve their cause?'

'Think about it, Scott,' Pravda said. 'You've been connected to everything that's happened since Carey was assassinated. Poking around, probing, keeping things to yourself, telling your authorities what you think of them; telling Chalmers what information you have on certain elites...compromising material that could end their careers. You might think you're getting your revenge on the Establishment after the way they treated you in 2016, but nobody likes having their noses rubbed in it. You must have upset some very powerful people.'

Tom's words came back to him: *Why did you tell Chalmers you had this evidence? Don't you think it could have been premature, especially as you say that some of it was bluff?'*

Tom was right about him having threatened Chalmers without prudent consideration, but Pravda and Yelena were wrong that it was a good enough reason to kill him.

'No, no,' Scott said, scratching his forehead. 'No, it's not me they want to silence. I'm a small fish floundering in an ocean. No, it's somebody else, somebody who can do much more damage to the status quo, the Establishment's comfort zone, call it what you will, than I could ever do with my investigation.' He thought of Chalmers. 'Besides, don't forget my insurance policy. I can't see them risking the exposure.'

Who was he trying to convince?

Pravda and Yelena, or himself?

Scott shuffled the papers around.

'I wish I could be as certain as you,' Pravda said. 'I think you should—'

'Oh shit!' Scott exclaimed. He banged the desktop. 'Shit! Shit! Shit!'

He took images of the passports, the bank statements and the email.

'How secure is your Wi-Fi in this place?'

'Ninety-nine per cent,' Yelena said. 'It's our own. Only for this office.'

He looked at Pravda. 'The Kremlin's tentacles?'

‘It can never be 100 per cent, but 99 is a reasonable assessment.’

So be it.

‘I can live with the one per cent,’ Scott said.

He uploaded the five images to the cloud account he shared with Sergey and sent him a text, deliberately in upper case:

> IMMINENT THREAT TO MR G’S LIFE. CHECK DOCS SENT TO CLOUD.
> DON’T ACCESS FROM RUSSIA

He gave out a long sigh, with a swarm of butterflies flying around his stomach.

‘It’s not me. It’s Gravchenko. I’m *sure* of it.’

Pravda and Yelena looked at each other as if to say, ‘Maybe he’s got a point.’

‘This fashion designer’s kill score is 100 per cent,’ Yelena said.

‘Then let’s hope I’m wrong,’ Scott replied.

5.15pm

‘Your heart rate is setting world records,’ Pravda said to Scott, as he put three bottles of beer on the table. ‘You’ve hardly said a word since we left the office and you’ve not stopped checking your phone for messages. Do you know the Russian proverb “a watched pot never boils”?’

‘Same in English,’ Scott said, as he lingered on his text to Sergey.

A power outage in the building had forced the three to take a break and find refuge at an open-plan bar on the ground floor of the local shopping mall, a short walk away.

Despite the crowds of shoppers, Scott considered it to be a safe space in which to continue their discussions. The exchanges between a Russian GRU General, his Major assistant and a British human rights lawyer couldn’t compete with the large discounts being given on the latest fashion items.

Besides, who'd have the ability to bug every unit and open space in a five-storey shopping mall, much less the inclination?

The text arrived from Sergey:

Situation secured

Scott closed his eyes and dropped his shoulders.

'Good or bad?' Yelena said.

Scott opened his eyes.

'Situation secured,' Scott said.

'Where is he?' Pravda asked.

'No idea,' Scott said. 'But he's secure. That's all I need to know.'

'But for how long?' Pravda said. 'We've got a very determined professional killer on the loose.'

'Uh huh,' Yelena said. 'And she's got a million-dollar incentive.'

They were right. But it was out of Scott's hands. He'd done all he could to warn his boss.

'Well, we'll just have to pray that someone gets to her before she gets to the man,' Scott said as he reached for his beer.

'Pffft.'

Yelena jolted and clutched her neck.

'I've been shot.'

She collapsed forward and smacked her head on her beer bottle, blood pouring from her neck.

'What the fuck?' Scott said.

'Pffft.'

Pravda, who was sitting next to her, collapsed to the floor.

The man fell sideways clutching his shoulder and toppled from his chair.

'Pffft, pffft, pffft.'

Scott dived to the floor, to get cover under the chairs and table.

A searing pain radiated up his leg.

'Pffft, pffft, pffft. pffft, pffft.'

Another searing pain in his leg as he dragged his whole body under the table.

Screams from the shoppers erupted, as more bullets peppered the area around Scott's table.

Yelena fell sideways on top of Pravda.

Pravda, gritting his teeth in obvious pain from his shoulder, edged Yelena under the table.

'Is she still breathing?' Scott said.

'Only just. Yelena, Yelena, come on, come on. Talk to me. Talk to me.'

Scott pulled off his jacket and tried to rip the sleeves apart. They were too well stitched. He tore out the lining and shredded it into strips, which he used to staunch the blood flowing from Yelena's neck.

The shooting stopped.

'What the...?'

He turned to Pravda. 'Can you take over? With that shoulder?'

'Of course,' Pravda said. 'It's only a flesh wound.'

It didn't look like it.

Scott gave the strips to him and eased out from under the table.

It was a war zone in their immediate area: people from adjacent tables lying on the floor, frightened to move, a woman trying to cover her restless two- or three-year-old daughter, chairs upturned, bottles and food littering the floor.

'Jesus!' Scott said. Unlike the Cuckoo restaurant, this was for real.

Elsewhere people were seeking shelter in the individual shop units.

Apart from the child crying, an eerie silence descended on the place.

Scott gazed up at the first floor balcony from where the shots had come.

A figure wearing a balaclava was fiddling with his or her automatic.

Where was security?

Where were the police?

More shots rang out.

The woman screamed as the child broke free and wandered into the open, bullets splintering everything in sight.

The shooter fiddled with the gun again.

It was sticking.

He crawled across to the floor to the child, pulled her down and dragged her under the nearest empty table. His own was occupied with Pravda nursing Yelena and the woman blocked his way to her table as she crawled with an outstretched hand to reach her child.

'My baby! My baby!' she shouted in German.

More shots.

Scott checked the balcony again.

A lone security guard was shouting something and pointing his pistol at the shooter.

The guard didn't appear to be wearing body armour.

An exchange of fire followed.

Scott seized the moment to edge the little girl her to her mother's outstretched hands, while interposing his body to protect her from the line of fire.

The shooter headed for the escalator going down to the ground floor, haphazardly spraying bullets over the balcony, causing more screaming and shoppers to run for cover.

Despite the lack of support from his painful and semi-useless leg, Scott picked up a chair for protection and hobbled after the shooter as he/she got off the escalator, with the guard in hot pursuit.

The shooter turned, took a steady aim and fired at the guard.

He dropped to the floor in front of Scott.

The shooter ran on and disappeared through a swinging side doorway.

Scott hesitated at the guard's body – lifeless.

He had a bullet hole in his forehead.

Scott limped after the shooter, using the chair as a shield.

Police sirens from outside pierced the air.

The swinging doorway opened into a long straight corridor with closed doors at intervals on either side, as far as the eyes could see.

Scott looked both ways and mentally flipped a coin.

He turned right and edged along the wall, holding the chair close to his chest.

A door opened five metres in front of Scott and on the opposing wall.

The shooter strolled out, the weapon pointing at Scott.

'Stop where you are,' a male voice said in broken English. 'Put the chair down.'

Scott hesitated.

So it wasn't Yelena's fashion designer.

The shooter raised the gun.

Scott obeyed.

'Move to the centre.' The shooter waived the weapon at him.

Scott did so.

More sirens from outside and shouting in the Mall.

'Listen to that,' Scott said. 'You're not going anywhere. The police have arrived.'

'On your knees,' the shooter said approaching Scott. 'Hands on your head.'

He eased down; his leg was agony and his trousers soaked in blood.

He was light-headed.

'You'll never get away with this.' It was all he could think to say.

'But *I* will, Scott Mitchell. *I* will,' said a female voice in Russian from behind.

Scott turned his head, his sight fading as more blood drained from his body.

A balaclava-clad woman towered over him, a gun in her hand.

'Gulyana Niyazova, I presume,' Scott said weakly. 'Or is it Simone Bisset, today?'

'Pffft, pffft, pffft.'

The woman fell forward onto Scott.

He blacked out.

Chapter 40

Day Thirty: 8pm, Budapest

Scott opened his eyes.

He couldn't focus.

Bright lights pierced his blurred vision. It was as if he was on his back a few feet below water level in the Mediterranean on a cloudless sunny afternoon.

'Where am I?' he said to himself in English.

'In hospital,' a female voice replied in Russian. 'City centre.'

He turned to where the sound came from and blinked a hazy figure into view.

Yelena was sitting by his bedside, with a bandaged neck and wearing a white hospital gown.

He was in a single ward.

She beamed at him.

'Either we're both dead or we're both alive,' Scott said, reverting to Russian.

'Alive and kicking,' she said. 'Well, *I* am.' She nodded at his leg, which was cradled in a pulley hanging from the ceiling. 'Not sure about you.'

He moved his leg, with difficulty, but at least he could feel it.

'How long have I been here?'

'Twenty-four hours.'

'How's the General?'

'Recalled to Moscow.' She didn't look happy. 'For a chat.'

'With the Kremlin?'

'Who else?'

'Good news or bad?'

She shrugged. 'Anybody's guess. He promised to call me as soon as he can.'

'Okay, so tell me what happened to you,' he said. 'The last time we met, you were dead.'

'Yeah, that's what I thought too. But the bullet went straight through my neck, in one side and out the other. Soft tissue damage. It didn't hit any vital organs and stuff: trachea, spinal cord, arteries, veins and all that shit.'

'Jesus. How often does that happen?'

'The doc said she'd only seen it once before. It was a 7.62mm bullet, clean in and out. The smaller 5.56mm is more likely to fragment inside the neck and rip into everything.'

Scott scanned the room: the leg sling, the machine monitoring his heart, the saline drip.

He turned back to Yelena.

'So has it been confirmed that it was your fashion designer who collapsed on me?' Scott said.

'Yeah, no doubt about it. Forensics found a scar on her upper thigh. A knife or something. We matched it to her Uzbeck medical records a few hours ago.'

'Confirmed by Moscow or France?'

'No. Nothing from them.'

What a surprise.

'And the shooter?'

'The sex maniac and husband, Bobby Pappalardo,' she said.

Scott frowned. 'Why would he do that?'

'Anybody's guess.'

'Did he escape?'

'That's one way of looking at it,' Yelena said.

'What do you mean?'

'They caught him alive. Chucked him into a cell and he woke up dead this morning. Hanged in his cell. A clear case of suicide…' She smirked. 'Not.'

'Jesus, Yelena. This killing just goes on and on. Will it ever stop?'

Her face saddened.

He slid his hand across the sheet towards her.

'Why do we do this stuff?' he said.

She nursed his hand with both of hers.

'My mum told me to get a professional qualification,' she said. 'I failed my accountants' exams so I joined the GRU and learnt how to kill people, professionally.'

He didn't know whether to laugh or cry.

She squeezed his hand. 'What's *your* excuse?'

He shrugged. 'I don't like taking "no" for an answer, I suppose.'

They stared at each other.

She began to cry, gently at first, then it increased.

Scott sat up as much as his leg would allow.

'Yelena, what is it? What's the matter?'

She sniffed. 'Can I hug you?'

She was sobbing.

He was stunned.

'Sure, of course you can.'

She leant into him and lightly put her hands around his neck.

He hesitated, then reciprocated, with physical difficulty.

She held him tighter as tears gushed down her cheeks.

'Yelena. What's the matter? Please. Tell me what is it?

She eased back to her chair, sniffed and wiped her tears with a bedside tissue.

'I never knew my dad. He left Mum when I was six months old. She never remarried. I'm an only child. I've never had any men in my life, never wanted them. Except the General. I've grown to love him like a father. I'd die for him...'

Scott welled up.

'And now *you*.' She crushed his hand between hers. 'You're the brother I never had. The only two men I've ever had any feelings for. I could have lost you both.'

'Come here, sis.' Scott held out his hands for her, as tears rolled down his cheeks.

She leant forward again and he forced himself, despite the pain, to embrace her, squeeze her.

'And we thought we'd lost *you*,' he said. 'The only sister *I'd* ever had. I'm also an only child.'

She gripped him tightly.

'And don't forget,' he said. 'If you hadn't saved my life in 2013 you wouldn't have had a brother.'

She eased back again and smiled.

The door opened and Sergey marched in, clutching a selection of newspapers.

Yelena quickly stood up.

'I'll see you later, Scott.'

'No, Yelena, you don't have to go.'

Sergey said nothing as he nodded at her and stepped aside to let her pass.

'No, that's okay. It's time for my meds,' she said.

She flashed a perfunctory smile at Sergey and left the room.

Sergey took Yelena's chair.

'You don't do things by halves, do you my friend.' He dropped the newspapers onto the bed. 'Take a look at these. I know you like hard copies.'

Scott selected an English tabloid. It was dated that day.

The headlines read:

UK LAWYER HERO IN BUDAPEST TERRORIST ATTACK

Scott began reading the lead article:

Scott Mitchell, Chief Counsel to the WPF charity owned by Russian oligarch Konstantin Gravchenko, yesterday single-handedly stopped an assassin from killing a young mother and her baby daughter who'd wandered away from her mother under a hail of bullets in a Budapest shopping mall.

Having been shot in the leg several times, Scott found the strength and courage to grab the baby to safety and return her unharmed to her distressed mother while being shot at by the assassin...

'The internet's lit up,' Sergey said. 'Teresa's made sure of that. Social media sites, Twitter's red hot, YouTube and loads of other places. Videos taken by the eye witnesses. All that stuff.'

'Yeah, well,' Scott said. 'That just about sums up social media in the 21st century. Why didn't at least one of the amateur photographers try helping the young mother with her kid instead of filming it?'

Sergey ignored the question and tapped Scott on the wrist. 'You're a superhero. A fucking superhero. Teresa got her SEO guys to whizz you and the WPF into pole position on Google. I've never known the boss to be in such a good mood.'

Something held Scott back from rejoicing.

Post-traumatic shock?

Or something else?

He couldn't get Yelena out of his mind.

He fiddled with the other papers: French, German and Italian. Their headlines seemed to be saying the same as the UK tabloid.

'Well,' Scott said. 'We'd better make the most of it, before my 15 minutes of fame turns into 15 months of notoriety again and the trolls say the boss set it up, along with the Cuckoo raid.'

Kevin Shaw's website came to mind.

Chapter 41

Day Thirty-four: 12.30pm, London

'So, how do you feel?' Tom said.

'I'm going stir crazy and I'm only two days into my prescribed "complete rest" regime; another 28 days to go,' Scott replied.

'Is Gravchenko happy with that? Out of action for four weeks?'

'He hasn't sent me a get-well card and flowers, if that's what you mean. But he appears to be a happy bunny with all this good publicity we're getting after the shopping mall incident.' A quick smile. 'So, yeah, I can't see him objecting to my taking four weeks off to recover.'

'In that case, you've got no worries. Relax...and serve your stir time.'

'Nothing to worry about, except slow death by frustration. Parts of my body may be knackered, but I can't stop my brain from continuously firing on seven of its six cylinders. They've been pumping 24/7 since the day after your father-in-law's assassination. They don't know what a "complete rest" regime is.' He sipped his wine. 'Still, that's enough of my woes. How's the family coping?'

Tom had invited Scott to lunch at The Anachronism, a retro-Edwardian style institution which shunned modern-day distractions, bowing only to Wi-Fi – his favourite eatery whenever he could spare the time in London. He'd secured a discreet alcove where they could catch up before going into the restaurant area.

'Thanks to *you* and your relentless search for the

truth,' Tom said. 'Stephanie's improving every day. Now she knows who assassinated her father and justice, of sorts, has been served, she's ticked an enormous box; not quite closure, but it's getting there. And Chrissy's doing okay, now she's back home with my folks.'

'That's kind of you, Tom. But I didn't do it all alone. Without Pravda's and Yelena's help...and yours of course...and Brett's, I wouldn't have got very far.'

'Okay,' Tom said. 'Let's settle for a collective effort.'

'And Jonathan, how's he?'

'Getting itchy feet again, but he'll stay with us for a while. Deep down he accepts that the thugs may still be looking for him.'

Tom took a mouthful of wine, licked his lips and stared at Scott.

'What is it?' Scott said. 'You look like you're about to tell Stephanie you've won the lottery jackpot but you've lost the ticket.'

'I'm afraid I've got to keep your synapses agitated,' Tom said.

Anything to prevent brain death.

'I'm listening.'

'Do you know a man called Sergey Ivanovich Sobol?'

'Yes, of course. It's Sergey, Gravchenko's right-hand man. Or at least that's Sergey's full name. There might be other men with the same names of course. Why?'

'Do you trust him?'

'Sure do. With my life. As much as I trust Gravchenko.'

'Does Gravchenko trust him?'

'I'd be surprised if he doesn't. I do a lot of Gravchenko's work through Sergey. Personal stuff, money matters.' Scott scratched his cheek. 'Tom, what's this about?'

'Bear with me for a minute.'

He didn't want to. He wanted clarity without further delay.

'Okay.'

'Is your Sergey married?'

'Yes, as far as I know. But I've never met his wife.'

'What's her name?'

'Oksana.'

'Do you know her full name?'

'I don't know her middle name, her patronym, but her last name is Nekrasova.'

'She doesn't use Sergey's family name?'

'He says she has an independent spirit.' He hesitated. 'Look, Tom, what are you trying to tell me. We're both lawyers. Your line of questioning is making me uneasy. Please, get to the point.'

'A woman called Oksana Alexandrovna Nekrasova, who's married to a man called Sergey Ivanovich Sobol, is the sole signatory on more than 25 bank mandates of nine offshore companies incorporated in Nevis, Bahamas, Marshall Islands, Cyprus and Croatia. The bank accounts are located in New York, Chicago and Pittsburgh, as well as Cyprus, India, China, Australia, New Zealand, Argentina and Panama. For the last two years they've all been receiving monthly payments ranging from $100,000 to $1.5 million. These funds are then disbursed in irregular amounts to more bank accounts in different company names in other countries; some offshore, others more transparent.'

Faintly audible alarm bells in the distance.

'And?' Trillions of dollars whizz around the globe every day. Nevertheless, the names coincidence was something Scott could well do without.

'And,' Tom said, 'the payments emanate from a Santorini account in West Africa – Nigeria to be precise.'

The noise from the alarm bells was deafening.

No, not Sergey. Surely not.

'I assume this is from the FBI via Brett,' Scott said. If it had come from Wyatt or Fraser Scott would have dismissed it as shit-stirring, but Brett was another matter.

'Have the FBI found any documentation purporting to evidence the commercial transactions underlying the bank transfers?'

'If they have, they've not disclosed it to Brett.'

In the absence of supporting documentation, the pattern of payments had the hallmarks of what the authorities called "suspicious activities".

Scott quickly ran through the possibilities:

1. The names could be a coincidence – but if Oksana's patronymic is also Alexandrovna, the chances of a coincidence of that magnitude would diminish substantially.
2. Sergey may not know what his wife is doing – insufficient information to form a reasoned opinion.
3. Sergey may know, but Gravchenko may not – again, insufficient information to form a reasoned opinion.
4. Gravchenko may have known about it, and have been turning a blind eye, if not actively promoting it, since inception – if so, Scott's world could be coming to an end.

'Are the FBI saying that this Oksana woman, and not Kabir Shastri, is the real moving spirit behind the operation?' While Scott and Pravda were satisfied that Santorini deserved its reputation as a laundromat, and that a relatively insignificant sum had probably been used to finance the murders of Carey, Costello and Zapatero, they were far from knowing who the company's ultimate puppet-meister was.

'No,' Tom said. 'It's still very much a smoke and mirrors situation.' He adopted an "I told-you-so" look. 'As I said when we first met, we're teetering on the tip of a very deep iceberg.'

THE END

If you have enjoyed this book and have a few moments to spare, I would really appreciate a short review on Amazon, or wherever else you bought the book. Your kind help in spreading the word is gratefully appreciated, as reviews make a huge difference to helping new readers find the series.

Sign up for Adrian's VIP newsletter to receive a FREE copy of his book, *Beyond the Law*, comprising a short selection of world-famous political conspiracies, plus EXCLUSIVE bonus material including periodical giveaways, information sheets about Russia and pre-release specials in respect of future books in the Puppet Meisters series.

Go to:
www.adrianchurchward.com/newsletter-sign-up

Acknowledgements

I am indebted to the professionalism of my editor Beth Jusino. Once again she had to nudge my ego back from fantasy land with my first couple of drafts before I finally realised that my original storylines were sowing the seeds of confusion at an alarming rate. It was only after my third attempt at redrafting the first 100 or so pages that I convinced Beth I was ready to be let loose on my devoted readers.

Even having been paroled by Beth, I wouldn't have been able to complete the book without the assistance of my dedicated beta readers: Sean Anderson, Sergey Markariyan, Toni Mooney, Jenny Parker, Michelle Willett and Kieran Wyers whose constructive suggestions helped further to clarify various aspects of the narrative.

A special thanks also to the Hilton Hotel Prague whose staff kindly allowed me, as somebody who literally popped in off the street, to inspect the Tyrolka meeting rooms complex which features in Chapter 4 of the book.

Finally, as always, I would like to thank Catherine at SilverWood for bringing this book to publication with her expert guidance, and with special thanks to Eleanor for the evocative book cover.

Lightning Source UK Ltd.
Milton Keynes UK
UKHW011834180221
379020UK00002B/32/J